Roger Taylor was born in Heywood, Lancashire, and qualified as a civil and structural engineer. He lives with his wife and two daughters in Wirral, Merseyside, and is a pistol shooter and student of traditional aikido. He is the author of the four chronicles of Hawklan, *The Call of the Sword*, *The Fall of Fyorlund*, *The Waking of Orthlund* and *Into Narsindal*, and the epic fantasies *Dream Finder*, *Farnor*, *Valderen* and *Whistler*, also available from Headline Feature.

Ibryen

Roger Taylor

First published in 1995
by HEADLINE BOOK PUBLISHING

First published in paperback in 1996
by HEADLINE BOOK PUBLISHING

A HEADLINE FEATURE paperback

10 9 8 7 6 5 4 3

ISBN 0 7472 5007 3

Printed and bound in Great Britain by
Mackays of Chatham PLC, Chatham, Kent

HEADLINE BOOK PUBLISHING
A division of Hodder Headline PLC
338 Euston Road
London NW1 3BH

To my wife and daughters

Chapter 1

The wind that brought the messenger was full of strangeness. For several days it had blown, no different from the wind that always blew at this time of year; loaded with subtle perfumes from the spring-awakening grasses and flowers that coloured the lower slopes of the mountains, and woven through with the whispering sounds of high, tumbling streams and the home-building clamour of the birds and animals that dwelt amid the towering peaks.

Yet, for Ibryen, the wind was different. It carried at its heart a faint and elusive song that possessed a cloak-tugging urgency during the day and reached into his sleep during the night, bringing him to sudden wakefulness. Thus roused, he would lie, still, silent, and expectant, with anxious magic hovering, black-winged, about him in the darkness that spanned between his sleeping world and his solitary room. But nothing came to explain this mysterious unquiet – no sudden illumination to show a way through the uncertain future before him, no new tactics to outwit the growing power of the Gevethen, no new words with which to encourage his followers. Nothing.

You expect too much, he thought irritably, on the third night of such an awakening. Or was he perhaps just tormenting himself with imaginary hopes? Was this disturbance no more than his clinging to some childish fancy that

1

all would be well in the end? Was he deluding himself that somewhere, something was preparing to come to his aid, rather than face the dark knowledge within him that he and his cause, and his men, were probably lost?

No. Surely it couldn't be that! Doubt was an inevitable part of leadership, he knew. It underscored his every action and he deemed himself sufficiently aware of his own nature not to have such a foe lurking in the darker recesses of the mind waiting to spring out in ambush.

Yet . . .?

He growled angrily to end the questioning. Then, though it was some three hours until dawn, he swung aside his rough blankets and, draping them about his shoulders, went to the door. As the night cold struck him, he took a deep breath and pulled the blankets tight about him. There was no moon, and the stars shone brightly through the clear air, as familiar and unchanging in their patterns as the mountains themselves.

And as ancient and indifferent, Ibryen mused, shivering despite the lingering bed-warmth in the sheets.

All about him, the camp, or, more correctly, the village, which is what the camp had developed into over the years, was quiet. Yet it would not be asleep. Around the perimeter and on the nearby peaks, eyes would be staring into the darkness, ears would be listening, waiting for that movement, that sound which would indicate the approach of some spy, or even the Gevethen's army. Briefly, his old concerns surfaced again. Practical and tactical this time. How long could such vigilance be maintained? How long could he keep up the spirits of his own followers? How long before the Gevethen discovered this place and launched a full attack? How long—

He dashed them aside and turned his mind back to

whatever it was that had wakened him in the middle of the night, and had been disturbing him during the day whenever he found himself between tasks. Maybe it's just spring coming, he thought, smiling to himself, but the whimsy did little to allay the peculiar unease that was troubling him. For it was still here – permeating the soft breeze that was drifting along the valley. Calling to him – a haunting . . .

What? He closed his eyes and leaned back against the door frame.

Urgency and appeal was all around him, faint and shifting, but distinct for all that. Yet it was not the urgency and appeal of his present predicament, nor those of his people whom he had abandoned. He curled his lip at the bitterness in the word. For a moment, memories threatened to flood in upon him, but he let the word go. That too was a well-worn debate, and that he had had no choice gave him no comfort.

The breeze returned its unsettling burden to him again. There was an almost alien quality in what he could feel – or was it, hear? It was as though he were listening to a creature from an ancient fable, articulate and intelligent, yet wholly different from him in every way. Images formed and re-formed in his mind, but none clearly, each dissolving as he turned his thoughts towards it like shapes within a swirling mist.

'Are you all right, Count?'

The voice thundered into his inner silence, rasping, uncouth and distorted, making him start violently. Only years of silent and stealthy warfare kept him from crying out. His questioner however was as shaken as he by the response.

'I'm sorry, Count,' he gasped. 'I didn't mean to startle you. I—'

Ibryen raised a hand to silence him. The man's voice was becoming normal in his ears – a tone scarcely much above a whisper – the tone he would have expected anyone to be using in the sleeping camp. He identified the speaker. It was unthinkable that he above all should have spoken as Ibryen had heard. It had been like the shattering of night vision by a sudden brilliant light. What had he been listening to with such intensity? He made no attempt to answer the question.

'It's all right, Marris,' he said to the dark shape in front of him. 'I was a little restless. I just came out to look at the stars.'

Marris cleared his throat softly. 'Fortunate that I wasn't one of the Gevethen's assassins,' he said sternly.

'I stand rebuked,' Ibryen replied good-naturedly. 'Though I doubt they'll take the trouble to send assassins if they find us.'

'*When* they find us,' Marris emphasised.

Ibryen reached out and laid his hands on the man's shoulders. 'I yield the field, old friend,' he said with a soft laugh. 'I'm retreating – returning to my bed to regroup my scattered wits. Wake me at dawn if I show any signs of licking my wounds too long.'

Marris bowed slightly. 'Sleep well, Count. The camp and all about is quiet.'

As Marris turned to move away, Ibryen said hesitantly, 'Have you felt anything ... strange ... in the wind, these last few days?'

Marris paused, his head bent to one side as he searched for the Count's face in the darkness while he considered this odd question. Then he shrugged. 'Only spring, Count,' he replied. 'Good and bad, as ever.'

Ibryen nodded. 'Sun on our skins again, blood moving in our veins, but the passes clearing of snow and the

4

need for renewed vigilance. Winter's not without its advantages.'

Marris gave a low grunt by way of confirmation. 'Twenty years since they came, five years since their treachery forced us to flee, and every year they come searching, stronger each time, and nearer finding us. Soon they'll come in the winter also.'

Ibryen frowned. Such comments from any other would have brought a crushing response, but Marris was too close a friend for him to invoke such defences. Five years ago it had been Marris who rescued him from the mayhem when the Gevethen's followers had stormed their country home and murdered his family. He was Ibryen's most loyal and trusted adviser, as he had been to his father. Blunt and fearless in his opinions, he was nevertheless enough of a realist to speak such words to his Count only when no others could hear. And Ibryen too was enough of a realist not to bluster in the face of them.

'It's constantly on my mind, old friend,' he replied simply.

Marris bowed again and let the matter lie. 'Catch what sleep you can for the rest of the night, Count,' he said. 'And take care, the air's deceptively chilly.'

Then, without waiting for a dismissal, he was gone. Ibryen stood for a moment staring into the darkness after him before he turned and went back inside. He had not noticed how cold it was outside until the warmth of the room folded around him. Briefly he toyed with the idea of returning to bed as he had said, but decided against it. Marris's unexpected arrival had completely scattered the strangely intense concentration with which he had woken, but the memory of it lingered and, as he thought about it again, so he became even less inclined to regard what he had felt as an idle fancy. Elusive and intangible it might

5

have been, but, whatever it was, there had been a hard, shimmering sharpness at its heart which declared it to be both real and outside himself.

The conclusion unsettled him however. A practical man, surrounded by more than enough problems and responsibilities, it was inappropriate, to say the least, that he should find himself considering such foolishness. What he needed was a good dose of normality. He dragged the sheets off his shoulders and threw them on to his bed as he moved back to the door. Outside stood a large barrel, full almost to the top with water. Stars twinkled in the motionless surface and, for a moment, Ibryen felt as though he were looking down on the heavens as their creator might have done. It was a dizzying perspective. Then he scattered his tiny universe as he plunged his arms into the near-freezing water and performed a premature morning ablution. Long, deep breaths kept his shivering at bay as he went back inside and towelled himself down violently. He was glowing as he dressed.

But, despite this assault, his memory of what had happened was unchanged. Pensively he fastened his swordbelt. He felt good. His body was awake and his mind was sharp and clear ... so how was it that a vague feeling which had been stirring at the edges of his mind should suddenly seem to him to be a call – for call it was, he was sure now, though from whom and for what he could not imagine. He had no ready answers. Strange things happened to people in the mountains, but this did not have the quality of something generated by a mind addled by shifting mists, or lack of food, or thinness of air.

It occurred to him unnervingly that perhaps it was some devilment by the Gevethen. They certainly had talents which seemed to defy logic and reason. But again, the call – he grimaced at the word – did not have the sense of viciousness, of clinging evil, which pervaded their work. Rather, it was clear and simple; beautiful, almost, despite the urgency that underlay it. All that was at fault was *his* confusion, his inability to listen correctly – as though he were a noisy child, pestering about something that his parents were already trying to explain. Perhaps he should stay silent, he decided, with an uncertain smile. Routine concerns were already beginning to impinge on him following his brief exchange with Marris and all too soon they would become a clamour as the village awoke and set about its daily life.

Compromise came to him. He would do two things at the same time. He would walk the outer perimeter, to check the vigilance of the guards and to encourage them, then perhaps he might clamber up on to the southern ridge to judge for himself the state of the adjoining valleys. These were necessary tasks which he could pursue without any sense of guilt, while at the same time they would give him silence and calm in which to ponder what was happening.

Dawn was greying the sky as he began the ascent to the southern ridge. It had been a valuable exercise, walking the perimeter. He had been challenged at every guard post and was now flushed with the quiet congratulations he had been able to give. He paused and, unusually, allowed himself a little self-congratulation as well. It was no small credit to his leadership that his people were so attentive so long into the night. It helped, of course, that all here had suffered appallingly at the hands of the Gevethen and were more than well-acquainted with their cunning and treachery. They knew that should a hint of the location of this place reach the enemy, then a pitched and terrible battle would be inevitable. And there would be little doubt as to who would prevail should this happen. The Gevethen were in power now, not only because of their ability to sway others to their cause but because of their complete indifference to the fate of those same followers. Wave upon wave of attackers would be sent against the camp until sheer attrition won the day. It was a dark image and, for all it was no new one, Ibryen frowned as he set it aside.

He glanced briefly at the lightening sky then quickly turned his eyes back to the darkness around him. He must be careful, of course. It was not necessary to fall over some craggy edge to injure oneself seriously in this terrain, a simple tumble would suffice, but by the time he would be moving from the grassy slopes on to the rocks proper it would be much lighter. For a moment he considered the wisdom of what he was doing. It was not essential that he personally viewed the adjacent valleys, any of his senior officers could have done it. But even as he reflected, he felt again a slight tension urging him forward. Whatever it was, it would not be ignored.

He set off, slowly.

Though he kept his attention focused on the shadowscape about him, and on his every footstep, he was aware that what had been disturbing him for the past few days and nights was truly there. It permeated his relaxed awareness, growing then fading but never truly disappearing, like the sound of a distant crowd carried on the wind. Words such as 'call', 'song', floated into his mind, but none were truly adequate.

As he had estimated, the sun had risen when he came to the rockier reaches of the ridge. It was going to be a fine spring day – not warm enough for idling in the sun, and probably very cold up on the ridge, but heart-lifting for all that. He sat down, not so much to rest as to think. Far below he could make out the village, small and seemingly fragile amid the peaks. It was not difficult for him to find it, but for a less informed eye it would have been no easy task. Turves covered both roofs and the shallow ramped walls built from the local rocks, and a random arrangement on either side of a bustling stream which twisted between large rocky outcrops ensured that the buildings were not readily distinguishable from the general terrain. A few trees and bushes completed the visual confusion. It was not perfect, but it was adequate. Caves would have been a wiser choice, but apart from there being too few suitable for the number of people involved, there was something deeply repugnant about the idea of being driven underground by the Gevethen. At least in these simple houses, Ibryen's followers could live lives that bore some resemblance to those that they had led previously. In other valleys, such crops as could be coaxed out of the thin soil were grown, and cattle and sheep were tended. Barring discovery, they could survive here indefinitely.

Instinctively, Ibryen looked up at the clear sky. When the Gevethen had first appeared, so too had a great many small, rather sinister brown birds. Among the rumours that had eventually sprung up to surround the Gevethen was one that they used these birds as spies and that through their piercing yellow eyes, everything in the land could be seen. It was palpable nonsense, of course; the birds had probably been carried there by accident – doubtless unusual storms on their normal migratory flights – for a few years later they vanished as abruptly as they had arrived. Nevertheless, the influence of the Gevethen was so grim and all-pervasive, that the rumour lingered uncomfortably, and no one had seriously demurred when it was suggested that the camp be disguised in such a way that it could not easily be seen from above. After all, it couldn't be denied that at the time of the disappearance of the birds, the Gevethen had seemed to be more uneasy, less well-informed of events, could it?

Probably coincidence, Ibryen mused unconvincingly as he returned his gaze to the camp below. Putting his hands on his knees, he levered himself upright, irritated at finding himself thinking about these old tales. He began climbing over the rocks.

The sun was well above the horizon when he finally reached the ridge. Snow-covered peaks shone far into the distance, brilliant and aloof, as if disdaining the frantic scrabblings of the mortals who flickered their tiny lives away so hysterically beneath their timeless gaze.

A cold wind struck Ibryen's sweating face as he clambered over the last few rocks. In years past he had delighted in striding out along such ridges. Now, concealment being an almost permanent obsession, he moved carefully, keeping low or otherwise ensuring that he did not present a conspicuous silhouette against the skyline. It was just another example of the Gevethen's pernicious influence, their gift of corroding even the smallest worthwhile thing.

Ibryen did not know what he had expected to find at the end of this journey, and the last part of the climb had been too strenuous for him to pay any need to the subtle urging that had drawn him here, but his initial response was one of disappointment. The view was, as ever, inspiring, but no great surge of understanding overwhelmed him, no sudden insight. Instead, he was just both hot and chilled as he normally was when travelling a little too quickly in the mountains. For the same reason he was also out of breath.

'Just sit down and relax,' he said to himself. 'Calm down.

There's still the valleys to be looked at.'

Sitting down carefully in the lee of a rock he turned his face to the sun. Perhaps he could simply luxuriate in the warmth for a little while, allow his many cares and responsibilities to fall away. But while he might do the former, the latter was almost impossible, reared as he had been to accept that responsibilities were part of his birthright as the Count of Nesdiryn – a necessary counter-weight to the privileges that went with that office. His parents however, had trained him for the ruling of a rela-tively peaceful and ordered land. They had not remotely prepared him for dealing with a people torn from within by such as the Gevethen, except in so far as they had died for their own inability to measure the depth of the Gevethen's treachery and inhumanity. Their deaths had been their last terrible lesson for their son.

Now, Ibryen's duties were both simpler and more oner-ous. No longer was he burdened by the innumerable ties of administrative and political need that ruling a land involved. Instead, he had become a besieged warlord whose least error, or lapse in vigilance, could see himself and his followers destroyed utterly, and the Gevethen given full sway over the land. And always, darkening even this deep shadow, was the unspoken question – what were the Gevethen's ultimate intentions? What could the acqui-sition of such political and military power as they con-stantly sought betoken, except ambitions beyond the borders of Nesdiryn?

However, while these considerations formed a constant, disturbing undertow to his life, none of them were immediately in Ibryen's thoughts as he lay back against the still-cold rock and, eyes closed, turned his face towards the sun. His new life was not without pleasures – simple pleasures that once he would have disdained or

11

even been oblivious to – pleasures such as the sun on his face and the solitary silence of the mountains. And he could indulge these for a few moments now that he was here and alone.

He had scarcely begun to relax however, when, unheard and unfelt, yet indisputably *there*, the mysterious call that had reached into his dreams to waken him and lured him to this eyrie was all about him. But still its message eluded him. Still it shifted and changed like voices in the wind, though now perhaps it was nearer? Louder? Clearer? Again, none of the words were adequate, yet all were true. Shapes formed in the sounds that were not sounds, and danced to the rhythm of the flickering lights behind his closed eyes – now solid and whole, now intangible and vague – jumping from time to time as Ibryen resisted the warm drowsiness that was threatening to overwhelm him and jerked himself into wakefulness.

Until a pattern began to emerge, tantalizingly familiar. It echoed around a sound that suddenly was truly a sound. Ibryen's mind lurched towards it, drawing it closer and closer, searching into it, clutching at the meaning that he could sense striving to reach him.

Abruptly it came into focus.

'Hello,' a voice said, close by.

Chapter 2

Ignoring curses and ill-aimed kicks, a large mangy dog dashed purposefully between the legs of the passers-by and out into the roadway. It began to bark ferociously at a passing carriage. The horses reared at this unexpected onslaught, almost tearing the reins from the driver's hands. The clattering hooves, the barking, and the raucous shouting of the driver – at both horses and dog – inevitably brought nearby pedestrians to a halt to watch the spectacle, and soon further cursing rose to swell the chorus as other carts, carriages and riders had to stop or take evasive action.

No one made any effort to seize the dog however, for not only was it large, it was moving very quickly, dodging the flailing hooves and the driver's whip with ease. Further, it had a look in its eyes that would have made even the sternest hesitant to tackle it; its lip curled back to reveal teeth whose whiteness testified to the fact that, ill-kempt though it might be, it had plenty of bones to chew on. To those late afternoon citizens who had the misfortune to understand, this above all identified the dog not only as feral, but as having come from the death pits. Who could say what impulse had drawn it into the heart of the city?

And who could say what impulse continued to guide it,

13

for instead of barking and fleeing as most dogs would have done, this one's attacking fury seemed to grow in proportion to the uproar it was causing. The driver soon stopped trying to beat it off with his whip as he needed both hands to control the two horses. Angry shouts began to emanate from within the now swaying carriage and the watching crowd both grew and widened under the contradictory effects of curiosity and fear. Other drivers in the street stopped their cursing and started backing away from the scene.

Then further cries came from a section of the crowd and several people leapt hastily out of the way as another dog emerged to join the first in attacking the carriage. The assault redoubled, the horses became frantic and the driver lost such control as he had. The swaying of the carriage increased until, after hovering for a timeless moment, it crashed over, taking the thrashing horses with it. The driver fell heavily on to the rough cobbled roadway and lay still.

The crowd became suddenly silent, and for a while the only sound to be heard in the street was the scrabbling of the terrified horses and the ominous snarling of the dogs as they paced to and fro in front of the destruction they had wrought.

No one moved to help the fallen driver. Indeed, eyes now fearfully averted from the scene, the crowd began to melt away. Slowly at first, then with increasing urgency.

A sudden crash halted the flight. It was the carriage door being flung back by the passenger. He began to heave himself up through the opening. Though not a young man, vigorous command and capability could be read in his grim face and the very sight of him seemed to chill the crowd into immobility.

'Stay where you are,' he said, his voice harsh and menacing. Even the dogs fell back a little, crouching low, though their snarling muzzles were even more terrifying than before. Half emerged from the carriage, the man disdained their menace and slowly scanned the crowd. It was as if he were memorizing the face of each individual there, or worse, already knew it. Those who failed to avoid his gaze could not tear their eyes away. The street stank of fear while, above, the already gloomy sky seemed to darken further, adding its weight to the sense of oppression that the man's presence exuded.

Then, into this silent interrogation came a flurry of movement and the two dogs, still snarling, began to crawl forward, their tails sweeping over the cobbles expectantly. The man in the carriage turned sharply towards the disturbance, his teeth bared as if in imitation of his attackers, but even as he did so, the cause was upon him. A lithe figure, ragged and dirty, was vaulting nimbly up on to the carriage. Disbelief came into the man's face. It was changing to anger when the newcomer reached down, seized his hair with her left hand and jerked his head back, unbalancing him. Then with her right, she plunged a knife into him. It was a deliberately wounding stroke.

'Just to catch your attention, Hagen,' she hissed, wrenching his head back further and slashing savagely at his flailing arms. 'This one should be for the Count, but really it's for my parents. I wish I could take more time over it,' and she stabbed him in the throat twice. 'Rot in hell.'

A futile hand clutching his wounds, Hagen straightened momentarily, then crashed back down into the carriage, the opened door slamming behind him. Even as he disappeared from view, the woman was running back into the crowd, the two dogs at her heels and the knife trailing blood. She made no sound but neither did she hesitate and the crowd parted hastily to let her through. The movement

15

seemed to break the spell that Hagen had cast and abruptly the street was alive with screaming, fleeing people.

The city was busy at that time of day, and those trying to escape found themselves impeded by others who were pursuing their normal errands or had been drawn to the scene by the noise. Abruptly, a shrill cry rang out above the others as a group of armed and uniformed horsemen appeared at the end of the street.

'Guards! Citadel Guards!'

As the cry passed along, the confusion turned almost to panic. The man at the head of the column stopped and looked at the milling crowd with a mixture of irritation and disdain. He was about to say something when the rider next to him took his arm urgently and pointed towards the overturned carriage.

'Captain! Captain Helsarn!'

The leader seemed about to transfer his annoyance to this new intrusion, but as he followed the trembling arm, his scornful expression suddenly became one of stark horror. He spurred his horse forward frantically, at the same time shouting out an order, his voice cracking. The Guards surged after him, and the group galloped along the street with complete disregard for whoever was standing in their way. Several people were knocked over, but none of them wasted any time in abusing the riders; rather, they redoubled their efforts to escape the scene.

Reaching the carriage, the Captain swung off his horse directly on to the upturned side. For a moment he struggled with the door before he managed to wrench it open, then he had to shield his eyes to see into the dark interior. A gasp of disbelief concluded his inspection and he dropped down into the carriage, pausing only to motion his companions forward to help him. After a brief, confused interlude of cursing and slipping, the bloodstained body of the slaughtered Hagen was lifted awkwardly from the vehicle and laid on the ground. Throughout, the Guards handled the body with a hesitant mixture of reverence and fear, as if at any moment it might spring to life and bring down some terrible wrath on them for their profanity in so touching it. The mood lingered even after the body had been laid down, as the men formed a circle about it as though preparing for a vigil.

It was Helsarn who recovered first. He glanced up and down the street and, in a sinister echo of the call that Hagen himself had made, he shouted, 'Stay where you are, all of you!' The crowd however, already motivated to movement by the murder of Hagen, and suddenly unified in their intention by the appearance of the Guards, had used their momentary paralysis to escape. Thus the Captain found himself addressing a dwindling number of distant and fleeing backs and a handful of individuals who were already converging on the carriage. Obediently, these all stopped, obliging him then to motion them forward angrily, while the rest continued their flight.

He opened his mouth again, but for a moment, no sound came as he searched for something to say. Finally he managed to demand, 'What's happened here?'

There was some dumb shaking of heads but the Captain was already bringing his thoughts to more urgent needs. He turned to one of his men, a heavy-set and powerful-looking individual. 'Low-Captain Vintre, get this carriage righted, then use it to bring the Lord Counsellor's body back to the Citadel.'

'And these?' The Low-Captain indicated the remains of the crowd.

The Captain frowned as though irritated at having to deal with such obvious matters.

17

'They're all under arrest, of course,' he snapped. 'They're witnesses. Bring them as well. They'll have to be questioned. I'll go ahead and tell Commander Gidlon what's happened.' He looked down at the body and briefly his inner fears showed through. Though he spoke softly to Vintre and did not move, his eyes flicked from side to side, as if spies and denouncers might be all around him. 'This is unbelievable. I hope someone hasn't struck a match in this tinderbox.'

The Low-Captain responded in kind, but more prosaically. 'Let's just thank our fates we weren't Lord Hagen's duty escort today.'

Helsarn's cold demeanour returned as he nodded, then he remounted and, driving his spurs viciously into his horse's flanks, galloped off down the street.

A little later, the carriage was upright again and, bearing both the injured driver and the dead body of Hagen, was following the same route as the Captain. It was a strange procession. Not that the sight of carriage, escort and prisoners was strange in Dirynhald, but normally it would provoke little or no response from the passing citizens. Now, however, despite the time of day, the streets were almost empty and such few people as were about were ill-at-ease and either stared fretfully or conspicuously averted their eyes and strode out purposefully.

It did not need Helsarn's words, 'match in this tinderbox', to heighten Vintre's nervousness further and he closed his men up and moved them to the trot, notwithstanding the discomfiture of the 'witnesses' jogging between the two files. News of Hagen's death had obviously run through the city as fast as legs could carry it, and who could say what consequences would ensue. It was a long time since there had been any serious, or even open opposition to the Gevethen, but though an insidious

18

mixture of sustained terror and familiarity was gradually sapping its will, the opposition was there, brooding and ominous – in many ways very little different in its demeanour now from that of the Gevethen themselves. Vintre's mind wandered . . . Perhaps this year they would at last find the Count and stamp out the remaining spark of resistance that his continued existence maintained.

A disturbance behind him brought Vintre sharply back to the grey street, but it was only one of the prisoners being dragged to his feet after stumbling. He reproached himself angrily for drifting into daydreams. Now was a time to be alert. Lord Counsellor Hagen had been the Gevethen's closest adviser, and his death would undoubtedly be used as an excuse for them to tighten further their grip on the city and its people. Whatever else happened, the next few weeks were going to be busy and brutal, and there would be plenty of opportunities for an ambitious young officer, not least for one who was first upon the scene and who was bringing in witnesses. Almost certainly that alone would assure him the Gevethen's personal attention. Excellent opportunities for sure – and a damn sight easier than trekking through the mountains searching for the Count, in constant fear of ambush.

Instinctively, Vintre straightened up and began making adjustments to his uniform. He brought his horse alongside the carriage and peered inside. Hagen's body was draped along one of the seats while the unconscious driver had been propped up in a corner. Without realizing that he was doing it, he made his face look concerned. It was as if Hagen's awful will, too cruel even for death's domain, might suddenly return to his corpse and open the eyes to find himself the object of a junior officer's ghoulish curiosity. Even in death, Hagen was frightening.

Only now did Vintre being to grasp the awful magnitude

of what had happened. There'd be more than just another purging of the citizenry, there'd be some rare jockeying for position at the highest level – for the ears of the Gevethen themselves – and who could say what benefits such a change could bring to lesser lights further down the chain of command? Vintre's ambition, already on the wing, began to soar. Yet, like a cloud about to obscure the sun, there hovered the thought – who could have done such a thing? Not, who, after all this time, would have dared assail Hagen of all people, in broad daylight and in a busy street? Or, how many could have been involved to turn over the carriage? But what *kind* of a person was it who could have stood face to face with Hagen, looked into those awful eyes, and not let their weapon drop from nerveless hands?

Vintre shivered.

Then they were at the Citadel.

Vintre shivered again.

Chapter 3

The rasp of Ibryen's sword being drawn echoed the hiss of his sharply in-drawn breath as he leapt to his feet. Despite the violent shock of hearing a voice when he had believed himself to be quite alone, some discipline prevented Ibryen's alarm from announcing itself any louder. The bright mountain daylight burst in upon him blindingly as he opened his eyes and, keeping his back against the rock, he held out his sword and swung it in a broad protective arc while they adjusted.

'Oh!' exclaimed the voice incongruously, amid this frantic scramble.

As Ibryen's vision cleared, he found himself looking at a small figure standing well beyond his sword's reach and shifting its balance from one foot to the other as if preparing to flee.

'I'm sorry if I startled you,' the stranger said. 'I didn't realize—'

'Who are you?' Ibryen demanded brutally.

The new arrival was a man. He was dressed in simple, practical clothes, though they were of a cut unfamiliar to Ibryen, and he had a pack on his back. He stood scarcely chest height to Ibryen and was very slightly built – frail almost. Further he seemed to be quite old. But all this signified nothing. Though he asked it, Ibryen knew that his question was of no import. Whatever answer was given, he already knew the truth. Appearances notwithstanding, the man was not one of his followers and could have only come here by stealth – considerable stealth at that, to have avoided the newly alerted guards. He must thus be a Gevethen spy or, worse, an assassin. Marris's remarks of a few hours before came back to Ibryen, now full of ominous prescience.

He could have been silently murdered while he basked idly in the sun!

Yet he hadn't been. This 'assassin' had announced himself. The thought made Ibryen feel a little foolish, though keeping the stranger in view he looked from side to side to see if anyone else had also reached the ridge unseen and unheard.

'I'm just a traveller,' the man replied. His voice was high-pitched but not unpleasant – indeed, it had an almost musical lilt to it. And he had an accent such as Ibryen had never heard before.

'You're not Dirynvolk,' Ibryen said, instead of the question he had intended.

The little man craned forward a little as if he was having difficulty in understanding the remark, then he smiled. His smile was full of white teeth that seemed to glint in the sunlight, and his eyes sparkled. It was a happy sight, but it was not the smile of an old man. Ibryen tightened the grip on his sword to keep at bay the softening that he was beginning to feel. Though they had long discarded any pretence, the Gevethen had won as much through smooth speech and manners in the early days as through the brutality and terror they now exercised and, even before his flight into the mountains, Ibryen had long schooled himself to be wary of smiles and bland, assuring speech.

22

'No,' the man was replying. 'I'm far, far away from where I was born.'

'You have a name though?'

The man nodded and said something. This time it was Ibryen who leaned forward, frowning, to catch the words. The man noted the movement and repeated his name. Ibryen shook his head as the sound eluded him again.

'You're not Dirynvolk,' he announced with finality. 'I'll call you Traveller.'

'As you wish.'

'What are you doing here?' Ibryen returned to his earlier brusqueness. 'Who sent you? How did you get here?'

A flicker of irritation passed over the little man's face. 'I don't think I wish to be spoken to like that,' he said. 'Least of all at the end of a sword. I'll go on my way if my presence offends you so.' He made to move away. Ibryen stepped forward and placed the point of his sword on the man's chest.

'You'll go nowhere until you answer my questions,' he said starkly. 'This is my land and strangers in it are not welcome.'

The Traveller looked down at the sword and then up at Ibryen. 'I'd never have guessed,' he said acidly. He waved an arm around the towering sunlit peaks that surrounded them. 'This all belongs to you, does it, swordsman?' He met Ibryen's stern gaze squarely. 'A wiser person might have been more inclined to say that he belonged to the land, don't you think?'

Ibryen almost snarled. 'A wiser person might perhaps be more inclined to avoid philosophy and answer my questions, in your position.'

The Traveller snorted disdainfully. 'What I am doing here is a fundamental question of all philosophies, is it not?' he said, even more acidly than before. 'As to who sent me. Ha! Well! A still deeper question. Though I presume you are posing it in the sense that I might be here at the behest of some employer, or even a powerful lord – doubtless one such as yourself who owns many great mountains . . .' he flicked the sword-blade contemptuously with his middle finger '. . . and a big sword with which to menace lesser fry.' Ibryen winced inwardly before this verbal onslaught but his expression did not change. 'However, avoiding the greater question, to the best of my knowledge I am here at my own free will, as presumably are you. And how I came here? I used these!' He lifted one leg off the ground in a dance-like movement, and slapped his thigh loudly. 'Now may I go?'

There was such authority in the voice that, for a moment, Ibryen almost acceded to the request. 'No, you may not!' he shouted, recovering.

The Traveller grimaced and shook his head. 'Not so loud,' he said, almost plaintively. 'I'm not used to people and I've very sensitive hearing.'

'I'm sorry,' Ibryen heard himself saying. The shock of the Traveller's sudden appearance was still unsettling him, and his mind was awash with conjecture about Gevethen treachery, but holding his sword at the chest of someone who was both older and patently no match for him physically was distressing him. His confusion was not eased by the fact that, despite his position, the Traveller did not seem to be in the least afraid. Ibryen lowered his voice when he spoke again.

'Only a few hours ago I checked the vigilance of my guards,' he said. 'It isn't possible that you came past them other than with great stealth. And stealth equals treachery in these mountains. You can only be a Gevethen spy and that means your death unless you can show why we should

24

let you live. Now tell me who sent you and why, and how you came here. And spare me any more of your sarcasm.'

Ibryen's quieter manner seemed to have a greater effect than his previous bluster. The Traveller screwed up his face pensively and the rancour had gone from his voice when he replied. 'No one sent me, swordsman. I know nothing of these Gevethen you speak of, though there are ancient resonances in the word which are rather unpleasant.' He pointed. 'I came here on foot across the mountains. It's the way I always travel. Fewer people, less noise. And my ancestors were mountain folk.'

Ibryen followed the extended arm. He was unable to keep the surprise and disbelief from his face when he turned back. 'You came from the *south*?' he exclaimed. His sword began to falter, but he steadied it quickly. 'There are supposed to be lands to the south, but the mountains are impassable even in summer. No one even attempts to go there. And certainly no one ever comes from there.'

The Traveller gave a disclaiming shrug. 'There are many lands to the south,' he said, as if stating the obvious. 'All rather noisy, I'm afraid, but that's the way it is with most people these days. As for the mountains being impassable, that's obviously not so. Though, in all honesty, I *am* well-used to mountains.'

Ibryen looked at the Traveller narrowly. There was nothing about him that suggested he was lying. But to travel from the south! That wasn't possible, surely?

'You're lying,' he said.

The Traveller shrugged again, but did not speak.

'Tell me the truth,' Ibryen said, forcing an interrogator's concern into his voice. 'The Gevethen have lured good men to their cause before now. What have they told you about us? What have they told you to do? How are they

25

paying you? Or are they threatening you, or your family?'

The Traveller frowned. 'I've told you once. I know nothing of these Gevethen. I know nothing of you. Not even your name.' He became indignant. 'It may offend your lordly dignity, *owner* of these hills, but you're nothing more than a chance encounter on a long journey. A possible companion with whom I might have whiled away a little time – learned a little, perhaps taught a little – before going on my way again.'

Ibryen stared at him in silence for some time, then, for no reason that he could immediately fathom, he lowered his sword. The Traveller looked at him intently, but did not move. 'If there's such danger from this enemy of yours, why are you lounging in the sunshine like a noon-day lizard?'

Some quality in his voice insinuated itself deep into Ibryen and forced out an answer that he had never expected to hear uttered. 'I thought I . . . heard . . . something,' he said uncertainly.

The Traveller let out a long sigh of understanding. He took a pace backwards and crouched down. He motioned Ibryen to sit. 'You heard something,' he echoed softly. He glanced down into the valley. 'Heard it in the night, I'd judge, from the distance to your village.' He began to rock to and fro on his haunches, humming to himself, seemingly oblivious to Ibryen, though from time to time, he looked at him narrowly.

'What could you have heard that would bring you from your bed and make you climb up here in the darkness?' The question was not addressed to Ibryen, it was simply voiced. Then one eye closed and the other opened wide and stared directly at Ibryen. 'A call, perhaps? A distant cry carried on the underside of the wind, clinging to the rustling of the leaves and the hissing of the grasses?

26

Bubbling in the chatter of the streams?'

The Traveller's voice brought vivid images into Ibryen's mind and a profound curiosity that over-mastered his concern at the sudden appearance of this stranger. He stepped forward and knelt down by the man's side.

'You heard it too,' he whispered. 'What is it?'

'I heard what I heard. The question is, what did you hear?'

Some of Ibryen's caution began to return. 'Enough to draw me here as you guessed,' he replied.

The Traveller's face became unreadable. 'Indulge me, lord. Tell me what you heard,' he said after a moment. 'It may be important.'

Ibryen hesitated, then, 'I'm not sure that I heard anything, although sound is the only word that can describe what I . . . felt. It was as though something were calling out – wanting help.'

The Traveller looked out across the valley. 'Help,' he said softly, turning the word over thoughtfully. 'You could be right. How strange. You seem to hear more keenly than I do.' Then he frowned as if at the deep foolishness of such a remark. 'Or . . . perhaps you hear beyond where I can. Perhaps you're . . .' He left the sentence unfinished. 'I think I'd like to know more about you, swordsman. May I impose on your hospitality for a little while? I can work – or entertain the children with stories. And I'm an interesting cook.'

Ibryen started at this sudden appeal. Despite his curiosity about the Traveller, there had never been any doubt in his mind but that the little man would be experiencing their hospitality for a while, whether he wanted to or not. Probably much longer than he intended. Whatever this man might be – spy or innocent traveller – his knowledge of the village's location made him a threat and he could

27

not be allowed to leave the valley. Ibryen kept this from his face however, as he stood up and sheathed his sword. 'You may indeed,' he replied.

They had attracted considerable attention by the time they reached the lower slopes of the mountain and a growing crowd was emerging from the village. The Traveller paused and furrowed his brow unhappily. 'A moment,' he said, laying a hand on Ibryen's arm. Ibryen stopped, wondering for a moment whether the little man was at last about to flee. He had been a pleasant, if silent, walking companion during their descent, with a keen eye for the easy way and, Ibryen noticed, a feeling for the right pace for his companion. But that had been just another puzzle, for though he seemed to be an old man, the Traveller was quite untroubled by the descent. 'I'm not used to so many people,' he went on. He was anxiously searching in the pockets of his tunic. 'Do forgive me. Ah!' Two small rolls of material appeared from somewhere and, after kneading them briefly between his thumb and finger, he put one in each ear. 'That's better,' he announced, with conspicuous relief, and strode out again.

Two riders were heading towards them. 'I'm afraid I'm causing a bit of a stir,' the Traveller said, manipulating the material in one ear. 'Your people are very alarmed.'

'You'll understand why when you've been here a little while,' Ibryen told him.

The riders, a man and a woman, reached them and dismounted in a great flurry. Both were red-faced and flustered.

'Count . . .'

Ibryen waved them silent. 'No fault of yours that I can see, cousins. The Traveller here has a tale to tell that should be worth listening to. He's come some distance and he's asked if he might stay with us for a while. I've offered him our hospitality.' Neither of the two arrivals made any attempt to keep the surprise from their faces, but Ibryen ignored the response and turned to the Traveller. 'Hynard is the son of my father's brother, and Rachyl the daughter of my mother's sister. They'll look after you while you're with us.'

The surprised expressions became indignant, then confused, as the Traveller advanced on them, hands extended in greeting. Rachyl's hand flickered uneasily about a knife in her belt, but before it could decide what to do the Traveller encased it in both of his and smiled at her. 'A delight to meet you,' he said. His tone forced a hesitant smile on to Rachyl's grim face but she looked at Ibryen unhappily as the Traveller turned to Hynard and greeted him similarly.

'If you'll allow me a moment, I must give my cousins their instructions,' Ibryen intervened, motioning the Traveller to stay where he was while he moved Hynard and Rachyl some distance away.

'How the devil—?'

Ibryen beat down Hynard's voice with a furious gesture. Hynard continued in an equally furious whisper. 'How the devil did he get through the passes?' he hissed.

'And why didn't you kill him right away?' Rachyl added, grasping his arm.

'I'd neither inclination nor justification for killing him,' Ibryen snapped back angrily.

'That he's here is justification enough!'

'That he's here is justification enough for keeping him alive, Rachyl. Use your head.' Rachyl's jaw came out fiercely, but Ibryen ignored the challenge. 'He's got a wild tale to tell and I think we should listen to it. If it transpires he's lying, then we need more than ever to know how he came here, don't we? Especially if there are ways to this place that even we don't know about. For pity's sake, we can kill him any time. He's hardly a fighting man, is he?' The two cousins cast a glance at the Traveller standing patiently some way away, apparently looking round at the mountains. Ibryen's reasoning was impeccable, but a stranger in the valley was nerve-wracking, for all that.

'What do you want us to do with him?' Rachyl conceded surlily.

For an instant, Ibryen's face bore the expression of a man facing insurmountable odds as he looked at his glowering cousin.

'Be pleasant. Be polite,' he said, with an effort. 'Watch him all the time. And watch what he watches. Listen to what he says and take note of everything he asks you. Tell him as little as possible but remember what you *do* tell him. And tell everyone else to keep away from him.'

'And if he tries to escape?' Rachyl asked expectantly.

'Don't let him!' Ibryen's tone was final. 'I hold you responsible for his well-being until we decide what to do with him. Is that clear?' Rachyl nodded curtly. Ibryen returned to the Traveller. 'You have my protection, but there's no point pretending you're welcome here. We're under siege from a terrible enemy and have been for many years now. People who appear from nowhere strike a deep fear into us all.'

'I understand.'

'I doubt it,' Ibryen retorted. 'Go with Rachyl and Hynard, they'll find somewhere for you to stay.'

'And they'll keep an eye on me.'

Ibryen nodded. 'And they'll protect you until we can talk further.'

'I'm grateful,' the Traveller replied.

'Do whatever they tell you to do and don't wander away from them.'

'I will. They both look very ... determined.'

Ibryen looked down at the Traveller. It would have needed no great perception to read the expressions on the faces of Hynard and Rachyl when they first arrived, for all they were now endeavouring to appear civil, and, in his brief acquaintance he had not found the Traveller to be anything other than very astute. He must know the danger he's in, he thought, yet his last remark was almost flippant. Either he's a complete fool, or he has greater resources than he appears to have.

He abandoned his debate and without further comment took Rachyl's horse and turned it towards the approaching crowd.

Chapter 4

Every part of Jeyan cried out for continued flight. She
wanted to run and run until Hagen's corpse, the Guards,
the city, this whole damned land was far behind her. But,
well away from the scene of the murder now, she forced
herself to slow to a walk as she emerged from an alleyway
into the busy street. The two dogs, Assh and Frey, who
had been running ahead, slowed without turning round.
Long-developed habit made Jeyan slouch and lower her
head to take on the semblance of one of the many indigent
street-dwellers that littered the city. But it was difficult.
Her whole body was shaking violently and she felt as
though her inner turmoil must surely be resounding
through the afternoon crowd like a clarion, drawing all
eyes towards her. Grimly she made herself stand still for
a moment while she stared at the ground, nudging a
mound of rubbish with her foot, as though searching for
something. Her passion and hatred had done their part in
giving her the courage to stare into the face of that creature, Hagen, and slay him – her shaking increased at the
recollection – but now her wits must ensure her escape.
And running was not the way. Running was the way that
would indeed draw all eyes, and thence the Guards, to
her. She allowed herself to start walking again, carefully
maintaining her slovenly posture. At the same time she

signalled to the dogs to move away. They obeyed immediately, Assh surreptitiously trotting ahead and busying himself sniffing amongst the piles of refuse that lined the street, and Frey dropping back and crossing to the other side to do the same. Though they were soon weaving casually through the passers-by, Jeyan knew they would be watching and listening, waiting for her least signal. She, in her turn, was listening for the sounds of pursuit or, worse, for the sounds of the street purging that must surely follow what she had done. In the shivering chill that followed the heat of her slaughter of Hagen, colder counsels were emerging from time to time. Much more than a street purging would follow on such a deed. How many innocent people had she condemned with her act? What trials had she unleashed on the city?

She gritted her teeth. No more than the city deserved, she thought. Hadn't the city stood by, timid and compliant, when her parents were hounded with lies and petty persecutions before finally being selected for trial and execution? Trial – the word made her want to spit – what an obscenity! All the forms and procedures, full of dignity and pomp, glibly displayed to cover and at once reveal the Gevethen's grinding cruelty. But that was the way they ruled – paying obsessive attention to the superficial details of the Law, while wilfully corrupting its very heart. Turning it into just another subtle instrument of torture. And so tainting it that even if the Count should return, he would find its ancient face disfigured beyond repair.

There would be plenty of trials after today's work. Jeyan had known this from the moment she began to contemplate it, but it was of no concern to her. Only by the merest chance had she been absent from her parents' home when the Citadel Guards came ... and it was the cowardly response of her erstwhile 'friends' that had set her on the inexorable way to today's deed. One after another, once-welcoming doors had remained implacably shut against her tearful pleadings as, frantic, she had gone searching for help. Angry voices had spurned her, threats had been made to hold her for the Guards, dogs had been set upon her. The greatest kindness she had received that day had been a loaf of bread thrust through a briefly opened shutter, and even that had been accompanied by a fearful, whispered injunction to go at once, to flee the city.

And there had been little kindness or help since, so frightened were the people. For once the Count had been swept aside and his remaining followers silenced, the secret denunciation had become the Gevethen's most insidious weapon. So pervasive had it become that spouse feared spouse, parents feared children, each feared his neighbour. Where there had been debate and laughter, there was now sullen silence. Where there had been warm and open faces there were now suspicious, uneasy glances. Even the least whisper seemed to reach the ears of the Gevethen, and the whisperer would be pursued and brought to account. There would be a well-rehearsed public trial, or the offender would simply be no more . . . Those who saw the Guards marching at night turned their faces away.

Yet Jeyan had survived. She had eaten the loaf while softly cursing the giver, then, with the vague idea that perhaps she might meet survivors from the masssacre of the Count's followers, she had fled into the Ennerhald: the labyrinth of crooked streets, broken buildings and crumbling cellars that were the remains of the old city from which grew Dirynhald. She had found only such as herself there however, together with those who had no place under either the Count's rule or the Gevethen's –

petty thieves and pathetic rogues and others whose grasp on the direction of their lives was, at best, tenuous.

For a little while, as the daughter of one of the Count's staunchest allies, she had found herself the focus of a group who talked boldly about rising up and ridding the land of the Gevethen. She was no longer alone. Hope blossomed again. But just as her father's name drew this band about her, so too, it drew the attention of the Gevethen and soon a whispering betrayer brought the Citadel Guards upon them. Jeyan's revolutionaries had neither the stomach nor the skill for such a conflict, and those who had not fled, had died.

It was the final severing of Jeyan from her former life – a terrible, learning time. Shortly afterwards, half-crazed at the destruction of this, her second family, she crossed another awful threshold by killing the betrayer. She gave him neither warning nor mercy and he had Gevethen coins in his mouth when he was found. Tales began to circulate of a wild, vengeful spirit that flitted through the night shadows of Dirynhald. A spirit that was as cruel as the Gevethen themselves.

By a dark irony, it was this notoriety that made those involved in the soft, silent network of opposition to the Gevethen reluctant to pursue their search for her.

From then on, Jeyan had walked alone, living by the harsh code of the Ennerhald, watching, listening, lying, stealing, and making only such acquaintances as need dictated. And, Ennerhald society, like any other, having its own hierarchy, she also learned to defend herself against those who would have preyed on her. She became horribly proficient with the knife she carried – agile and fast but, worst of all, quite without hesitation. She was greatly feared.

Not that she was even aware of the opinions of others

for, above all other things, her thoughts were dominated by a single vision – a vision of the Gevethen, dead, and dead by her hand. She nurtured it obsessively. Only the rumours and, later, the knowledge that the Count had survived and was in the mountains with many of his followers, prevented her from sinking into rambling insanity.

Now the obsession and the skills and the temper that the Ennerhald had bred in her had come together and set her on the road to attaining that vision. And she had taken that first simple, practical and bloody step with relish. She had struck a blow close to the Gevethen's heart. It was a rehearsal for a future event. Consequences were irrelevant.

Rain began to fall, a few large drops heralding a spring downpour as the clouds that had been lowering over the city all day abruptly released their charge. The pace of the street changed and, with considerable relief, Jeyan took the opportunity to change her shambling gait to one more matching her mood. It carried her through the now-bustling crowd without remark. The two dogs went their own way; in so far as they were noted at all, they were assiduously avoided.

Then Jeyan was gone from view. It would have taken a keen observer to note her action, as she disappeared down an opening that gaped in front of a derelict building. Free of the public gaze at last, she slipped nimbly under the stone steps that led down from the street and, wriggling through a hole in the wall, scarcely visible in the gloom, resorted again to outright flight.

Sharp eyes and practised but cautious feet carried her through a confusion of dank and disused cellars, lit only by occasional shafts of light which struggled through long-forgotten windows and gratings, and the holes and cracks that years of neglect had brought to the wooden floors above. Such slight sound as she made was well-hidden by the incessant dripping and splashing of the rainwater which found its way into the darkness through a myriad more devious and destructive routes.

Once or twice she caught a glimpse of other shadowy figures moving through this twilight world but she paid them no heed, nor they her save to avoid her.

Away from the open street and moving at her own pace through ever more familiar terrain, Jeyan's trembling began to abate. A cloak of unreality still hung about her however, as the enormity of what she had actually done seeped into her. Hagen dead! And by her hand! The Gevethen's cruellest lieutenant no more. How many murdered innocents had she avenged today? Hundreds . . . thousands? It didn't matter. He was gone.

Abruptly she stopped. Alone in the darkness she found herself searching for a flicker of regret, remorse. But the only regret she could truly feel was that Hagen's death had been so quick, so merciful. Worse, it had been banal and ordinary, just like that of any other man – now alive and thinking himself so for ever, now gone, all fears faced, all fleshly needs and ills ended, all ambitions dust. His face had shown only surprise and . . . irritation.

Rage filled her. Irritation! He should have suffered more. He should have been harrowed as he harrowed others, should have felt himself dying slowly from the inside out as his victims did, felt his screams choking him because he was too afraid to utter them.

Her victory was not enough.

She swore under her breath and clenched her teeth. She was rambling, thinking thoughts such as these. It was sufficient that he was dead. It was sufficient that the people would know that the authority the Gevethen vested in him and which, in his arrogance, he had deemed to be a shield against all ills, had failed him. It was sufficient too that the Gevethen would know that. Would know that their protection was imperfect, that a random stone might unshoe a horse and bring down a king.

She took out the knife and gripped it tightly until her arm ached. Would that she could come within arm's reach of them as well.

The moment was cathartic and as it passed, she felt much calmer, although a faint tremor still seemed to be shaking her whole person – body and mind. She sheathed the knife and set off again.

Within a short while she came to a place where the floor above had collapsed completely. The destruction was old. Well-established bushes and shrubs now grew out of the cellar floor, and swathes of grasses and climbers festooned the ramps of rubble and broken timbers that partly filled the opening. The rain had stopped but the air was filled with an elaborate tattoo as the vegetation above continued to shed the water that it had intercepted.

Despite the gloomy sky, the area seemed unusually bright after the darkness of the cellars and, as was her normal habit, Jeyan waited, silent and still, all senses alert until she was quite satisfied that nothing was to be seen, heard, or felt there that should not be. Then she clambered through the dripping foliage and, pausing again to reassure herself further that all was safe, she emerged into the remains of one of the buildings that lay at the fringe of the Ennerhald. Around her were the decaying remains of the roof and floors that had collapsed many years before. Like the debris in the cellar they were scarcely recognizable under the vegetation that was repossessing the site.

From here, Jeyan moved through a large and spacious hall. Who could say what it might once have been?

Banqueting Hall, Meeting Hall, Court? Perhaps it was not even part of the old city, for, just as the Gevethen rotted Dirynhald society from within, so people edged nervously away from the unsettling presence of the Ennerhald and thus it spread outwards, slowly but relentlessly encroaching on the city that had supplanted it. Now, whatever its past, the roofless building, its stained and lichened walls perforated by circular openings and pocked with holes where floor and roof-beams had once rested, was just a chasm – another way from here to there; its only significance now as a quick escape route – should need arise.

Vaulting through a window, Jeyan glanced from side to side quickly, then straightened up. All around were other, smaller buildings, all decaying. Here and there some had collapsed across the narrow street, while others leaned forward as though to whisper profundities to their neighbour opposite, and were actually touching one another. They formed bizarre arcades. Once the Ennerhald had been as distant from her life as the moon, but now it was her land. Here, the Gevethen's writ faltered, whether by design or through indifference did not matter. Here no Citadel Guards, no soldiers, strutted and brutalized, no officials of the new order wove their endless webs of petty regulations to control the every deed of every individual. The only enemies here would be her own kind, and few of those troubled her now.

As she walked along, she put her fingers to her mouth and gave a loud but very short whistle. The sound bounced sharply from wall to wall, stirring the silence. Somewhere a bird fluttered up in alarm. Within a few moments, Frey and Assh appeared, one bounding through a window, the other sneaking up silently, belly low, behind her. Jeyan knelt down and embraced them. Tails wagging, they nuzzled her. These were allies that she could truly trust. Their damp fur stank but Jeyan was a long way from being disturbed by unpleasant smells now.

'Well done,' she whispered passionately. 'Well done. Tonight we'll celebrate. We'll eat.'

It was some time before she reached her destination. She had, in fact, many places which she had made suitable for living in, and many other places which she knew to be safe from anything other than the most determined search. Today however, she had chosen the one she liked the most, the one she was inclined to call home and where she preferred to spend most of her time. It was situated at the southernmost edge of the Ennerhald, farthest from the city. Just as the Ennerhald at its opposite end seemed to be encroaching on the city, so here the forest that ran south towards the mountains also seemed intent on repossessing its ancient terrain. The strange atmosphere that pervaded the deserted city became eerie and watchful here as root and branch did their work, and man-made shapes gradually crumbled or disappeared under foliage and vegetation.

Further south, the forest was bounded by a fast-moving and dangerous river that tumbled violently out of the mountains. Further south still, the empty land that lay between the river and the mountains was regularly patrolled by the Gevethen's army for fear that the Count might perhaps seek to ford the river and move through the forest to attack the city. But the forest, like the Ennerhald itself, was ignored – or avoided.

At one time, Jeyan had considered moving into the forest completely, but she rejected the idea. While perhaps it might have been safer, it would have provided an even more alien and isolated existence than the one she now had; also, there would have been a feeling of desertion, treachery almost, in abandoning the city completely: she could see no life ahead of her that did not involve active opposition to the Gevethen. As it was she had acquired enough forest lore to trap the occasional animal or bird, and forage roots and fruit to carry her over those times when a street purging or a curfew or some other activity that brought unusual numbers of Citadel Guards on to the streets, made venturing into the city to steal food too dangerous.

Her chosen sanctuary was in the centre of a long block of buildings that had once perhaps been dwelling houses, though there was so little in common between the architecture of the Ennerhald and that of Dirynhald that few could have argued the point. Certainly the buildings were unusual: a motley arrangement of unsymmetrical roofs covered them while inside was to be found a seemingly incoherent mixture of large and small rooms, set at many levels and joined by twisting stairways and winding corridors. Some of the rooms reached up through two and more storeys to disappear into the elaborate roofspace, some had curved and undulating walls, while others were rigorously straight. Here and there the faint remains of huge wall paintings could be made out and cold-eyed carvings of both people and outlandish creatures guarded unexpected places. Not that the history of the buildings or their builders concerned Jeyan. It was sufficient that parts could be made warm and dry and that they had many entrances and exits which could be well-disguised.

Before she slipped through the bushes that were growing out of an opening in the wall, she routinely looked to see if a particular loose branch had been disturbed. It never had been in the past, but that did not prevent her from always checking. Then she sent the dogs in. Branch or no branch, if someone more cunning than she had gained access then they could debate their cleverness with

Assh and Frey first. She heard the dogs scuttling around noisily, sniffing as though they had never been there before, then they ran back out to her. All was well.

Later, as night rolled over the forest and into the Enner-hald, Jeyan pondered the day. Dried from the soaking she had received earlier, and warmed by the food she had eaten, she had expected to feel replete and relaxed, able to stretch out like the two dogs, and rejoice in what she had achieved. But no ease came. Instead, a shadow of the trembling that had possessed her as she fled from the city, remained. Its buzzing-insect persistence filled her entire body, kept her restless and tense, almost as though a thunderstorm was pending.

Perhaps one was, she thought. Regrets at what she might have unleashed flickered again at the edges of her mind, but were overshadowed by both a cold satisfaction and the simple survivor's acceptance that what was done was done, for better or worse. All that mattered were the consequences for herself.

Consequences.

Now there would be change. The whole structure would have been shaken. Not damaged beyond repair, by any means – there would be others to take Hagen's place – but where change existed, so did chance, and so did opportunity. But so too, did danger. None of the crowd would have recognized her, of that she was sure, and most would have presumed her to be a man. But word must inevitably reach the Gevethen that Hagen's killer was a street creature, and from that it would be but a step to presume that she hailed from the Ennerhald. The only question that remained was how determinedly would the Gevethen seek out the murderer of their closest and most able counsellor. Forays into the Ennerhald had been made in the past, but its winding streets and innumerable buildings and hiding places would have absorbed an army far larger than the Gevethen's city companies, and rarely had such ventures yielded anything other than a handful of pathetic souls too feeble or witless to run.

But this time, it would be different. This time, vengeance would be sought.

The trembling threatened to return. Out of hard-learned habit, Jeyan used it to bring herself to her feet and, snuffing out two of the candles that illuminated her adopted sanctuary, she moved across the room to the pile of blankets that served as a bed. As she sat down, she clicked her fingers and the two dogs woke immediately and looked at her, ears pricked. She beckoned them and embraced them when they came to her.

'We must be careful, dogs. More than ever. Watch and listen. Smell them coming.'

Assh yawned and Frey scratched herself and, with a final squeeze, Jeyan dismissed them. Both of them slumped down alongside her. The physical contact with the dogs was important to her. If only she could be as they were, she thought, lying back. Unaware of the future, and probably the past, also. Responding only to the needs of the moment. Now awake, now asleep; now fierce, now quiet. Their calm seeped into her. The single, tiny candle that remained reduced her world to a small domed enclave surrounded by darkness. For a moment, memories of times long gone returned. Times when the world was not only safe but inviolable, when the only danger was an angry look from a loving parent. Once, such memories used to make her weep. Then she had learned to sneer at her youthful naivety. Now she felt only anger and sadness.

And again, hatred for those who had brought this about. As it did almost every night, her vision of the Gevethen perishing at her hand returned to soothe all ills and to

44

sustain her. Tonight, it was more intense than ever. Jeyan was more like her dogs than she knew: she had tasted her prey's blood and she wanted more.

As she felt sleep overtaking her, she reached out and extinguished the remaining candle.

Across the room, resting on a makeshift table, lay a small mirror which she had stolen one day – hardship had not laid vanity fully to rest. For a brief moment, the blackness that the mirror reflected shifted and changed. When it stilled, staring out from the mirror, cold and unblinking, was a solitary watery eye.

Chapter 5

Even as Vintre looked at the dark gates of the Citadel,
they opened. The sudden movement made him start. He
had not even considered the greeting that would be waiting for him as a result of the news that Helsarn had carried
ahead, but the absence of the rigid formality associated
with the opening of the gates disturbed him, so imbued
was he with the Gevethen's obsessive insistence on order
in all things. Further, for a moment, it seemed to him that
the gates were gaping like the mouth of some ancient
creature come to take vengeance on those who had had
the temerity to so handle the murdered body of the Lord
Counsellor. The impression was so vivid that it made
him gasp and he raised his hand quickly to his mouth to
disguise the response as a clearing of his throat.

Silently he reproached himself for this foolishness. The
reaction however, gave him a measure of the shock he
was suffering at this ominous event. Be careful, he thought
sternly. Very careful. Keep hold of the reality of what's
happening. For all the aura that had hung about him –
that indeed had been assiduously cultivated by him –
Hagen had been only a man, and now he was just another
corpse, one person less in authority to be feared. Doubtless an awful vengeance for his slaying would be determined by the Gevethen, but that was a mere detail. All

47

he had to remember was to look for opportunities in the re-ordering that must occur in the immediate future.

He took one advantage immediately. In the absence of the usual formal challenges, he led the column through the gates without stopping. The outer courtyard was crowded with people – Guards, officials, servants – but Vintre ignored them as he rode on, causing them to scatter. He had already noted Helsarn standing on the steps that led to the guardhouse by the inner gate. Just joining him was the bulky figure of Commander Gidlon, the most senior of the five Commanders of the Citadel Guards. He was red-faced and struggling frantically to button his tunic.

Fooling around with the servants again, eh, *Commander*? Vintre thought caustically. Getting caught out at that, plus the shock that Helsarn had just delivered to him – and a little good fortune – might well see another gap being made in the higher ranks of the Gevethen's aides, he mused. But Vintre kept any sign of this speculation from his face, adopting an expression of stony-faced shock as he halted the column and dismounted.

Gidlon, tunic awry, ignored his salute. He ran clumsily down the steps and threw open the carriage door. The driver's unconscious body slowly tumbled out into his arms. Gidlon uttered a startled cry at this unexpected embrace, for a moment fearing that it was Hagen himself. It took all Vintre's self-control to bite back an hysterical laugh at the sight. By the time he had reached his flustered Commander, the driver's body was sprawled on the ground.

'Get this offal out of here,' Gidlon was shouting at no one in particular, kicking the body.

Helsarn stepped forward, quickly selecting three gaping Guards from the gathering crowd. 'Take him to the physician straight away, and stay with him,' he ordered, his

48

manner cold and forceful and markedly at odds with his Commander's. 'Mind how you carry him. Tell the physician he's to be tended carefully – he'll have to be questioned thoroughly later.' He turned to the crowd. 'The rest of you, get about your duties.' Unusually, the order had only a limited effect. For a moment Helsarn considered repeating it then rejected the idea. It was perfectly obvious that though he had only spoken to Commander Gidlon, the news of Hagen's death had flown through the city faster than he had galloped. Even now it would be spreading through the Citadel like a cold wind bringing news of premature winter.

As the men set about removing the driver, Gidlon swung himself up into the carriage. Its springs creaked a little and the horses' hooves clattered as they responded, then there was a sudden silence across the whole courtyard. The sounds of the city outside drifted in to fill it. When Gidlon emerged, there was blood on his hands, and his face was as pale as previously it had been flushed. Very slowly he stepped down from the carriage. Vintre noted that his tunic was now straight and that he had regained much of his normal control. For a moment, he felt a twinge of sympathy for his Commander. He would not have relished breaking such news to the Gevethen, and it certainly wasn't a matter that could be left to some underling.

Gidlon looked at Helsarn. 'Get the physician here immediately,' he said. Helsarn motioned urgently to Vintre, who ran off in the direction taken by the men carrying the driver. Gidlon gestured towards the people that Helsarn had arrested.

'They did this?' he asked incredulously.

'Probably not,' Helsarn replied discreetly. 'It was only people running away that made me turn into the street.

These were all that were left by the time we realized what had happened – the nosy and the stupid.'

Gidlon scowled and bared his clenched teeth viciously. 'I told him repeatedly not to go into the city without his duty escort,' he said, though he was talking to himself, weighing consequences.

'Lord Hagen was Lord Hagen,' Helsarn sympathized coldly. 'More than once he's dismissed me and my men, and he wasn't a man to be argued with. There's no reason why any reproach should be levelled at you, or any of us.'

'Reason doesn't come into it,' Gidlon snarled. 'Get these people locked up, we'll question them later. Then start making preparations for a full purge of that part of the city. That'll be the least that follows this.'

He looked into the carriage again as if for confirmation of what he had to do next. Then, preening his tunic nervously and straightening up, he said, 'I'll have to go and tell *them* what's happened.' Helsarn said nothing. Gidlon took a deep breath. 'Find the other Commanders and tell them to meet me outside the Watching Chamber right away.'

'And the Lord Hagen's body?' Helsarn asked uncertainly.

'Do whatever the physician says when he gets here,' Gidlon said over his shoulder as he walked with heavy deliberation towards the inner gate.

It took Helsarn only a few moments to set in train the instructions that Gidlon had given then he turned his attention again to the watching crowd. No grief was to be seen. That was not unexpected. It was highly unlikely that anyone felt any but, in any event, those who worked in the service of the Gevethen soon learned to become masters of their faces. Nevertheless, he could smell their

50

uncertainty and fear. Who could have done such a thing – that was indeed a frightening thought which he himself did not care to reflect on too deeply at the moment – and who could guess what would flow from it and who would be arbitrarily snatched up in it? His first instinct was to scatter them with a blasting order, but instead, he said quietly, 'Go about your duties. Say nothing and encourage no gossip. All that is necessary for you to know will be revealed in due course. It will be expected of you at such a time in particular to fulfil your duties without deviation and without error.'

This simple, cold statement had more effect than any amount of raucous bawling. Everyone there knew that mistakes, however slight, could sometimes be used as the basis for all manner of accusations. The crowd slowly melted away, leaving Helsarn with the carriage and the remainder of his Watch. Others drawn to the gathering turned about when they saw the crowd dispersing and then the courtyard was empty except for the occasional individual earnestly pursuing some errand with his eyes fixed firmly forwards.

As he surveyed the effect of his words, Helsarn reminded himself that he too was not inviolable in these changed circumstances. Better perform his duties as near as possible to what was normal, he thought. He dismissed six of the Guards to attend to the stabling of the horses and formed the others into an honour guard about the carriage.

Then came an interval of eerie silence. Even the sounds from beyond the wall were waning, as if the whole city was beginning to hold its breath.

The sound of footsteps broke into Helsarn's thoughts. He recognized them before the person making them appeared. Physician Harik's strides, like the man himself,

51

were long, relentless and purposeful. They never varied. He could hear too the fainter sound of Vintre trying to match this testing stride without too much loss of dignity. The soft-soled boots for the Citadel Guards had been one of the Gevethen's whims. 'Best the people do not hear you coming,' they had said. Perhaps it was a dark joke, but no one laughed.

Harik's tall, lank form came through the wicket in the inner gate, with Vintre slightly behind and burdened not only by his shorter stature but by a long and awkward bundle that Harik had obviously thrust upon him. Helsarn flicked an order to two of the Guards who rushed forward and relieved their Low Captain of his charge. It was a stretcher. Harik cast a glance over the scene then acknowledged Helsarn with a cursory nod before turning to the carriage. He laid a reassuring hand on one of the horses then moved to the open door and stepped inside. Helsarn wanted to walk forward and see what was happening, but Harik intimidated him almost as much as the Gevethen, albeit in a different manner.

Harik's face was, as ever, expressionless when he emerged. Taller than Helsarn he bent foward, bringing his face very close. 'Gone to whatever hell he's made for himself,' he said. 'Long gone.'

Helsarn had difficulty in meeting the enigmatic grey-eyed gaze but he could not restrain a start of surprise. Harik was the last person from whom a remark such as that might be expected.

'What shall we do with the . . . his . . . the Lord Counsellor's body?' he said, cursing himself inwardly for stumbling thus.

'Bring him to my Examining Room.'

Helsarn confirmed the order with a nod to Vintre. 'Will anything about his wounds tell you what happened?' he asked, still unsettled by Harik's manner and anxious to sound coherent and in control.

'Little other than the precise manner of his dying,' Harik replied, looking directly at him again. 'But doubtless they'll wish to hear it.' Harik rarely referred to the Gevethen as anything other than 'they', and though he gave the word no special inflection, it was nonetheless full of meaning. 'I doubt the wounds will tell me much about who did it.' His gaze intensified. 'Your province, I think.'

Hagen's body was gingerly taken from the carriage and placed on the stretcher. Harik looked down at him, bending only at the neck, as if to distance himself from the sight, then he produced a cloth from somewhere within his robe and placed it over the dead man's face. The tension amongst the watching men seemed to lighten perceptibly. It lightened further as the body was carried away.

Helsarn stared after it for a moment, then, cursing himself again for his folly, he dismissed the Watch with an order to remain in their quarters and, leaving a solitary Guard to tell Gidlon where he was going, he set off after the retreating physician. A rare figure he'd have cut, standing on the steps waiting for something to happen when Gidlon returned! Whether he liked it or not, he had become the Lord Counsellor's escort and he must attend his every moment for, sure as fate, he would be interrogated about it by the Gevethen themselves.

By the time he caught up with the stretcher party, they had passed through a broad-arched doorway in the inner wall of the Citadel and were moving along the corridor that led to Harik's Examining Room. This was the same room that Harik had used when he was the Count's Physician, and the area around it still had an open and airy feeling that had long passed from the rest of the Citadel. It was many years since Helsarn had been here and, as he took in the scents of the place, they transported him back to the time when he had been a wide-eyed and ambitious junior cadet in the Count's Guard. He scowled under the assault of the peculiarly vivid memories that were suddenly surging through him. Far too much darkness lay between that time and now. Far too much pain, too much cruel learning.

'You're troubled?' Harik asked, noting the change in countenance.

The question brought Helsarn sharply back to the present. He tested the question for treachery. There would be none, he decided. Whatever else he was, Harik was beyond all Citadel politics. Nevertheless, caution was essential.

'How could I not be after such an atrocity?' he replied stiffly. He thought he saw the flicker of a smile on the physician's face – or was it a sneer? But if there was anything there at all, it did not linger, and Harik was merely nodding when Helsarn looked more carefully. The short journey was completed in silence.

Harik's examination of the body did not take long and Helsarn stood through it with stoical impassivity, though it was an effort. Not that he was particularly squeamish about knife wounds or, for that matter, most forms of violent injury, but there was a disturbing quality about Harik's combination of cold-blooded efficiency and delicate gentleness.

Harik straightened up when he had finished and pulled a cloth over the body. He stood for some time looking down at the now anonymous form. 'Doubtless they'll want his body accorded some special respect,' he said eventually, without looking up. 'Have your men take him to the buriers. Tell them to put him in the cold room until I have instructions about what's to be done.' He paused

54

and tapped the edge of the examination table thoughtfully. 'Take him now. There's nothing else to be done and I must take them a report straight away.'

'Did you discover how he was killed?' Helsarn asked bluntly.

'There was a knife wound in his shoulder, but he died from two stab wounds to the throat. I doubt you needed my expertise to tell you that,' Harik replied.

'I didn't examine him other than to confirm that he was dead.'

Harik continued: 'They were delivered from above, very powerfully.'

'A big man, then? Strong?'

Harik looked straight at him. Once again Helsarn found it difficult to hold the grey-eyed gaze. 'Strength lies unseen in many unexpected places, Captain. It merely awaits the right key to release it.'

Helsarn frowned. 'A big man, though?' he persisted.

Harik turned away, a faintly weary expression on his face. 'Probably,' he said off-handedly. 'And it was done with a knife about so long and so wide.' His two forefingers then a finger and thumb demonstrated. 'About the same size as the daggers that your Guards carry.'

Helsarn's stomach lurched and his knees started to shake. Casual remarks such as that could be disastrous. In present circumstances they could spiral out of control and lead to any conclusion – even a purging of the Guards. His voice was almost trembling when he spoke. 'Knives like that are carried by every thief in the city, not to mention all the old Count's Guards,' he said, too quickly. He cleared his throat. 'It won't be necessary for you to make such a . . . comparison . . . in your report, will it?'

Harik eyed him again. 'No,' he said simply. 'Just a statement of the size. Conjecture will be for others. As will everything else. Such as I can do I've done.'

As he was about to leave, Helsarn remembered the driver of Hagen's carriage. He enquired about him.

Harik indicated a door. 'He's in there, with your Guards. I only had time for a cursory examination when he arrived. I'm going to have a proper look at him now. He seems to have had a severe blow to the head. He may not regain consciousness, and if he does there's no guarantee he'll remember what happened.'

'You must do whatever's—'

Helsarn's words froze as Harik's gaze fixed him again. There was no mistaking the anger in it, for all that it was gone almost immediately. He left the sentence unfinished. The driver was in secure hands and he could be dealt with any time. All that mattered now was being ready for the Gevethen's response to what had happened.

When Helsarn had left, Harik began cleaning the examination table. Part way through he stopped and his impassive face became briefly both tragic and triumphant. 'Still there,' he said, very softly. 'Strength lying unseen. Still there. Waiting for the right key.' Then he was himself again, cleaning up the debris left by the Lord Counsellor Hagen.

Helsarn was not unrelieved to be leaving Harik's rooms. The atmosphere of the place still tugged him back to times long gone and he did not like it. As he and the men carrying the stretcher returned to the inner courtyard, he felt the old associations drop away from him. In their place came a renewed unease. It took him only a moment to realize what it was. Silence. Normally the Citadel was alive with activity as officials, Guards, servants went about their business. In addition, he felt as though he were being watched. That, however, was no great mystery. He *was* being watched. As he glanced around at the buildings lining the courtyard, faces quickly vanished from almost every window.

It occurred to him then, that the silence was wrong. Gidlon must have informed the Gevethen about what had happened by now. There should have been a massive response. Why wasn't the Citadel alive with the sound of clattering feet and rattling weapons as the Guards prepared to set out on a major purge?

A deep, echoing boom scattered his thoughts and made him start violently. Though he had not heard it for many years, he recognized it immediately. It was the great Dohrum Bell, a growling, ill-balanced and ill-tuned monster that hung from the rafters of the Citadel's main tower. It had not been rung for so long because the vibrations it caused shook the very fabric of the tower itself. Now however, its rumbling tones seemed appropriate to the event.

Nine times it tolled, and when it fell silent its fading resonances seemed to draw Time after them, stretching each measuring heartbeat out into an eternity.

Helsarn and the stretcher-bearers had slowly come to a halt as the bell rang, and now stood motionless in the middle of the courtyard. He was about to order them to move off again when a high-pitched voice, cold, gratingly soft and quite unmistakable, folded itself around him. It merged with and was followed by another.

'Carry him on your shoulders, my children ...'
                                      '... my children.'
'Such as he should not ride so near the dusty earth ...'
                                      '... the dusty earth.'

Helsarn stiffened as he turned towards the voices, then

slowly dropped down on to one knee and lowered his head in submission. Standing at the top of a broad flight of steps leading to an ornately canopied doorway, their mirror-bearers about them, stood the Gevethen.

Chapter 6

Ibryen found the crowd in the same mood as Hynard and Rachyl when he reached it. A bubbling mixture of anger and guilt and no small amount of fear that a stranger should have apparently breached their careful defences.

He did not dismount, but beat down their many questions with a forceful gesture.

'I don't know who this man is or how he came here,' he shouted. 'But he's come down off the ridge of his own free will when he could easily have fled, and for what it's worth, my feeling is that he's no enemy.'

His words addressed their fears, but did not allay them, and the questions surged up again. He became sterner. 'What I learn, you'll learn, in so far as it's safe for many to know, as with everything we do,' he said. 'But I'll need to question him carefully and at length. For the time being he thinks he's a guest and he'll be treated as such . . .' There were cries of disbelief and some scornful laughter. Ibryen scowled. 'That he's here at all tells you he's someone unusual,' he said forcefully. 'Perhaps our defences are not what we thought. Perhaps some of us may have earned a reproach for carelessness. I don't know. I'd have sworn not, only a few hours ago, but I'll find out more and quicker if this man is treated as a would-be ally than as a definite foe.'

It was not a popular conclusion, but the questioning faded into an uneasy silence.

Ibryen moved his horse to start shepherding the crowd back down the hill.

'Go back to your normal duties now, there's nothing to be done here.' There was still some hesitancy. He paused, and looked at the crowd intently. His voice was kinder, more resigned, when he spoke. 'Besides, guest or no, enemy or no, he's confined to the valley now, like the rest of us. He'll not leave until we all leave.' He twisted round in his saddle and pointed back to the approaching trio. 'Unless you think he's capable of escaping from Rachyl's care,' he added, grinning. All eyes turned towards the approaching Traveller and his escort. Rachyl was taller than Ibryen and powerful as only a woman so inclined can be. Few of the men in the valley would have aspired to match her combination of strength, mobile athleticism and sheer brutality in unarmed combat. Even fewer would have been inclined to match her armed. The sight of the Traveller's slight frame between Rachyl and Hynard – himself not a small man – together with Ibryen's abrupt change of manner broke what tension there was left in the crowd and it began to disperse.

Ibryen rode on down towards the village, motioning the growing number of new arrivals to turn about. Just before he reached the village he saw the form he had been expecting from the beginning. He reined his horse to a halt and dismounted.

'Someone woke you,' he grinned.

'How can a man sleep when his Lord prowls about the night, climbs alone to the ridge and then returns with a stranger?' Marris replied. 'Not to mention the din of the entire village talking about it. I'd be surprised if they don't hear it in Dirynhald.'

Ibryen's lightness vanished and he laid a hand on his old friend's shoulder. Gently he turned him round and began walking with him towards the village, leading his horse. 'I prowled the camp last night because something was troubling me. While I was thinking about it, I took the opportunity to test some of the sentries. They were awake and alert. Then I went up on to the ridge because I was still troubled.' He made his voice reassuring. 'It was no foolish act. I was careful and I knew that even if I didn't solve my . . . problem . . . I'd at least be able to see the state of the passes. Incidentally, they're clearing rapidly, we must extend the posts again.' Marris's face began to wrinkle irritably at what he took to be a distracting ploy. Ibryen made a gesture which asked him to be patient, then told him quickly and without embellishment, of his encounter with the Traveller.

Marris's eyes opened wide. 'From the *south*?' he said. 'Ye gods, it's not possible. He must be some kind of spy. Some foreign mercenary the Gevethen have found. An assassin.'

Ibryen shrugged slightly. 'Except for the fact that he could have killed me while I was half-dozing in the sun, and he didn't.'

'He was that close?' There was both concern and reproach in the question.

'That close,' Ibryen admitted, offering no excuse.

'Perhaps he didn't know who you were,' Marris said, but dismissed the conclusion even as he spoke it. The Gevethen were hardly likely to send out an assassin without giving him a likeness of the victim. 'He's probably just a spy, then. Thinks he's going to be able to get away from here when he's learned enough.'

'Possibly,' Ibryen conceded. 'But what's to be learned here, that couldn't be learned from up on the ridge? All

61

the Gevethen need to know is where we are. Our numbers and dispositions are of no interest to them. Besides, he could have walked past me as easily as stop and speak to me.'

They walked on in silence for some way.

'I need to talk to him,' Marris said eventually.

'We all need to talk to him,' Ibryen agreed, then, as an afterthought: 'It'll be interesting to see what effect he's had on Rachyl by the time they get here. She was all for killing him on the spot.' He chuckled, and Marris cast a glance skywards.

They had reached the building that served as head-quarters for the organizing of the Count's new domain. Irreverently dubbed 'the Shippen' by most in the village, though still assiduously referred to as 'the Council Hall' by the Count, this was set at the foot of what was apparently a small knoll. It was largely covered by grassy ramps, and looked little different from any of the other buildings in the village. Inside however, it consisted of a large and roughly circular hall with several smaller rooms leading from it. These served as temporary sleeping quarters for duty guards, or as stores, meeting rooms or whatever suited the current need – some were kitchens and wash-rooms using water diverted from the stream that wound through the village. The walls of the hall, though of roughly hewn stone, were closely jointed, and rose up to form a high curved ceiling before continuing downwards to find support on a single central column. During the day the whole was lit by daylight carried in by ingenious arrays of mirrors and lenses – a common feature of Nesdiryn architecture. The Council Hall was a considerable achieve-ment, especially considering the haste with which it had been built and the difficulties then facing the newly arrived and bewildered fugitives.

Ibryen gave his horse to a man who emerged from the deepset doorway, then entered the Hall. Silence greeted him. Gone was the constant sound of the stream and the irreducible murmur of the many tiny sounds of the valley. It was a feature of the place that Ibryen particularly appreciated, for although the village was not a noisy place, his followers being all too aware of the need for silence in the echoing mountains, such noise as there was could not penetrate the hall's dense walls.

He motioned Marris towards a long, solidly built wooden table. 'They'll be here soon,' he said, sitting down and leaning forward on to his elbows.

Without preamble, Marris asked 'What problem was troubling you so badly that it dragged you out of bed and sent you wandering the valley and the ridges?'

The sudden question caught Ibryen unawares. He started a little, then stammered as he replied. 'Nothing. I... nothing important. I just...' The reply foundered under Marris's gaze. 'I don't know,' he ended flatly. He knew that he could not keep his concern from Marris for long. The old counsellor knew him too well, and would pry gently but relentlessly into the reasons for his seemingly eccentric actions until he obtained satisfactory answers. More importantly, Ibryen felt the need to talk to someone about what had happened. But where to start? And what to say?

He held up his hand in a plea for a tolerant and silent listening. 'Something's been disturbing me for a few days now,' he began. 'Even waking me up in the night. I've no way of describing it. I'd call it a sound, but I can't hear it – not as I normally hear things, anyway. I'd call it a feeling, but it's sharper and clearer than that. I thought at first...' He shrugged unhappily. 'I don't know what I thought. One of the reasons I went up on the ridge was to be

63

completely alone for a while, to think – to listen – to clear my mind.' He fell silent.

'And?' Marris prompted after a little while.

'And I'm not a great deal wiser,' Ibryen replied. He looked at Marris directly, knowing that he was looking at someone who, if necessary, would put his loyalty to the Dirynvolk, and certainly to the people of the village, before any personal loyalty if he judged that his Count was no longer fit to lead. 'Except that I'm certain now that, whatever it is, it's not some folly on my part – a pending sickness, or the remains of some unspoken fancy. For all it's intangible and elusive, it's real. Just like the wind blowing on your face is real, even though it can't be seen, or grasped, or smelt.'

'But we all feel the wind,' Marris said.

Ibryen nodded slowly in agreement.

'Perhaps we could all hear this if we knew how to listen,' Ibryen retorted, adding thoughtfully, 'if we had the right faculties. Some of us have keener senses than others. Can see better, hear, even smell.'

The conversation was interrupted by the arrival of Hynard and Rachyl, escorting the Traveller.

'We must talk again. I'll need to think about what you've told me,' Marris said hurriedly as the trio walked over to them.

'I'd not have mentioned it to you otherwise,' Ibryen replied firmly. 'I *need* your thoughts. But do nothing until you've spoken with this man. When I mentioned the sound to him, he—'

'You mentioned this to a *stranger*?' Marris's eyes widened in horror. Ibryen quickly waved him silent as he stood up to greet the new arrivals.

The Traveller was gazing about the place with undisguised curiosity. Rachyl's face, already grim when she entered, darkened further at what she obviously took to be yet more spying by this intruder. She shot an angry look at Ibryen who returned it with one of his own that told her to keep her thoughts out of her face.

'Traveller, this is Corel Marris,' Ibryen said.

The Traveller bent forward slightly as if listening for something as he took Marris's rather tentative out-stretched hand. 'Corel,' he said softly, pronouncing it in an oddly ringing fashion as though he were testing it in some way. He seemed satisfied. 'This is an interesting place,' he went on, his manner genial. Reaching up, he very cautiously, and only partially, removed one of the small rolls of cloth from his ear. Ibryen and the others watched him uncertainly and in complete silence. After a moment, the Traveller nodded. 'More interesting than I think you realize,' he said. 'Perhaps there are Sound Carvers in your lineage somewhere too.' He hummed a few notes, very softly, nodding to himself as he did so. His smile broadened appreciatively.

Rachyl, fretful still, shifted her feet and cleared her throat quietly. The Traveller jumped, and with a sharp in-drawn whistle of distress, hastily thrust the cloth back into his ear. All the others started slightly in response, then there was an awkward pause.

'Please sit down,' Ibryen said, to end it. 'Would you like some food, or something to drink?'

'A little water, perhaps.'

Ibryen glanced the request towards Hynard, meticulously avoiding Rachyl's gaze.

'It's many years since I've been in this part of the world,' the Traveller said, before anyone else could speak. 'But seeing this place brings back many memories.' His manner became quite intense. 'Circumstances have constrained you to such simplicity here that the underlying roots of your architecture are exposed quite vividly. There are signs of many cultures here. All made distinctly yours.' He hummed to himself tunelessly for a moment as he looked around the Hall again. 'And your use of mirror stones is very good. A marked improvement.'

Ibryen felt an uncomfortable mixture of pride and irritation at this unexpected praise.

'It serves our needs,' he said simply. 'We're quite pleased with it.'

The Traveller stopped humming then uttered a series of soft but very rapid whistles. As he finished, his eyes widened and his face broke into a broad smile, as yet again he glanced around the Hall. This time however, his movements were sudden and erratic, as if he were following the fate of the sounds he had just made. Both Rachyl and Marris found themselves imitating the man as they tried to follow his gaze.

Then he was still, and looking at Ibryen. 'You should be more than pleased, Count,' he said. 'There are ancient traits running strong in your people yet. You've built more than you know here. Perhaps one day—' He stopped abruptly. 'I'm sorry,' he said, smiling at his hosts. 'I'm not used to people – to talking so much. I'm afraid I'm chattering on about things you're not interested in when you probably want to ask me all manner of questions.'

Rachyl cleared her throat again.

Marris nodded, as if to accept the point, but unbalanced by this voluble newcomer, he merely made a vague circling gesture about his ear. 'Are your ears troubling you?' he asked. 'We've a good physician here.'

The Traveller looked puzzled for a moment, then his hand went to the cloths sealing his ears. 'Oh no,' he replied. 'My ears are fine. It's just that with being in the mountains so long, my hearing's . . . very sensitive.'

Another awkward silence descended on the group. It was broken by Hynard returning with a large ewer of water and a handful of earthenware beakers. Catching Ibryen's eye, he filled one and offered it to the Traveller, who took it gratefully.

'Who are you? Who sent you? And how did you get here?' Rachyl's impatience got the better of her as she seized one of the beakers and filled it hastily, splashing water on the table.

The Traveller's eyes shone as he peered over the top of his beaker. 'Ah, you have the gift of creation, young woman. Look, jewels as bright as your eyes, to form a necklace for your lovely neck.' He pointed to a string of water drops arcing across the table. They shone brilliantly in the sunlight that was being carried into the Hall, and cast rainbow shadows.

Marris and Ibryen exchanged identical wide-eyed glances full of equal proportions of surprise, amusement and anticipation. Hynard's mouth dropped open. As did Rachyl's, the beaker clattering against her teeth. Then, after a moment's uncertainty, she caught the looks of her comrades, and coloured. She brought the beaker down on to the table with a bang, sending another small fountain of water into the air. Her mouth slammed shut and her jawline stiffened as she jabbed a determined forefinger into the table. Her words had to fight their way past clenched teeth.

'Don't you . . .'

The Traveller reached forward and laid a hand briefly on Rachyl's. 'Don't be angry,' he said gently. 'It was just a compliment.'

Ibryen interceded quickly. 'Compliments are a rarity here,' he said. 'And, sadly, confined for the most part to praising fighting attributes rather than anything else.' He

67

became more purposeful. 'But Rachyl's questions are as valid as when I asked them up on the ridge, and we need to know your answers.'

The Traveller nodded. 'I can appreciate that more now,' he said. 'But my answers are unchanged. I am . . .' He pronounced his name. As Ibryen had done when he first heard it, the other three listeners leaned forward to catch it, then shook their heads and looked at one another in confusion.

'Well, you're not from anywhere around here, that's for sure,' Marris said after a moment.

'We'll continue to call you Traveller,' Ibryen said authoritatively and a little impatiently. He motioned the Traveller to continue.

'My homeland's a long way from here. I've travelled to and through many places over the years, but I've come here now from the land you probably know as Girnlant.'

The reaction was as Ibryen's had been.

'Girnlant's supposed to be to the south,' Rachyl burst out. 'It probably doesn't even exist. No one could possibly get over the mountains.'

The Traveller snorted slightly. 'Girnlant exists well enough,' he said, and dipping a finger in his water he began drawing a crude map on the table. At the top were a series of peaks representing the mountains. 'You're here,' he announced, poking a glistening spot above them. 'And Girnlant's down here.' A broad sweep finished the map. 'It used to be one land once, but there are about twenty or more states there now . . . all of them at least as big as Nesdiryn.' He sat back, adding with some heat, 'Just because you can't walk to the moon doesn't mean it doesn't exist, girl.' Rachyl bridled at the word 'girl' but Ibryen's look kept her silent. The Traveller fumbled in a purse at his waist and eventually produced a coin. He put it on the table and flicked it towards Rachyl. 'That's from one of them. Somewhere in the middle. Here.' He prodded the map again. 'I can't remember the name of the place.' Rachyl examined the coin cursorily then handed it to Ibryen. On one side was a mountain, on the other a ring with a number in it.

'It's not gold,' he said, handing it to Marris.

The Traveller chuckled. 'Not a golden people, I'm afraid,' he said. 'Somewhat burdened by their religion.' His mood became suddenly sadder. 'Heavily burdened when I left them, although before I headed north I did hear that the individual who was causing the problem had died, or been killed, so maybe all's well now.' He shrugged to himself reflectively. 'People have a great capacity both for self-deception and for doing harm to themselves. It's such a shame when you look at what other things they can do.'

'Some foreign coin tells us nothing,' Rachyl sneered.

'It tells us he's been somewhere a long way from here,' Marris said, fingering the coin thoughtfully. 'It's vaguely familiar. I've seen something like this before. When I was a boy, I think. It certainly doesn't come from any of our immediate neighbours, nor from any land that I've ever been to.'

'It means nothing,' Rachyl insisted forcefully. 'Except that he's a foreigner, which we can tell just by listening to him. What we need to know is who sent him and why.'

'I'd swear he never got past the sentries.' It was the first time Hynard had spoken. He had been in command of the inner posts through the night, and though less forthcoming than Rachyl, he was deeply disturbed by the mysterious arrival of the Traveller. 'They were fully alert when you came round, Ibryen, and they were even more so afterwards. He's either better than anyone I've ever known,

69

or he got up on to that ridge by some unknown route.'

'Or he came from the south,' Ibryen offered.

The Traveller did not speak. Silence seemed to radiate out from him, deepening further that which already filled the Hall.

'Why are you here, Traveller?' Ibryen asked, almost whispering into the heavy stillness. For the first time since he had arrived at the Hall, the Traveller seemed uncertain. 'No flippant answers, please,' Ibryen added. 'I'm sure you've got some measure of our problem here by now, and our natural concerns about you.'

The Traveller looked straight at him. When he spoke, his voice was strange and his words seemed to contain more than they said. 'Do you not think that you and I should discuss this alone?'

'No!' Rachyl and Hynard replied urgently at the same time, albeit almost whispering, like their lord.

Ibryen held out a restraining hand, and thought for a moment. He reached a decision. 'I make no excuses for my lack of care, other than that I'd no cause to imagine anyone would be up on the ridge. But I was idling in the sun – eyes closed, half-dozing – when he spoke to me. I was quite unaware of anyone near me. He could have killed me, or turned and left, just as easily as speak to me.'

Hynard and Rachyl watched him unhappily. He turned to the Traveller. 'I trust the judgement of my friends and kin here completely. That's how we've survived so long against the Gevethen. Whatever it is that drew us together up there, whatever you and I have to discuss, we can . . . *we must* . . . discuss it before them.' He glanced quickly at Marris. 'However strange.' There was reservation in Marris's eyes, but he said nothing.

The Traveller gave a disclaiming gesture. 'As you wish,

70

Count, but in such matters, the reactions of those who lack understanding can be . . . unpredictable.'

Ibryen looked round at the others. 'Say what you have to say, Traveller,' he said.

Chapter 7

When the Traveller spoke, each listener heard him differently. It was, at times, as though his voice came from many directions at once and his words were often filled with meanings far beyond that of their seeming content.

'This is no flippant answer, Count,' he began. 'But I can't tell you truly what has brought me here. I *am* a traveller. I've always been one. I need little to live on and I've got more than enough wit to be able to find what little I do need. I go from place to place as the whim takes me. Whether some other hand guides me is a question none of us can answer.' He ran his finger idly through the watery map he had sketched on the table. 'But I was disturbed by the events I encountered in Girnlant, for all I was merely on the fringe of them. There was something in the air . . . faint and distant, but there, definitely. Something beyond the immediate comings and goings of the people involved, something deep, ancient . . .' He paused and for a while stared into space as if he were trying to recall some long-forgotten memory.

Rachyl leaned forward and rested her head in her hand, a deliberately weary look on her face.

'It disturbed me much more than it should have, considering the number of political and religious squabbles I've been witness to over the years,' the Traveller went on, ignoring the silent comment. He looked around the Hall though not so much at it, as at the mountains beyond the stone walls. 'But then, I came to realize on my journey north, many things have disturbed me over the last twenty years or so, more than perhaps they should have done. There seems to be an unease about the world that wasn't there when I began my journeying long ago. It's as though something's creeping into the normal tides of change. I don't know whether it's good or bad. Maybe it's both.' He turned to Ibryen, puzzled but confidential, man to man, as if he were talking to someone equally knowledge-able. 'I'll swear I even heard the Sound Carvers singing again. Singing about a returning to the Ways, to the Heartland, but . . .' He slumped a little, and for a moment he looked like a weary old man. Then he gave a resigned shrug. 'It was probably a dream. The Sound Carvers are long gone, aren't they?' Ibryen said nothing. Rachyl glanced at Hynard and discreetly tapped a finger against her temple.

'No, young woman,' the Traveller said, without looking at her. 'A Teller of Stories I can be, if need arises, but I'm no more touched in the head than someone who thinks the mountains go so far south that they ring the globe to become the mountains of the north.' He was his old self again, taunting. Rachyl glowered at him, but Ibryen intervened before she could speak.

'I don't understand what you're saying,' he said, a hint of irritation in his voice as he frowned at Rachyl. 'Religious or political happenings in a distant land are of no concern to us, nor, with respect, are your vague feelings of unease. We've much more than unease to live with all the time here. And I've no idea what Sound Carvers are. We need sensible answers to our questions, not fireside tales.'

74

The Traveller half-closed his eyes for a moment. 'Indulge me, Count,' he said, a firmness in his voice that seemed quite out of character to his slight frame. 'Nothing presses you at the moment. And, for all I came of my own free will, you consider me your permanent prisoner, don't you?'

Ibryen frowned at this cold exposure of his thinking. 'We're all prisoners here, Traveller,' he said.

'Then you've time to hear me out.'

'We don't have time for childish nonsense,' Rachyl said angrily. 'There's plenty of work to do around here just surviving. We can't be idling our days away listening to—'

'Be quiet, Rachyl!' Ibryen was suddenly angry. He slammed his hand on the table, making everyone jump. The Traveller grimaced and pressed the pieces of cloth further into his ears. Ibryen levelled his finger at Rachyl, though his voice softened. 'Your services against the Gevethen and to me are beyond any conceivable reproach, but there are times when more than a strong arm and a stout heart are needed. I allowed you and Hynard to stay and listen to this man because things have happened lately of which you're unaware. Strange, puzzling things, which must be discussed thoroughly and on which thoughtful judgements must be made: family judgements as much as war judgements. They may or may not be important matters, and they may or may not involve this man, but I need your help now as much as I've ever needed it in battle. This is a time for a different kind of courage, Rachyl. Set aside your anger for the moment, and listen. Listen truly.' Rachyl's face twitched unhappily, and briefly, she seemed to be contemplating a reply. In the end however, she simply nodded her head.

Ibryen looked round at the others. 'Let's all listen truly. I said before that the very fact that this man is here is a strange happening in itself. Think about it.' He lowered his voice. 'And before you choose to dismiss his words as so much nonsense, let me remind you of the fearful and mysterious powers that the Gevethen themselves possess. Albeit they use them rarely, they're beyond any explanation I can fathom. We forget too easily what they are like in the bustle of our daily practical concerns.' This sobered his audience. He held out a hand to the Traveller. 'Finish your tale, please,' he said. 'But remember your own words: the reactions of those who lack understanding can be unpredictable. And you must include me in such a group while you talk as you do.'

'I accept the reproach, Count,' the Traveller acknowledged. 'I told you I'm not used to dealing with people, still less explaining things when my own thoughts are far from clear.' He picked up the coin and looked at it for a moment, then placed it back in the purse on his belt. 'You're not the only one who stands in need of the advice of others.'

He leaned forward, resting his elbows on the table. 'If the Sound Carvers are not even part of your lore, then I can see that talk of them would serve no useful purpose. To some they're merely a legend, but that they existed is no more a matter for debate for me, than the existence of this coin.' He tapped his purse. 'My ancestry's of no relevance here, but the line of the Sound Carvers is strong in me, and it's thanks to them that I have . . . skills . . . not given to most people. Skills of hearing and the making of sound.' He gave an airy wave of his hand to close the subject. 'However, returning to your questions. Many years ago, I was travelling in a land far to the north of here when I came to a village which was overlooked by a mighty castle built in a cleft between two mountains. Towers and spires soared up behind a wall that seemed

76

to have grown out of the rock itself, and set in the wall was a massive gate. Sealed, it was, the villagers said. Had been so in living memory and beyond, but I was welcome to look at it. Indeed they took a pride in it, for it was covered with such carvings as you could scarcely imagine.' He stopped and hummed to himself gently, then smiled. 'I'm sorry,' he said, recollecting himself. 'I feel happy just to think about that land and its people, and its splendid castle. I remember the day so vividly. Sharp and frosty, with a wintry sun washing soft shadows everywhere as I walked up the long road to the castle.' He smiled again, then his voice fell and he leaned further forward. 'When I reached the gate, I stood for a long time just staring at it. It was magnificent. From the top to the bottom, I doubt there was a space the size of my hand that didn't have something carved on it. Patterns within patterns – some, huge and sweeping – some, intricately detailed and so delicately carved that looking at them made me feel I'd be carried down and down into them, falling for ever.' He paused, wide-eyed and reflective. 'And, whatever that gate was made of, even the finest lines were as sharp-edged as if they'd only just been cut. So complex was the work that it took me some time to realize that it was no abstract patterning, but a vast history. Tableaux and text, intimately woven into one. Such stories were written there. Loyalty and treachery, heroism and cowardice, the sweep of the fate of nations, the touch of a child's hand – all there. Even tales from my own childhood, told anew. And questions answered that I'd often asked, but still more posed to spur me forward. Then, as I drew close, to study one part of it . . .' he hesitated momentarily, as if judging how, or perhaps even whether, to continue ' . . . I heard it.' He glanced at his listeners, but despite this strange pronouncement, they were all attentive, captivated by the manner of his telling. 'I heard it singing at the touch of my breath misting in the frosty air. Telling again the tales that were carved there, and more. So much more.' He touched his ears. 'For while my sight is as dim as yours, my hearing is beyond your imagining. I heard tales of the making and shaping of all things. Of the harmony that pervaded all things and its end with the coming of a corruption which was as old as the first making itself. And I heard too of the defeat of the One in whom this corruption took form yet how, in His very defeat, He knew victory, for He saw that His teachings had been spread far and wide, and learned well.'

Something in Ibryen told him to urge the Traveller forward to matters of greater moment, but he paid no heed to it.

'I've seen many wondrous things on my journeys but nothing ever like that gate. The memory of it has stayed with me always. The stories – the histories – it told me, return to me constantly. And more and more they return to me as my ... unease ... grows. I have a sense of powerful forces moving; of the world being shaped yet again. As though what happened then might be happening again.' He paused. 'It's almost as if He who carried the corruption had returned.' He shook his head, dissatisfied with this conclusion. 'Or perhaps was trying to return.' He frowned, still not satisfied. 'Whatever it is, it's deeply disturbing and it won't go away. Indeed, it seems to grow stronger by the day.' He fell silent for a moment, preoccupied, then he sat up suddenly, bright again, like a parent anxious to reassure his children after a frightening tale. 'Still, that's no concern of yours, is it? Suffice it that I was travelling through these mountains on my way back to that sealed castle and the Great Gate to study what I should have studied when I was there last, when I heard the call that brought me here.'

He looked at Ibryen, seeking permission to continue. Ibryen nodded.

'For days now, I've heard the cry clinging to the edges of the wind,' the Traveller told them. 'A sound such as I've never heard before, though I've been taught that such things exist. A sound which is said to be an echo here of happenings in another world.'

Ibryen sensed Rachyl's restraint faltering.

'Listen,' he said to her, very softly, laying a hand on her arm. Then, to the Traveller, 'Explain.'

The Traveller waved Ibryen's injunction aside. 'I'm pursuing my thoughts as best I can,' he said. 'I told you I'm far from clear in my mind about what's happening and why I'm here when I should be journeying north. And I've certainly no words of simple clarity for you.' He settled back to his tale. 'I don't know whether this exists in your lore or not, but it's said, by people wiser than I, that what we see about us is far from the totality of things; that there are many worlds other than this, all sharing this time, this space. Worlds – perhaps an infinity of worlds – that exist between the very heartbeats of all we think to be to be whole and solid.' He gave a slight shrug. 'It's not a thing I can deny or confirm, though I believe matters could well be thus, for all the . . . disturbing nature . . . of such an idea. It's also said that there are pathways between the worlds, many pathways, though few have the gift to travel them.'

Ibryen frowned at what seemed to be mounting eccentricity in the Traveller's story. His expression released Rachyl.

'You'll be asking us to believe in Culmadryen next,' she sneered.

The Traveller looked at her sharply and mouthed the word to himself.

'Cloud lands,' Marris said, by way of explanation.

'Children's tales, like everything else you're telling us,' Rachyl added caustically, turning to Ibryen. 'What are we wasting our time like this for? We should—'

'No.' Marris's voice cut across her plea. 'Hear him out.'

Rachyl gritted her teeth and threw up her hands in disbelief. 'I suppose *you* believe in Culmadryen too, do you?' she taunted viciously, standing up and leaning towards Marris provocatively.

'Enough!' Ibryen shouted furiously. 'Rachyl, you're dismissed. Go to your—'

'It's all right.' Marris's voice over-topped Ibryen's anger. His restraining hand was towards Ibryen, but his gaze was squarely on Rachyl. 'She's telling the truth as it happens. I do believe in Culmadryen.' The certainty in Rachyl's posture, already strained by Ibryen's anger, faltered. 'Sit down, girl and do as you've been asked. Listen.' The soft purposefulness in Marris's voice pushed a glowering Rachyl back on to her seat. He pressed on, in the same tone. 'I don't know what they are, how they can be, or what kind of people live on them, but I believe in them just as I believe in you and this Hall and the mountains around us. Because I've seen one.'

A small flicker of desperation passed over Rachyl's face and she looked rapidly around the gathering as if in search of some more sane witness. Marris snapped his fingers to draw her attention back to him. 'It was a long time ago and a long way from here. I couldn't even tell you where it was now. I was only a child, and my father was a restless soul in those days. He travelled us all over the place, keeping us fed and clothed by mending pots and pans, helping with the harvest, doing anything that came to hand.' His eyes became distant. 'But I remember that day. Bright and sunny, like today. Me clutching my father's hand, people running out of their houses, then just standing there gazing upwards – a straggling crowd in a sunlit street full of crooked shadows. And there it was, floating high above us and just beyond the village, slow and majestic.' He echoed the Traveller's words. 'A city of towers and spires rising from a bright, white cloud. Everyone was standing still and silent, as if to move or make a noise would be a desecration. I remember thinking they looked as though they'd all been trapped in a painting, and I was the only one left who was real.'

He smiled at the memory, then, recollecting himself, glanced round the watching faces and cleared his throat awkwardly. 'It was a long time ago, as I said,' he declared gruffly, by way of apology for this whimsy. 'And I've never seen one since. But they're real enough.' He spoke exclusively to Rachyl. 'Sadly, you've learned many things that you shouldn't have had to, over the last few years, Rachyl,' he said. 'And you've not learned things that you should have done. One of these is to understand that we know very little about most things and probably nothing about a damn sight more, and that if we want any semblance of control over our lives them we must keep not only our eyes and ears open, but also our minds and our hearts.'

He turned back to the Traveller. 'But your tale's rambling far and wide,' he said, with a hint of reproach in his voice. 'You must have a measure of our concerns by now. Address yourself to them.'

'I am,' the Traveller said. 'Truly.' He looked at Rachyl, subdued again by Marris's revelation. 'Why did you speak of Culmadryen?'

Rachyl gestured vaguely. 'I've no idea,' she replied. 'It just came to mind.'

'And how long is it since such a fancy came to mind last?'

Rachyl hesitated. 'I've no idea. Years, I suppose.'

The Traveller's eyes narrowed and he looked at her intently as though searching for something. Rachyl edged away from the scrutiny.

'Well, here's a strangeness for you, fighting woman. The clouds that sustain the cities of the Dryenvolk high above us are not really clouds, though they seem to be, changing shape and changing colour like the true clouds around them. They're known as Culmaren, living things that are said to exist both here and ... in the worlds beyond. What we see is but a reflection of something whose true perfection blooms elsewhere.'

'That *is* the stuff of children's tales,' Ibryen said gently, but the Traveller raised a hand and shook his head.

'Like Marris, I have seen Culmadryen,' he said. 'Not often, but more than once. And I've met Dryenvolk too. Talked with them, high in the silent, distant mountains where no people go and where the Culmaren reach down for the sustenance that they need in this world. There's mystery in the Culmaren that eludes even the Dryenvolk themselves, and their knowledge of it is great. It sustains them in many subtle ways and they revere it even as they use it.'

He turned and spoke directly to Ibryen. 'Count, I came here because of the cry I heard. It was faint and distant and very strange, as I've said, but it had a quality of need about it. It also had, shall I say, an aura about it, such as I've only heard in my contact with the Dryenvolk. You told me that something similar had drawn you up on to the ridge, for reasons you did not understand. Well it's not possible that you heard the same as I did. Not possible. That gift hasn't been given to you. But I'm beginning to suspect you may have an even greater gift. I think you heard that part of the cry of the Culmaren that comes

82

from beyond. I think that you may have the skill to reach across the worlds. Perhaps even to move between them.'

There was a stunned silence.

'There *was* need in what you felt, wasn't there? A great need,' the Traveller insisted, before Ibryen could speak. Ibryen nodded. His mouth was dry. Like Rachyl, he wanted to denounce this strange little old man as deranged – too long alone in the mountains – too long alone in life. But the word *need* chimed through him. Every part of him cried out, Yes! But there was more than need. Something out there, wherever that might be, was *in extremis*, was reaching out. And it had touched him.

The Traveller sat back, seemingly satisfied at last with his conclusion, although his manner radiated great excitement. Ibryen now felt all eyes turned to him, waiting for his verdict. Instead, he returned their questioning.

'Rachyl, what do you make of our visitor and his story now?' he asked.

Caught unawares, it took Rachyl some time to compose herself. So violently had her moods swung since she first met the Traveller that she was deeply uncertain about what she had heard.

'I don't know,' she said. 'I'm dizzy with it all. Only moments ago I'd have laughed to scorn the idea of Culmadryen being anything other than a tale for children. Now I've been told they exist. They actually exist.' She looked uncomfortably at Marris. 'And told by someone whose word can't be doubted. And if *they* exist, then what else is possible? But other worlds around us – here, now! How can I credit such a notion?'

'Hynard?'

Hynard ran a hand through his hair and shook his head violently, as if in the hope that he might wake to find that he had merely been dreaming. But no such solace came. 'I'm no wiser than Rachyl,' he admitted. 'Things have been said which sound like nonsense, yet which ring true. But even ignoring that, all the time I'm thinking about simple practical matters. How did he get here? I'd swear it's not possible that he could have got past the sentries and the traps, even at night. Just not possible. *Unless he came from the south as he claims.* In which case he's truly a very... unusual... person. And if he didn't, if he's been sent here by the Gevethen and somehow avoided the sentries, why didn't he just flee with his information, or kill you while he could?'

Rachyl took charge of their predicament. 'We've duties to do and we need to think,' she said, her voice a mixture of appeal and brusqueness. 'May we leave, to do both?'

Ibryen nodded. 'But speak to no one about any of this,' he ordered. 'No one.' As they rose, Ibryen held out a detaining hand and addressed the Traveller. 'Where did you camp last night, and which way did you come up on to the ridge, precisely?'

The Traveller thought for a moment and then told him.

Ibryen gave his cousins an order. 'There's enough of the day left. Take a party, find his tracks and follow them back as far as you safely can, in time to return here today.' The pair looked relieved to be given a simple task to perform.

'I leave no tracks,' the Traveller said, with some indignation. 'I have respect for the mountains.'

'If you camped, you left signs,' Hynard announced. 'Even if it was only the scooping-up of snow for water.'

The Traveller gave a conceding nod. 'Well, if it'll make you easier in your mind,' he said.

'It will, greatly,' Ibryen said.

When Hynard and Rachyl had left, Ibryen sat silent for

a while, then rubbed his eyes wearily. 'Too early a start, too long a day,' he said, standing up and motioning Marris and the Traveller to follow him. He led them out of the Hall and into the afternoon sunshine. There were more people than usual in the vicinity of the Hall, but they were all moving away quite briskly. Ibryen smiled as he detected Rachyl's hand in this dispersion.

'I'm not sure that it was the wisest thing to do, inviting those two to listen to all that,' he mused.

Marris pursed his lips and spoke reassuringly. 'It would have been unwise to leave them out. They'll say nothing, you know that. And they'll think a lot, you know that too. They'll bring something to the debate that you and I might well not see.'

'I've caused you a great many problems,' the Traveller said.

'Problems?' Ibryen echoed with a slight smile. 'No. I think perhaps all you've done is rearrange the ones I already had.' He became practical. 'You'll have to stay in my quarters until we find a proper place for you, and I'll have to arrange a guard detail for you.'

'I've no plans to leave at the moment,' the Traveller said. 'If you remember, I invited myself here.'

'You did indeed,' Ibryen agreed. 'But I don't think you realized then that it was a prison you were walking into.'

The Traveller smiled. 'I invited myself,' he repeated.

They walked on in silence for some way then Ibryen said simply, 'Why?'

'I told you why,' the Traveller replied.

'You told me some nonsense about my having a gift to hear things from another world.'

'Nonsense? You believed it in there.'

'You're a fine story-teller. I half-believe it yet,' Ibryen said.

The Traveller pointed back towards the Hall. 'Rachyl's your kin, isn't she? And some part of her heard the same call that you did.'

'Just because she mentioned the Culmadryen?' Ibryen asked sceptically. 'Coincidence, that's all.'

The Traveller was dismissive. 'In my limited acquaintance with her, I'd say she's more interested in arm-wrestling, sharpening blades and laying ambushes than whiling her time away recollecting the days when she played with dolls and listened to magical tales at her mother's knee.' He jabbed a finger towards Ibryen. 'She heard, Count! Far less so than you did, but she heard nonetheless. It's in your blood. A special attribute, a talent, a gift, call it what you will, but we have to find out about it.'

'Coincidence,' Ibryen repeated, with some force. 'For all I know, you just wove your entire tale around her casual remark, and you're continuing in the same vein for some devious purpose of your own.'

The Traveller seized his arm. He had an unexpectedly powerful grip. Marris stepped forward urgently, but the Traveller let go immediately. 'I may be wrong in my judgement of you, Count,' he said fiercely, 'but I don't think so. And know this: I don't lie, I don't fabricate fictions, I don't seek to deceive. I'm too old to have even the slightest interest in scheming and plotting and the petty seeking after temporal power, though where I can I'll try to help those who find themselves under the heels of those who do. And the greatest strength that any people can have against such, is knowledge.' He stepped forward and stood directly in front of Ibryen. 'I know nothing of the enemy – this Gevethen – you face, except such as I've gleaned from casual remarks. They overthrew you by treachery and force of arms, and now hold your people in thrall by the same means. Am I right?'

'In essence, yes,' Ibryen said. 'Though you could add ruthlessness and terror to your list.'

'It's nothing new,' the Traveller said, then he waved his arm around the valley, and said, acidly, 'But what do you expect to do against them with *this*?' Ibryen started at this sudden jibe, then his jaw jutted and his shoulders rose up menacingly.

'You're fighting a hit and run campaign, aren't you? And you live in mortal terror of your little enclave here being discovered,' the Traveller continued in the same manner. 'You're going to die here, all of you, eventually, unless you do something drastically different from what you're doing at the moment.'

'That's enough!' Ibryen began furiously.

'No, it's not,' the Traveller ploughed on. 'I haven't begun yet.'

Ibryen made to step forward and seize him, but Marris caught his arm. 'Let him finish,' he said softly.

'But . . .'

'Let him finish!'

The Traveller cocked his head on one side as if listening intently to something. He looked at Ibryen thoughtfully, then spoke again, more quietly. 'I don't know whether the Counts of Nesdiryn are warriors by tradition, or whether circumstances have made you one, but you need no military education to *know* that you cannot defeat the Gevethen going on the way you are. You know it's only a matter of time before they find you and come in force.'

Ibryen listened grimly.

'But they don't even need to find you, do they? All they need to do is let you keep venturing out to harry their force and take a few of you each time. I doubt they give a fig for any casualties they take, but a warrior lost to you strikes at the heart of everyone here, and most of all at yours. Insidiously, wearing you down, drip by drip. How many more such blows can you take, Count, before your heart breaks and you and all your people fall?'

Ibryen swore violently and lifted his hand to strike the Traveller across the face.

Then he was in darkness, thunder all about him.

Chapter 8

Helsarn did not move. Indeed, he was scarcely capable of moving. Though he could not see anything, he knew that the Gevethen were approaching him – they sent fear before them like a shadow. At the edge of his vision he could see the legs of one of the stretcher party. They were shifting as Hagen's body was hoisted up on to their owner's shoulders as the Gevethen had ordered, but all Helsarn could see was that they were trembling. A visible reflection of his own inner feelings. He was glad he could not see the man's face.

'Stand firm, my children . . .'

        '. . . my children.'

'Hold him steady and strong as he held you . . .'

        '. . . held you.'

'Where will this city, this land, be without the likes of him, brother?'

'Where indeed, brother?'

'Chaos may ensue.'

'Chaos.'

'Sure of touch, perceptive of heart, gentle arbiter of our will . . .'

        '. . . our will.'

'Such men are as water in the desert, as diamonds in the mire.'

'Rare beyond price.'

'Where shall such as he be found?'

'Who would seek to wound us so?'

Both voices came together to speak this last: cold, piercing and dissonant. They spoke again.

'Who, Captain Helsarn?'

Helsarn had had comparatively few dealings direct with the Gevethen, but they had been enough to teach him that no bravado could disguise his feelings from them and it would be folly to try. Hagen himself had bent the knee before them, and he was not Hagen. The question skewered him like an icy spear.

'I do not know, Excellencies,' he said, his voice steadier than he had hoped. 'People have been brought here from the scene for questioning, but I fear the true culprits had escaped even before we knew what had happened.'

'Merely fled, Captain. Not escaped. Escape is not possible. Such a deed carries the inevitable destruction of the doer at its very heart. Time will bring him to us.'

Rain began to fall. Helsarn could feel large, cold drops striking his bent back. They threatened to release the violent shivering that he was holding pent within him. Dark robes came into his vision. The Gevethen were in front of him.

'Rise, Captain. We would look on your face . . .'

'. . . your face.'

Helsarn forced his legs to respond, but the fear of the consequences of disobedience only just outweighed the fear of facing his masters.

Pale moon faces and drifting watery grey eyes hovered in the darkness of the hooded robes before him, while white and flaccid hands floated against it, having what appeared to be a life and will of their own, moving in ways quite divorced from anything that was being said.

The Gevethen were identical.

They were never apart.

When they moved, they moved as one. Sometimes like shadows, each of the other, and sometimes like reflections, opposing one another, unsettling and disorienting for any who saw them.

When they spoke, one voice would often follow the other, trailing behind like a lingering echo, though at times, they would speak simultaneously, and then their voices were jarring and jagged, tearing through the hearer like a barbed weapon.

None knew from whence they came.

Nor could any surmise what they thought.

Since the ousting of the Count, they had set aside all that might have drawn away from their disconcerting appearance, wearing now only simple black robes, undecorated save for the shattered half of a small iron ring which hung about the neck of each on a fine black chain. Frequently, the restless hands would carry fingertips to run delicately over this broken remnant, then they would linger down the palm of the other hand, and sometimes across the face. And, at times, after this, each would touch the other, as if to assure themselves that they were truly there.

The only colour to be seen about them lay in red, voluptuous mouths, as full and sensual as their garb was ascetic and spare.

And where went the Gevethen, there went their mirror-bearers: mute servants whose own gaze, fixed, as it seemed to be, on some other place, was almost as disconcerting as that of the Gevethen themselves. They moved elaborately about their masters as if dancing to music that they alone could hear, carrying black-edged mirrors which they shifted and turned constantly. Sometimes these were held so close as to form almost a shield wall, while at others they straggled in loose, fluttering skeins as though they were being swept out by a buffeting wind. When talking to one another, the Gevethen would often address their images instead of each other until the conversation appeared to exist only between the images, and reality and reflection became indistinguishable.

Occasionally a soft, hissed command would send the mirrors into a frenzy, quivering and changing for no reason that was readily apparent. Always however, they were arranged so that many images of the Gevethen paraded in front of the hapless onlooker. Who the mirror-bearers were, and how they had come by their appointment, no one knew, and no one enquired. They disturbed Helsarn. They disturbed everybody, as did all the Gevethen's servants.

Helsarn came to attention and fixed his eyes forward. The Gevethen being shorter than he was, he hoped that way to avoid looking directly at them. Who could tell what they could see when they looked into a man's eyes? Or, worse, who could tell what *he* would see? It was said that men had been driven insane by their gaze. But he knew that the attempt would be in vain; the gaze of the Gevethen was not to be avoided. The rain began to fall more heavily.

The mirrors twitched and the many heads of the Gevethen, tilted and viewed their Captain.

'He is true and loyal.'

'He served the traitor Count.'

'He was not cherished, nor did he cherish. And he has the mark of Hagen about him.'

'He let the Lord Counsellor die.'

There was a long silence. The heads tilted again. Grey eyes, streaking now in the rain, washed over Helsarn. He began to sweat.

'He will account in time, will you not, Captain?'

'I am yours to command, Excellencies.' Helsarn tried to keep the fear out of his voice.

There was a long silence, then:

'Indeed.'

'Indeed.'

The scrutiny was gone. The mirrors drifted sinuously after the Gevethen and all attention was turned to the body of Hagen. A floating gesture from the hands brought the stretcher unsteadily down again and the two figures, rain falling grey and straight about them, bent over it like riverside willows. Fingertips touched, and there was a soft muttering.

'Bring the Lord Counsellor to the Watching Chamber...'

'... Watching Chamber.'

'We will guide you...'

'... guide you.'

Then, Helsarn felt the focus return to him. Two voices spoke as one.

'Captain, we require the Physician Harik to be with us now.'

Abruptly released, Helsarn saluted smartly, turned on his heel, and started off at the double across the courtyard. He did not dare to look back, but as he passed a window he saw a reflection of the Gevethen and their mirror-bearers passing into the shade of the ornate canopy, followed by the Guards struggling to keep the stretcher level. Even as he looked, the images of the Gevethen seemed to stare back at him, probing still, urging him forward.

Get used to it, he thought. There was no worthwhile future to be had here other than by their side, and on the whole, they looked after their own well enough. It was not as satisfactory a conclusion as he would have wished, but he was spared any further inner debate by the appearance of Harik coming around the corner. With the hood of his cloak pulled up against the rain he looked even taller than ever.

'Where?' the Physician asked before Helsarn could deliver his message.

'The Watching Chamber,' Helsarn replied. He fell in beside him, matching as well as he was able the long steady strides. It was uncomfortable for him. He felt the need to speak. After the Gevethen, even Harik seemed approachable. 'They came out for him. Into the courtyard. Into the light,' he said.

Harik glanced up at the Citadel's main tower. 'Tolled the Dohrum too. Nine times,' he said, apparently ignoring Helsarn's remarks. 'Could have brought the tower down on their heads.' He became pensive. 'Nine times, eh?' And after a moment, he intoned softly to himself, 'In the ninth hour of the Last Battle . . .' His voice faded.

Helsarn craned forward. 'Pardon?'

Harik shook his head. 'Nothing. Just the beginning of a story I used to know,' he replied. 'Came to mind for some reason.'

Helsarn felt almost as though he had shared a great confidence with the Physician. Harik never made small talk. He must be as shaken as the rest of us, he thought. Probably scared witless under that stony exterior. Yet even as the idea came to him, he knew it was wrong. Harik might well have been shaken by the death of Hagen, but any fears he had would almost certainly be for other than his own skin. He was that kind of man. This insight merely added to Helsarn's discomfort and he made no effort to continue the conversation as they walked across the courtyard and up the broad steps that led to the entrance the Gevethen had used. Guards opened the doors and snapped to attention.

Inside, the silence seemed even more intense than that which had pervaded the courtyard. Though more spacious than the corridors that served Harik's quarters, those they were walking along now, in common with most of the interior of the Citadel, were claustrophobic, menacing almost, as though the air itself were afraid to move for fear of bringing down retribution. This had, in part, been brought about by the gradual but relentless removal, or defacing of the many pictures, sculptures and furnishings that had adorned the place in the time of the Count. But added to it was the indefinable but quite identifiable quality that the Gevethen brought to everything they touched. Like a disease-bearing miasma, it clung to everything.

Even Harik seemed as though he were having to wade through some unseen resistance, and Helsarn had almost to remind himself to breathe. He pulled out a kerchief and tried to disguise his unease by wiping the rain from his face. The Guards that were posted at intervals along the corridors were so still and pale that it seemed that the earlier passage of the Gevethen had turned them to stone, and such servants and officials as the pair encountered were moving very resolutely, very quietly, and with their eyes fixed firmly on the floor.

They came at last to the wide corridor that led to what had once been the Count's Audience Chamber. Elaborately decorated, with its arched ceiling lit by daylight brought along the Citadel's many mirrorways, it had once been as welcoming and open as the Count himself. Now the mirrorways had been sealed and the decorations draped with dark cloths, and the effect was of a descent into darkness. Count Ibryen's Audience Chamber had become the Gevethen's Watching Chamber.

Helsarn was relieved to see Commander Gidlon waiting by the tall doors at the far end, but his relief became concern when he realized that, apart from the door Guards, he was alone. Where were the other Commanders? He cursed inwardly and began preparing a list of names should punishment be called for. What had his men been playing at? He was not assured as he reached Gidlon. His Commander was pale and trembling, and very agitated. Quickly, he said, 'I sent men to find the other Commanders, sir. They should have been here some time ago.'

Gidlon scowled, as if he were being pestered by an irritating child. 'They're organizing the purging,' he replied off-handedly as he acknowledged Harik. 'Their Excellencies wish you to enter, Physician.' He nodded to the rigid Guards. They opened the doors and Harik entered.

Helsarn was about to relax a little in anticipation of a long wait in the gloomy corridor while whatever the Gevethen wished to transact with Harik was completed, but Gidlon urgently motioned him to accompany the Physician. The order disconcerted him momentarily, but using another salute to disguise any outward sign that might betray his alarm, he strode after Harik.

Like the greater part of the rest of the Citadel, the Audience Chamber had been transformed into the opposite of what it used to be. Where there had been light and openness, there was now darkness and oppression. The low dais where the Count had sat on formal occasions, and the few gentle steps by which it could be reached were no more. They had been replaced by a high throne platform, bounded by sheer curving sides, on which the Gevethen could stand aloof, overseeing all and quite unapproachable.

The windows having been curtained and the mirrorways

sealed, such light as there was came from a host of small lanterns. These hung at many levels from the ceiling, rested in niches and alcoves, swung from brackets which jutted, spiky and gibbet-like, from the walls, and stood also on slender, twisted columns which grew at random from the floor like so many storm-blasted trees. The lanterns burned with a cold, unwelcoming light, which heightened shadows rather than brought illumination, and they flickered from time to time, though no draught of air could find its way into the place. They also tainted the air with a fine, throat-catching smoke.

Multiplying the images of these lanterns were mirrors. Like the lanterns they reflected, many were hung from the ceiling and the walls while others leaned crookedly against one another in balanced arrays around the floor, some reaching up into the hazy ceiling. There were mirrors of all sizes, set at many angles, but they brought only further confusion to the scene.

Helsarn did as he always did when he entered the Watching Chamber; he tried to focus on the Gevethen – to concentrate on the heart of all that flickered about the hall. For even when the Gevethen themselves were motionless – which was rarely – the mirror-bearers continued their elaborate ballet about them so that the images of Nesdiryn's new Lords moved constantly. And all movement in this unsettling gloaming flew from mirror to mirror, deep into their flat and glistening depths before returning, unchanged, save that left had become right and right, left.

Helsarn's eyes thus moved automatically upwards to the top of the high throne platform. It stood dark and empty however, and for an instant, the confusion of the hall threatened to disorientate him. Then he saw that the Gevethen were at the foot of the platform, as were his men, though they were no longer carrying Hagen's body. Keeping a discreet distance behind, Helsarn followed Harik, his eyes fixed on the group ahead, trying to make out what was happening. As ever, there were other figures standing about the hall. These were yet more mirror-bearers, and some of the strange servants who tended the Gevethen. What function they fulfilled no one knew, and, like the mirror-bearers, their seemingly soulless manner disturbed all who had contact with them. Helsarn found their current inaction particularly unsettling. How could they not be drawn to what was happening?

When he reached the foot of the throne platform, he saw that four of the mirror-bearers were crouching on the floor. They were carrying their mirrors on their backs, to form an uneasy table on which was laid Hagen's body. The Gevethen, hands clenched in front of them, were swaying back and forth slightly. Helsarn kept some way away from the scene, suddenly superstitiously fearful of what he might see reflected in that smooth and shining bier.

'He is gone, Physician, is he not?'

'Our right arm has been hacked from us?'

'The Lord Counsellor is dead,' Harik said flatly.

Hands floated towards him, beckoning. 'You cannot draw him back?'

'Quicken those dead eyes?'

'Make supple these stiffening limbs?'

'He is dead,' Harik repeated. 'He would have died from those injuries had I been at his side when they were struck.'

'By his side. Ah!'

'Ah!'

Briefly all the images turned to Helsarn. He stiffened.

98

Then they were gone and a score of images of the Gevethen were peering up out of the mirrors on which Hagen rested, as though they were waiting to receive him. There was a long silence. Helsarn became aware that the dark figures about the hall were slowly gravitating towards the scene.

Innumerable pale faces turned to one another and spoke in hoarse whispers. 'Shall we go after him, brother? Into the darkness. Beyond.'

'Those Ways are tangled and broken, brother. We would be lost.'

'He tests us yet.'

'He tests us yet.'

'We must have faith . . .'

'. . . faith.'

'Nothing can be done, but to lay the Lord Counsellor to rest.' Harik cut across the hissing dialogue. The images were gone and a myriad grey eyes were focused on the Physician.

'How can he rest? His work here scarce started. So many promises unfulfilled.'

Fingertips touched the harsh face. They lingered.

'Will you not bring him back?'

'I cannot,' Harik said. 'Nor could any that I have known, wiser than I by far.'

Though Harik's manner was unchanged, and his voice still flat and without any semblance of emotion, Helsarn sensed a battle of wills being fought. Not for the first time he felt almost as frightened of Harik as he did of the Gevethen. What was there in this man that he could stand against these two when even the strongest and most ruthless quailed?

He glanced around the hall discreetly. As ever, lights and shadows were moving and changing at the will, or the whim, of the mirror-bearers. All that appeared to be motionless were the dark and silent shapes of the servants. Yet, though he saw no movement amongst them, Helsarn knew they were drawing closer.

The Gevethen were muttering softly to each other – or were they singing?

Then, whatever tension there was between Harik and the Gevethen was gone and the two figures were bending over Hagen's body again.

'He is truly going.'

'Leaving us.'

'We must delay no further.'

And the mirrors were alive with beckoning hands urgently drawing the spectators forward.

'Come!'

'Come!'

'All of you . . .'

'. . . of you.'

'Pay your respects . . .'

'. . . respects.'

'The Lord Counsellor must enter the Ways before his spirit is lost.'

'Grieve not.'

'His wisdom will guide us still.'

Then, scarcely knowing how he came there, Helsarn found himself in a line moving slowly past the body: mirror-bearers, unfolding from around the Gevethen then returning to them, the Guards who had carried Hagen from the carriage, and all the others in the Hall who had at last silently come together. Only the Gevethen and Harik did not move, standing respectively at the head and the foot of the dead Counsellor. As each person passed, Helsarn noticed that they laid a hand on Hagen's forehead and the Gevethen mirrored the gesture. It was no Nesdiryn ritual and Helsarn had not noticed who began it, but he felt constrained to do the same. It took him a considerable effort of will. Not because Hagen was dead – he had handled plenty of corpses in his time – but because, even in death, he was frightening. Yet even as he looked, he saw raindrops, caught in the cold lantern-light and resting whole and undisturbed on the dead face. They looked like tears and they added, for Helsarn, an unexpected and almost incongruous poignancy to the scene.

Throughout this eerie wake, the mirror-bearers moved constantly, transforming the motley handful of mourners, now into a throng, now into a line that spiralled off into a lantern-lit infinity. Then, abruptly, they were still and their mirrors turned about. For a moment the Hall was suffused only with the light of the lanterns that were truly there. Individuals were individuals again, with no gliding reflection moving independently. Only the Gevethen, side by side, white-faced and watery eyes glistening, seemed like reflections. The sudden cessation of all movement, and the disappearance of the milling images twisted a spasm of panic inside Helsarn.

'Know then our trial . . .'

'. . . our trial.'

And the movement began again. The group of eerie servants and mirror-bearers about the body began to disperse as silently as it had gathered. Helsarn could feel the eyes of the stretcher-party looking at him, waiting desperately for him to make some move that would enable them to leave this place. The Gevethen were talking softly to one another again.

When they fell silent, he ventured cautiously: 'What do you wish to be done with the Lord Counsellor's body, Excellencies?'

'Leave us, Captain,' came the simultaneous reply from both of them. 'All that can be done here has been done. Now the Lord Counsellor must enter the Ways.'

Questions formed in Helsarn's mind, but he did not voice them. 'As you command, Excellencies,' he replied.

The eyes turned towards him, as did rank upon rank of others, motionless and staring. 'It was pertinent that you who bore the awful burden of finding the Lord should attend these obsequies. That your tongue did not swell and choke you rather than bring such news to us speaks well of your courage and loyalty. We will question you later, Captain. And your men. And too, those others of our children who were present. Culprits must be found. Retribution administered as he would have wished. The disease that was the way of the Count Ibryen survives still, despite our blessed rule, and we must be ever vigilant in seeking it out. The perfection and order of true justice that Nesdiryn, and beyond, require, will elude us for ever while this corruption remains amongst us.'

Then the eyes were gone, and a limp hand was dismissing him. The stretcher-party needed no urging, and at his soft-spoken order, they formed up and marched from the Hall. Harik looked at the Gevethen then at Hagen's body, then turned and left without waiting for a formal dismissal.

The light in the corridor beyond the Hall, though dull, was almost dazzling after the oppressive gloom of the Watching Chamber, and it took Helsarn a few moments to adjust to his vision being free of the endless, shifting images.

Uncharacteristically, he dismissed the stretcher-party with congratulations for their conduct in the Hall, albeit he ordered them to return to their quarters immediately, pending further orders.

Gidlon, pacing anxiously in the background, strode up to him as they left, but Helsarn turned first to Harik, just emerging from the Hall. Behind the Physician he could see the Gevethen and the mirror-bearers forming a tight circle about the corpse.

'What about the body?' he asked. 'It can't just be left there.'

Harik looked past him. 'I know no more than you,' he said coldly. 'Doubtless if we're required for anything we'll be called.'

'But—'

Harik shrugged and strode off without comment. It seemed to Helsarn, staring after him, that the Physician's stride was more urgent than usual. Whatever relationship he had with the Gevethen, he wanted to be away from this place as quickly as possible.

'Captain!' Gidlon's hissed command ended Helsarn's reverie. 'What happened in there?'

Helsarn cast a quick glance at the door Guards and, motioning Gidlon to follow him, began walking back along the corridor. As they gradually moved towards the light, Helsarn told Gidlon all that had happened. When the tale was finished, Gidlon's immediate comment was the same as Helsarn's. 'What about the body? It can't be left there.'

And Helsarn's reply was largely the same as Harik's. He shrugged, as respectfully as he dared. 'We'll just have to wait Their Excellencies' pleasure.' He changed the subject; he had no desire to dwell further on what had happened in the Watching Chamber. 'What orders did they give about the purging?' he asked, seeking refuge in matters practical.

'Full curfew with immediate effect. Although from what I've heard, there's hardly anyone on the streets even now

103

– everyone's run for cover. And we're to purge from that street as far as the Ennerhald.'

'Do you want my Company out?'

Gidlon shook his head. 'They might be needed for questioning. I don't want them scattered all over the city when they're asked for.'

They had reached the main door. The sky was still overcast, but Helsarn still had to screw up his eyes against the light. The rain had stopped though the courtyard was full of the sound of overflowing gutters and gullies. As they moved to the top of the steps, the Dohrum Bell began to peal again. As before, it tolled nine times. The sound shook the ground under the two men's feet, and shivering concentric circles of agitation formed in the many puddles littering the courtyard.

Chapter 9

Jeyan woke as she normally did – as soon as light began to appear. As usual, Assh and Frey were already awake. It had been a bad night, punctuated by periods of half-sleep, with her mind full of heart-wrenching memories of childhood and her parents. Fully awake, she would have fended off such visions as though they had been Citadel Guards, but caught thus, she was defenceless and was sorely hurt when morning came.

Throat tight, she lay for a while staring upwards, waiting for the pain to pass. In the low, early-morning light, it was possible to make out marks on the ceiling that might be the remains of a painting: probably a cloudscape of some kind, she had decided once, though at times she thought she could also make out the lines of buildings and streets. In her sourer moments, she took them for stains caused by rainwater blown into the floors above through shattered windows.

Now, however, she saw nothing, for she was lingering still in her night thoughts, at once reluctant and desperate to leave, to close and bar again the door that separated her from her past.

As was often the case, the dogs determined the matter for her, Frey walking over and putting her muzzle wetly in her face. Jeyan swore at her and scrambled out of the disordered blankets. With a sudden rush, Frey pushed past her, plunging in search of a spider that had inadvertently scuttled out into the open during the disturbance. The impact tumbled Jeyan over on to her back and she swore again. Before she could sit up. Assh bounded over, tail wagging low along the floor. He stood looking down at her intently until she was obliged to wriggle out from under him. She had no sooner stood up however, than she flopped down on to a chair, her face wearily in her hands. She felt awful. A whirl of black humour came to her aid. Probably caught something off Hagen's last breath, she thought. Someone as foul as him must surely be diseased through to his very heart. No normal person could do what he did without becoming so.

She looked down at her hands, half-expecting them to be stained where she had seized Hagen's hair to yank his head back, or where his blood had splashed on her. There was nothing to be seen however, and such blood as had struck her had either washed off in the rain, or merged into the dirt-mottled background of her clothes.

Yet she was still uneasy. Everything after the killing should have been a song of triumph, but there was a strained quality to her. There was no true sense of release, of freedom. It worried her that the trembling that had suffused her yesterday still lingered, fluttering deep within her – it wasn't as if it was the first time she had killed someone. And from time to time her hand still twitched as she recalled the impact of the blows she had struck.

She took out her knife and looked at it. As she held it, she began to feel quieter. Hagen was dead. Dead! And *she* had done it! The world could not be other than better for such a deed. True, others would probably follow in his steps – her lip curled as she recalled the names of her father's erstwhile friends who had bowed before the

Gevethen, pleading to serve – but none would ever again pass through the streets of the city with the aura of invulnerability that Hagen had exuded.

She pressed the knife into the table slowly. 'Invulnerable,' she said, laughing viciously. 'Not while you're flesh and blood. Not while there's a joint in your armour. Not while someone can get within arm's length of you.'

The last remains of her uneasiness disappeared under the clarion cry that now filled her. She was herself again. Her momentary weakness had been caused by those treacherous wakings in the night that had tried to take her back to a world long gone, and beyond any recalling. She twisted the knife, gouging a piece from the table as she dashed aside even the recollection. She must not allow herself to be so undermined. She had faced *real* dangers in her time and doubtless would again, especially after what she had done – it was ludicrous that she should risk being felled by a mere memory. She needed all her wits to be firmly secured in the present. Perhaps one day, when the Gevethen were destroyed, gentler times would come again, but she dismissed these thoughts as she had dismissed the others. Times past and times to come were of no value to her if they impaired what was here and now.

She sheathed the knife and stood up. The dogs came across to her.

'Better see what we've started,' she said to them, snapping her fingers and indicating the door. The dogs ran off. From the first she had taught them to leave the building as she did, never by the same way on two consecutive occasions. Now they had ways in and out of the building that even she did not know about.

Outside all was still, save for a slight breeze. She looked up. Clouds littered the blue sky and the sun was warm on her grimy face. Perhaps once, celebration might have rung out within her at this but now, sight and sensation were of tactical value only. They gave her a measure of what places in the Ennerhald would be light, what places dark, where she might safely go without being seen, where she might not, what traders, what beggars, would be about and where.

In the distance, beyond the forest, the mountains gleamed, many peaks still snow-capped. For a moment she was drawn to the idea of setting off towards them with a view to joining Ibryen and his followers. It was not the first time such thoughts had occurred to her and, as on all other occasions, she quickly rejected them. Amongst other reasons, it would not be the easy journey it appeared to be. The mountains were further away than the sunshine painted them, and there was the river to cross, with the Gevethen's army guarding the obvious crossing points and constantly patrolling the rolling land on the far side. And other, more subtle, ties restrained her. She looked around at her immediate surroundings. This was her world. She understood it, she could use it. Here, she, and she alone, determined the time and order of combat. She found little to be relished in the prospect of skulking far away in the mountains, ambushing the Gevethen's men, when the heart of the problem lay here in the Citadel and nothing would truly be achieved until it had been cut out.

But despite this judgement, there still lingered the faint hope that one day she would look towards the mountains and the Count and his army would slowly emerge from the forest. She laid the notion aside more gently than she had most of her other reflections that morning.

As she moved through the Ennerhald, it seemed to her that it was quieter than usual. Fewer of its denizens were abroad and even the birds were less boisterous than they should have been on such a day. Her senses, already heightened by the previous day's work and the knowledge that some form of retribution would probably already be afoot, became even sharper. She moved slowly and cautiously from shadow to shadow, each footstep as silent as she could make it, ears and eyes fully alert. The dogs too, tails and heads low, moved stealthily, refraining from many of the bouts of urgent curiosity that usually marked their journeying. The pack was hunting.

Steadily they moved closer to the area where Ennerhald and city merged uncertainly, until she came at last to a building with five towers that stood high above its neighbours. Two of the towers had partly crumbled and stood jagged against the sky. The remainder were intact. All were covered in ever-thickening ivy as Nature quietly strove to regain her own. Noiselessly Jeyan slipped inside, then, pausing briefly for her eyes to adjust to the comparative darkness, she made her way towards a long winding flight of stone steps. As she started up them, Frey ran ahead of her and Assh lingered behind, vanguard and rearguard. At intervals, the stairs opened out into landings with doorways leading to the various floors, but she continued past them. Some of the doorways led only to vertiginous drops, the floors that they once served having long since collapsed, while others led to floors that were treacherously rotten. She had learned from terrifying experience in her early days in the Ennerhald to be very circumspect before venturing out on to untested timber.

Eventually she reached the highest landing. A circle of arched openings led out on to a parapet. Frey was waiting for her dutifully, standing at the top of the stairs. Jeyan patted her then dropped down on all fours and crawled out on to the parapet. This was not for fear of tumbling off, as the parapet wall was whole and solid, but the towers were visible from many parts of the city, not least the

Citadel, and any movement above the wall was at risk of being seen. Further, this was a part of the Ennerhald into which the Citadel Guards would venture if the mood so took them. It was not a place to which she normally came, for this reason, together with the fact that there was only one way in and out, though she had determined to use the dense ivy, now draping the parapet wall, as an escape route if need arose. Today however, she needed to peer into the city before she ventured into it, and this was by far the best vantage point. It had come to her as she made her way through the Ennerhald that the silence was so unusual because the steady murmur of the busy city which normally pervaded everything, was absent.

She came to a jagged hole in the wall. Once, rainwater had run through it, washing along a carved stone channel to discharge through the mouth of a leering head, but some chance had long since carried the channel away and taken part of the wall with it. Carefully she lowered herself on to her stomach and positioned herself so that by reaching out and parting the ivy she could peer through the opening. From here she could see part of the city, including a view directly along one of the long, straight avenues that led to the Citadel.

What she saw confirmed her suspicions. The city streets, which should have been busy with people going about their business, were deserted. As she watched, a group of horsemen appeared and trotted along the avenue in the direction of the Citadel.

She retreated and moved further round the parapet to another, similar opening. Everywhere that she could see was deserted save for groups of Citadel Guards and, on foot, columns of marching men: the army, she presumed. It was an ominous sight, but she registered it coldly. The Gevethen must have ordered a full curfew as a precursor to a purging – probably a bad one, with house-by-house searching. Anyone foolish enough to be found on the streets was likely to be killed on the spot or, worse, taken away for 'questioning' first. Excuses would be futile. Once, an entire household had been massacred as they fled their burning house during a curfew.

For a moment a spasm of guilt threatened to shake her as she thought about what her deed had released on the city, but it passed. The city had not helped her when she needed it; now it must take the consequences of so readily accepting the Gevethen's rule. Even before she had been driven into the Ennerhald she had seen clearly that no civilized proceeding would bring the loathsome pair down, so the people would have to tolerate ever-increasing brutality until they too chose to awaken to this realization.

The only question that formed in her mind was, why were the army there? Ostensibly, the army and the Citadel Guards worked together and held one another in mutual regard as the two pillars that supported the Gevethen. In reality there was little love lost between them. The army thought of the Guards as privileged milksops who, despite the occasional foray, avoided the real business of dealing with the Count in the mountains, and who did little or nothing to ensure the safety of Nesdiryn's boundaries, now under some threat from nervous neighbours since the Count's overthrow. The Guards in their turn viewed the army as an adjunct to their own power, a body of fairly worthless expendables necessary to prevent the Count from escaping the mountains and for keeping the population beyond Dirynhald under control until such time as the Guards were sufficient in number to handle the matters properly themselves. The Gevethen, creators of both, played their own game.

Jeyan did not need to think about the answer to her

111

question. If the army and the Guards were patrolling the city together, then the operation underway was a large one. She crawled to a third outlet. It told her nothing new, although she could make out foot patrols moving from house to house in one street. She allowed her high vantage to separate her from the nightmare that would be transforming those houses, as familiar, sheltering rooms became cruel, enclosing traps, as protecting arms were rendered impotent and pathetic, as precious possessions were smashed or stolen, as loved ones were humiliated and degraded or beaten and dragged away.

How far would the purge spread? she asked herself. Usually a purge was confined to a few streets either side of the place where some untoward event had occurred, but with the army having been brought in, this was obviously going to be much bigger than that. She pictured the streets around where she had laid her ambush and, not for the first time showing an unwitting affinity with her enemy, decided that the purge would be in a broad sweeping arc from the scene of Hagen's death to the edge of the Ennerhald.

It was obvious that she could not venture into the city today. All she need concern herself with, was whether the purge would bring the army or the Guards into the Ennerhald itself. It was a risk, she decided. Even if the pickings here were likely to be few, the seeming inability of the Guards to cleanse the place utterly was a point of sneering disdain that the army frequently levelled at them. She must leave immediately.

Assh and Frey, who had padded softly from doorway to doorway as Jeyan crawled around the parapet, suddenly growled. Jeyan spun round and raised a hasty hand for silence. It was a familiar gesture, at once grateful and urgent. But she was wide-eyed with alarm. There should be nothing up here that would disturb the dogs. Then, to her horror, voices drifted up to her. Several voices. From below. And there were other noises. Nothing was individually distinguishable but it was unmistakably the sound of a large body of men. It needed no great powers of deduction to decide that the purging had indeed been carried into the Ennerhald. She thought she could hear horses, but whether it was the army or the Guards below was of no import – she was trapped. Quickly she scuttled round to an opening on the side of the tower away from the city. She could see nothing, however; the old outlet merely offered her an ivy-framed view across the Ennerhald. The only way she could find out what was happening below was to stand up and peer over the parapet, or perhaps go partway down the stairs and look out of one of the windows. Although she knew that the chance of her being seen doing this was slight, it was far more than she was prepared to risk. Like any solitary animal that both hunted and was hunted, Jeyan was obsessively careful in her contacts with her own kind.

Slowly she pushed her head forward as close to the opening as she could. At least she could listen to what was happening below. One hand still held the dogs silent. They lay down gently, ears pricked, hackles raised, and eyes fixed on their pack-leader. Patient as Jeyan had learned to become, the dogs could out-wait her tenfold.

She screwed up her eyes as she tried desperately to make out what was happening. Her thoughts were racing. Surely whoever it was would not bother to climb up the towers? In the past when Guards had come into the Ennerhald, they had confined themselves to rooting out basements and ground floors, risking dubious stairways and upper floors only in pursuit. All she had to do was remain silent and eventually they would go away. She cursed herself for coming so close to the city. It had not been necessary. She had food and supplies enough scattered about the further reaches of the Ennerhald to last for a long time before she needed to risk going into the city to steal anything. Indeed, by using her knowledge of the forest, she could have remained away from the city indefinitely. She clenched her teeth in anger. What could have prompted her to commit such a folly? It was not necessary to witness the fact to know that drastic action would be taken against the people following Hagen's murder. That was as inevitable as the rising of the sun. And, by the same token, whatever that action might have been, there was little or no possibility that she would have been able to enter the city safely today even if she had wanted to.

That it was vanity that had over-ridden her native caution never occurred to her. To know that she had wanted to revel in seeing the Gevethen's men thrashing impotently through the city as a consequence of *her* actions – the great and powerful bending before her will – would have been to give her a measure of the brittleness of her strength that she could not have borne.

Shouts began to reach her. Orders.

If only she could see!

Carefully she reached into the opening in the hope that moving some of the ivy might improve her view. As she began to push the thick tendrils aside however, two birds, startled by this intrusion into their roost, took violent flight, bursting noisily out into the Ennerhald quiet. Jeyan snatched her hand back and only just avoided crying out. Below, the noise faltered, then more orders were shouted. The dogs began to growl again. Jeyan silenced them and, without hesitation, crawled quickly back into the turret room. Silently instructing the dogs to stay where they were, she started making her way down the stairs. She *must* know what was happening.

It was not long before she found out, for echoing up the stone steps came the clatter of feet. The heavily shod footwear confirmed that the intruders were the army but Jeyan had no inclination to ponder such niceties. Panic and seething rage welled up inside her in equal proportions: the one urging her to flee back upwards in the hope of finding some cranny where she might avoid detection, the other urging her to rush on down, knife drawn, and kill as many as she could before . . .

Before what?

'Before dying, donkey,' came a colder assessment, cutting through the frenzy stirred by these alternatives.

Or worse.

Images of cruel, jeering faces and unstoppable hands threatened momentarily to paralyse her, turning her insides to lead. Then the approaching footsteps stopped and she was released. There was some shouting. She could not make out what was being said, but she heard the fainter answer from outside.

'Right to the top, you blockhead!'

Legs shaking and pulse racing, Jeyan turned and ran back up the stairs. Almost immediately she ran into the dogs sidling warily down. The sight of them at once sobered and heartened her. The dogs looked to her for many things and she must not infect them with her fear. Whatever she chose to do, they were going to have to fight their way out. Baring her teeth, she slipped between them and, placing an arm about each so that they could feel her anger, she hissed, 'Go!' and pushed them down the stairs.

Within seconds, the sound of the ascending footsteps was replaced by a frantic uproar as Assh and Frey, propelled by gravity, the will of their leader and no small amount of natural malice, leapt at the throats of the leading soldiers. Both men were badly hurt before they even knew what it was that was attacking them, and those immediately following fared little better. Six men had been ordered up the tower to see what had disturbed the birds, and the last two were turning to flee as the dogs savaged their legs and sent them tumbling headlong before pounding over them to escape from the building.

Jeyan listened to their progress with a grim delight. The dogs would be safe, she was sure. They were big, strong, and very dangerous animals, well-used to fending for themselves. Either on its own was a disconcerting match for a man with his wits about him, let alone someone clambering up an unknown and narrow stairway in the half-light.

And they carried something else with them which would double the havoc they caused. Jeyan did not have to wait long before recognition of it reached her, for as the sounds of the rout in the stairwell faded away, they were replaced by sounds from outside, drifting in through a nearby window.

'Death-pit dogs!'

The phrase, increasingly high-pitched, was repeated several times but was soon lost in panic-stricken uproar. Jeyan clenched her fists and grimaced, willing the dogs on to mayhem. Amid the din she could just detect a voice desperately trying to impose order, then there was barking, and a terrified neighing, and it was gone.

The noise went on for a long time, though Jeyan knew from its tone that Assh and Frey were safely gone. In fact, they had done their worst and fled before the panic even reached its peak. The fear of death-pit dogs – their savagery and the diseases they carried – was a weapon such as the Gevethen themselves might have envied.

Gradually, and only with a great deal of shouting and cursing, order was restored. Jeyan listened tensely as the sound of footsteps and voices came once again up the stairs, but she soon realized that it was only the original party decamping – or being removed, by others. There were several agonizing cries of pain. Jeyan smiled. Her only regret was that she had not been able to watch the dogs at their work.

'Welcome to the Ennerhald,' she whispered softly. What a pity it was that the rest of Dirynhald did not give these creatures the same reception.

She waited for a long time after the soldiers had left before even considering moving down the tower. The trembling that had persisted for so long after her attack on Hagen seemed set to return, even more overwhelmingly than before. But that act had at least been planned – fretted over for months before it became clear in her mind, and then perhaps as long again before she could find both the courage and the opportunity. This today had been so unnecessary – so pointless. It disturbed her deeply that she could be so foolish. Had she not learned yet? Trust no one, trust nothing – least of all chance. If she did not think – did not use her wits – how much longer was she going to last here? And how many times was she going to have to learn that lesson?

Eventually, as the unnatural silence of the Ennerhald that day returned, she ended her vigil at the top of the steps and crawled carefully to the opening that she had first looked through. Hands still shaking, she parted the ivy and peered through. The sight was little different from what it had been before. The streets were still deserted save for groups of Guards and soldiers. One group she noted was moving along the avenue that led to the Citadel.

117

It was too far away for her to make out any details, but the column looked uneven and disordered, and the officer at its head was definitely walking his horse.

Carrying bodies, are you? she thought. Helping your wounded?

She must give the dogs some of her meat tonight.

The thought of the future seemed to calm her. The Ennerhald was still her place. She'd made a mistake today, a serious one, but that was perhaps understandable after what she'd done yesterday. She would be able to do nothing in the city for some time and if she wanted to know what was happening then she would have to content herself with listening to the gossip of such of the Ennerhald inhabitants as she knew. Now she needed distance. She needed to be away from the confines of this place with its isolating height and its rotting floors and its visibility from the city.

She crawled back to the stairs and started to move down them, all senses vivid and alert even though the soldiers had long departed. She missed the scratching click of the dogs' pads as she descended, and she placed each foot down slowly and silently before committing her weight to it. Even the rustling of her clothes seemed deafening.

Some way down from where she had released the dogs, she came across bloodstains. Patches on the floor, still wet, showed the skidmarks of army boots and told her how much had been spilt, but the most vivid were the sprays splashed over the walls. She saw in her mind the dogs' bone-crushing jaws gripping and then the fearsome, neck-breaking shake that so effortlessly dispatched rabbits and other small creatures unlucky enough to draw out the hunter in them.

For a moment she felt a spasm of pity for the men who

had suddenly encountered this slavering and merciless terror, but she crushed it. They shouldn't have been here. They should have left her alone. Nothing else was to be said. Nevertheless, she tip-toed past the blood with a look of distaste on her face.

When she reached the bottom of the stairs, she let out a long breath. She had not realized how oppressive the close walls of the stairwell had become. She must get away from here as quickly as possible now. Make herself safe, near the forest, stay there for a few days – let things settle down.

A noise jolted her back to the present. As she turned, three men, in the dirty brown uniform of the Gevethen's army, emerged from the shadows to confront her, swords drawn.

Chapter 10

The thunder rolled on and on into an infinite, dwindling distance. Then there was nothing except an empty, timeless and drifting darkness, unaware and at peace.

All was silence.

Silence.

And, abruptly, it was over.

Ibryen opened his eyes and found himself gazing up into Marris's startled face. He made to sit up but Marris's hand on his chest forbade it.

'Just rest a moment,' his old friend ordered, quickly recovering his composure after the suddenness of Ibryen's awakening. Ibryen swore, pushed the hand to one side, and struggled upright. He was in his own room and on his own bed. And the curtains had been partly drawn.

'What the devil . . .?' he began.

'You fell over,' Marris replied before the question was finished.

The answer did not improve Ibryen's mood. 'Fell over!' he bellowed. 'Fell over!' He swung his legs round and stood up. 'What do you mean, fell over? I don't fall . . .' The room swayed perilously and he flopped down on to the bed immediately, Marris catching his arm. He shook it off.

'Give yourself a moment.'

Ibryen looked up. It was the Traveller. His voice was soothing and reassuring without any cloying hint of pity, and at its touch the room became still.

'What happened?' Ibryen asked again, this time of the Traveller.

'I'm afraid I made you angry and when you tried to hit me, you . . . fell over,' came the reply.

Marris nodded in confirmation but Ibryen looked at both of them suspiciously as he stood up again, this time slowly. The room remained stationary. He motioned to Marris. 'Open those curtains, for pity's sake,' he said irritably. He began checking himself for signs of injury.

'You're better now?' the Traveller said, as light filled the room, though, to Ibryen, the remark sounded more like an instruction than an inquiry. The memory of what he had been doing before he collapsed suddenly returned to him. He had to force himself to meet the Traveller's gaze. 'I remember trying to strike you,' he said uncomfortably.

'I provoked you,' the Traveller said. 'I told you, I'm not used to dealing with people. Sometimes I speak when I shouldn't.'

'You did indeed provoke me,' Ibryen agreed. 'But my conduct was inexcusable, and I apologize. I don't know what came over me.' He put his hand to his forehead and moved to the door. 'Nor why I should collapse like that.' Fear welled up inside him. Such a thing had never happened to him before. Was he ill? It didn't bear thinking about. He couldn't afford the luxury of sickness now or, for that matter, at any time.

He stepped outside into the sunlight. It felt good. *He* felt good. The others followed him. 'Perhaps too little sleep and too strange a day,' Marris offered hesitantly.

Ibryen gave him a sour look and sat down on a grassy

122

bank. 'Don't be ridiculous,' he replied, just managing to keep enough humour in his voice to avoid offence. 'I'm not some dizzy young girl up dancing too late.' He closed his eyes in an effort to remember fully what had happened. 'I recall raising my arm, then something . . . hit me. No. Something swept me up. Tumbled me over as though I were a leaf in a gale. And there was a great din all around me. Like a rockfall, but louder. Then it was all gone and everything was . . .' He left the sentence unfinished.

'I heard nothing,' Marris said, into the silence. 'One moment you were lunging at him, the next you were measuring your length on the ground. Not a sound anywhere. Not even from you as you fell.'

Another thought came to Ibryen. He motioned Marris to sit down beside him. 'Did anyone see this?' he said softly and anxiously. Any hint that he was unwell could have a profound effect on morale.

Marris shook his head and replied equally softly. 'No one saw anything.' He pointed. 'We were just over there; those rocks kept us out of sight of most of the village. And once we were satisfied you'd only fainted we got you on your feet and here in seconds.'

'I didn't faint,' Ibryen snarled through clenched teeth, then: '*We?*'

Marris indicated the Traveller. 'He's stronger than he looks,' he said, without amplification. He turned sharply to the little man. 'You say you've got keen hearing. Did you hear anything strange when he fell?'

The Traveller looked unhappy. On an impulse, Ibryen held out a hand to countermand Marris's question. 'What did you have to do with all this?' he asked.

'You're all right now,' the Traveller said quickly, though again it was more of an instruction than a question.

123

'There's nothing to worry about. Really.'

His evasiveness made him the immediate and intense focus of both men. Ibryen looked thoughtful. 'You're right,' he said. 'I'm fine now. No dizziness, no sickness. Not even a headache. It's as though nothing had happened. In fact, apart from being concerned about what *did* happen, I feel very well. Almost as if I'd had a long and relaxing sleep. I'll ask you again, what did you have to do with all this?'

'He never touched you,' Marris said to him, but more in the spirit of providing relevant information than pleading in mitigation. His eyes remained firmly on the Traveller. Under this scrutiny the Traveller folded his arms and began looking up and down and from side to side – anywhere rather than directly at his questioners.

Ibryen recognized the signs and changed tack. 'I'm truly sorry I tried to hit you,' he said. 'It was unforgivable for many reasons, but you struck straight through to the heart of everything we have here and I lashed out. So many unsettling things have happened today, I suppose I was on edge, and your words were too close to something I suspect I don't want to think about.'

The Traveller's expression became pained as he listened and then, slowly, he looked up at the surrounding peaks, his face full of a poignant longing. He was about to speak when, following yet another impulse, Ibryen said, 'You're free to go.'

Marris started but stayed silent, though it was patently an effort. The Traveller sagged, as if he had been struck a telling blow. 'Yes, I know,' he said quietly, sitting down between the two men. 'I always have been. Nothing you could do could keep me here against my will.' It was a simple statement, quite free from challenge or bombast but it was too much for Marris.

'You think you could have escaped from here?' he said, with some indignation. 'Past Hynard and Rachyl and a great many more like them scattered on sentry-watch all about this region? And every one of them knowing about you and watching you like hunting birds? I think not.'

The Traveller seemed to be gently amused. 'I didn't say I could fight my way out of here,' he said. 'Heaven forbid.' He smiled broadly as if suddenly relieved of a burden. 'Besides, I'm not so old that I can't think of better things to do with Rachyl than cross swords with her.'

Marris, about to extol further the vigilance and prowess of the Count's followers, found his mouth dropping open at this unexpected turn in the conversation. Ibryen fared little better. Despite their more pressing concerns, he and Marris exchanged disbelieving glances.

When Ibryen caught his breath, he said, softly and urgently, 'I'd advise you to keep even a hint of *that* fancy to yourself, Traveller. Rachyl has a highly developed sense of . . . maidenly honour.' Instinctively he looked over his shoulder as though glowering retribution for such thoughts might be standing there.

'Oh yes,' the Traveller replied, still smiling. 'I'm not *so* inept in my dealings with people that I hadn't discerned that.'

Marris growled, 'Don't change the subject, Traveller. Explain what you meant.'

The Traveller looked surprised. 'About Rachyl? I'd have thought—'

'About how you could have left here at any time,' Marris interrupted sternly, still defensive.

The Traveller looked at the mountains again and his smile faded. 'There's nothing to explain,' he said. 'I was about to say that I came here of my own free will and that I'd leave similarly, but there are times when I wonder about such things. I fear I'm no freer than you, really. Your Count's offer of freedom is more binding than his chains.'

Marris looked set to become angry at what he took to be continued evasion. Ibryen interceded. 'It was a contentious remark,' he said. 'An explanation wouldn't go amiss. And you still haven't told me what part you played in my . . . falling over.'

The Traveller looked down at his hands and hummed softly to himself. 'I was just travelling. As always. It's strange, I rarely have a destination. I find they're troublesome – they entangle, they impede, they mar. But I'm not a passer-by, you understand. After what I'd seen and heard in Girnlant . . . so many years of strangeness, unease . . . taking almost physical form.' He paused and hummed a little more. 'I had to go back to that castle and look at that Gate – read it – study it – learn. Something in me prodded me forward. Held my feet to the path. And led me here. Not halfway to my goal and a strange hint of the Culmadryen in the air draws me down off the ridges.' He looked at Ibryen intently. 'And draws a man who perhaps hears beyond, up on to them.' He stood up quickly, and spoke decisively. 'This is the message that I heard, hung about with the aura of the Culmadryen, Count. Plain and simple. "Help me. Help me. I am nearly spent".'

Ibryen's eyes widened, but Marris grimaced and smacked his hands down on his knees. 'This is madness,' he said to Ibryen angrily. 'I don't know who he is, or how he got here, but he's raving. And you're on the verge of . . .' he hesitated and selected his words carefully '. . . doing something foolish.' He leaned towards Ibryen, almost pleading. 'If you try to release him you'll have a mutiny on your hands.' He shot a glance at the Traveller.

'And, your orders or not, someone'll kill him before he reaches the next valley.'

Ibryen merely nodded in response to this outburst. 'But he's not leaving, are you, Traveller? He won't leave because helping us is a necessary part of his journey. Because he's found the same trouble here that he found in Girnlant.'

'What?' Marris exclaimed incredulously. 'The Gevethen causing problems on the other side of the mountains?'

Ibryen's brow furrowed. 'No, obviously not. But perhaps the same . . . moving force, behind them. The same spirit. Am I right, Traveller?'

The Traveller did not reply.

'I am right,' Ibryen concluded. He put his hands to his temples, as if that might quieten his thoughts. 'Tell me the truth, Traveller, and tell me now. What did you just do to me? What did you do that gave me all these thoughts that are swirling round up here?'

The Traveller cast the briefest of glances up towards the mountains – a final parting, Ibryen thought – then met his gaze squarely. 'I defended myself against you, that's all. I'm sorry. It was a reflex.'

'You never touched him,' Marris burst out with a violent gesture of denial. Ibryen restrained him gently.

The Traveller ignored Marris's anger, but spoke directly to him. 'I'm from the line of the Sound Carvers, Corel Marris,' he said. 'The Song alone knows, I've few and poor skills as a Carver myself, but such as I have are beyond your attaining or even understanding. I'm not a warrior – I am what you see – small and weak, though I'm older than you might think – but when I'm threatened I use such tools as I have to defend myself.'

Marris turned to Ibryen for help.

'Let him finish,' Ibryen said.

The Traveller thought for a moment. 'Just as a stone carver might defend himself with his mallet and chisel if he were suddenly attacked, so did I.'

'You never touched him!' Marris protested again, even louder than before.

Frowning, the Traveller reached up to touch the rolls of cloth in his ears, then he looked at Marris and opened his mouth. Marris immediately clamped his hands over his own ears, then, with an oath, he leapt to his feet and began looking round urgently at the mountains.

'What was that?' he said, after a moment, cautiously lowering his hands.

'What was what?' Ibryen asked, looking up at him in some alarm.

'That noise. Like a . . . rockfall . . . thunder. I've never heard anything like it!'

'What noise? I heard nothing.'

'But you must have!'

Ibryen shook his head.

The Traveller took Marris's arm. 'Only you heard it, Corel. Just as before only your Count heard something similar. It was me. My carver's mallet and chisel,' he said softly and with regret. 'Not intended to be used as a weapon, but effective enough when need arises. All things can be used as weapons – you, above all, know that, warrior. The essence of a weapon lies in the intention of the user, not its maker.'

Curiously childlike, Marris allowed the little man to sit him back on the grassy bank. He clung to his litany. 'You didn't touch me. I don't understand.' Ibryen watched them wide-eyed, trying to grasp what he had just heard.

'And I couldn't explain,' the Traveller went on. 'It'd be easier for you to learn to speak to the birds and have one tell you how it flies than for me to tell you about the

Carving. Easier by far. All you can do is accept me as I am. What you heard, you heard. And you alone. Just as before, only the Count heard.' He picked a blade of grass. 'Does it concern you that you don't *truly* know how even this inconsequential thing has come to be? Why it is what it is? Why this shape, why this colour, why this place? No. You accept. This is all you can do with my poor skills.'

Marris looked from the Traveller to Ibryen and back again, then put his head in his hands. There was a long uncertain silence. 'Perhaps there's a sickness come into the place,' he said eventually, half to himself. 'A sickness to confuse our minds. I've heard it said that some can carry an illness without suffering it themselves. Is that what you are, Traveller, a plague-bearer? A new horror sent by the Gevethen to drive us all into insanity?'

But there was none of the fear in his voice that should have accompanied such a question and, despite his own confusion, Ibryen frowned at his old friend's pain. He turned to the Traveller. 'Help him,' he said.

'I can't,' the Traveller replied. 'Besides, he needs no help, any more than you do. He's suffered change not hurt. He's old in his body, not his heart. What I am and what I can do is a strain for most people to accept if they're unfortunate enough to find out about it. That's one of the reasons why I keep myself to myself. But if I'm any judge, you're both too well-centred to avoid the reality of what you've experienced for too long, however strange it might be.' His voice was unexpectedly resolute.

Marris neither moved nor replied. The Traveller sat down again. 'Still, it's better you know than not. Especially as it seems I must stay here.'

Ibryen tried to collect his thoughts. 'I told you, you're free to go,' he said, still watching Marris, concerned.

'You also told me why I have to stay,' the Traveller replied.

Ibryen gave a shrug of indifference then, registering the remark, he turned back to him sharply. 'What do you mean?' he asked, frowning.

'I mean that you were right. There's a feeling about this place that's very like what I found in Girnlant.' He became pensive. 'A feeling that I've been finding increasingly, almost everywhere I go, now I think about it.'

Glad of something to focus on, Ibryen reiterated Marris's comment. 'The Gevethen couldn't possibly have had anything to do with whatever happened in some country on the far side of the mountains. Apart from the fact that few here have even heard of Girnlant, they've been here for twenty odd years and they rarely leave the Citadel, let alone the country.'

'I know that,' the Traveller said impatiently. 'What did you say? The same moving force – the same spirit. Didn't I tell you, back in your Council Hall, I've had a feeling of an unease creeping into the world. A feeling of something awful returning. Something that was described on the Great Gate. Marris and you aren't the only ones struggling with change – that's why I was going with a destination in view.' He tilted his head back, as if scenting the air. 'You were right. It's here too. I feel it in every word you speak. The resonances of these Gevethen of yours cling to you and stink of it. How couldn't I have heard it before?'

'I was talking without thinking,' Ibryen retorted, increasingly concerned about Marris's stillness.

'You were speaking your thoughts as they came to you,' the Traveller announced.

'Damn you, shut up,' Ibryen snapped, waving the Traveller aside. 'Marris, for pity's sake, what's the matter?'

'Give him a minute, and he'll be—' the Traveller interrupted angrily.

Ibryen rounded on him. 'I told you to—'

Marris suddenly straightened up, then leaned back on the grass, taking his weight on his elbows.

'Are you all right?' Ibryen asked.

Marris looked up at the clouds drifting slowly overhead, and then down at his hands, resting on the grass. Idly he pushed a solitary blade from side to side with his forefinger. 'Yes, I think I am,' he said. 'Bewildered and confused. And with more questions than answers, but yes, I'm all right.' He looked at Ibryen. 'And you, Count,' he said. 'Are you all right after what you've just heard?'

Ibryen did not reply.

Marris plucked the blade of grass then sat up and rested his chin in his hand. 'That noise you made – or made me hear, Traveller. Brought back memories. Thoughts I haven't had in years.' He smiled to himself. 'When I was a child, I used to think what could be the smallest thing that would start an avalanche. What could it possibly be that would send boulders the size of a house crashing down a mountainside? I remember I decided in the end that it might be nothing more than dust blown by the wind.' He held his thumb and forefinger slightly apart. 'One tiny speck rolls into its neighbours, which roll into their neighbours, and so on and so on until down comes everything. Then I thought, but what could cause the breeze?' He pursed his lips and blew the blade of grass from his extended palm. It twisted and turned erratically as it floated to the ground to meet its approaching shadow. 'Then I gave up. So many tiny things, each smaller than the last, where could it possibly end?'

Ibryen looked at him uncertainly. Marris caught his expression. 'Don't worry, Count,' he said, smiling. 'My brains aren't addled yet though I'll concede they're well stirred up.' He pointed at the Traveller. 'Dust in the wind, aren't you, old man?' he said. 'Come to start an avalanche.' The Traveller tilted his head on one side. 'It's very strange,' Marris went on. 'Only a few hours ago, the future was merely a dim reflection of the past, dwindling into the far distance. Things would go on as they've always gone on since we came here. We'd fight and run, hide and prepare, think, fret, worry. Then fight and run, hide and prepare. Over and over. Until in the end . . .' he pointed at the Traveller again ' . . . like he said. We'd lose. We'd make a mistake. They'd find us and crush us. Or, more likely, a stray arrow would bring you down – a missed footing – anything. Then me, Rachyl, Hynard, all the rest, one after the other. Inevitable, sooner or later.' His demeanour, at odds with the content of his speech, was almost jovial, then it became suddenly dark, and he drove his fist into his palm. 'We set our future in stone. Made it immutable, unavoidable.' He looked up at Ibryen and his voice was vicious with self-reproach. 'We nearly betrayed our people, Count. When we closed these mountains about us for protection we closed our minds as well. Ye gods, how could we have done it?'

As Marris spoke, Ibryen felt the words cutting through his own confusion – the confusion that had been growing since the eerie skill of the Traveller had been demonstrated and which had worsened abruptly with the Traveller's revelation. But it was not easy to accept. 'We could have done nothing else,' he said defensively, holding on to matters he understood.

Marris levered himself to his feet and recanted a little. 'Perhaps not, who can say? But it's not important. We are where we are, and how we came here's of no consequence except in so far as we can learn from it. What matters is that from here we can change the future that we'd set for ourselves.'

Marris's sudden and uncharacteristic optimism chimed with something in Ibryen but it was nameless and unspecific, and years of patient, cautious opposition to the Gevethen prevented it from soaring. 'Obviously we're where we are,' he said. 'But what's different?'

Marris pointed at the Traveller again. 'He is,' he said. 'He's slithered through our precious defences – from a direction we thought impossible, on the rare occasions we thought about it at all – to remind us that there's a world beyond here and Dirynhald – that there are powers other than sword and spear – that somewhere the great cloud-lands still fly.'

'All of which means what?' Ibryen was almost shouting.

Marris sagged a little. 'I don't know,' he said, more quietly. 'Except that if he slipped under our guard, per-haps we can slip under theirs. Somewhere there'll be a way. We mustn't continue doing what we've always done just because we've survived so far doing it. We must find a way that's . . .' he looked upwards as though the answer might be written in the sky for him ' . . . different,' he decided, though with a look of anti-climax on his face. 'A way that doesn't fight them on their terms. A way that slips by them, through them, unnoticed – that finds them dozing in the sun on the ridge, thinking themselves safe.'

'But—'

Marris held up his hand to prevent Ibryen's response. 'Let me finish,' he said, very softly. 'Please. I must say this while it's in my mind, even though it's still forming.'

Ibryen waited.

'We mustn't be afraid of this wild thinking, Count. Somewhere in it there's victory for us. Yet even now I can feel the last five years of careful habit clamouring to dash it away, to keep everything as it was, to carry on as normal. But it's wrong – so obviously wrong. And it grieves me that I, who had the arrogance to act as your mentor in such matters, shouldn't have seen it sooner.'

Ibryen interrupted him. 'I'll accept no reproach from you, Corel,' he said. 'Few of our decisions have been made without the thoughts of us all being well-aired, but *I* accept responsibility for everything we do. We're safe, we're strong, our casualties have been comparatively slight and, as far as we can judge, our presence disturbs the Gevethen constantly, slowing down whatever plans it is they have against our neighbours. What we've done – what we do – isn't something that can be lightly cast aside.'

Marris took his arm. 'Nor would I,' he said. 'But it's not enough. It's not enough to survive and *slow* the Gevethen down. To defeat them, to free our people, we have to do what we do, *and more*. And it's on that *more* that we must concentrate.' He turned to the Traveller. 'What you did to us, can you use it against the Gevethen's forces?'

The Traveller retreated a step, arms extended. 'No,' he said unequivocally. 'I'm no fighter. Besides, what I did was an abuse of my gift. Using it like that in the heat of the moment is one thing, wilfully using it as a weapon is another.'

'You said you'd help.'

'And I will, if I can.'

'But . . .'

'No!'

There was refusal in his tone that few could have gain-said, but Marris was not one to surrender easily. 'What *can* you do then?' he demanded angrily.

The Traveller looked at him a little uneasily. 'I think I've already done two things,' he replied. 'One by accident, one deliberately. You yourself said that just by coming here I've made you think. Made you turn your minds to things that you never dreamed existed. Shaken loose thoughts that have been stagnant for years.' Ibryen found himself being studied. 'That was the accident,' the Traveller went on. 'The deliberate help I've given you, I suspect, is the message I gave you before. The message that gave form to what you'd already heard.'

'What!' Marris exclaimed. 'That nonsense about the Culmadryen?'

'Was what you said just moments ago only air, then?' the Traveller responded, himself suddenly angry. 'Have your everyday needs swamped you already? Have you so soon given up your search for the way that can't exist, that'll bring you the Gevethen?' He did not wait for an answer. 'I don't know what the call I heard means for any of us, but that's what it said – "Help me, I am nearly spent".' He levelled a finger at Ibryen. 'And he heard it in ways as alien to me, as my ways are to you. That's where your way lies, Count. Into the Unknown. That's the direction that cannot be – that crosses all others no matter which way you turn – and that's where you must go.'

'What are you talking about?' Marris stormed. '*You* must be the way. You could use this power of yours to distract their forces. Unhorse their riders, scatter their infantry. Don't you realize what a weapon like that—'

'No!' There was force in the voice now that even Marris could not oppose. 'I am not a warrior. I do not fight, except in need, and then only to escape. *Do not mention this again.*' His final emphasis slammed Marris's mouth shut.

A cloud moved across the sun, throwing the group into shadow. Only when the sun returned did Ibryen find a response. 'Neither of us understand,' he said, stepping to the defence of his Councillor. 'You overwhelmed both of

135

us effortlessly. You must explain.'

For a moment the Traveller seemed inclined to turn and walk away, then he gave a helpless shrug. 'By its very nature, a way that doesn't exist, a direction that cannot be, isn't amenable to explanation, is it?' he said. 'It's to be stumbled upon. It's to be the Unseen already clearly before you. I spoke as I was moved, and *you* must act as you are moved. I can't add anything further.' He held out a peace offering to Marris. 'If I were able to attack the Gevethen's forces in some way, would it really be any different from what you've already been doing? Perhaps there would be a temporary advantage, who can say? But if not, where would you be then? Still doomed.' Marris bridled, but did not reply. The Traveller went on: 'To you, my gift is strange and powerful. To me, it's something delicate and fragile, easily damaged – a trust to be cherished and tended as I constantly strive to improve my poor skills. It's neither weapon nor magical power. There is no magic – nothing that just wishing makes it so; you know that, you're not children. There are only those many wonders which for the moment lie beyond our knowledge.' A hint of reproach came into his manner. 'And didn't you say that the Gevethen themselves have strange gifts – powers, if you must – of their own? Powers which you also do not understand, presumably, yet which you'd have me ride to war against. Would you ask me to die for your cause?'

Though the words were spoken simply and without rancour, Marris closed his eyes and turned away as if he had been winded. 'I'm sorry,' he said, after a long silence. 'I didn't think.' He shifted uneasily. 'I started the day worried enough because the Count had wandered up on to the ridge in the dark – something he's never felt the need to do before. Since then, confusion's followed on

136

confusion.' He cleared his throat. 'I was afraid.'

'Ah.' The Traveller breathed out the exclamation as if he were recognizing an old friend. He fiddled with the cloth in his ears. 'Fear, everyone understands,' he said. 'It's been a strange and difficult day for us both, Corel Marris. I'd not expected to find myself cramped in a valley and involved in a war when I came across a stranger enjoying the morning sun. I was merely going to pass the time of day with a fellow traveller.'

The two men looked at one another in silence for a long time.

'What would the dust know of the avalanche?' Marris asked rhetorically.

The Traveller did not reply, but frowned and reached up to adjust the cloth in his ears again. 'Someone's whistling,' he said. Both Ibryen and Marris stiffened. The Traveller looked up and pointed. 'Over there. It's getting closer.'

With increasing concern the two men turned to follow his gaze. Almost immediately a faint, staccato whistling reached them. Ibryen straightened up and motioned the Traveller to follow him. 'It's the alarm,' he said. 'Someone's approaching.'

Chapter 11

Some instinct stopped Jeyan from reaching for her knife as she saw the three soldiers. Instead, she casually pulled her ragged jacket about her to ensure it remained out of sight. A picture of what must have happened formed in her mind in an instant. It was almost certain that those purging the city knew two dogs had played a part in the killing of Hagen. Even though she had seen people frantically fleeing the scene as she herself had fled, there would have been plenty present who would willingly have provided that information later. That, and the fact that it had been a lone assassin. So although small packs of death-pit dogs were not all that uncommon, and despite the mayhem that those two had wrought to this trio's comrades, whoever was in charge had had wit enough at least to consider the possibility that perhaps the tower was occupied by more than them alone. He'd also had sufficient sense not to risk any more men on those narrow stairs.

She began to tremble again – a mixture of genuine terror and blazing fury at having allowed herself to be trapped. Her eyes flickered across the three men and their levelled swords. A sudden dash, low and fast between them and she could be away.

Perhaps.

139

But the men were watching her both intently and calmly, as though whatever she chose to do, they were a match for it. As well they might be, probably mistaking her for a scrawny youth. And they kept moving – as did their swords – not in a jerky and tense manner, betraying alarm, but almost relaxed. Gaps came and went, but the scrutiny never faltered.

She couldn't do it! There was too much rubble and tangled foliage on the ground for her to risk scrambling between them, she told herself, but part of her knew that the moment for action had simply slipped from her and her fury flared anew.

But she had other resources, and when she spoke she lowered her voice slightly and slurred her words to make them difficult to understand. If they thought her a youth, so much the better, and it would be useful if they thought she was simple; heaven knew, there were enough such in the Ennerhald. She did not have to fake the tremor in her voice.

'Have they gone? Have you killed them?'

'What?' said the nearest soldier, a large man wearing an insignia on his uniform that marked him out as some kind of leader. He leaned forward as he spoke, but did not lower his blade.

'Have they gone? Have you killed them?' she repeated. 'The dogs.' She made her eyes vacant and let her mouth drop open. 'They chased me in here.' She pointed shakily up the stairs and began to gabble. 'I'd to go right to the top. I nearly fell through a hole in the floor. They ran off when you came. I heard a lot of noise. I was frightened.'

The men's demeanour changed perceptibly, and they exchanged knowing glances, though they came no closer, nor conspicuously lessened their guard.

'What would they be chasing a half-wit like you for?' asked the leader.

'For the bones probably,' one of the others interjected, a stocky individual with broken and discoloured teeth that made him look peculiarly repellent. 'There's no meat on it.'

The others laughed unpleasantly. 'You can't get meat here, sirs,' Jeyan started off again. 'Not meat. I have to beg to eat, sirs. In the streets. The Guards allow it. I don't bother anyone. But I've never had meat for a long time. People don't give you meat – not fresh anyway. Sometimes there's some around the stalls and at the back of the shops, when they can't sell it. It's not nice, but—'

'Shut up,' said the leader irritably. 'Don't speak unless you're told to.'

'No sir, I won't. I won't.' She looked around anxiously. 'Did you kill them? I heard a lot of noise. They were death-pit dogs, you know. When they bite you, they—'

'I told you to shut up!'

Jeyan cowered, hands twitching to her head and face.

There was a brief consultation between the soldiers. 'Is there anyone else up there?' one of them asked. Jeyan shook her head dumbly. 'Are you sure?' She nodded.

There was more consultation. 'Finish the damn thing off and let's get out of here. They're a pox, these people. This place needs a real cleaning out, it's a cess-pit.'

'Maybe, but sooner you than me. It's a big place and I wouldn't fancy working round the pits. We'd better take this one in with the rest of the rubbish we've found down here; there's no saying who's checking up on us today. Let the officers sort out who's who.'

'Can I go now?' Jeyan intervened.

The leader sheathed his sword and stepped towards her, his hand drawn back to strike her. She cowered again. He relented at the last moment and seized her arm instead.

'You can go to the Citadel with the rest of your friends,' he said, yanking her towards the doorway.

Jeyan dug her heels in and began wriggling fearfully. 'No, no!' she cried. 'Have you killed them? I'm not going outside unless you've killed them. They chased me. They're death-pit dogs. They're . . .' The soldier swore and tightened his grip about her arm. 'You're hurting. You're hurting. Are they dead? Are they dead?'

The other soldiers were laughing at their comrade's plight and, for a moment, Jeyan thought that he was going to lose his temper and start beating her. She lessened her struggling and began leaning on him.

'Thump it for pity's sake, and let's get off.'

'Yes, and you can carry it,' retorted Jeyan's assailant, transferring his anger to his adviser. 'Come on, damn you,' he said, returning to Jeyan. 'It's all right. We killed the dogs. They're not there any more.'

'Where are they?'

'They're outside. Come on.' The last remark was accompanied by a violent jerk that pulled Jeyan off her feet. The others sheathed their swords and, still laughing, followed them out into the sunlight.

'Where are they?' Jeyan demanded, looking round anxiously. She began resisting again.

The leader stopped and made a pantomime of looking around. 'Oh dear, they mustn't have been as dead as we thought,' he intoned to the increasing mirth of his friends. 'Now come on!' He swung his hand at Jeyan's head, but in partly releasing her to do this she slipped away from him slightly and the blow barely caught her. She tumbled to the ground however, howling, thinking frantically how she could elude her captors now that she was out in the open.

'They'll come back,' she whined. 'They'll come back. They'll tell him what's happened and he'll send them back for me. They kill people. He's taught them to. They always do what he tells them.'

The laughter faded abruptly and the three men looked at one another significantly. 'Who are you talking about?' said the leader, bending down and dragging her to her feet. 'Who'll send them back?'

'Don't hit me, please.'

'I'll do more than hit you, you dozy little sod. Just answer my question. *Who*'ll send the dogs back?'

'Him!' Jeyan exclaimed fearfully, pointing. 'Him. The big man they belong to.'

There was such alarm in her voice that all three spun round in the direction she was pointing as if expecting to see Hagen's murderer about to fall on them. One partly drew his sword. Jeyan found herself pulled off her feet again. 'Who're you talking about?'

'Him! Him! The one who owns them. They go everywhere with him.'

The questions became urgent. 'Who is he? Where is he?'

Jeyan shook her head and pointed again, mimicking increasing terror. There was another hasty conference, more serious than the last and with some head-shaking and hesitancy, then the leader decided. 'Show us.'

Jeyan shook her head violently. 'I'm afraid,' she said. The soldier struck her across the face. This time the blow caught her fully and sent her sprawling facedown on the ground. It was a long time since she had been touched by anyone other than the two dogs and she was finding her response to the manhandling she was receiving difficult to contend with without retaliating. Now, for a moment, her face smarting and her ears ringing, a screaming, manic anger threatened to overcome her judgement and she nearly snatched out the knife. She came to herself just as her hand closed about its hilt and managed to release it as, once again, she was dragged to her feet.

'The one you've got to be afraid of is *me*!' said the leader. 'Now take us to this man.'

The reluctance of the others gave itself clearer voice. 'We should get some help. If this fellow killed Hagen, he's not going to be some puny little simpleton like this one. And I don't fancy dealing with those dogs.'

The soldier holding Jeyan gave a snarl of disdain and struck his companion on the chest with the back of his hand. 'What do you mean, *if*? A big man and two mad dogs. Who the hell else could it be?' His manner became more conciliatory. 'Come on, move yourself. The dogs caught us all by surprise before. They won't do it again, will they? What do we need help for? One man and two dogs against *us*!' The man wavered and the attack was pressed home, this time with a prodding finger. 'I'm damned if I'm going to hand *this* prize over to that bastard captain who thought it such a joke to leave us here. "Wait till nightfall," he says with that sneer of his. And still less am I going to hand it over to those snots in the Guards. We catch the man who killed Hagen, and there's plenty of good things will be lined up for us. Reward, promotion, soft city duty instead of flogging through the mountains. Whatever we want.' He concluded by laying a fraternal hand on his companion's shoulder.

The wilting reservation gradually became a shrug of bravado. 'You're right,' concluded the reluctant soldier, brown teeth smirking. He made to cuff Jeyan. 'Come on, hero. Show us where this great assassin skulks.'

.144

'Don't hit me any more, please,' Jeyan whined. 'I'll show you. But you'll keep the dogs off me, won't you? I don't want the dogs to get me.'

The teeth affected a pained expression. 'I don't mind taking on death-pit dogs and some Ennerhald lunatic, but I don't want to put up with that whingeing all the way.'

The leader did not reply, but gave Jeyan a telling look and shook her to silence as they set off. After a little while and a few stumbles by Jeyan, he tired of holding her arm and let her walk just ahead of him, though he drew his sword and the two others came closer. From time to time, Jeyan stopped and looked around as if thinking where she should go next. In reality however, full of blazing anger and hatred, she was luring them deeper into the Ennerhald. The further they went, the more they would be moving into her own territory, with its many hiding places and secret exits and entrances. Sooner or later they would become careless and then she would be away. With good fortune, a swift stroke would wound the leader to slow down any pursuit. Discreetly she checked her knife.

They continued in silence, moving along the winding, uneven streets and past decaying buildings with blank-eyed windows and crumbling thresholds. Eventually, the strangeness of this long-dead city within a city began to unsettle the three soldiers.

'This place is giving me the creeps,' the teeth said. 'It feels bad. There's more places for an ambush here than in the mountains. There could be an army around us and we'd never know.'

His complaint received no sympathetic hearing. 'Shut up,' snapped the leader.

'We should go back. What if killing Hagen was just to lure us into the Ennerhald – the army, that is. A trap.'

145

A hand caught Jeyan's arm and the short procession stopped as the leader turned to deal with this query. 'Then you can bravely cut your way back to the Citadel and raise the alarm, can't you? Who's going to lay traps for us here, you idiot?'

There was little note of banter in his voice as he vented his own growing concern on his subordinate. That's right, Jeyan thought savagely. Quarrel. Fight amongst yourselves. Give me the least chance to bring one of you down. Surreptitiously she looked around, but there was nowhere immediately by that would serve as an escape route.

'I was only . . .'

'Only what? Thinking? Don't, it's bad for you, leave it to me. You just keep your wits about you.'

Jeyan waited for an angry response but nothing happened. The recipient of the abuse merely glowered. Then the leader turned his irritation back to Jeyan and gave her a powerful push in the back. 'Come on you, move! We haven't got all day. How much further is it to where this individual lives?'

'Not far,' Jeyan said.

'How far?'

'Not far. I think. I don't know. I don't come round here much. I'm frightened. He's dangerous. He—'

'Yes, we know. He kills people.' The leader seized Jeyan's jacket with one hand and pulled her forward so that his face was almost touching hers. Jeyan screwed her eyes tight and turned away, genuinely fearful that, so close, he might realize that she was not the youth she had been taken for, but a woman, with all that that implied for her. She had no doubts about her inability to contend with someone so strong, no matter what they chose to do. The edge of the sword came terrifyingly to her throat.

'Well, so do I. And *I'm* here, right now, lad. Do you understand?'

Ironically, relief flooded through her at this conclusion. He hadn't noticed. She nodded as frantically as the menacing blade would allow until she was eventually released. 'Not far, not far,' she gasped, pointing. 'Round the corner, down the hill, through the—'

There was another angry push. 'Just move.'

They set off again, moving further and further away from the city, the three soldiers watchful and uneasy, Jeyan forming and discarding plans for her escape. Having felt the strength of the leader and studied him a little, she was having reservations about being able to use her knife against him. It was sharp, but the uniforms were stout leather and robust-looking, and might be difficult to penetrate with a direct thrust. Further, the jerkins rose to cover most of the throat. She would have to attack a hand, or the face – the one small, fast-moving and not immediately disabling, the other precious little bigger and protected by deep and ancient reflexes. Whatever she did, she mustn't let them get hold of her once she made her attempt to escape. She must keep her distance, use her speed and knowledge of where she was to flee and hide. She began to be very afraid.

'This is a waste of time. This idiot's no idea what he's doing or where he's going. We could be wandering round for hours. I'd no idea how big this place was. I say we take him back now. Get back to the purge, before everything worth taking's gone.' It was the third soldier talking this time. The teeth nodded in agreement but did not speak.

The leader halted and paused. He looked at Jeyan grimly. The third soldier's opinion meant more to him than Teeth's. 'Let's give it a little longer,' he said eventually. He

147

pointed his sword at Jeyan. His voice was chillingly calm. 'Listen carefully, boy, and understand. You may be near the end of your life. You take us to this man *now*, or I'll open you from neck to crotch, very slowly.' The sword point followed the words.

Jeyan felt sick, and the trembling that had so dominated her after the death of Hagen, returned in full. All she could do was nod again. She held out a shaking hand. 'Down there. Across a square at the end, there's a big building on the corner with . . .'

The sword prodded her forward. 'Just take us.'

She began to walk a little more quickly, disguising her increased gait, by tripping and stumbling forward nervously over the uneven ground. There were plenty of places around here that she knew. If she could get away she had no doubt that she would be able to elude the three men, and in their present mood it was unlikely they would follow her far into the maze of buildings and streets. But she could not delay much longer; that same mood was becoming dangerously unanimous and increasingly impatient. She stumbled again. As she recovered she turned and beckoned them forward apologetically.

They came to a pile of rubble strewn across the street where a building had finally succumbed to time, and collapsed. She scrambled up it agilely bending low and using her hands. She stopped at the top and, crouching, turned as if waiting for her captors to catch her up. The leader came first, but having one hand encumbered by his sword his balance was unsteady. Jeyan turned away as if looking where they must go next. At the same time she ran her hand frantically over the rubble, feeling for a suitable stone. For a moment it seemed that she would not find anything and, in mounting desperation, she looked down. The approaching leader noted the movement.

'What're you doing?' he said, stopping to steady himself.

Jeyan drove her hand into a pile of debris, oblivious of the damage to her hand and, with a wild sweep flung stones and dust into his face. He swore, and his hands came up to protect himself. His flailing sword unbalanced him and also became a momentary threat to his companions. Jeyan did not wait to see the outcome of her actions. She dashed down the far side of the mound, reaching the ground in three strides, and headed towards a nearby building. She was impeded only slightly by the fact that she had landed awkwardly on her ankle as she leapt down from the rubble, though she was aware of the pain and could feel her body's resources mounting to carry her through this moment regardless, incurring a debt which would demand payment as soon as she was safe.

The sounds of abuse and vigorous action followed her and she did not look back until she had clambered through the window she had been heading for. All three men had recovered from their surprise and whatever damage she had caused them, though the leader was rubbing his left arm across his face as he ran. There were plenty of potential missiles lying about her and for a moment she was tempted to stand and repeat her assault. The speed of her pursuers' approach dispelled the idea even as it formed, but she did pause long enough to place her fingers in her mouth and emit a piercing whistle. The sound made the three men falter where a barrage would not have done, and Jeyan turned and fled into the building.

These men were not slow-witted denizens of the Ennerhald nor startled citizens from whom she might be begging or stealing however, they were soldiers of the Gevethen's army and had seen active service against the Count in the mountains and in patrolling Nesdiryn's other borders. Further, though Jeyan did not know this, they were strongly motivated by the knowledge of what would befall them if they returned to their Captain empty-handed and with the puling excuse that they had allowed a mere youth to escape their charge while he had led them a merry dance through the Ennerhald.

The leader was through the window even as Jeyan reached the doorway at the far side of the room, and the others were immediately behind him. Jeyan's natural fleetness and her intimate knowledge of where she was should have carried her steadily away from her pursuers, but the pain threatening to seize her ankle took this advantage from her and as she ran along passageways, turned rapidly into doorways and scuttled through openings, she found that she could not elude them.

Dappling sunlight shone through a hole in the ceiling of a wide hall, and hovering pollens and seeds caught in its beam danced and whirled as Jeyan flickered through it, then rose, as in alarm, in the wake of the three soldiers following close behind. As the motes leisurely returned to their own gentle orbits, the fading sound of the chase suddenly stopped. Jeyan had sped through a cluster of small, many-doored rooms and finally escaped from the leader's relentless intent.

No less than six walls and four doors faced him when he finally came to a halt. He beat down his companions' oaths before they were uttered, as he moved to each door in turn, head forward as he sought for any sound that might tell him which way Jeyan had gone. Finally he himself swore and slammed the last door shut violently. Dust fell from the damaged ceiling, spattering on to his shoulder.

'Gods, I don't like this place. We should never have let him bring us here. We should've taken him back instead. We—'

The look on the leader's face ended Teeth's reproach.

150

Apart from the direct threat in it, it reminded him that they would all suffer punishment if this matter was not resolved satisfactorily.

A whistle reached them, making them all start, but it was not possible to say where it came from within the confines of the room.

'That's twice. He's calling those bloody dogs!'

'Shut up!'

'He's there! Outside!' The third soldier was up on his toes peering through a high window.

As Jeyan glanced quickly back, a rending crash exploded into the silence of the Ennerhald and wrapped itself chokingly around her pounding heart as, with agonizing slowness, a door burst open under the impetus of the leader's charge. The three men tumbled out. They lost the merest fraction of time before they recovered balance and turned to continue the chase.

Never before thus harried, Jeyan was beginning to be driven by stark terror. It marred her judgement. Fatally – she turned the wrong way. Realization struck her instantly, as did the knowledge that there could be no turning back. The narrow alleyway into which she had run was sealed by a wall which she could not possibly scale and the only doorway would lead her into a room whose exits had been long blocked by collapsed floors. Nevertheless it was the only place she could go and she turned into it with scarcely any hesitation. Inside, breath wrenching and trembling violently, she drew her knife and crouched low behind the remains of the door hanging by a solitary hinge. She had no time to decide what to do before a gasping figure lurched unsteadily into the room. Desperate beyond all thinking, Jeyan, clenching the knife in both hands, thrust herself upright, driving the knife towards the intruder's throat.

Only his reflexes saved the leader as, unbidden, his left arm extended to deflect the blow. The action saved his life, but his arm was cut almost to the bone. The suddenness and ferocity of Jeyan's attack sent him reeling, clutching his arm. As he tried to recover his balance, he stumbled on the debris that cluttered the floor and fell heavily, losing his sword. Jeyan too was unbalanced by the unexpected impact, but she recovered almost immediately and turned to face the next man silhouetted in the doorway. She was vaguely aware of a dirty smudge across his shadowed face as discoloured teeth were bared in a menacing grimace, but she had eyes only for the extended sword. Like a cornered animal she danced from side to side looking for an opportunity to slither past this menace, but the sword point followed her unerringly.

Driven now by forces beyond her control she was coming inexorably to a state that would lead her straight into a desperate charge regardless of all apparent danger. And feeding this was the fear leaking from the soldier, for though Jeyan could not see his face, he could see hers even in the dull light, and it was a mask of awful and primitive hatred against which his sword seemed to be more an emblem of futility than a weapon. The sight brought into awful clarity for him all the qualms about the Ennerhald that he had been having since they had left the towered building so comfortingly near to the city.

Jeyan's mind took in everything before and around her, unbearably heightened in intensity and framed in a silence which shuddered to the pounding rhythm of her heartbeat: the felled and wounded soldier at the edge of her vision, slowly struggling to recover, the man and sword hesitating directly in front of her, and the third figure hovering at his shoulder. There were no details, only a single whole.

And there was only one way.

Yet, even as she began to launch herself forward, the scene changed. The soldier outside turned, his actions laboured and slow. Eyes widened in fearful realization and the sword came up in defence.

Then, like a suddenly clearing mist, the silence was gone; torn away and replaced by a screaming frenzy of noise and terrifying movement. Assh's bone-crushing jaws were at the sword arm of the third soldier but he was hurled brutally to the ground and hacked down with a single blow. His assailant however, had no opportunity to celebrate this victory, for even as his sword struck the felled dog, Frey was on his back, tearing at his throat. The two fell to the ground in a floundering mass of limbs and fur and foaming blood.

Distracted by the commotion behind him, Teeth's attention wavered and he turned. He hesitated for the merest instant then drove his sword into Frey's side. He was too late to save his companion however. And too late to save himself as Jeyan, already half-crazed by her own plight, seeing her only friends butchered, was swept away by a primal, uniquely female lust to destroy the destroyers at any cost.

The long-abandoned room which had known no disturbance in generations save the excursions of occasional small animals, was filled with a high-pitched, wavering cry that was no longer human as Jeyan, imitating Frey, leapt on to the soldier's back, and drove her knife repeatedly into him.

So frenzied was the attack that the man did not have time to make even a token resistance, and he was dead before he hit the ground, Jeyan still stabbing him frantically.

She was still stabbing and screaming when a powerful hand seized her shoulder. A terrible sight, with eyes blazing, mouth snarling and her face covered in blood, she swung round to strike at this new intrusion.

A fist, swung with a combination of skill and sheer panic, struck her squarely on the chin, and the noise in the room died abruptly.

Chapter 12

Though he had motioned the Traveller to follow, Ibryen strode out at a pace that the little man could not follow, short of running, which he did not seem disposed to do. Marris, with an odd combination of politeness and lingering suspicion, hung back with him though he was patently anxious to be by his Lord's side.

There was suddenly more activity in the village. Armed people were appearing in considerable numbers and though many were apparently just concerned about what was happening, at least as many again were following some well-ordered drill, dispersing themselves to what were obviously pre-arranged locations about the valley.

'It's not an army coming,' the Traveller said to Marris in a surprised voice, as they stood to one side to allow a group of armed men and women to run by.

Marris gave him a brief, puzzled look, then treated the statement as a question. 'No,' he said. 'It would have been a different call. This is a messenger.'

'But not expected, I gather from your tone?'

Marris did not reply. They were at the Council Hall where Ibryen was at the centre of a large, agitated crowd. It parted as Marris reached it though the arrival of the Traveller did little to ease the tension and Marris kept close to him as they walked up to the Count.

'What's *he* doing here?' came a voice from somewhere. An echo of agreement bubbled out from all around the crowd.

'He's waiting, like the rest of us,' the Count replied sternly.

'He's seen too much.'

'How did he get here?'

Ibryen stamped on the questions before more came. 'You've all heard by now what I said before unless everyone's suddenly given up gossiping. When he's been properly questioned, what we know, you will know, if it's possible. Right now, Rachyl and Hynard are checking to see if he's told us the truth about how he came here. In the meantime he's in the charge of myself and Marris and he's to be offered the courtesy due to a guest until we say to the contrary.'

The answer was not popular, and there was some muttering, but there was enough humour mingled with Ibryen's sternness to prevent any further questions being pressed. The Traveller shifted his feet uncomfortably however, and fiddled with the rolls of cloth in his ears.

'Are you all right?' Marris heard himself asking.

The Traveller nodded, but frowned. 'The noise isn't easy to deal with, and some of your companions here are quite clear in their minds what they'd like to do with me.'

'Don't worry, it's just talk,' Marris said, as reassuringly as he could, then, giving him a knowing look, added, 'talk you're not supposed to hear. They're nervous about you.' He paused and peered into the distance like the rest of the crowd. 'They'd probably be even more nervous if they knew what you could do.'

His remarks did not calm the Traveller. 'Do you think we could go inside?' he asked, looking from Marris to Ibryen. Ibryen gave a curt nod and, with a hint of reluc-

156

tance at being taken from this impromptu vigil, Marris led the Traveller into the Council Hall. As the door closed behind him the Traveller let out a noisy breath of relief. Marris jumped to a conclusion.

'You're going to find life here very hard if you think that was noisy,' he said. 'You should hear the din when they're arguing.'

'It's not that,' the Traveller said. He was wandering about, as though looking for something. 'Noise I can cope with if I have to. My not-hearing is almost as good as my hearing at times.' He smiled ruefully as if at some private memory, before concluding, 'It was the hostility.'

'I told you. That's just talk. You're in no danger, especially as the Count's given you his personal protection. Besides, you can look after yourself well enough, can't you? Even if you don't like doing it.'

'I can, but . . .' The Traveller paused by a table and, after trying one or two, selected a seat which he twisted round slightly. He did not continue with his reservation. 'While in many ways I'm different from you, in as many ways I'm also the same. If I'm startled suddenly or menaced in some way, then I lash out, just as you do – without thinking. And the crowd out there was menacing me.'

'But—'

The Traveller silenced him with a look. 'You must understand. I don't eavesdrop, but I couldn't help myself. I heard every word, felt every nuance that that crowd uttered and it frightened me badly for all your and the Count's assurances. People are such dangerous animals.' He shuddered. 'I'm talking about a reflex response. Something I've no real control over. I – my body – will use whatever noise it finds around it to use as a weapon. What I did to you deliberately was the merest touch and was taken from sounds that *you* probably couldn't even hear.

157

The noise of that crowd on the other hand, was like a vast armoury full of all manner of potentially lethal devices. I was concerned I might do great harm without intending to, both to other people and myself. That's why I wanted to get away.'

His sincerity was all too apparent. 'I can't pretend to understand,' Marris said, 'but I'll take your word for it. That *merest touch* of yours was alarming enough.' He gave the Traveller a stern look. 'I know you told me not to mention it again, but we need all the help we can get. Are you sure that you can't—'

'Certain,' the Traveller replied before the question was completed. He wrapped his arms about himself and shuddered again. 'You don't know what you're asking.'

Despite the Traveller's obvious distress, Marris was half-inclined to pursue the matter, but the little man closed his eyes and cocked his head on one side. He seemed to be approving something. 'This is a melodious seat,' he said with a smile. 'You sit there.' He pointed without opening his eyes. 'Your visitor's a little way to come yet.' At a loss to know how to respond to any of these remarks, Marris remained silent and sat down where the Traveller had indicated.

As the two men sat motionless, waiting, it seemed to Marris that the silence in the Hall was deeper than ever, as though their very presence had drawn all the sounds from the place and transformed them into absolute stillness. Such quiet should have unnerved him, but he felt only calmness. The Traveller sat with his eyes still closed and his head bowed, nodding occasionally as though he were asleep in the cool shade of his favourite tree, with the scents and sounds of a summer garden all about him.

How sad that something like this should end, Marris thought.

The Traveller pursed his lips and moved a solitary finger in a delicate plea for silence though Marris was not aware that he had made any sound. The silence returned and flowed through him, a deep and gently overwhelming tide.

Time ceased to exist.

Then, as if at the touch of some unknowable moon, there was change again, and the Hall was as it always was. For a moment, Marris felt its silence to be a great clamour.

The Traveller smiled again. 'Good,' he said. 'I needed that after all this upheaval.' He looked at Marris. 'You did well. There's something in the blood around here, without a doubt.' Before Marris could reply, the Traveller was on his feet. 'He's almost here now.'

As he spoke, the Hall door opened, throwing a sunlit path across the floor. Along it, in a wash of sound, came Ibryen followed by two men who were carefully guiding a third, heavily blindfolded. The path vanished as the door closed and Ibryen spoke to the escorts who gently removed the third man's blindfold and then disappeared into one of the rooms off the hall. The Traveller beckoned the Count and indicated the table at which he had been sitting. It was the gesture of a host, at once authoritative and welcoming, and Marris's visible surprise was compounded when Ibryen obeyed it, walking protectively by the new arrival who was screwing up his eyes and blinking as he grew used to the light in the Hall. He was a young man, but his drawn face and haunted eyes betrayed hardship that was already ageing him beyond his years.

'There'll be food and drink for you in a moment, Iscar,' Ibryen said as they both sat down. 'You look exhausted. Did you have any more problems than usual on the way?'

But Iscar's attention was on the Traveller. 'Who's this?' he demanded bluntly.

'Do you know him?' Ibryen asked in return. 'Have you

159

seen him about the city, the Citadel? Or heard chatter of anyone similar?'

Iscar gave the question no thought. 'No, never,' he replied immediately and unequivocally. 'Who is he? How did he get here?'

'In due course,' Ibryen said. 'But, as ever, only if we consider it safe for you to know.' The answer seemed to satisfy Iscar, but he kept looking uncertainly at the Traveller. 'Now tell us what's brought you here so early.'

Iscar leaned forward across the table as if to give his message less distance to travel.

'Hagen's dead!'

'Dead?' Both Marris and Ibryen echoed his last word. Then there were a few moments of stuttering confusion which Iscar ended brusquely.

'The only tale we have, but it's from several good sources, is that two death-pit dogs panicked the horses and turned his carriage over. Then as he struggled out of it, someone ran out of the crowd and stabbed him.'

'Some*one*?' Ibryen said, snatching at the first thing that came to him.

'So the rumour goes,' Iscar confirmed. 'Two wild dogs and one man – and him only a youth apparently. Just jumped up on to the carriage and stabbed the devil.' His hand mimicked the action and he bared his teeth in grim appreciation. 'We've no idea who it was.'

There was a brief buzzing silence.

'Hagen dead,' Ibryen said wonderingly. 'I can't believe it.' He could not keep the shock from his voice as he asked the question that had just been answered: 'And no one knows who did it?'

'Not as far as we can find out.'

'Is there a chance it could be one of your people, taking matters into their own hands?'

Iscar gave a faintly helpless shrug. 'It's a possibility, I suppose,' he said. 'We work in small, separate groups for fear of us all being betrayed at once, so there must be some doubt.' He was frowning and shaking his head even as he spoke, and he went on more certainly: 'But no, I can't see it being any of us. It was such a bizarre, almost random attack. Killing Hagen is everyone's fantasy, but even when it was discussed it was never seriously considered. Certainly no plans were made. It was obvious that such an act – if it could be done – if people could be found to do it – would have to be a precursor to a larger action, precisely for fear of what's happening right now.'

Ibryen's face darkened at the reminder. 'What *is* happening?'

'The city's under full curfew and they're purging all around where it happened.' He hesitated. 'House by house. They've brought army units in to help. I only just managed to get out.'

Ibryen's expression was pained and, briefly, he turned his face away from this stark telling. The silence of the Hall closed about the group.

'Whoever did it cost the city a fearful price,' Iscar said into it dully.

No one spoke for some time.

'It must have been some demented soul driven past his wit's end,' Ibryen conjectured eventually, his voice full of conflicting emotions. He glanced at Marris. 'Dust in the wind,' he said. 'But what'll be left standing after *this* avalanche?'

'Hagen murdered.' Marris spoke for the first time. His face was pained. 'News for celebration if ever we heard such, except that the consequences for Dirynhald don't bear thinking about.' It took him an effort to force the next words out. 'Still, they're set in train now and must be lived with, whatever they are. Apart from that, my only regret is that I wasn't able to kill him myself.'

The talking stumbled to a grateful halt as the two escorts entered with food and drink for Iscar. He ate greedily while the others sat back, engrossed in their own thoughts. As Iscar finished eating at the same speed as he had started, Ibryen signalled for more food to be brought. 'Things are getting worse are they?' he asked.

Iscar coloured and hastily declined the offer. 'I'm sorry,' he stammered. Now, guilt-stricken, he looked like the young man he was. 'Food's getting scarcer and scarcer. In fact, everything's getting scarcer. The Gevethen are blaming you and neighbouring states, but it's the incompetence of the people who are running things now. Or malice. A lot of the farmers near the city have been expelled and their farms are just lying fallow. It beggars belief.'

Ibryen laid a fatherly hand on his shoulder. 'One thing we're fortunate in here is that we're not short of food yet,' he said. 'Not much variety, I'll grant you, but it's good simple fare. Eat what you can while you're with us and relish it. Get back some of your strength, you're going to need it, and your going hungry won't fill the bellies of your comrades in the city. If you think it's safe you can take some back with you when you leave.'

The reassurance seemed to ease Iscar just as giving it seemed to help Ibryen, the one exhausted and fretful following his difficult journey, the other still trying to come to terms with the startling news he had just received.

'What shall we do, Count?' Iscar asked as he regained his composure.

'What have you already done?'

'Nothing,' Iscar replied hastily. 'Everyone's stunned and

the city's closed. All we could think of was to let you know what had happened.'

Ibryen nodded slowly. 'Have there been any signs of disturbance or disaffection amongst the Guards or the army?' he asked.

'No. The only thing out of the ordinary was that they tolled the Dohrum Bell twice,' Iscar replied. Both Ibryen and Marris straightened in surprise at this, but Ibryen simply asked how quickly the army had been brought in to help with the purging.

'Almost immediately,' Iscar replied.

Ibryen frowned. 'No one can accuse the Gevethen of being incompetent when it comes to controlling their fighters.' He thought for a moment. 'You're right to have done nothing. The world can't be other than a better place with Hagen gone from it, but I fear that any precipitate action would be foolish at best. It occurred to me that perhaps the killing was part of a rebellion by the Gevethen's own people. But from what you say, it seems that it was nothing more than a random act by someone deranged.' He put his head in his hands. 'It's good that something like that can suddenly strike so close to the Gevethen's heart – perhaps it'll teach them about the vagaries of chance, or about the consequences of using force to repress a people, though I doubt it – but it's tragic that neither we nor you are in a position to take any tactical advantage from it. Tragic.' Wilfully he sloughed off the mood and became authoritative. 'You and your people must concentrate on surviving until the purging's over. Stay still and silent. Take no risks. Some other time will come.'

He would have preferred a more rousing conclusion. Marris echoed the sense of anticlimax. 'The death of such a man in such a way should have heralded great events.'

163

'Perhaps it does,' Ibryen said thoughtfully, 'if we've got the vision to see them. Many things today are different from what they were yesterday, aren't they?' He looked at the Traveller. 'Perhaps what we need to do is look and listen to what's happening beyond the immediately apparent.' The idea intrigued him. 'With Hagen gone, there'll be a rare scrambling for position amongst their followers. Right from the top to the bottom. Change all the way through. And who can say what that'll bring?' He spoke to Iscar again. 'Tell your people to watch and listen. To find out what promotions are being made, what new rivalries begun, what quarrels.'

'And what scores are being settled,' Marris added.

'But take great care,' Ibryen went on. 'We know to our cost that the Gevethen have more unseen and unknown servants than liveried ones and the change will affect them too. Take care who you bring new to the cause.'

'Informers are a problem we're well aware of,' Iscar said with a hint of reproach in his voice. 'The death pits contain more than just the Gevethen's victims.'

The mood around the table changed perceptibly at this dark observation. Iscar's attention returned to the Traveller, though he did not speak.

Ibryen addressed the unspoken question. 'Nothing as momentous as your news has happened here, Iscar, and what *has* happened I can't tell you about. But change has come here too, and a new strategy is under way that will take us directly to the heart of the Gevethen.'

Iscar's eyes widened and he made to speak but Ibryen's hand held him silent. 'For the time being, I can tell you neither the time nor the events that will mark this, but inform your people that it will come when they least expect it and they will have their part to play in it.' He leaned forward earnestly. 'Suffice it that the Gevethen will be attacked from a direction that they did not even know existed.'

Iscar glanced quickly at the Traveller and then at Marris, but the Traveller was gazing idly around the Hall, apparently indifferent to the conversation, and Marris's face was unreadable.

'You must rest now,' Ibryen said, ignoring the mute appeal. 'Leave me your messages to study and I'll reply to them before you go.'

It was an end to the brief conference. Iscar struggled for a moment with the questions that Ibryen's announcement had loosed in him, but left them unasked.

A little later, Iscar was resting in one of the rooms off the Hall, while Marris and the Traveller were sitting with nothing to do other than watch Ibryen as he read through the papers that Iscar had brought. Marris was restless, several times catching his muscular fingers on the verge of beating out a devil's tattoo on the table. As Ibryen turned over yet another page, Marris's patience ended abruptly. 'What did you tell him that for?' he hissed.

Only Ibryen's eyes moved as he looked over the page at his questioner. 'I'm reading,' he said.

'What did you tell him that for?' Marris repeated.

'Let me finish,' Ibryen replied, with an edge to his voice which stopped Marris pressing his question further, but made him even more restless than before. Finally Ibryen laid down the papers and pushed them across to Marris, his face grim. 'Morale's better than we deserve,' he said, holding up a hand to prevent Marris from speaking. 'It's not easy living here, but it doesn't compare with what our people in Dirynhald are having to tolerate. Living in squalid daily hardship and helpless in the face of a terror that can arbitrarily snatch them from their firesides at any time without even the vaguest pretence of lawful authority. We forget too easily that for some of them each passing moment is a nightmare, each passing footstep, each knock on the door the possible harbinger of untold horror.'

'But why did you tell Iscar we had some great plan in hand?' Marris blurted out, though less forcefully than before.

'Because we have,' Ibryen replied.

'What!' Marris exclaimed.

'Because we have,' Ibryen confirmed. Marris's face showed surprise and alarm in equal proportions. 'It's all right,' Ibryen said. 'I've not taken leave of my senses.' He cast an uncertain glance at the Traveller. 'In fact, it may be that I've just come to them. Hear me out, then you can say whatever you want.'

He became both urgent and purposeful. 'There's nothing in what I'm going to say that you haven't fore-shadowed countless times yourself, Corel. Whenever I've said "if", you've always replaced it with "when", haven't you? A dark joke between us – mentor and pupil. Now, after what's happened over the last few hours, I think – no – I *know*, we must accept that you were in the right.' Without turning from Marris, he indicated the Traveller. 'Whoever this man is, from wherever he's come, his assessment of our position is beyond reproach. We've accepted that already, haven't we? Accepted that we're doomed here unless we do something radically different from what's been our strategy since we escaped the city.'

'A *successful* strategy,' Marris interposed pointedly.

'Yes, I know, I know,' Ibryen hurried on. 'But doomed for all that. Attrition will finish us, even if luck stays with us. There's no other outcome possible. We must grasp that

166

at any cost. Our strategy's served its time. Now we must change it.'

Marris managed not to demand, 'To what?' though it lit his face.

Ibryen turned to the Traveller. 'I'm far from clear in my mind why I've allowed you to be privy to all this but that's by the by, now. Today should have been as any other day when winter's almost gone and spring's almost here. Everyone in this valley knew what was expected of them, and why. Nothing was purposeless. And tomorrow would have been much the same. And the day after. Only a gentle and steady change like the season itself, with occasional storms and showers as we laid plans to draw our enemy's forces out and harry them or returned to some victory celebration. On and on. But instead, the cycle's been broken. Where there should have been silence has come the din of two messages. One from you, strange and enigmatic, from a direction unknown to us, and one from our own kind, blunt and simple, telling us of the greatest blow against our enemy that we could ever have expected short of their actual death.' He paused for a moment, staring fixedly ahead. 'Whatever else these messages have told us, they've blown the mist from our eyes and left us gazing unblinking at the truth.'

Unexpectedly, he smiled. The smile was strained, how-ever. 'But where's it left us, apart from dazzled? We can do nothing about Iscar's message other than at once cele-brate and grieve, though I can try to encourage and hear-ten my people with a few words.' He tapped the papers that lay spread on the table in front of Marris, untouched. 'But while we must conduct ourselves as before, for our safety's sake, it seems we need a completely new strategy – one which cannot be attained by continuing as before.

A paradox. So we must look for the way that can't exist, mustn't we?' The Traveller looked uneasy. Ibryen did not release him. 'How should I attend to the message that you've brought, Traveller?'

The little man hesitated. 'I doubt I'm the one to advise you in such matters, Count,' he said eventually. 'I'm not . . .'

'. . . used to people.' Ibryen finished his plea for him. 'Yes, I know. You've mentioned that once or twice already. Nor are you a soldier. But most of the people in these mountains who are fighting for me weren't soldiers when they arrived, so that's of little consequence. The fact is, the wind that brought you here, left you. Tell me again the message you heard, and tell me what I must do.'

Marris looked at him anxiously, increasingly concerned about the direction of the conversation. For a moment, the Traveller looked as if he was considering fleeing the Hall, but it passed. 'I don't know what you must do, Count, but the message, more and more clear to me now as I look back, was, "Help me. I am nearly spent." '

Ibryen leaned forward intently. 'You said that what you heard was hung about with the aura of the Culmadryen.' He laid a hand on the papers. 'I have to read between the lines of these letters to see into the hearts of my people and discover the truth. Now, tell me *everything* about what you heard so that out of the plethora of change that's swept over us today I can perhaps find one small thing that will point me towards action.'

Marris's gaze flickered between the two men.

The Traveller sniffed and shook his head. 'I don't think I can,' he said weakly.

Ibryen was unyielding. 'You have no choice. You must tell me what you know for sure, and what you think, however unsure, and any speculation that comes to mind.

You must tell me everything whether you think I'll understand or not.'

The Traveller did what Marris had assiduously been avoiding doing, he drummed a flurrying tattoo on the table with his fingers. It ended with a resounding slap. Ibryen waited, his gaze allowing the Traveller no escape.

'What I know for sure I've told you,' he said eventually. 'The call was faint and distant, rising and falling on the wind and echoing and re-echoing off the crags and pinnacles, but it was plain and simple, and it was crying for help.'

'A sound?' Ibryen asked.

The Traveller frowned. 'Of course it was a sound, what else could I hear?' He relented abruptly with a moue of self-reproach. 'But not such as you could hear, I think, nor in a language that you could understand.'

'What language was it in?'

The Traveller gave a chuckle like a parent being asked an honest but impossibly taxing question by a child. 'I'm not as my forebears were, Count, but like them, and unlike you, I'm not separated from my own, or, for that matter, from many other things by the limitations of language as you know it. What I heard was spoken in what you would call the language of the Culmaren.' Strange resonances filled the word 'spoken', bringing together song and rhythm and dance and joining and many other images into a totality of meanings which made both Ibryen and Marris catch their breaths.

Ibryen closed his eyes and lowered his head, moved by what he had just felt, and floundering for words that would carry him forward. When he looked up he spoke slowly, carefully, for fear that such clarity as he had would stumble over some facile phrase and slip away from him.

'The Culmaren are the clouds on which the Dryenvolk build their cities?' he laboured.

The Traveller nodded. He too was listening intently, partner in Ibryen's caution. 'They look like clouds, but ...' he abandoned the explanation. 'The Dryenvolk don't build,' he said. 'They shape, they form, they tend and – you would perhaps use the word, grow – their cities – their lands – from the Culmaren.'

Ibryen frowned and struggled on. 'Why would such ... a thing ... such a huge thing ... be crying out in distress in our mountains?' He gestured towards Marris though he kept his gaze on the Traveller. 'Marris has seen one of these cloud lands, but only once, and I've never even heard of one passing over Nesdiryn, or over any of our neighbours for that matter. How can it be that one of them is now so near to us and apparently is suffering in some way, with none of us having seen any sign of it?'

Now it was the Traveller who was struggling. 'I don't know,' he said. 'I've met and spoken with Dryenvolk on occasions, but I know very little about them. As to the Culmaren, they themselves admit that their own under-standing is marked more by ignorance than knowledge, and I've only the merest fraction of the knowledge that they do have. However, such as it is, I'll tell you, but expect no great revelation.' He gave Ibryen a school-masterly look. 'The Culmaren is both a whole and many parts just like ... a tree ... or a person. But unlike a tree – or us – each part is also a whole in itself, sentient after its way, and quite entire. It can take many forms seemingly at its own will, and in the hands of those who know how to use it. Many forms. But it's deeply mysterious and, I suspect, its true nature's far beyond the understanding of anyone of this world. And the bond, the affinity, between the Culmaren and the Dryenvolk is scarcely less strange.

I'd call it a caring, but the word is inadequate. And perhaps it's more a need, a mutual need.' He gave a shrug and waved his hands dismissively. 'I don't know. I'm weaving a tale now, speculating not instructing. I'm sorry.'

He was abruptly silent, but as Ibryen made to speak, he began again. 'Tell me now what it was that *you* heard, that took you up on to the ridge, to the alarm of your adviser here?'

Ibryen started a little at this sudden counter-thrust. 'I . . .' he began, with a stammer. 'I don't think I can.'

'No,' the Traveller declared, school-masterly again and refusing the answer. 'You must. You must.'

Marris, still watching in silent concern and forcing himself to listen with as open a mind as he could, felt himself torn between indignation and amusement at this insistent harrying of his Lord.

The Traveller's words pinioned Ibryen, wilfully burdening him with a duty to explain as the Traveller had explained. 'But I heard nothing . . . plain and simple,' he said, pleading mitigation in advance and using the Traveller's own words. A flick of the Traveller's hands hurried him on relentlessly. 'Indeed, I *heard* nothing. I was just disturbed – made uneasy.' He was almost spluttering. 'It was as though something inside of me was demanding attention. Sometimes it was clear and sharp, at others, vague and elusive.' He threw up his hands. 'This is impossible!' he exclaimed.

'I'll decide what's impossible,' the Traveller said powerfully, almost menacing now. 'There's more in your words than you know. Finish them.'

The two men stared at one another.

'Finish!' the Traveller snapped, ending and winning the duel.

Ibryen turned his head away for a moment, then went

on as if he had never stopped. 'When it was clear, there seemed to be a need in it, an urgency. It wanted something. When it was vague, it was as though I could . . . sense . . . without hearing, many voices crying out.' He fell silent.

The Traveller hummed to himself, his brow furrowed. 'Is it with you now?' he asked eventually.

Ibryen gave a rueful grunt. 'It was at the limit of my perception when I lay alone in the darkest part of the night, and when I was surrounded by the stillness of the mountains. Now, there's too much turmoil, too much upheaval.'

'I could still it for you,' the Traveller said. 'Quieten the turmoil. Let you listen in peace.'

'No!' It was Marris. His elbow resting on the table, he levelled a finger at the little man, though his words were for the benefit of Ibryen. 'You'll get courtesy and honourable treatment from me until the Count says otherwise, but you'll get no trust – few do. You're getting further and further into our ways, but we've still got to find out whether you're who you say you are, or at least, whether you've come here from the south as you claim. And as for this . . . gift of yours, that's beyond me utterly and you'll do nothing until I've got the measure of what deceits you can practise with it.'

Ibryen's face was impassive. Marris's warning was timely.

'It was only a suggestion,' the Traveller protested in an injured tone. 'Don't you want to know what's going on?'

'Yes I do, very much,' Marris retorted. 'And I want to hear someone telling me about it, *plain and simple*, without any descant from you.'

'It's not going to be that simple.'

'Make it so.' Marris's conclusion was of parade-ground finality.

The Traveller conspicuously refrained from replying, but turned his attention again to Ibryen. 'Is there anything else that comes to you when you think about the call you heard?'

Ibryen shook his head. 'No.' The Traveller's head tilted at the equivocation in his voice, but he made no prompt. 'Though there was a quality about it that was oddly beautiful at times.' He frowned, reluctant to say what came next. 'But it came and went so independently – it was so indisputably at once inside and beyond me – that more than once I had doubts about my sanity.'

Marris reached out to lay a reassuring hand on his arm, but Ibryen waved it aside. 'It's odd,' he went on. 'What's happened over the last few hours would give anyone cause to doubt their sanity, but I'm easier in my mind than I've been for days. More confused and bewildered and even alarmed I'll grant, but still easier without a doubt. Rachyl, Hynard, you,' he motioned to Marris, then extended his hand casually to embrace the whole Hall, 'everything about us and everything that's brought us to this time, is so solid and sustaining. A single burrowing doubt nurtured in my own darkness might have brought me low, but all this isn't so easily destroyed.' He ended his declamation with an airy wave.

'I've done as you asked,' he said to the Traveller. 'Told you what I can, as best I can. Now . . .' he leaned forward and his eyes were piercing '. . . whoever you are, you've clattered through my thoughts like a mad horse in a market-place, and they're far from recovered yet, though you've done me no harm that I can see, other than wind me. Now I've deliberately set words in stone by telling Iscar what I did. Done it in complete ignorance of what

173

I was going to do, but in complete faith that something was imminent. My judgement, not yours. But now I have to find that something. Turn conjecture and speculation and airy phrases into hard-edged practical details that can be measured in fighters, resources, plans and counter-plans. Details which my people can see leading us to the Gevethen's heart.

The Traveller had held his gaze throughout, although his eyes were unfocused, as though his entire concentration was elsewhere. As Ibryen finished, life returned to them. He shook his head unhappily. 'I can't help you further,' he said 'I—'

Anger broke through on to Ibryen's face and his fist thumped the table. 'You can! For all that's happened since I met you, all I have now that I didn't have before is the soft silver thread of the call that reached even into my sleeping hours and drew me up on to the ridge. You must—'

The Traveller stopped him with a sharp gesture, his face lighting with realization. 'Silver thread,' he echoed. The words flew up into the arched silence and shimmered around the Hall like tiny excited birds. They returned and hovered about him, waiting, breathless. 'Soft silver thread,' he repeated, looking at Ibryen as though he had never seen him before. 'Yes,' he said. 'A way is there. Perhaps. I'll help you find it.' He glanced at Marris. 'But I doubt you'll like what I have to say. And as to where it will lead . . .'

He shrugged.

Chapter 13

Everything was pain.

Jeyan stumbled and fell as the rope about her ankle suddenly tautened again. Harsh cords biting into her wrists prevented her from breaking her fall and only at the last moment did she manage to twist round and take the impact on her arm and side instead of her face. Exhausted from the chase, howling inside at the death of her companions, and throbbing from the blows she had received, the fall winded her and she made no effort to rise. Instead, she closed her eyes in the hope that she would never have to open them again.

The mood however, was transitory and, as a tugging at her ankle brought her back to the bright day and the silent Ennerhald, it was replaced by a black and vengeful hate. She rolled over to face her tormentor. As previously, she had been brought down because he too, had stumbled. She tried to kick him as he struggled to rise, but her legs were leaden and would not respond.

Had she been able to deliver a blow of any power, the soldier could not have stopped her, for the gash that she had slashed in his arm was long and deep, and was bleeding profusely despite his attempts to bind it. His strength was failing almost as fast as hers.

Seeing both his comrades and the two dogs slain in the

narrow alley, and having managed to subdue the object of his pursuit, the soldier's immediate intention had been to kill Jeyan. But the pursuit, the two dead bodies and the wound in his arm bore graphic witness to this individual's ferocity and cunning; however improbable it seemed, this scrawny youth must indeed have been Hagen's assassin. To kill such a person in battle anger would be to deprive the Gevethen of their prey – and that could bring untold consequences down upon him against which no plea would be heard. But to return with Hagen's murderer bound and helpless; that was another matter. There would be reward for that indeed. And now, two less with whom to share it.

Whether it was fear or greed that motivated him, the intention to deliver his prisoner alive was now firmly locked into his mind and, despite his weakening condition, a determination, fully the match of Jeyan's own, was keeping him moving forward.

He had fastened the rope around Jeyan's ankle to his belt, as a precaution against dropping it, and as he scrambled painfully to his knees Jeyan managed to jerk it. He lurched forward, instinctively reaching out with both arms. The wounded arm collapsed as soon as it took his weight and he pitched forward with a cry as blood burst out of his crude bandage. Unfortunately, the effort had spent all Jeyan's immediate resource and she could take no advantage of the situation. Instead, she rolled on to her back and gaped sightlessly at the blue sky fringed by the ragged canyon walls of the Ennerhald buildings.

A numbing blow struck her arm. The soldier had recovered and, lying on his back, he had been able to deliver a powerful kick. Somehow Jeyan did not cry out, but she arched up and made no effort to keep the pain from her face.

'If I have to, I'll kill you, boy,' the soldier said as he wrestled with the binding around his arm. 'Make no mistake. I don't *have* to take you back alive. There'll be plenty who'll identify you as Lord Hagen's killer when your body's stretched out in the Citadel Square for public exhibition.'

Jeyan twisted her pain into a balefully glittering knot and dropped it into the well of hatred which now had almost total possession of her. It overflowed. 'You'll be in hell before me, you piece of Gevethen filth,' she spat, through her bruised and bloodied mouth. 'Look at your arm. You're bleeding like a stuck pig. You're dying. Go on, porky – die – squeal and die.' She swung a feeble foot at him but missed. The soldier was no Citadel fop however, and Jeyan's goad merely helped him to recover. By way of recompense he delivered two more kicks, both harder than the first.

With unexpected agility he was on to his knees and then his feet and a powerful hand was dragging Jeyan painfully upright. Her legs could hardly support her. 'Be quiet,' the soldier said, shaking her. The very softness of his voice carried more menace than any roaring curse. 'I've had worse hurts than this further from safety before now. If you want to stay alive, just keep quiet and hope that I don't feel myself about to pass out, because if I do, I'll make sure you don't escape by pinning you to the ground with your own knife.'

He gave her a violent push that sent her sprawling again, then he yanked her upright by her bound hands. 'And the next time you go down, boy, I'll kick you until you get up. I can kick you all the way to the Citadel if I have to.' He snarled into her face. 'In fact, it's something I'd enjoy doing.' He dropped her again.

Jeyan had no doubt that he would at least try to fulfil

this threat. She shook her head frantically. 'No more, no more. I'll do my best to walk, but I'm dizzy,' she gasped.

They had gone only a few paces when the soldier faltered and propped himself against a wall to avoid collapsing again. Jeyan made no attempt to escape, however. The rope around her ankle was a very effective restraint. From somewhere she found another resource.

'I'm sorry I cut you with the knife,' she said plaintively. 'You frightened me, chasing me like that. I didn't know what to do. I just lashed out. And the dogs – they're my friends, they look after me. They'll attack anything that threatens me.'

The soldier, clutching his bleeding arm, glowered at her, but said nothing.

Jeyan slumped against the wall alongside him and stared down at the arm. 'It's bad, isn't it?' she said guiltily.

Still no reply. Exaggerating her distress, she went on, in rasping breaths, affecting kinship in suffering. 'Look, we're both lost here. I don't know where I am. I only know a little bit of the Ennerhald – near the city. I usually beg – I never come this far in – there's all sorts of strange people in here. And I don't know anything about Lord Hagen. I didn't even know he was dead. And there's scores of dogs round here. Fierce dogs. People use them for protection. Why don't you let me go – save yourself before you lose too much blood.'

She bent forward to look into his eyes. She had been hoping that his silence meant unconsciousness, but it was not the case. He was wide awake and alert. With an effort, she kept the disappointment from her face, and nodded towards his injured arm. 'Look, the blood's coming out with your heartbeat. That's bad. I know it's bad when it does that. Go and get help before it's—'

A ferocious back-handed blow across the face ended her plea.

'Keep quiet, I told you!' The soldier snatched at the rope attached to her ankle, partially unbalancing her. She lurched into him, taking some satisfaction in bumping into his injured arm. It cost her another blow which left her on her knees, her head ringing. She pushed herself upright again. To her horror, the soldier was staring at her intently.

Let him not see I'm a woman, she thought frantically, all her fears re-doubled. She dropped her head. A hand gripped her chin cruelly and jerked her upright so that the inspection could be completed. 'What's the matter?' she asked tremulously, the grip blurring her words. 'You're hurting. I'm trying to do what you want. I can't help falling over.'

The hand twisted her head round to look along the crumbling street. Over the broken and crooked rooftops at the end could be seen the five towers of the building where she had started that morning. 'Don't worry about being lost, boy. You recognize those, don't you? All we've got to do is keep walking towards them, isn't it? Then even I know the way.' He shook her head viciously, making it throb. 'What were you doing there? Enjoying the purging? You'd have been better to run and keep running after what you did. The Gevethen see everything, and they can reach everywhere, believe me, I know. Whoever paid you to kill Lord Hagen did you no favours.'

Jeyan did not need to be reminded where they were, she knew exactly, and it was imperative that she get away from her captor as soon as possible. 'I didn't kill Lord Hagen,' she protested. 'I didn't kill anyone – I've never killed anyone. Why would I—'

Her head was jerked round again. The soldier's face was barely a hand's width from hers and his scrutiny was

179

as intense as before, though it was apparent to her that he was having difficulty in focusing.

Squeal and die, pig, she thought vehemently, though no sign of it appeared on her face.

The soldier growled through clenched teeth: 'Your dogs killed our men in the tower. You led us a dance all over this place just so they could do the same again. And I've seen you use that knife of yours. You killed Lord Hagen all right – I can smell it all over you. We know our own kind, don't we? We brothers in blood, we're different, aren't we? No hesitation, just . . .' He jabbed a finger into her chest and seemed to gather new strength. 'But keep it up, keep it up. Shout your innocence as much as you like, you'll have plenty to shout about when the Gevethen's Questioners – Hagen's people – his *loyal* people – start working on you.' He came even closer, malevolently confidential now. 'They always enjoy their work. It frightens *me* just to be near them, and it takes a lot to frighten me, I can tell you. But I might ask if I can come and watch after what you've done. Then again, perhaps they'll do it in the Citadel Square for everyone to see – bit by bit, nice and slow, just to discourage any others who might be thinking the same way.'

For the first time since she had been captured, Jeyan's fear threatened to become screaming panic; her knees and bowels began to yield as the scene described by the soldier appeared before her, lit vividly by his wide and shining eyes. Then the gaze was gone as the eyes screwed tight; the soldier's relish in this anticipated celebration fading before more pressing needs.

When they opened again, there was simple puzzlement in them. 'But there's something odd about you,' he muttered, shaking his head to clear his vision. 'Something odd. I can't grasp it, but . . .' He grimaced and pushed

180

himself off the wall. He was swaying. Jeyan was little more steady herself and the throbbing in her arm from the kicks she had received was merely the focus of the pain that suffused her entire body. She looked around at the familiar landscape, her haven, her hunting ground, now almost mocking her as blank-eyed windows and shattered doorways gaped, indifferent to the drama being enacted before them. And beyond, the five towers, which had once held her high and invulnerable to view the city at her will, had become a menacing hand, signalling to all where she was to be found – even she was not totally immune to the soldier's fears – the Gevethen see everything.

Then she changed.

So far she had been contending with the fears of the moment, but the soldier's gleeful reference to the Questioners and what lay ahead had set light to truly deep and awful terrors. And too, lurching inside her was an emptiness which Assh and Frey had once occupied. Their mother had attacked her when she stumbled into her lair in search of a refuge of her own, and she had killed the animal. Following who could say what instinct, the pups had trailed after Jeyan and she had tended them. They had been with her ever since, at once free and bound. Despite her other fears, the emptiness was bleak and awful, and such as she had not felt since her early days in the Ennerhald following the death of her parents. Now, as she stared at the soldier, his shadow swaying raggedly over the uneven ground, and felt the gaunt hand of the towers at her back beckoning the city to her, the emptiness welled up and became one with the terror. Their combined momentum pushed her beyond anywhere she had ever been before. She would not be taken alive into the city. Either she escaped from this failing butcher here and now – or she died.

She dropped to her knees and slumped forward on to her elbows. 'I can't go on,' she said. An exasperated gasp of pain and weary anger greeted her. Head lowered, she watched the unsteady legs out of the corner of her eye. They were covered in blood and more was dripping constantly, some splattering on to soiled boots, some on to the sun-dried roadstones, cutting new rectangular valleys along the ancient weathered joints.

The sight awoke no compassion. Rather it rekindled the bloodlust that had filled her in the dismal little room where she had been cornered.

Drip, drip. *Squeal and die, pig.*

Affecting to make an effort to rise, she took her weight from her hands and clenched them to her as if in pain. As she did so, she surreptitiously took hold of the rope that was fastened to her ankle. It tautened as the soldier tottered back with a view to delivering a kick and, unconsciously, he took support from it. The tug rang through Jeyan like a signal and, animal now, she gathered all her pain and rage into a single intent and hurled herself at him. Already off-balance, and suddenly losing his unwitting reliance on the rope, the soldier staggered back. Bound hands flying at his face and mouth screaming, Jeyan crashed into him. When she felt him toppling under this impact, she relaxed and lifted her feet off the ground so that her entire weight landed on him as he struck the ground. Immediately she hammered her clenched fists into his face, then jumped to her feet with the intention of stamping on it. Reflexes rolled the soldier out of the way, but the defending arm that he raised was his injured one and it took the full force of Jeyan's descending foot. Crying out, he flailed it desperately, knocking Jeyan off her feet as she tried to stamp on the arm again. Then there was only milling, blood-spraying confusion, with

Jeyan wriggling and thrashing wildly to do what hurt she could, where she could, and to prevent the soldier from retaining any grip he succeeded in fastening on her. In so far as she was aware of what she was doing, she was also trying to snatch her knife from the soldier's belt. And as they rolled over, so the rope faithfully measured out the consequences of their every move, entangling them, releasing them, gripping tight, flying loose. Then it was around Jeyan's hands and across the soldier's face and as she threw her weight to one side again, so it wrapped itself painfully about her hands binding her to her enemy even more firmly than before. Only when she twisted and turned her hands to free them did she realize that at the same time it had looped itself about the soldier's throat and that his uninjured hand was clutching at it.

Freedom came into sight. She could escape this nightmare. A touch of the future came to her: showed her herself snatching cached supplies and running, running, deep into the forest, far beyond any search. All it needed now was one last effort.

Ferociously, and oblivious to the pain in her hands she twisted the rope tighter and tighter, leaning backwards and driving her heels into the ground for purchase.

So absorbed was she in the destruction of her captor that she did not see the figures appearing round a corner of the crooked street. Nor did she see them suddenly start running towards her. Only when hands that were not her own came into her narrow, desperate focus did the world become again anything other than a protesting skein of twisting fibres. And only as they gripped her wrists and forbade them movement and a knife sliced through the rope, jerking her loose, did she return to the Ennerhald.

And to the Citadel Guards surrounding her.

Chapter 14

It was night and Iscar had gone. For all the solace that his journeys to the valley offered him of being free to be himself again instead of watching his every word, his every gesture, albeit within the confines of the Council Hall, the responsibilities that he voluntarily bore on the Count's behalf would allow no true respite and once he had eaten and was sufficiently rested he sought Ibryen's permission to leave.

As he was escorted, blindfolded again, out of the valley, to begin his dangerous return to the choking claustrophobia of the city, he took with him not only food and news of the well-being and renewed determination of the Count and his followers, but also the reiterated pronouncement that the Gevethen were soon to be attacked, 'from a direction they do not even know exists'. Further, and to Marris's unspoken but increasing alarm, Ibryen had extemporized about the message.

'Hagen's death is but the start.'

Unusually, this message was not to be wrapped in ciphers, to be discreetly passed to the Count's followers in the city; it was to be spread far and wide, to as many people as possible. It was to become part of common gossip – the many-headed monster that could not be silenced and that had no heart to slay.

Whatever elation Iscar carried back to the city, it was not to be found in the room in the Council Hall where Ibryen sat, part of a stern circle. Marris and the Traveller were on either side of him and Rachyl and Hynard sat opposite. The atmosphere was tense.

Lanterns lit the room and hid the bright stars that the Hall's mirrorways carried through the darkness and strewed across the ceiling. In the daytime, or in the absence of the lanterns, the room seemed to be open to the air, so faithful was the picture. It was unlikely that a finer example of mirror art existed even in Dirynhald but the craftsman who had built the ways, almost on a whim and with unpromising materials left over from other work, declared that the quality was attributable more to good fortune than any skill on his part. He was deeply pleased for all that, though he was hesitant about doing new work for some time after.

Rachyl and Hynard had only just returned with their team from the southern ridge and their manner was oddly strained. Food stood untouched on a small table in front of them, though a pitcher of water had twice been emptied, some of it across Rachyl's face and neck as she had performed an impromptu and sulky ablution when Ibryen had directed her and Hynard immediately to the room on their return.

'Did you find anything?' Ibryen asked Hynard almost as soon as the door closed.

'Oh yes,' Hynard replied significantly. 'His tracks.' He nodded at the Traveller. 'You're some climber, old man,' he said. There was reluctant admiration in his voice.

'I'm small and light, and I'm used to mountains,' the Traveller replied. 'It all helps.'

Hynard pursed his lips and gave an acknowledging nod as at a considerable understatement. 'There was some faint sign on the ridge, but it was clear enough,' he went on, addressing Ibryen. Then he paused. 'And we could see his trail in the snow across the Hummock.'

'Ye gods.' Marris's stern expression cracked into amazement in spite of himself, and Ibryen's eyebrows rose.

'The Hummock! You're sure?' he asked, wilfully keeping his voice low.

'We're sure,' Rachyl replied on Hynard's behalf. 'We had Seeing stones with us and everyone made damned certain about what they were looking at.'

The Traveller shuffled his feet uncomfortably. 'I did tell you where I'd come from,' he said weakly, adding again, 'and I *am* used to mountains. Can we get on now?'

'You did indeed tell us,' Ibryen conceded, ignoring the request. 'But you'll understand our doubts, I'm sure. Had anyone asked me, I'd have said that in so far as any approach was even expected from the south, the Hummock was the best possible defence we could have had.'

Ibryen looked at his two cousins, Rachyl with her flushed and dirt-streaked face and Hynard, also only now cooling down after what must have been a rapid climb and descent. There was an unfamiliar uncertainty about them both. It was not difficult to surmise its cause. Sceptical and suspicious, at times almost to the point of obsession, they would have led their team up on to the South ridge largely convinced that nothing was going to be found and that the Traveller was beyond doubt some kind of spy. It would have been unsettling for them to find the first small indications that someone had been up there recently. And then to see the footprints still surviving in the snow on the Hummock! That must have been profoundly unnerving. He could see the members of the team on the ridge, looking and looking again across the Hummock in the hope that some other explanation might come to them before they accepted the reality of what they were seeing.

He must be careful with them. Rigid things shatter, he thought. It was an old memory. As a child he had had a formal training in arms as befitted his station and, for a little while, he had been taught by an old man who, though much respected by his peers, used techniques which were frighteningly effective yet strangely soft and subtle. He had never seen the like since and none of his subsequent instructors had made such an impression on him. 'Relax. Let go. Only dead things are rigid,' the old man used to say. 'And rigid things shatter. Shatter suddenly.' He would clap his hands explosively and laugh. He laughed a lot. Ibryen had enjoyed his training but had never understood what he was being taught, always throwing himself massively into either attack or defence, invariably to crushing defeat and always much to the old man's amusement. 'Don't be upset,' he would say. 'What little I've truly taught you, you'll understand when you need it. There's no hurry. Some things can come only with time.' Then he would always add, 'But you've learned more than you realize.' There had been a great affection between them and Ibryen had been deeply distressed when the old man had died. Even now, he often thought about him, always remembering his kindly ways but always too, with the feeling that an opportunity had slipped away from him which would not come again.

Yes, he must be careful with Rachyl and Hynard. Circumstances for his followers demanded a meticulous attention to the procedures that had grown up over the years. To veer away from them was to jeopardize the whole community. That was an article of faith. But had it become mere blind ritual? Had Rachyl and Hynard become strong, supple and well-founded like great trees, or had they become dead stumps, stiff and useless, mere obstructions to be walked around? Would they crumble and disintegrate into ineffectiveness at the wrong touch?

Patience, he counselled himself. Let them ease fully into the present. Put time between the now and the frightening discovery that there had been silent footsteps at their back.

'Iscar's been,' he said abruptly. When the first rush of surprised exclamations petered out he motioned Marris to recount the reason for the premature visit.

Both reacted to the news of Hagen's death with unfeigned and noisy delight, the only regret being from Rachyl who, like Marris, mourned the fact that she had not been able to kill him herself. Their mood sobered a little as Marris went on to tell them about the purging that had been set in train as a consequence, but still they were uplifted. This was a worthwhile blow, well struck.

'What a pity they didn't toll the Dohrum Bell a little more,' Hynard exclaimed at one point, his face alight. 'It might have brought the whole tower down on their wretched heads and solved all our problems at once.' His dark humour was as infectious as it was inappropriate, the more so because the same idea had occurred to both Ibryen and Marris when Iscar had told them of the bell, though neither had voiced it.

Released in some way, Rachyl and Hynard simultaneously downed more water and then began to eat. Ibryen smiled. The footsteps along the Hummock were a little further away already.

'What are we going to do with him, then?' Ibryen asked into a lull that followed Marris's telling and the subsequent questions. His cousins stop chewing and frowned at him. He flicked a hand towards the Traveller. Their four eyes followed his direction, then became uncertain again.

Hynard swallowed. 'It takes some accepting, but he's at least telling the truth about the direction he came from. I can't say I trust him, but that's no insult the way we are here. I'll give him the benefit of the doubt. I'll even guard his back if he needs it.'

Ibryen looked expectantly at Rachyl.

'And me,' she said after a pause. Then she spoke to the Traveller directly, as if anxious to make amends for her earlier manner. 'But you can't leave.' She waved the words aside apologetically. 'I mean, you mustn't leave. If you're captured by the Gevethen's men, they'll torture you until you tell them everything.'

The Traveller smiled and, leaning across to her, took her extended hand. 'Don't fret,' he said quietly. 'When I go, it'll be through the mountains. There'll be no one there.' Rachyl looked at him strangely then, with a slight start, withdrew her hand sharply and put it awkwardly in her lap. She cleared her throat.

'What are you going to tell everyone about him?' she asked Ibryen, hastily reverting to her usual forthright manner.

Ibryen glanced at Marris. One of the lanterns hissed and flickered briefly, trembling the edges of the shadows in the room. When he spoke, Ibryen's voice was steady and careful. 'I told you when the Traveller first arrived that things had happened of late that you weren't privy to and that I needed your help and courage. That's still the case.' He outlined the assessment of their future in the valley as it had revealed itself to him through the day. Both of them protested at length, but the logic that had swayed Ibryen and Marris, eventually swayed them also. Time and attrition would destroy them as surely as an attack by overwhelming odds. It was a cold, frightening realization that dashed utterly their exhilaration at the news of Hagen's death, and it left them in the same predicament as their leader. If their current strategy was destined inexorably to failure, what else could be done?

Ibryen did not let them languish. 'Everything that's happened to date has been necessary for us to reach this point. Have no doubts about that. We could have done nothing else. Now we're ready for change, and we will do the following. Raids against the Gevethen's troops will stop. We'll simply continue to observe their—'

A protest from Rachyl stopped him but he held up a hand to silence her. 'Listen! I don't know what the next few weeks are going to bring, but we continue only with what is *valuable* from the past. We can't afford to lower our guard, to slip into carelessness, but what is merely habit or convenience must be abandoned, and all minds must turn towards looking at events afresh.'

Rachyl swept aside his demand for silence. 'We can't *not* fight!' she burst out. 'We've got to—'

'We've *got* to do nothing!' Ibryen said angrily. 'Just listen, as I've asked. This isn't going to be easy for any of us to accept, but understand, *we've no choice*. We change or die.' Rachyl seemed set to continue her protest but Ibryen allowed her no opportunity. He was with his old instructor again – understanding flickering about him, solid yet elusive. He spoke as his thoughts formed. 'Change, in the form of a random assassin, has intruded on the Gevethen. Let them cope with that as they may – the greater disruption Hagen's death causes, the more likely that mistakes are going to be made. Those few knife-blows won't bring the Gevethen down, but they'll have shaken the entire edifice of their power, just as the Dohrum Bell shakes the Citadel tower. If we continue as

191

we've always done – a spring offensive – moving out, raiding and harrying, then that consistency, that normality will help to support them while they recover. But if suddenly we're not there, and rumours are flying around the city that an attack is to come from some unexpected direction and that Hagen's death was planned as part of it, what then?'

The argument unsettled Rachyl, but she clung on. 'We could tie up part of the army, leave them fewer men to purge the city with.' She dismissed this herself as soon as she spoke it, however. The Gevethen's army was no skilled fighting force, but it *was* large. Whatever happened in the mountains it was unlikely that it would have any serious effect on the numbers available to purge the city. Added to which was the fact that the purging was under way *now*. Any venture that the Count's followers could mount would be weeks away. She shifted ground. 'And what do we do if they come looking for us?'

'Let them come,' Ibryen replied off-handedly. 'We watch and wait, as always, but that's all. Obviously if they look like coming too far we'll intervene. But we'll fight them defensively. Like a token force, left behind to guard a camp. Let them do the attacking. They'll not like that in this terrain.'

Defeated for the moment, Rachyl picked up a piece of bread and began slowly breaking it up. 'But . . .'

'But how are we going to overthrow the Gevethen if we do less than we're already doing?' Ibryen finished her question. Feeding herself with small pieces of bread, Rachyl gave a soft grunt of agreement.

Ibryen's mood darkened. He spoke carefully. 'While you were away, we travelled this same ground many times.' He indicated Marris and the Traveller. 'No logical conclusion is to be found. So we are faced with two choices

– despair and die – or pursue a course of action that has no apparently logical basis.'

Rachyl's eyes were fixed on him, thumb and forefinger slowly rotating an almost non-existent piece of bread into her steadily grinding front teeth. Hynard was sitting very still, his head craning forward intently as though to miss some tiny detail of what was being said would plunge him into darkness. Neither spoke.

Ibryen continued. 'This has been a desperately long day. We're all such a distance from where we were when we woke this morning. An assassin brought change to the Gevethen, the Traveller has brought it to us. And what's been unmade can't be remade.' He forced himself back to the subject that he was evading and tumbled into it. 'I intend to go with the Traveller up into the peaks to try to find the source of the sound that drew him here and the source of the strange call that's been disturbing me these last few days.'

'What!' Rachyl spat crumbs. Hynard gaped.

Ibryen hung on to the reins of his tale with grim determination. 'Marris will take command in my absence and you will pursue the tactics that I've just outlined. Company commanders will be—'

'Are you crazy, Ibryen?' Rachyl spluttered, standing up. She filled the small room like a thunder cloud. Her earlier softening towards the Traveller vanished instantly. 'You can't go wandering about the mountains with a complete stranger, looking for some vague . . . *noise*.' She gesticulated violently. 'What are you going to do *if* you find it? *Shout* the Gevethen out of the country?' She swore and threw down the crust that she was waving incongruously at the Traveller. 'He's probably heard some rutting animal, and you've probably got indigestion,' she diagnosed. 'And we've still no idea who he is. He might well have come from the south, but that leaves us none the wiser about why he's here.'

'Sit down, Rachyl.' Ibryen's quiet tone brought her to a blustering halt but she did not sit. Ibryen turned to Hynard expectantly.

'I think Rachyl's raising some valid questions,' Hynard said unsteadily after a momentary hesitation. His diplomacy warmed Ibryen.

'I understand your concern, Rachyl,' he said. 'Marris has already been over the same ground with me at length – great length.' He had hoped to be conciliatory but her looming presence made him frown. 'Will you sit down, please. This room's too small for you to flail about in.'

Replying with a scowl of her own, Rachyl sat down but perched herself bolt upright on the edge of her chair so that she was only marginally less intimidating than she had been standing. 'Whose idea was this?' she demanded, loath to concede anything further.

'Mine.' It was the Traveller who spoke. His tone was unexpectedly serious. Rachyl's hand shot out, its extended forefinger moving between Ibryen and the Traveller while she struggled to find words to express the realization of her worst fears.

Ibryen took the initiative. 'What's he going to do, luring me up into the mountains, Rachyl? Murder me? I told you, he could have done that already when he first spoke to me.'

Rachyl moved effortlessly to her next thrust. 'The way he can climb he could just abandon you and be off to the Gevethen with everything there is to know about us here.'

'He could have left any time he wanted to.' This time it was Marris who spoke. He gestured to the Traveller as Rachyl faltered again. 'Show them.'

The Traveller pulled a sour face.

'Show them,' Marris insisted. 'Rachyl and Hynard are nothing if not realists. Cut through all this blather, we're wasting time.'

'What do you mean, he could have left?' Rachyl asked indignantly of no one in particular.

The Traveller looked at Ibryen for support but found none. 'Marris is right,' the Count said resignedly. 'I know you don't like doing it, but they'll grasp the significance of what it means at least as fast as we did and then we'll be able to get on. Do it.'

Hynard's eyes narrowed suspiciously during this exchange, but Rachyl was becoming increasingly agitated. Half-standing, she levelled her finger at the Traveller again but spoke to Ibryen. 'I don't know what you're talking about, but if he . . .'

The Traveller opened his mouth slightly. Ibryen was vaguely aware only of a faint humming but Rachyl stopped abruptly and sat down with a thud, her eyes glazed and fixed. Hynard started turning towards her then he too became still.

'What have you done?' Ibryen said, suddenly concerned. 'That's not what happened to me.'

'Nor me,' Marris added.

'This is less distressing to me, if you don't mind,' the Traveller said haughtily, his voice echoing oddly. 'And also kinder to them. Besides, the circumstances are different. And the materials I have to work with. Go and stand behind them.' This instruction was given to Marris in a tone that brought him immediately to his feet and carried him across the room. As he moved behind the two cousins, they were themselves again. Hynard finished turning towards Rachyl while she completed her declaration: '. . . tries any fancy tricks on me, don't think either his age

195

or your protection will . . .' She stopped and blinked. 'What the . . .! Where's . . .?'

'I'm here.'

Both jumped up and spun round at the sound of Marris's voice. Rachyl's chair clattered over. Marris stepped back hastily, arms extended as Rachyl's hand moved instinctively to the knife in her belt.

'Sit down.' The Traveller's voice, though not loud, filled the room and halted this sudden flurry. His two subjects obeyed the command without hesitating, but seeing the shock in their eyes Ibryen did not wait for any questions. 'Marris just walked behind you, that's all. For the last few seconds you've been . . .' he struggled '. . . asleep, for want of a better word.' He lifted his hands in denial. 'Don't ask me what was done, or how, but that's what happened.' Pausing, he looked at them both shrewdly. *Rigid things shatter*. Had the Traveller's demonstration been too sudden, too severe? 'Are you all right?' he asked.

Hynard blinked several times and then opened his eyes very wide. 'Apart from seeing someone vanish, yes, I think so,' he said.

'Rachyl?'

'Yes, fine, fine,' she said, though her voice was unsteady. 'Just a little shaky at finding someone suddenly behind me, that's all.' She shuddered noisily and put a hand on her knife again. It was obvious to Ibryen that both of them had been more badly affected than they were admitting, but their straightforward responses eased his concerns. He repeated his previous remark. 'I don't know what he did or how he did it, and I suspect he couldn't explain it to us even if he wanted to. But you've felt it now. I've no doubt at all that he could have slipped through the entire camp unnoticed at any time if he'd wished. And I know for a fact that his strange gift can be used to far more destructive ends than sending people to sleep for a few seconds. He gave me and Marris a much more violent demonstration of what he can do earlier.'

Rachyl, who had been glaring at the Traveller, and receiving only a smile in return, looked sharply at Ibryen at this. Understanding made its way through the angry confusion in her eyes and her voice became excited and earnest. 'We could use it to—'

'No, we couldn't,' Ibryen interrupted quickly, anticipating Rachyl's conclusion and fully reassured now, seeing her turning so readily to tactical matters. 'We've discussed this at length already. Apart from the fact that this isn't the Traveller's war, and using his gift as a weapon carries a special toll for him, it would merely be an extension of what we're already doing and wouldn't change the ultimate conclusion. We go the way I've said. I go into the mountains with the Traveller in search of whatever's brought him here, and you and the others remain here, to watch, defend and think.' He held out both hands in a gesture of openness. 'I'll not bandy words,' he said. 'This is an act of faith. There's no apparent logic to it except the logic of defeat if we continue as we are. Nothing may come of it, but we all know the value of our instincts out here, and I'm following mine now. They reason too finely for my thinking wits to follow and I must simply trust them.'

There was a brief silence, then Rachyl said, 'You were right, it has been a long day. I feel as if the last five years were in another lifetime.'

Hynard nodded. 'Nothing will turn you from this?' he asked with finality.

'Nothing that I've heard or thought of so far,' Ibryen replied. 'But if you can think of anything, I'm listening.' He became matter-of-fact. 'When you came back you were prepared to give the Traveller the benefit of any

197

doubt you had. I respect your caution but, when you've got over the shock you've just had, I think you might find yourselves on the way to trusting him. However, that's not important. Consider this: what's to be lost by my following this ... fancy? Spending a few days, perhaps a few weeks, in the mountains? Nothing. And what's to be gained? Who can say? But no harm can possibly come of our re-ordering our thoughts; of making ourselves more ready to respond to change, can it?'

Hynard looked doubtful. 'Put like that it all seems innocuous enough. But I'm not happy about you wandering the mountains on your own. It's been a long time since you did any serious mountain work. With all due respect to our ... guest ... good climber he might be, but can he carry you on his back for any distance if need arises?'

Marris's nodding did nothing to prevent Ibryen's indignation mounting at this slur, but Rachyl intervened before he could give it voice.

'Don't worry,' she said to Hynard. 'I'll be going with them.'

Ibryen's mouth dropped. 'I think not,' he said with massive authority. Rachyl's gaze fixed him. There was a strength in it that he had never known before.

Change reforges. The thought came to him unbidden.

'This isn't a matter for debate, Cousin,' she said. She waved an arm around the small gathering. 'This is as it was when we were in the Shippen this morning. This is family. It's imperative that we all agree. But it's also got to be accepted by the Company Commanders – by every one of our people here, if it's not going to do anything other than shatter morale.' She looked at Marris then Ibryen. 'I presume you've given some thought to what you'll be telling them?'

Marris made no reply and, after considering improvising, Ibryen told the truth. 'Not fully,' he admitted. 'We wanted to know what you thought first.'

'You mean you wanted to see how we'd react,' Rachyl translated.

This time Ibryen did not reply. Rachyl grunted significantly. 'Well,' she went on, 'this is what we've all agreed here. You, the Traveller and myself go in search of this mysterious whatever it is that's calling you into the mountains, while the valley contents itself with watching and waiting under Marris's command.' It was a summary, not an opening argument, but before Ibryen could say anything he was once again the focus of Rachyl's attention. 'All that remains is how long this business is supposed to continue, and what's to be told to the others, because you can't tell them what you're really doing.' Marris and Hynard turned to him expectantly.

Suddenly defensive, Ibryen said, 'I can't lie.'

'You can't tell the truth either,' Rachyl said bluntly. 'Not and hope to retain any sense of authority. Loyalty can go only so far. It's been hard enough for us who've known you all our lives, and *I'm* trusting you rather than understanding. You can't ask it of anyone else, it's too much.'

Before Ibryen could reply, Hynard had taken up the challenge. 'We'll have no trouble in announcing that the Traveller's from the south. In fact, we'll have to. The others will have spread it all over the valley by now, so we haven't got much longer before the Hall's full to bursting.'

'I asked you to say nothing about all this,' Ibryen said angrily.

Hynard retorted in similar vein. 'You asked us to say nothing about the discussion in the Shippen, and we didn't, in spite of some considerable pressing. But there were six of us went up on the ridge – the duty stand-by team and us – and the sight of those footsteps across the Hummock couldn't have been kept quiet for any length of time no matter what we, or for that matter, you said.'

For a moment the two men held one another's gaze, then Ibryen broke the contact with an irritable wave. 'Finish what you were going to say.'

Hynard pressed on. 'I think all we can say is that the Traveller is what he says he is – a traveller, journeying from Girnlant in the south to . . .' he shrugged '. . . some place – his home perhaps – in the north. We can say he's an expert mountaineer – also true, and witnessed by others. And we can say he's offered to help us find a way through the mountains that'll help us to come at the Gevethen from some unexpected direction. Again true, after a fashion.' He looked at Ibryen for approval but received only a stern nod. 'Rachyl's going with you will reassure everyone who might have doubts about the Traveller's real intentions. As for a change in tactics, a policy of watch and wait following Hagen's assassination and pending your return shouldn't present any problems. In fact, using nothing as a means of further disturbing the Gevethen is quite brilliant.' Ibryen tilted his head on one side and searched Hynard's voice for any signs of irony but he found none, and Hynard did not seem to notice the scrutiny though he was a little hesitant about his next words. 'All this you can say without lying. But I agree with Rachyl that you should make no mention whatsoever of the Traveller's strange powers and this . . . call . . . you've heard. Nor should we mention anything about the Culmadryen. I'll trust you . . .' He glanced at Rachyl and received some form of assent. '*We'll* trust you absolutely, but in the name of pity, take care – in every way. Keep your feet on the ground because it'll all come to edges, points and physical courage in the end, and we need you here, clear-headed and clear-sighted, directing events from the centre.'

Ibryen's residual anger at their confrontation faded before the unexpected power of Hynard's exposition and he felt more than a little ashamed of his behaviour. He cleared his throat uncomfortably. 'It seems that change is truly in the air,' he said, managing a smile to cover his awkwardness. 'I've never heard you string so many words together before. Certainly not to such effect.'

'I don't think you'll fault them either,' Marris said.

'I think you're right,' Ibryen agreed, then to Rachyl and Hynard he said simply, 'Good. Very good. Thank you both,' before turning to the Traveller. 'Does any of this give you offence?'

The reply was unexpectedly sour. 'The whole thing gives me offence, Count. I belong in the cold high peaks, alone with my thoughts and carving the sounds I find there. If you remember, I told you the tale from the Great Gate about the defeat of the Ancient Corrupter, and how even in the very moment of defeat He knew victory, for He saw that His lessons had been spread both wide and deep throughout humanity.' He looked down into his hand which was curling first in to a claw and then into a fist. 'He's here now, as if those arrows and spears had never brought Him down. He's here, standing sweet-tongued at our shoulders, turning the rich skills of fine people towards a myriad forms of hurt and deceit when they should be celebrating just being – just being.' He looked up from his hand and round at each person in turn. 'But I'm as much one of you as I'm not, and I'll help you as I've promised. At least you too are offended by what you do and you'll turn from it as soon as you can.'

There was a discreet knocking at the door. Ibryen, the nearest, stood up and opened it. A man was standing there, his manner at once respectful and determined. Behind him, the Council Hall, its arched roof lit by dozens of lanterns, was full of silent people, also waiting.

Chapter 15

By an irony that she would not have appreciated, it was fear of the Gevethen's all-pervading power, and the ambition of their servants that fed upon it, that saved Jeyan's life again that day. Citadel Guard Captain Aram Helsarn, routinely supervising part of the purging, intercepted the army company withdrawing from the Ennerhald with their dead and injured and their wild tale about death-pit dogs lurking in one of the buildings. 'I left three men on guard, just in case there was anyone about,' the captain confided shrewdly to demonstrate that it was not only the Guards who were adept at dealing with city-spawned events. But Helsarn had affected a patronizing indifference to the incident and parted from him with a cursory nod of sympathy for his losses which verged on the insulting.

When the column had moved on however, Helsarn uttered a prayer of thanks for the idiocy of his army compatriot and, taking a dozen of his best men, headed rapidly for the Ennerhald and the five-towered building. The reputation of death-pit dogs was coloured by their undoubted ferocity but was disproportionate to their real threat. Helsarn knew, as did most who had ever had to enter the Ennerhald, that while a pack might occasionally attack a lone individual, they would not attack a large group, nor would they wait in pairs to ambush people. And they certainly wouldn't linger about on the upper floors of buildings! A will far more purposeful than brute-hunting instinct was behind the attack or he was a mirror-bearer.

The destruction wrought by Assh and Frey was easily found, and Helsarn could scarcely keep the excitement from his face when the trail of the three soldiers was also located. He actually glanced casually away for fear of what would be seen in his eyes when he heard, 'There's someone with them, Captain.'

They had someone captive and they were going for the assassin! An inveterate schemer, an account quickly formed in his mind of Hagen's murderer overpowered by the Citadel Guards who, sadly, arrived just too late to save the three brave soldiers left by the army captain. Due honour could be given to the army provided that due reward went to him – and his men.

His elation began to wane as the trail became harder to follow through the twisting stone-paved streets, and he was beginning to consider alternative schemes such as waiting for the return of the three men and their prisoner, when sounds of a gasping struggle drifted to him through the Ennerhald silence.

It took four of the Guards to drag the manic Jeyan from her prey and contain her. Finally, already drained as she was, a single blow rendered her unconscious. She received several others before she hit the ground and Helsarn had to intervene to prevent further harm coming to his prize.

Descriptions of Hagen's assassin had varied considerably, all the witnesses' views being radically distorted by the significance of the event, but a substantial number had referred to him as being lightly built and nimble, and to his having a scruffy, unkempt appearance. Helsarn noted that the figure lying at his feet could fit such a description, but he was genuinely puzzled when he compared the youth's slight frame with the bulk of the desperately wounded soldier. Then one of his men removed the crude bandage from the man's arm only to be sprayed with pumping blood before hastily retying it. So it had been a lucky knife thrust that had evened the odds, had it? But where were his companions? They wouldn't have abandoned him with such a prisoner, surely? Perhaps, seeing the worth of his captive, the soldier had killed them – that was more likely, that's where the knife wound had come from. His conviction grew as the soldier gasped out, 'My prisoner!' as soon as he recovered his voice, but subsequently faltered as the saga of Jeyan's capture was hastily revealed. Not least because the telling was frequently punctuated with an all too genuine, 'Dangerous, very dangerous, not what he looks like. Be careful.'

Helsarn made reassuring noises. 'We'll have to get you back to the Citadel and proper help. That wound's bad.' He shared a professional joke with the fading man, patting his shoulder in a comradely manner. 'We don't bother carrying field dressings when we're on purging duty, do we?' His men laughed and the injured soldier smiled faintly.

Still, there's no point in hurrying, Helsarn thought. If he received help soon enough, this man might survive and that would present political problems with the army about the prisoner which were best avoided. Responding thus to his thoughts rather than his words, he affected to ponder something for a while then crouched down and asked, 'Where are your comrades? We should find them. They may not be dead after all, they could just be wounded, like you.'

The soldier waved his good arm about vaguely and began muttering incoherently. Helsarn bent low over him, as though listening carefully, until the man slipped into unconsciousness.

'Shall we look for these others, Captain?' one of the men asked him as he stood up.

Helsarn glanced around and gave a dismissive shake of his head. 'They could be anywhere,' he said. 'It's probably like he said, I doubt they're in any better shape than he is, or they'd be here. We'll get the army to look later. It's their problem if they lose their own men anyway. Let's get these two back to the Citadel.' Indicating Jeyan's body, he gave a grim warning to his troop. 'This could be the one we're after. Tie him up properly and watch him, but make sure he doesn't get hurt any more. He's the Gevethen's. We deliver him to their table trussed and in good condition; how they carve him is their concern. We lose or damage him and . . .' He drew his finger across his throat. 'If we're lucky.'

Thus when Jeyan groaned out of black and fevered nightmare into black and icy consciousness the following morning, she had few more extra bruises about her than when she had fallen to the Guards – not that that lessened the pain that was throbbing through her. She did not move, however; she always lay still when she woke to darkness – it was a long developed habit. For some time, confused images and thoughts spilled through her mind to tumble wildly amid the jabbing rhythms of her pain, urging her to thrash and scream, but still she did not move.

As some semblance of true consciousness began to emerge, her hand groped cautiously for a small hooded lantern that she always kept near to wherever she was lying. Her hand fell on cold damp stones. Only as she flinched away did it come to her that she did not know where she was. And following this, without the mercy of even a pause, the events of the immediate past crashed in upon her with agonizing clarity. A sickening terror filled her. The trembling that had never been far from her since she struck down Hagen, returned in full vigour. So fierce was it now that all semblance of control was torn away from her on the instant. It was as though some desperate spirit within her was seeking to end its pain by rending her frame utterly.

The duration of such racking cannot be measured by the moving of the sun and the beating of hearts: without beginning or end it is beyond and outside the lumbering progress of such crude contrivances. Yet their inexorable momentum cannot be denied and eventually the awful, buffeting tide receded, leaving Jeyan abandoned and empty save for a faint but all-pervasive tremor.

Where was she?

What had happened to her?

There was a dank coldness all about her, and she was lying on her side on a hard, uneven surface. Carefully, and finding new pains with each movement, she eased herself on to her back and stared up into the blackness. Slowly, a hazy greyness appeared above her. For a while it seemed to be moving and changing shape but, gradually, as her eyes adjusted, it became still. It was a door grille.

Even as she stared at it, the greyness started to brighten and yellow. She blinked to reassure herself that this was not just another trick of her eyes in the darkness. It became brighter still. Unsteady, swinging streaks of light began to slice between the bars and sweep across damp stone walls. Oozing fungal blossoms glistened briefly – gross, winking eyes. Shadows leapt frantically from side to side unable to escape from the hanging array of calcified skeleton fingers and cobwebbed tendrils that pinioned them to a low-arched ceiling.

And with the light came sounds – footsteps, voices, the clattering of . . . arms?

Keys!

Almost before she realized what was happening, the grille had swung away from her to be replaced by a tall and widening slash of light, unbearably bright after the almost complete darkness. She lifted a hand to her eyes for protection and thus had only a fleeting impression of the figures who had brought the light.

'It's awake. And it's not manacled!' The harsh voice was as intolerably loud as the light was bright. There was also a startled urgency in it and immediately a weight pinned Jeyan to the floor while something was clamped tightly about her wrists. Then she was being dragged to her feet. Her legs, shaking and unnerved, would not support her however, and she slumped painfully to her knees unbalancing her captors. A blow and an oath followed, knocking her to the floor. She sensed another blow pending.

'That's enough,' said a stern voice. 'Pick him up and carry him if he can't stand.'

'Prisoners are my responsibility, Captain.' There was venom in the word, 'Captain'.

The voice softened dangerously. 'Indeed they are, Under Questioner,' it said, emphasizing *Under*. 'And it'll be you who explains to the Gevethen why this very particular prisoner was damaged before they had a chance to interrogate him in person.'

There was a tense silence, followed by some rebellious muttering then several hands dragged Jeyan to her feet once more. Of the journey that followed, she had only a vague, kaleidoscopic vision: her swinging manacled hands,

208

her own stumbling feet between those of her escort, swaying lanterns and flickering torches, uneven stone steps,
damp and lichened walls. And many doors, stout and
studded with great bolts. And too, noises. People in pain.
She shook her head so that the pounding in it would not
let her hear.

Then she was gathering her faculties. Looking around
she saw she was being marched along a passage which,
though still oppressive and ill-lit was wider than those
she had just passed through. She was somewhere in the
dungeons of the Citadel, she deduced; this conclusion only
served to terrify her further.

The procession halted and there was a hiss of in-drawn
breath and a nervous curse. The hands that had supported
her so far now forced her down on to her knees. Those
around her also knelt. She looked along the passage to
see what had caused this sudden halt though she could
make out nothing other than an eerie pattern of dancing
lights and shadows some way ahead. As she tried to focus
on them, a hand from behind forced her head down.

'Don't move, don't speak unless you're told to,' the
voice said fearfully. She had no urge to disobey, not least
because the hands still gripping her were beginning to
shake.

The shifting lights drew nearer, mottling and rippling
across the stone floor like a moving mosaic. The hands
holding her began to shake even more.

Then, two high-pitched, echoing voices spoke.

'This is the one, Captain Helsarn . . .?'

'. . . Captain Helsarn?'

'I believe it could be, Excellencies, though I was not
certain enough to disturb your Night Vigil. He and his
two dogs killed and injured several soldiers in the Ennerhald and he is much stronger than his size indicates. We

209

were bringing him to you now to know your pleasure.'

'Pleasure?' The two voices spoke at once – grating.

Jeyan felt the focus move from her briefly.

'We know only the burden of office and duty . . .'

'. . . and duty.'

'To know your will, Excellencies,' Helsarn clarified, a little too quickly.

'Ah . . .'

The focus returned to Jeyan. Something touched her head. She squirmed away from it. There was a dark humourless chuckle.

'He is strong is he, this cruel slayer of our right arm?'

'Slayer of our valiant soldiers.'

Jeyan felt as though the voices were wrapping about her throat, choking her. The touch was on her head again, but this time she could not escape it. Something inside her was preventing her from moving. The touch became a hand. It stroked her matted hair as though she were a pet dog. The action repelled her but still she could not move. Then there was a hesitant pause in the hand and a brief stillness in the lights patterning the floor. Another hand was laid on her head, though this one was motionless, like a blessing, or, in truth, like a mockery of a blessing, for though it made no movement, it was as repellent as the first.

'Ah . . .'

The humourless chuckle gurgled into the stale air again, and the two voices came together.

'Stronger than you know, Captain. That which has wrought such hurt has indeed youth, but is not one.' Both hands began to move.

'Are you, woman . . .?'

'. . . woman?'

'*What?*'

Jeyan felt the violent start behind her even as she sank deep into herself at this exposure. She was vaguely aware of attention moving away from her again. Helsarn made no attempt to keep the fear from his voice.

'Forgive me, Excellencies. You . . . your revelation . . . startled me. I . . . I . . . have not your vision. I . . .' His words stumbled off into breathy silence.

The lights patterning the floor became absolutely still. Then: 'And too, she is indeed the slayer of our beloved Lord Counsellor. His blood is on her. His death perfume.' Then, intimately, to Jeyan: 'A rare cloak you wear, child.' The hands caressed her head.

'You have done well, Captain. Unchain her and withdraw a pace.'

'Excellencies, he . . . she is most dangerous. She's responsible for the deaths of several men as well as Lord Hagen.'

'Your concern moves us, Captain, but He guards His servants always.'

The Gevethen did not repeat orders and even as they were speaking, hands were fumbling with the manacles about Jeyan's wrists. They vanished, but Jeyan could hear them rattling behind her as the Under Questioner struggled to stop his hands from shaking. She became aware of the mirror-bearers moving around her.

'Let us look upon you, child.'

Almost to her horror, Jeyan felt a slender thread of rage and hatred slithering sinuously through the roaring terror that was filling her. She was at *their* feet, alone save for the wretched mirror-bearers. And, whatever else they might be, the mirror-bearers were not warriors. The spirits of Assh and Frey seemed to possess her. One powerful leap, and rending hands and teeth could perhaps halve this loathsome pair. One brief, desperate endeavour with

211

all its attendant chances in this narrow, congested passage – a shard from a shattered mirror, a defender's dagger carelessly held – and who could say what might be achieved? Assh and Frey were no more, and she herself was already one of the dead. Better she perish here in bloody, purposeful action than suffer the torments that were undoubtedly being prepared for her! But though the desire suffused her, hard and sharp in its intent, and crying out for release, no part of Jeyan would respond. It was as though her body were no longer her own. And indeed it was something other than her will that raised her head to look at the objects of her long hatred.

Like an unholy constellation, a score of pallid moon faces hovered above her, white hands gliding amongst them like lost birds. Watery eyes searched into hers. Loathing joined the hatred that was possessing her, screaming now at her impotence.

'Ah.' The many heads nodded as the two voices grated together again. All the birds perched protectively on the shattered rings.

'We hear your song.'

'She is kin.'

'She in one of us.'

'She is ours.'

'She is His . . .'

    '. . . His.'

The birds were in flight again, beckoning. Jeyan's legs straightened, unbidden. The many Gevethen swirled and twisted and then there were but two, side by reflecting side, in the lantern-lit passage. But fringing them was a multitudinous and bedraggled escort. As Jeyan looked at this scarecrow troop, fearsome staring eyes and gaping mouths turned to peer back at her. Only when the figures lifted their arms in reply to her own unintended salute

212

did she recognize them as herself. She, who had stayed silent through her suffering since her capture, let out a small cry. The scarecrows reached to their own faces in sympathy.

Then the escort turned away. The Gevethen were leaving.

'Follow us, child . . .'

       '. . . child.'

'There is much to be learned . . .'

         '. . . to be learned.'

'Follow.'

Chapter 16

A fine grey drizzle marked the start of Ibryen's journey. He had wakened to it at his normal hour and had deliberately turned over and gone back to sleep. The previous day had been long not only metaphorically, in the changes it had spawned for him, but actually, in the length of time he had been awake. It had been drawn out to its fullest by the impromptu meeting in the Council Hall of almost every member of the community who was not on duty.

Ibryen's followers formed a disciplined fighting unit, but they were such because they were also free individuals and stern in their defence of that freedom. Many procedures and practices, both formal and informal, had developed over the years in an attempt to ensure that the tensions, inevitable within such a community, were identified and aired before they could erupt into any seriously destructive form. For the most part these functioned well enough, but still much depended on the judgement and demeanour of Ibryen, Count of Nesdiryn by ancient statute and by common acclaim. When he opened the door of the ante-room where he had been talking with Marris and the others, to see the main chamber of the Council Hall filled with a large and silent crowd, he was both intimidated by what he knew he had to do, and heartened by the patient demeanour of his people.

As all there knew, he would have been acting fully within his authority if he had dismissed the gathering out of hand, harshly even, and instructed the various Company Commanders to attend on him the following day. Instead however, he gave a courteous acknowledgement to the man who had knocked on the door and stepped into the hall, signalling to the others to follow him.

Immediately, a questioning murmur began to rise from the crowd, but as he sought for somewhere to stand where he could see, and be seen, Ibryen spoke the honest thought then dominating his mind. 'If you can, sit please.' His hands beat them gently down. 'It's been a long and strange day for us all, and I've a feeling it's going to be some time before it's finished. I'm not inclined to spend the rest of it on my feet. Besides, you make the place look too full, standing up.'

His easy-humoured remarks and the consequent shuffling and rearranging of benches and tables lightened the darker tones of the atmosphere that had been building.

Not that the meeting went without difficulty. Studiously avoiding any reference to the Traveller's strange gift and the mysterious call that had drawn him there, Ibryen explained the events of the day and submitted his intentions to the meeting as he had just agreed them with his cousins. He avoided too, the bleak analysis of the future of their present form of resistance that the day had forced him to face starkly.

Even without these mysterious and dark elements, the tale and its conclusions provoked extensive debate. There was universal delight at the news of Hagen's death, but the presence of a stranger in the valley struck at the very roots of the community and the way it conducted itself, and even such news could not completely sweep aside concerns about the Traveller. Ibryen deliberately did not

216

allow Rachyl and Hynard to say too much at first, sensing that it was the evidence of those who had accompanied them up on to the south ridge that would be the most telling. And so it proved, though tempers flared more than once, culminating in a circle suddenly clearing as Seeing Stones were angrily thrust into the hands of one individual by the leader of the team, with the advice, 'Go and look for yourself,' uttered in a tone that was far more menacing than the words themselves.

A signal from Ibryen prevented his cousins and Marris from intervening. Now above all, it was imperative that he receive his authority from his people and not they from him.

'Go on!' the man blasted to the entire meeting. 'Get up there and look. Do you think that I – that any of us – wanted to see footsteps coming across the Hummock? Like it or not,' and he pointed at the Traveller, 'that man came from the south.'

The balance shifted and a reluctant acceptance began to seep into the crowd. The debate turned, almost grate-fully, to Ibryen's proposals that he should go into the mountains and that there should be no harrying raids against the Gevethen's army this spring. As Hynard had predicted, the inclusion of Rachyl in his party stilled most of the doubts about the wisdom of Ibryen accompanying the Traveller, and the idea of unsettling the Gevethen by using rumour and inaction, eventually appealed greatly.

'I intend to be away for no more than about two or three weeks,' Ibryen concluded. 'In the meantime, though no raids are to be mounted, all training must continue as usual, while vigilance must be re-doubled. There's always the chance that the Gevethen might seek to draw atten-tion away from problems in Dirynhald by mounting a large expedition against us.'

This caused a stir, but Ibryen quietly crushed it before it gathered momentum. 'That's no more than we've expected and trained for every year. As agreed many times before, Marris has command in my absence. Has anyone any objection to that?' There was no reply but the ensuing silence was unsatisfactory. He smiled and ploughed through it. 'Yes, I know. He's stricter than I am. But you all know your duties. Fulfil them properly and then the absence of Rachyl and me will only mean that our force is two fighters the less. Its heart and head will remain unaffected.'

Fastening his cape to keep the seeping rain out, and hitching his pack on to his back, Ibryen felt markedly less confident in the cool grey morning than he had in the warm gloaming of the Council Hall. He looked around at the mist-shrouded peaks. Still, the reasoning that had brought him to this point was sound enough even if it was directed at no particular conclusion. And too, he realized, the cause was still with him. Faint but quite definite, the strangeness that had carried him up to the ridge with such unforeseeable consequences was all about and through him. Not a sound, nor anything that he could define in words, but wilful and clear for all that, and tugging at him relentlessly. It was more urgent than before.

'What do you hear, Count?' It was the Traveller. Ibryen looked down at him in surprise. He had his pack on his back, much larger now than it had been, and he was wearing exactly the same clothes as the day before except that they were fastened more securely and a hood engulfed much of his face. Dressed thus it was even more difficult to judge how old he was.

'Will you be dry in that?' Ibryen asked.

The Traveller patted his attire in a proprietorial manner.

'Drier and warmer than you by far, old man.' Ibryen's eyebrows rose at the epithet but no indignation could bloom in the light of the Traveller's joviality. 'Had it for years. Made for me by people who know about mountains.' He winked knowingly. 'And I've added one or two little things of my own.' He returned immediately to his question. 'Can you hear anything?'

Ibryen answered him seriously. 'Only the sounds of the camp in the rain. And my own clothes creaking.'

'But . . .'

'But it's there,' Ibryen admitted, accepting the prompt. 'No sound, but . . . something. And either it or my perceptions have changed. It's clearer than it was, I'm sure, if clearer makes any sense.' He countered with the same question. 'And you? Can you hear anything?'

'Oh yes,' the Traveller replied darkly. 'We mustn't delay further.'

Ibryen was about to press him when the little man put his fingers to his mouth and blew a penetrating whistle, followed by a bellowing shout. 'Come on, Rachyl. Move yourself!'

Ibryen flinched openly. He was about to advise the Traveller that it was not an act of wisdom to address Rachyl like that when his cousin appeared almost immediately, hastily fastening her cape about her. Ibryen prepared to intervene but, unexpectedly, she said, 'I'm sorry, I'd forgotten to pack one or two things.' As they set off, she peered around into the mistiness and pulled a face. 'I'd have preferred pleasanter weather,' she said.

'Better this way,' Ibryen replied. 'Fewer people will see us leave and we won't have to fret about being caught against the skyline.'

When they reached the Council Hall, Marris and Hynard were waiting for them with some of the Company

219

Commanders. There was little left to debate however, and their parting remarks were confined to minor details about the first part of the journey and the amount of supplies they were carrying. It was territory already well covered and quite unnecessary.

'Mark your trail well,' was Marris's final offering, also unnecessary. 'We'll expect you back within the month. After that we'll come looking for you.' Then, after some cursory farewells, the trio left.

For the next few hours they walked on in silence. Neither the weather nor the terrain were conducive to conversation as the three trudged steadily up steep, grassy slopes and thence over tumbled piles of shattered rock and scree, all rendered treacherous by the rain. Thoughts were thus concentrated on the immediate problem of where to take the next footstep. Eventually they reached the ridge where Ibryen had rested on the previous day. It was greatly changed, the vast panorama of sunlit peaks having been swept into oblivion and replaced by rain-streaked greyness. Following the Traveller's signal, they moved into the lee of an overhanging rock and sat down. The Traveller threw back his hood and puffed out his cheeks.

Ibryen and Rachyl exchanged an amused glance. 'I thought you were used to mountains,' Ibryen taunted.

The Traveller shook his head ruefully. 'Not at this pace,' he replied. 'You two will wear me out.'

Rachyl nodded sagely, lips pursed. 'We're not mountain folk by birth, but we spend almost all our time either fighting or training amongst these crags. I suppose we move a lot faster than you're used to.'

The Traveller looked from one to the other, his expression pained. 'You mean this is the best you can do?' he asked.

Rachyl's face became indignant, but Ibryen laughed

softly and raised his hands in mock surrender. 'I think you're fighting beyond your weight, Rachyl,' he said, then, turning to the Traveller: 'I'll admit to being the slowest, so I'll have to ask your indulgence – younger to elder.'

This time the Traveller laughed. It was a sound full of joy. 'Indulgence granted, Count,' he said. '*I'm* certainly not going to fight beyond my weight. I'll leave that to the young folk.'

He gestured for silence. 'Let me listen for a moment to see if I can get some indication of which way to go next.' He looked at Ibryen significantly, but made no further comment. Ibryen closed his eyes.

Slowly silence formed about him. Then, for the briefest instant, it seemed that he could hear the trembling movement of each raindrop cutting through the air, followed by its splattering impact against the rocks. A low pulsing rumbling in the background he sensed was Rachyl, though no reasoning could have led him to that conclusion as he knew she would be sitting still and silent as the Traveller had asked. But scarcely had this impression formed than it was gone, and the silence returned.

And with it, the call. No stronger than it had been when he had been waiting for the Traveller an hour or so earlier. But it was clearer. As was the urgency that hung all about it. Suddenly he was filled with a desperate fear, and his mind was awash with strange images: duty, a long struggle ending, failure, an endless caring. Yet, though they could have been, they were not his. And there were other feelings too, deeply alien, for which no words could begin to exist. *We mustn't delay further*. The Traveller's words came back to him, full of force now.

Then a new fear arose. This time he knew it for his own. Had the years of leading his people in their seemingly futile resistance against the Gevethen finally taken their toll and plunged him into insanity?

He opened his eyes. Rachyl was gazing into the mist, one hand idly playing with a lock of damp hair. The Traveller was sitting with his head slightly canted and his hand still raised for silence. His eyes flicked towards Ibryen and he moved a finger to his lips.

The call and the urgency that impelled it slipped away, as though a door had quietly been closed. Yet, faint though they were, they were still there.

The Traveller lowered his hand and turned to Ibryen, eyes searching into his intently. 'Frightened?' he said.

Ibryen started and, his hand coming to his head, the truth gasped out of him before he could think what to say. 'Yes,' it said. 'What's happening to me?'

'What?' Rachyl enquired, coming wide-eyed out of her own reverie.

The Traveller abandoned Ibryen and turned quickly to her. 'What were you thinking about, Rachyl?' he asked.

She smiled. 'Just day-dreaming,' she replied. 'Just thinking about Marris and his Culmadryen. I always thought they were just tales. It's hard to imagine such a thing. A city, a whole land, floating in the clouds. What kind of people would live in such a place? What would they live on? What kind of a society would it be?' She leaned her head back against the rock and looked up into the rain. 'Would they know what the wind was if their land always moved with it?'

The Traveller clapped his hands in delight. 'Magical questions, every one,' he said, but neither answered nor pursued any of them. 'Keep them always in your mind so that more will gather around them. Then, maybe, who knows?' He tapped the side of his nose and winked then returned to Ibryen.

'What has frightened you?'

Again, Ibryen answered without hesitation. 'Doubt.'

The Traveller shook his head. 'Doubt, a man like you has always. Be specific.'

'Doubts for my sanity.'

He should not be speaking like this in front of Rachyl! But the Traveller was hustling him forward.

'Tell me what you just heard – what touched you. Quickly. While you can.'

Ibryen did his best, but the words he managed were barely shadows of what he had felt and after a few moments he waved them all away angrily. 'It's no use. It's just a waste of time. Perhaps I am going mad after all.'

'No,' the Traveller said, quietly but categorically. 'I think not. And neither do you.' He clenched his fist and held it out in front of Ibryen. As he spoke, he slowly uncurled it. 'Who can say what a bud feels as it unfurls to find itself no longer in the dark, but bathing in the sunlight?'

Ibryen looked at him suspiciously then quickly glanced at Rachyl. However, there was no hint of mockery in the little man's demeanour and Rachyl's expression was unreadable. Was she judging him? What of his authority if she should carry tales of this conversation back to the camp? Then, it occurred to him, why should she not judge him? If he couldn't face her judgement, he had no right to ask her loyalty. The conclusion made him feel almost light-headed.

The Traveller's strange observation was still hanging in the damp air.

'A bizarre analogy,' Ibryen replied.

The Traveller looked at his hand. 'More of a metaphor, I'd have thought. And rather a good one too,' he said in mild dismay, though he was immediately serious again. 'You can't hear what I hear and I can't explain it to you. I can't feel whatever it is that's pulling at your insides, and you can't explain *that* to me. The only common ground we have are these poor words and the pictures we can make with them.'

'All of which means what?' The question came from Rachyl and it was bluntly put.

'All of which means we go that way,' the Traveller said, pointing. He stood up and began walking without further comment. The others scrambled hastily to their feet and, pausing only to mark the trail, set off after him. 'Sorry,' he said, when they caught up with him. 'I forgot.' His brow furrowed thoughtfully. 'If I get too far ahead, just call out, I'll hear you.'

'We don't call out here,' Rachyl said sternly. 'And see *you* don't. Whistle like this if you need to signal.' She blew a short, staccato whistle similar to those that had greeted the arrival of Iscar. She became patronizing. 'It's much harder for the enemy to work out where the noise is coming from. We've a great many calls that we use, but you don't need to know about them. Just remember not to shout out.'

The Traveller nodded interestedly. 'Who taught you that?' he asked.

'Marris. Why?'

'Whistle me something.'

Rachyl glanced at him uncertainly, then whistled four notes. The Traveller frowned and then clicked his fingers. 'Friend coming,' he announced in triumph.

Rachyl did not seem inclined to join in his celebration. 'How the devil did you know that?' she demanded.

'It wasn't easy the way you were whistling it,' the Traveller retorted. 'The dialect's strange – from north of here, I'd say – but your accent's very fetching, quite charming.' He took her arm confidentially. 'Don't be offended,' he said, 'but your intonation's a little shaky, and it can be very misleading. And watch your rhythm. And your accents.'

Rachyl's face was darkening. 'Is there anything else?' she asked, unequivocally rhetorical.

'Well, now that you mention it . . .'

Ibryen interceded. 'Are you familiar with this way of signalling?' he asked, stepping between them both quickly. 'I knew it wasn't Marris's invention, but even he didn't know where it had come from.'

'Such a long time.' The Traveller pulled his hood forward so that his face could not be seen. 'It's not just a means of signalling,' he said. 'It's derived from a language. A beautiful language once – maybe still is somewhere, I suppose, though I doubt it.'

'You sound sad,' Ibryen said.

The Traveller shrugged. 'Not really,' he replied, though his face was still hidden. 'When I heard it yesterday, it started jostling all sorts of old memories, but I was so preoccupied with everything else that was happening I gave it no heed. Now, hearing it up here, I see a long, winding line going far back through time. A line decked with flags and battle pennants and shrouds and loving sheets – so much. It *is* sad that the last time I heard it, it was as a battle language, and it's that that's come down to you.' His hood edged back and a smiling face emerged. 'Still, I'm happy to be reminded of it, even if you are grunting it.'

Rachyl's face, which had been softening, began to harden and Ibryen intervened again. 'Would you teach it to us properly?' he asked.

The Traveller stopped. 'I suppose I could try,' he said after a long, pensive pause. He looked at the rocky slope rising ahead of them and disappearing into the mist. 'But you're asking me to climb a mountain steeper than any you'll find around here.'

Rachyl prodded a finger at him. 'It seems to me you're very free with your abuse about our efforts, but full of ... metaphor ... when it comes to actually doing anything.'

The Traveller set off again, drawing in a hissing breath. He spoke to Ibryen. 'Of all the sounds I've ever heard I don't think there's anything quite as unpleasant as a woman's taunt, Count, don't you agree?'

'I never provoke them,' Ibryen replied, siding with his soldier. 'If you wish to live recklessly then who am I to gainsay you?'

'Are you deserting me, Count?'

'Yes. As you appear to be losing I've realized where my better interests lie.'

'Weather's breaking,' the Traveller said, pointing ahead.

'Full of metaphor,' Rachyl said to Ibryen, conspicuously stretching the word as they began to clamber up another rocky slope.

Ibryen looked at Rachyl surreptitiously. As is the way with women who take to fighting, she was as ferocious and determined in combat as any man. Indeed, she was greatly feared amongst the Gevethen's soldiery and the sight of her suddenly joining the fray had more than once tilted cautious withdrawal into full-blooded retreat. But she was also far more ruthless both in her vision and her actions, and tipped rapidly into cruelty at times. It was a trait that Ibryen watched for constantly. He wondered at times what would become of her if peace ever came, but it was a fruitless speculation and he never dwelt on it. Here, she was better the way she was. The future would have to take its chance with her as would she with it. Nevertheless, he had been concerned that her stern and suspicious temperament would prove a considerable burden on their journey, for all she seemed to have begun accepting the Traveller after having seen his footsteps across the Hummock. He was pleased therefore with the relationship that was emerging between them. There was a tension in it, but they were sparking off one another. It was a good sign.

And as if in acknowledgement of this happier thought, the sky ahead started to lighten. Then the rain began to peter out. Not that it made the travelling any easier, for the rocks were still treacherously wet and for some time no one spoke as once again they found it necessary to concentrate on progressing safely.

They stopped from time to time, apparently by common consent, though Ibryen, who frequently found himself slipping behind, suspected that it was because the Traveller was keeping a particular eye on him – or, perhaps, a particular ear, he mused as he caught up with Rachyl and the little man again, puffing loudly.

'Not got the right pace, yet,' he said, lowering himself on to a rock.

Rachyl looked as if she were about to say something caustic, but refrained.

'My fault,' the Traveller said. 'I keep forgetting. It's some time since I mixed with people, but it's a *long* time since I walked through the mountains with anyone. A very long time.'

Ibryen ventured a question. 'Where do you come from?'

The Traveller smiled and gestured to the north. 'You didn't altogether lie when you told your people I was on my way home. The place where I was born was north of here.'

'Was?' Rachyl enquired, picking up the word immediately 'What happened? Was your village destroyed? A war? A disaster?' Ibryen raised an eyebrow in surprise at the uncharacteristically maternal note in Rachyl's voice, but the Traveller just shook his head, unperturbed by this gentle barrage.

'No, no,' he replied with a chuckle. 'I was moved about a lot when I was a child. Along and through the Ways, from hollow hill to hollow hill. It was inevitable, I was quite unusual.'

Rachyl's eyes narrowed.

'Rachyl doesn't respond well to being teased,' Ibryen said quickly.

The Traveller laid an affectionate hand on Rachyl's arm. 'I wouldn't dream of mocking such an enquiry,' he said. 'But I suspect my childhood – if that's what it was – is quite beyond anything you could understand, even if I had the wit to describe it to you, which I doubt.' The hand patted the arm. 'I don't know where I was born, but don't concern yourself. There's no village or mansion lying ruined at my beginning, either by brutal war or brutal nature.'

Rachyl withdrew her arm. 'Perhaps the land had a name though,' she said.

'Oh yes. We called it . . .'

But the word he spoke eluded both Ibryen and Rachyl, though it left Ibryen with a sense of mountains even more commanding than those around him, and ringing to their hearts with strange music. He craned his head forward as the impression slowly faded, as if reluctant to lose it.

It seemed to be having a similar effect on Rachyl, though, more earth-bound than Ibryen, she recovered sooner. 'Perhaps it had a name that *we* could understand,' she persisted, with heavy emphasis.

'Possibly,' the Traveller replied. 'But I don't know what it was. And it might well be different now. You know how ephemeral words are.'

Rachyl made to speak again, but Ibryen, laughing,

228

spoke first. 'I think that's all you're going to learn, Rachyl. You'll have to be content with the hollow hills filled with music.'

'Everywhere has a name,' Rachyl insisted, heatedly. 'A proper name that ordinary people can say.'

The Traveller prodded the rocky ground by his side. 'What's this called, then?' he asked.

Rachyl's chin came out. Ibryen stood up. 'I'm rested now, thank you. Let's get on while the weather's clear.' He started walking. 'Mark the trail would you, Rachyl.'

Within a few paces the Traveller was alongside him. Lowering his voice, Ibryen said with disclaiming sternness, 'If you persist in provoking Rachyl she may well throw you over the edge of somewhere very high before I can stop her, or, I suspect, before you can do one of your tricks. Life in the mountains has made her quite abrupt in both judgement and execution at times.'

Though there was some seriousness in his comment, his manner was ironic and he had expected a light-hearted response. The Traveller however, looked quite grave. 'I understand,' he said. 'But just as you seek to understand those closest to you in your land, so must I here, for this is my land – the land to which I belong – and this is my journey, my song. Who knows what tests lie ahead? You might think I'm strange with my crude Sound Carving, but you should see yourself as I see you with your *deeply* strange inner hearing.' His face became almost grim. 'I need to know what I need to know. Just as Rachyl changed to serve you, so she – and you, and me – will change to serve whatever end has drawn us together.' A broad smile banished the gravity. 'But no hurt will come of that. Change is what you make of it.'

He made a signal for silence as Rachyl reached them. She seemed to have set aside her irritation at the

229

Traveller's previous manner but Ibryen recognized the mood and knew that matters had only been postponed. 'We've several choices when we get to the top,' she said. 'Have you any idea which way we're going to go?'

'No.' The two men spoke simultaneously. Ibryen motioned the Traveller to move on alone.

'Are you all right?' he asked Rachyl when the Traveller was well in front of them.

'Yes,' Rachyl replied with an edge to her voice that said quite the opposite.

Ibryen spoke straight to what he took to be the heart of her concern. 'He's very strange,' he said. 'The more so to us because we've had to force ourselves into a very conservative way of living just in order to survive. But you don't need me to remind you there are many strange things in this world.'

'*That* strange?' Rachyl said, glancing significantly at the retreating figure ahead of them.

Ibryen could not forbear smiling at her manner, but her question had to be addressed. 'You've not forgotten the Gevethen already, have you?' he replied, equally significantly. 'The way they speak now, their mannerisms, their ability to sway people – or terrify them. And that business with the mirrors. Vanity we thought at first, if you remember – a foolish but harmless affectation. A trio of servants carrying decorated glasses, and two eccentric advisers making sly glances at them, then later, openly preening and posturing before them.' His eyes widened at the memory. 'And look what that turned into.' He trailed off into an awkward silence which neither of them seemed to know how to end.

Eventually Rachyl said, 'You're right, of course. We don't forget, we just don't bother remembering. It's too disturbing. But when you squeeze several years into a few words, it's all there again, isn't it? The horrific unreality of it all.' She looked up at the Traveller, now on the lightening skyline. 'He's still strange, but at least he seems to be human.'

Ibryen reached out and stopped her. He looked into her face. 'The Gevethen are human enough,' he said. 'Only creatures like us, permanently in thrall to the darker side of their natures, could do what they do. They're in all of us. That's why they frighten us. Sicken us.'

Rachyl held his gaze, but her face was again unreadable. In the end it was Ibryen who turned away. Waving a hand towards the Traveller, he began walking again, reiterating the Traveller's own remarks. 'We're probably very strange and frightening to him. He doesn't avoid people for no reason presumably. We should try to remember that. And as for what he's doing, or why, all we can do is judge him by his deeds, and try to understand him while he tries to understand us.'

Rachyl's hand moved unconsciously to a knife in her belt. 'It's difficult. One minute I take him for a sprightly little old man, the next – I don't know. When I think of what he did to Hynard and me, and the things he talks about, I feel quite afraid of him. Then . . .' she was surprised '. . . it's almost as if he were my own age. Vigorous and strong.' She stopped uncomfortably.

'By his deeds, Rachyl,' Ibryen repeated. 'I've trusted him this far because he's had ample opportunity to do us all great harm and he hasn't taken it. I'll continue trusting him for the time being, but not to the point of foolishness. Not to a point beyond reason.'

'And you think trailing after mysterious . . . noises . . . that only you can hear, isn't beyond reason, isn't illogical?'

The bluntness of this sudden question shook Ibryen. He saw the Traveller, a considerable way above them now, stop. Somewhat to his own surprise, he answered immediately. 'It's not illogical for me, because whatever's pulling at me is as real as the air around us. I know it makes no sense to you and that you're just trusting me, and too, that it's taking a toll. But judge me by my deeds as well. And whilst we might be searching for something that doesn't exist – a mirage – the reason why we're going – the strategy, Rachyl – none of that's beyond reason, is it? Looking for another way, unsettling the Gevethen by doing nothing. The least we'll gain, all of us, up here and back down in the valley, is a breaking of our rutted thoughts – a re-examining of what we think we already know. And perhaps somewhere in that will be the tiny thing that'll change our direction.'

As the stark question had shaken Ibryen, so his answer silenced Rachyl and they did not speak again until they reached the waiting Traveller. 'Do you want to rest again?' he asked Ibryen.

The Count shook his head. 'No. I'll be fine now. I'm getting my climbing legs back. Let's get to the top and decide which way to go from there.'

The weather continued to ease, occasional strips of blue sky appearing through the thinning cloud. A breeze was blowing as they reached the top of the rise. As Rachyl had said, several alternatives now faced them, for the far side of the rise dropped down into a valley while on either flank, hulking peaks shouldered down towards them.

Rachyl, first to the top, authoritatively directed the others to one side so that they would not appear against the skyline. 'There's no one about,' the Traveller protested. Rachyl looked at him and then motioned him to follow her. He gave Ibryen an arch look as he obeyed. Ibryen sat down and closed his eyes. The call was still there, but it was different.

Rachyl led the Traveller around a small outcrop towards a pile of tumbled rocks. As they drew near she placed her hands on his shoulders so that he could only move where she dictated. Finally, she pushed him almost to his knees and then the two of them were peering around the edge of a boulder. Her hand was pointing. 'Those two peaks,' she said, whispering as though they might be overheard. 'The most northerly of this region and the nearest to Dirynhald. The Gevethen regularly post small companies of troops on them, just to watch. The passes being the way they are, almost certainly there'll be some there now, and their seeing stones are as good as ours.' She sneered. 'I understand they call them their elite, though we have no difficulty killing them from time to time when they're being particularly troublesome. But we never forget them, nor the fact that they also send small scouting parties and even individuals looking for us.' Pressure on the Traveller's shoulders emphasized these points. Now a powerful hand came to rest on his neck. It exerted no pressure, but it was quite resolute. 'You must understand. Any serious hint of where the village is and the Gevethen will bring their every resource against us. We'll not survive such an attack, and who can say what horror the Gevethen will go on to without the fear of the Count at their backs?' The grip became more forceful and Rachyl's voice even softer. 'You may know a great deal about mountains and all manner of things, but I know *these* mountains and the particular dangers *we* face here. Ibryen has his own concerns at the moment, which I won't pretend to understand. I've got just *one* – to make sure that he, and the village, come to no harm. If you do anything to jeopardize either, then notwithstanding his protection, I'll kill you before you can purse your lips to whistle. Do you understand?' With what limited movement he was allowed, the

Traveller nodded. 'Good. Don't dispute with me again in such matters,' Rachyl concluded, releasing him and slapping him on the shoulder with ominous heartiness.

'Quite a sophisticated communicator,' the Traveller confided as he returned to Ibryen.

'Oh yes,' the Count replied, having deduced the possible nature of the conversation from Rachyl's posture as she led the Traveller away. 'She can explain things very well at times.' He bent close and lowered his voice. 'I should have impressed it on you more seriously before. Listen to what she says very carefully; she tends to mean what she says, and she's a very dangerous person.'

The Traveller gave a slight gesture that inferred both acknowledgement and dismissal, then asked, 'Which way?'

Ibryen looked at him for a moment, concerned that perhaps he had not fully appreciated the significance of the advice he had just been given, then he held out a tentative hand. The route would carry them into the valley on the far side of the rise they had just climbed. The Traveller nodded. 'Yes, I think so too. But the sounds I can hear are getting weaker. Are you sure?'

Ibryen grimaced. 'As I can be,' he said. 'But something's changing. Something's happening. It's going beyond.' Pain filled his face. 'We must hurry.'

Chapter 17

As the procession wended its way through the shadowed passages and hallways of the Citadel, the force that Jeyan could feel impelling her limbs gradually lessened. Though she could scarcely begin to order her thoughts, strands of curiosity began to filter into the swirling fear that was consuming her. That she was alive after being twice captured was bewildering, but that she was alive after facing the Gevethen themselves was almost numbing. It needed little coherent thought however, to realize that she had been allowed to live because some torment was being prepared for her.

Her knees started to buckle. If only she could think properly! But the reflected images dancing all around her snatched thoughts away even as they formed. For, like prancing flank guards, the mirror-bearers were making her escort herself as array upon array of ragged scarecrow figures marched and wheeled through the flickering gloom alongside her. Now staggering, now slouching, now staring at her, wild-eyed, now in lines curving into a dark unseeable distance.

Only two things had any semblance of constancy – the retreating backs of the Gevethen, and even these disturbed, moving as they did, now together, now like reflections of one another. Occasionally they turned and their moon faces displaced the ranks of scarecrow guards so that they seemed to be converging on her from every direction.

Then she was walking up steps, and carpeting appeared under her feet. Briefly, hints of bright early morning daylight slanted down on to the troop. They bounced off the mirrors like glinting spear points and the movement of the bearers faltered momentarily.

Senses heightened by terror, Jeyan caught the change and, like a desperate animal, suddenly hurled herself at one of the mirrors. As she touched it, it turned to one side and she passed by it only to run headlong into the wall of the passage. The impact sent her staggering backwards and the mirrors folded back around her as she tumbled to the floor. The ceiling became a panoply of struggling scarecrow bodies hovering over her. Slowly they began to descend, threatening to bury her. As she raised her arms to protect herself, so they all reached down to her.

Then, white floating hands were gliding amongst the flock and it was dispersed. The tattered army groped to its knees.

'There are many ways in which you can be bound, child.'

'Always there is choice.'

'But there is no way in which you may be free of us.'

'You are one of us.'

'We are your future.'

'We are *the* future.'

Though no signal was apparently given, the scarecrow army vanished and Jeyan found herself in a gloomy corridor. Ragged shafts of daylight were fingering in through ill-closed shutters and curtains, but they illuminated little, and merely served to dim the few lanterns that were lit. In two lines on either side of her the mirror-bearers stood,

236

stone-faced and motionless, eyes on some unknown distance and the tools of their mysterious art turned about and stood in front of them like shields. Save for three of them, so that as Jeyan oriented herself she was watched by four Gevethen. Hunching forward and peering at them blearily, she forced herself to stand.

A riot of thoughts rushed into her mind simultaneously, paralysing her. She must attack them now, do what hurt she could. She must flee while these bizarre bodyguards were frozen in ceremony. She must stay and plead a case – deny everything – how could a mere girl have killed the great Lord Counsellor Hagen? She must admit the deed and beg for mercy. The Gevethen were speaking.

'How long will your future be . . .?'

'. . . your future be . . .?'

'How long will it seem . . .?'

'. . . will it seem . . .?'

'Questions for you alone . . .'

'. . . alone.'

'Ponder well.'

'Always there is choice.'

They turned away.

And the escorting army was back, waiting only her will to march forward again. Though the Gevethen's echoing words had been spoken flatly, without emphasis, there was a terrible menacing finality in them. *Always there is choice. How long will your future be? How long will it seem?* The fear inside her became icy. Brittle shards of rational thought began to form in the stillness.

She could not hope to escape from this place by some mindless dash. Whatever these creatures were who served the Gevethen so strangely, they moved very quickly. There had been only the slightest contact with the mirror she had charged at before it had twisted away from her. And even if she evaded them, how could she hope to escape from the Citadel, a building she had only been in on a few ceremonial occasions long ago? She had no idea where she was. She was trapped in the enemy's lair – at its very heart.

The word changed its character even as she thought it. She was at the heart of all the ills that had happened to her. *Their* heart.

The hatred within her rose to displace her fear for a moment. She must be like Assh and Frey – the thought hurt – she must be silent and endlessly patient. She stepped forward. Her scarecrow escort matched her stride.

Jeyan's decision to abandon any reckless escape attempt was fortunate. Helsarn had been doubly shaken: first by the revelation that his captive was a woman and, secondly, that he had failed to discover it himself. It was only a matter of time before courtiers and advisers and, not least, army and Guard commanders, were milling about, seeking to glean to themselves some credit for the capture, and it was essential that he not only keep his name clearly before the Gevethen as the principal actor, but also ensure that no mockery or disdain could be linked with it. He had therefore taken vigorous action to divert attention away from any possible damage to his reputation. Jeyan's true captor, desperately weakened by loss of blood, had lapsed into unconsciousness as Helsarn's company had pursued their deliberately leisurely way back to the Citadel, and he had died during the night despite Physician Harik's best endeavours. As a sop to the army, Helsarn would give some credit to the man for his assistance in the capture.

Thus, though the Gevethen had given no specific commands after they led Jeyan away, Helsarn had taken

Commanders' powers to himself and quickly marshalled enough men to seal the immediate exits to the Citadel and all the corridors along and adjacent to the route which would carry the Gevethen back to the Watching Chamber. It was not a massive operation, but it was elaborate and detailed and proved to be an impressive and highly disruptive piece of impromptu organizing. It more than adequately served to stamp Helsarn's name firmly on the events of the day. Further, the levying of armed men to his back gave discreet notice to both his peers and his superiors that in the changes which must follow the death of Hagen, Helsarn was an individual determined to gain improvement – an individual better as an ally than a foe.

Of course, Helsarn knew, there was always the possibility that this woman had had nothing to do with the killing of Hagen, or even the knife attack on the soldier, though he doubted it. He had felt the ferocity of her intent as she had swung on the rope that was strangling the man, and he had seen the difficulty his own men had had in overpowering her. A man who fought like that was bad enough, but a woman . . .! He did not care to dwell on the matter. Nor did he concern himself too much with the possibility of Jeyan's innocence. The Gevethen seemed certain that she was the one who had murdered Hagen and that was sufficient. In any event, she was an extremely dangerous individual and was best out of the way. People like that always had to be dealt with sooner or later.

Thus, as Jeyan, hedged about by ephemeral and shifting images, made her unreal journey through the Citadel, she was shadowed by Helsarn and Vintre and various other of his more trusted men, all ready to offer far harder-edged restraints if need arose. As they neared the Watching Chamber, Helsarn took the risk of moving his group forward to walk alongside the mirror-bearers as a formal armed escort. When they reached it there were only the statue-like door Guards waiting.

Excellent, Helsarn thought. His late and wilfully unobtrusive arrival at the Citadel the previous night, coupled with the fortuitously early intervention of the Gevethen this morning had outflanked the Citadel's elaborate network of gossips and informers very effectively. He could almost hear the frenzied whispering hissing like a winter wind through the Citadel in the wake of the Gevethen's procession, and the clamour of frantic footsteps being drawn towards the Watching Chamber. Footsteps that would pace and tap anxiously as they ran into the cordon of Guards he had thrown around the Gevethen's progress. Now he and his men would be able to guard the door to the Watching Chamber. For a while at least, all would have to answer to him for access to Nesdiryn's Lords. He was careful however, to keep even the faintest hint of triumph from his face. The Gevethen appeared to be paying him no heed, but he knew from past experience that it would be a mistake to assume he was not being watched.

The doors opened like an expectant maw to reveal the gloomy interior of the Watching Chamber. The Gevethen turned to Helsarn. He dropped down on to one knee immediately, and lowered his head.

'Such happenings do not fall to chance. You find favour in His eyes,' they said, voices grating. 'And so you find favour in ours, Commander Helsarn.'

'I am nothing without your guidance and your grace, Excellencies,' Helsarn managed to say, though he was scarcely able to contain his elation. Commander! Just like that! Plans for the future unfurled recklessly in front of him. He swept them aside. Now was not the time. That which had been bestowed with the merest word could be as easily removed. Now he must listen.

'We are in Vigil, Commander.'

The mirror-bearers closed about them and they were gone. As Helsarn looked up, the doors of the Watching Chamber were softly closing. He had a momentary glimpse of Jeyan. Unexpectedly he felt a twinge of pity for the slight figure, trapped behind the mirrors and being swept into the darkness. He dared not even speculate on what fate was going to be meted out to her. His concern faded quickly however, turned to nothingness by the touch of his burning exhilaration.

As he stood up and straightened his tunic, Vintre appeared in front of him, saluting rigidly. 'My congratulations on your promotion, Commander.'

Good, Vintre still had wit enough not to bring the familiarity of their long acquaintance to this scene. Helsarn returned the salute. 'Thank you, *Captain* Vintre,' he replied. He looked in turn at each of the others, still standing motionless. 'All those who have helped in this will be duly noted in due course. Now we must guard their Excellencies against intrusion while they interrogate the prisoner.' He nodded to Vintre. 'Open the exits and corridors again. Tell the men what has happened and order them to return to their normal duties. I'll speak to them as soon as circumstances allow.' As Vintre was leaving, Helsarn called him back. He allowed himself a smile. 'And if anyone's hoping to see their Excellencies, tell them that they're in Vigil. All must wait.'

'Until?' Vintre queried.

Helsarn shrugged his Commander's shoulders helplessly. 'Until the Vigil's over,' he replied.

Vintre paused before he left. 'What about the purging?' he asked.

'What about it?' Helsarn retorted. 'It'll have to continue

until decreed otherwise. I doubt we'll be thanked for relaxing it just because the murderer's been caught. The people have to be shown the consequence of standing idly by while their Excellencies' servants are brutally cut down.'

When Vintre had left, Helsarn stood his men at ease around the entrance to the Watching Chamber. He would have given a great deal to be away from there and somewhere where he could exult in private about his sudden advancement, but, he reflected, here he was still before the eyes of the Gevethen: here he stood, for the time being, between them and all others. And here he could think and plan quietly, free from the responsibilities of his normal duties and anxieties about who might be reaching their ear.

He did not have much time for reflection; very shortly, the sound of a characteristic footfall reached him along the sparsely lit corridor.

'Physician,' he said, as Harik's tall lank form emerged from the gloom.

'*Commander* Helsarn, I understand,' Harik replied with a cold politeness that turned the new rank into an insult. 'I'm not amused by your Guards blocking half the corridors in the Citadel and keeping me from my duties.'

Helsarn became expansive. 'My apologies,' he said. 'I had to make a hasty decision. Their Excellencies were personally escorting Lord Hagen's murderer from the cells. A very dangerous person. I couldn't take any risks.'

Harik gave a non-committal grunt. 'He's in there now, is he?'

'She is.'

'She?' Harik started and his stern impassiveness flickered. Helsarn enjoyed the effect and let it show in a smug smile. 'Yes, she,' he confirmed.

Harik recovered quickly, yet though his armour had closed about him again, he radiated concern. 'What state is she in?' he asked.

'Better than that soldier she knifed,' Helsarn retorted as though he were punching the questioner.

'A little more dispatch in bringing him to me and he'd be alive now,' Harik replied with the same force.

'Exigencies of the service, Physician,' Helsarn said off-handedly. 'If she hadn't cut halfway through his arm he'd be alive too.'

Harik's jaw tightened but he did not pursue the matter further. 'I must see her right away,' he said. 'I'm not satisfied about—'

'Prisoners aren't your concern, Physician,' Helsarn said, not allowing him to finish, 'unless they have some form of contagious disease. You know that well enough. I'm surprised you should make such a request. This one's fit enough, rest assured. She and her dogs have left others dead in the Ennerhald by all accounts, and it took four of my men to restrain her.' He leaned forward, his voice low and filled with a deliberate mixture of surprise and indignation. 'She even tried to attack one of their Excellencies' mirror-bearers as she was being escorted here.' But this provoked no response, as Harik was fully in control of himself again. Helsarn straightened up. 'Besides, their Excellencies are in Vigil. It's more than my life's worth to disturb them.'

Helsarn looked past the Physician, footsteps could be heard approaching. 'Ah, more anxious petitioners doubt-less,' he said, then, with the polite urgency of someone with weightier matters pending he concluded his conversation with a rhetorical, 'Is there anything further I can do?'

Harik turned and left without comment. Helsarn

243

laughed softly to himself as he watched the retreating form. It was rare indeed to see Harik's guard slip. This was proving to be a remarkable day. Then he signalled his men to line up across the corridor, and, lifting a finger to his mouth for silence, stepped forward to meet the advancing crowd.

As the doors to the Watching Chamber silently closed, Jeyan's scarecrow army swung away on either side of her and evaporated into a tapering distance, leaving her alone, eyes blinking, as she tried to orient herself amid the confusion of lights and shadows and strange shapes. The Gevethen too, slipped into the distance, mirror-bearers silently moving about them, a strange soft-shelled tortoise of a creature shifting and changing as it slithered across the shining floor. Then there was a sudden flickering and they were gone. Jeyan swayed and reached out to steady herself against a mirror standing nearby. It was part of the bottom tier of a complicated tower of mirrors. To her horror, it swayed as she touched it and she snatched her hand away. A tremor passed through the entire edifice. There was a sound like that of a reluctant hinge echoing down a long passageway, and the hall became alive with dancing lights. Looking up instinctively, it seemed to Jeyan that the whole edifice was about to topple on to her, but it was merely an illusion caused by her leaning back too far and almost immediately she fell over.

As she scrambled to her feet, a figure, oddly mobile in the still-moving lights, loomed up in front of her. It reached out to her as she lifted a hand to defend herself, then it retreated as she did. She snarled as she realized that it was only another mirror, but it was gone before she could gather her wits fully. It was replaced by two others. Jeyan spun round, looking to flee, but crouching, twisting forms were all about her except on one side. As she edged towards it the corralling figures moved with her.

Then she was in front of the throne platform. Its curving sides drew her gaze upwards. From the top of it, a host of Gevethen looked down. They swayed hypnotically. Then they were beside her, their features and forms subtly twisted by the strange reflected journey that had brought them there.

'Child.'

The two voices grated through her.

'You have a name?'

She did not answer. The two figures looked at one another, red lips pouted in mocking sorrow.

'Do you think that our knowing your name will put you in our power, child?'

'Or that not knowing it will protect you?'

'Do you think we are magicians?'

'Conjurors and mountebanks?'

Regretful heads were shaken. 'A superstitious primitive. A simpleton. The great Lord Hagen has been destroyed by a simpleton.'

'It does not seem possible.'

'But it is so. The scent of his dying is all about her. What could he have thought, our proud Lord Counsellor, to find himself impaled on the cruel thorns of this ragged sapling from the Ennerhald?'

'This ragged simpleton.'

'With no name.'

'What could he have thought?'

'He was surprised. He was irritated like a peevish child.' The words, sneering and venomous, spat out of Jeyan, driven by an anger goaded beyond restraint by the nerve-jangling tones of the Gevethen. 'He could not believe what was happening even as I killed him.'

245

'Ah!'

'And my name is Jeyan. Jeyan Dyalith.'

'Ah.'

'The child of the traitor.'

'No!'

'A tainted line. We were right to expunge it.'

'To root it out.'

'To lop it off.'

'Tainted.'

'No!' Jeyan screamed and swung the edge of her fist at the nearest moon-faced image. On the instant it was gone and her fist struck only the fist of her own reflection. The impact made her recoil violently. Then the mirrors were all about her and she was staggering to and fro, lashing out wildly, a jerking hobby-horse leading her own wild scarecrow round dance. Someone, somewhere, was clapping out a beat for the buffeting mirrors.

Abruptly, and without signal, it was over. Jeyan slumped to her knees. Aisle upon devout aisle of kneeling figures appeared beside her. But still she was filled with a rage sufficient to hold her terror at bay. 'Come within arms' reach and I'll surprise you too,' she snarled.

'Would you?' The pallid faces and floating hands were beside her again, though the voices still came from the swaying figures above. Nevertheless, their sudden reappearance and an oddly plaintive note in the voices, shook Jeyan. As she struggled to rein in her passion, her mind began to race. She must escape this place. But the problem was the same as it had been before. Even if she could escape this room, how could she escape the Citadel? And, in any event, how could she escape this room? These mirror-bearers moved with uncanny and alarming speed. And, incongruously, she did not even know where the door was.

'Excellencies, forgive me,' she heard herself pleading. 'I have been so long in the Ennerhald. And so alone. A madness must have seized me. A madness that required the payment of blood debt for the murder of my parents by Lord Hagen.'

'Blood debt!' The tone was awful. Jeyan cowered, truly fearful now.

'You do not know the meaning of the words, child.'

'When He comes to collect His blood debt, then you will know.'

'All will know.'

'Great will be the winnowing.'

'The levelling.'

'And where will you be with your petty vengeance, mote, amid this dusting storm?'

'Safe under a sheltering wing?'

'Or crushed utterly and scattered into oblivion?'

Jeyan had the feeling of a great power having been released. A power before which she could not hope to stand. A power which at best she could only seek to avoid. 'I don't understand, Excellencies,' she managed to say. 'Who are you talking about? Who . . .?'

In-drawn breaths like the sound of a rushing wind filled the hall, mirrors domed up over her and the power that had marched her from the dungeons returned to throw her face down on the wooden floor. She could not move any part of her body. It was as though a great hand was pressing down on her and that with the least effort she could be extinguished absolutely.

'It is beyond greater minds than yours to understand such things.'

'Seek not to know His name, lest you feel His touch . . .'

'. . . His touch.'

Struggling though she was under the unseen weight,

Jeyan heard a quality in the Gevethen's voices that frightened her more than anything she had ever experienced
before. It was fear. The Gevethen were afraid! How could
there be anything – anyone – who could strike such fear
into this awful pair? But the impression was momentary,
swept aside by the fearful weight now pressing her into
the floor.

'Forgive me, Excellencies,' she gasped. 'Forgive me.'

The pressure did not ease but there was a faltering in
the atmosphere as though her faint plea had sufficed to
catch the attention of the Gevethen amid their own fearful
concerns.

'Forgive me, Excellencies.'

For an instant, the pressure increased sharply and a
gleeful malice was all about her. Then it was gone and
the scream of terror and pain that had been forming
inside her leaked into the shadow-streaked gloom as a
whimpering sob.

There was a long silence, broken only by Jeyan's
gasping.

'You distract us with your lies, child.' The voices were
steady again.

'Do so at your peril.'

'You stray into regions where Death itself is the least
of terrors.'

Hesitantly, Jeyan pushed herself into a kneeling position. She dared not speak and all thought of escape had
gone. She knew now that, however it was achieved, the
Gevethen could exert a power over her person unlike
anything she had ever known, or even heard of. The spirit
that had taunted the soldiers in the Ennerhald in the
hope that her fleetness would carry her from harm, was
silent. Now she must look only to survive the moment.

'Jeyan Dyalith, do not lie to us.'

'Nothing can be hidden.'

'We have known of you always.'

Denial rose in Jeyan but she neither moved nor spoke.

'As we peered into the darkness we felt your vengeful spirit blooming.'

'Saw it glowing in the night, along the Ways.'

'A black magnetic star, luring us forward.'

'Watched you.'

'Wanted you.'

'You are kin.'

Jeyan could remain silent no longer, but she forced her voice into courtesy. 'Excellencies, I am Dirynvolk. You are from another land. I cannot be your kin.' Then, with an effort, 'I am not worthy to be your kin.'

Amusement descended upon her like a cloying mist. 'True. But that is mere flesh, Jeyan. You *are* kin to our spirit. True kin. You are one of the chosen. We are few. Power will be given to you beyond your imagining. You will stand with those destined to bring order to an ill-created world where now there is only the squabbling ferment of a myriad petty tribes and chieftains. You will stand with those who will re-create the world in His image, with those before whom all others will bow, with those who are destined to prepare the Way for the coming of the One True Light.'

To her horror, Jeyan felt a distant thrill stirring in response to this enigmatic call.

'I don't understand,' she said, searching amongst these strange words for something that might enable her to get away from this bizarre, disorienting hall, with its flickering lights, and its silent moving shadows.

The amusement returned. 'It is not necessary. Does the axe understand the tree?'

'Does the plough understand the soil?'

'You are the blade.'

'You are the tool.'

'We the wielder.'

'Clearing the ancient tangled roots, the foetid by-ways.'

'Making pure and whole.'

Jeyan could do no other than remain silent. Such questions as struggled through her jangling thoughts she dared not ask, fearful of what had happened before. It came to her that perhaps all this was no more than a subtle torment. Perhaps the Gevethen were playing some elaborate game with her. How far would it go? Would she be lured to within a fraction of some greatness, only to have it snatched from her, and then be delivered into the hands of the Questioners? Zealously placed there by the soldier she had killed, images of a protracted public execution filled her mind. She wanted to vomit, so awful was the sudden terror. Yet, instead, she clenched her fists and gritted her teeth. She was where she was. She was not on the gallows. She must, above all, retain control of herself, of her thoughts, if she was to avoid such a fate. At the worst, she realized coldly, she must find some weapon with which she could end her own life. A simple edge across her wrists and she would enjoy the same fate as the man who had brought her here. The irony almost amused her. The finality of the decision quietened her. Carefully, she stood up.

The mirrors shifted and all about her were the strained images of the Gevethen, watching, waiting, bird hands hovering.

'How can this be?' she asked, looking up at the figures crowding the throne platform. The Gevethen around her gazed up and then down and were gone. She was alone, save for the silent mirror-bearers. There was a long pause.

'You are kin.'

'You are chosen.'

'I killed the Lord Counsellor Hagen. Was he not chosen?' She braced herself for some brutal impact. But none came.

'He was flawed.'

'He served his turn.'

'One more fitting dispatched him.'

Stepping to the edge, she said, 'Am I not to be punished?'

'Is the axe to be punished, for felling the tree?'

'The plough for turning the soil?'

She leapt. 'But I did what I did of my own free will. No one urged me. No one bought me.'

Laughter, cold and humourless, rose to a climax that filled the hall. The mirrors about Jeyan began to tremble.

'Take the Lord Counsellor to her chambers . . .'

                             '. . . her chambers.'

Chapter 18

After a little scrambling over the rocky crest of the dip between the two mountains, the descent into the valley took on the atmosphere almost of a family jaunt. Although on occasions the Traveller seemed to drift off into a reverie, there was a vigour and a sprightliness in his step which, his companions saw by contrast, had been conspicuously absent when he was in the village. The sky began to clear.

Ibryen and Rachyl moved uncertainly at first. It was a valley on the fringe of their domain and the head of it was routinely patrolled, even though it was, for all practical purposes, inaccessible to the Gevethen. 'There's no one about,' the Traveller assured them, though in more carefully measured tones than he had used before. Years of caution when moving through the mountains had taken their toll however, and his reassurance was politely ignored. Only as they moved further down from the ridge did Ibryen and Rachyl begin to feel easier.

'Keep a careful note of our route,' Ibryen said, as they began to stride out down a long grassy slope. 'It's fine today, but it could be mist and rain when we come back.'

Rachyl acquiesced, but with that air of polite toleration reserved by the young for respected elders who tell them the obvious. Both Ibryen and the Traveller noted it and exchanged knowing looks.

On the whole they did not talk a great deal as they moved along the valley, though at one point Rachyl stopped and gazed round at the enclosing peaks. Not, this time, with the shrewd-eyed warrior gaze that searched into shades and crevices, alert for the subtle wrongness, the movement, the shape, that should not be there, but almost with wonder. 'Probably no one's ever been here before,' she said, speaking softly as if she were in a holy place.

'No people,' the Traveller confirmed. 'At least not for a very long time. Certainly before ideas like Nesdiryn and Girnlant came into their thinking. Perhaps, as you say, never.'

He stopped and joined her in her study. 'Who knows. Perhaps some solitary wanderer, with his own joys and burdens has stood right here and felt them come into a different perspective, just like you are. Mountains are very good at doing that. That's one of the reasons I like them.'

Rachyl did not seem too sure. Ibryen took her arm and gently urged her forward. The last thing that Rachyl needed was a new perspective on her life, especially the last few years. Circumstances had made her a soldier and it was the best thing she could be until the need for soldiering was gone. 'What are the other reasons?' Ibryen asked the Traveller, anxious to draw Rachyl back to the present.

'No people,' the Traveller replied, slapping his stomach with both hands and then holding them out in a wide embrace. 'No people and no people.'

Ibryen laughed. 'I'm sorry if we give you such offence. Shall we walk in our bare feet to preserve the ancient silence?'

'I'd hear the grass bending under your feet,' the Traveller laughed in return. 'Listen!' he put a hand to his ear. 'I can hear the voices of the countless tiny creatures that dwell here, the tumbling of Marris's tiny pebbles on their way to the avalanche, the wind twining around the high peaks and sighing through the tangled gorse, the fluttering wings of nesting birds, the scuttling feet of moles and rabbits and . . .'

Ibryen and Rachyl were listening spellbound, there was such joy in his voice, when, abruptly, he stopped and tilted his head forward, a hand raised for silence. He turned from side to side intently as if searching for something. Alarmed, both Ibryen and Rachyl reached for their swords and, turning back to back, began scanning the surrounding slopes. Then the Traveller sagged slightly and his look of concentration became one of resignation.

'What's the matter?' Ibryen whispered, his hand still on his sword. 'Can you hear someone coming?'

The Traveller held out his thumb and forefinger. 'Twice now,' he said. 'Twice I'd swear I heard the Song.' Ibryen frowned. 'Sound Carvers, Count. My ancient kin. But so faint, so far away. The faintest wisps – deep, deep down, beneath the creaking roots of the mountains themselves.' He gave a little sigh and was himself again. 'Imagination I suppose,' he decided. 'We see what we want to, we hear what we want to. The Sound Carvers are long gone, aren't they, Count?' He snapped his fingers and set off walking. 'Ah, I forgot. You've never heard of them, have you?'

Ibryen wanted to question the Traveller about these strange ancestors, but the little man was gathering speed and was already some way ahead. For a moment he was inclined to call after him, but decided against it. His interest was little more than idle curiosity; he had nothing to offer the man in what was plainly a disturbing, if not

255

distressing matter. Rachyl was starting to stride out with a view to catching up with him, but Ibryen motioned to her to slow down. There was a quality in the Traveller's posture that said he wished to be alone for a while.

Eventually they caught up with him. He was sitting on a rock, swinging his feet, and seemed to have recovered from whatever had unsettled him. Ibryen met his concerns head on. 'Are you all right?' he asked. 'You seemed upset before. That's why we left you to walk on.'

The Traveller smiled broadly and gave an airy wave. 'A touch of nostalgia, a whimsy, a mishearing – it happens when one reaches too far. I should know better. But I thank you for your thoughtfulness. It's very pleasant to be reminded that not all people are braying oafs.' He looked at Rachyl. 'And that some of them are quite lovely.'

Ibryen responded as he had before when the Traveller had offered Rachyl his heavy-handed compliments – he started in alarm. He also prepared to move quickly, this particular compliment having been uttered to Rachyl's face. Any man in the village foolish enough to speak thus would soon have measured his length on the ground, nursing a bruised jaw, or worse. Somewhat to Ibryen's surprise however, Rachyl merely levelled a finger at the little man and said, 'Stop that!' like a matriarchal school-teacher. The Traveller drew in a sharp breath and patted his heart in a gesture of mock pain. Rachyl turned away, and became apparently engrossed in adjusting a strap on her pack. Ibryen eyed her carefully. He could swear she was blushing. The hearty companion in him laughed and jibed, but the leader of his people grieved that his cousin's life had been so needlessly distorted. Images of the life she should have led burst upon him. He allowed them no sway, and they passed leaving only a dull ache behind,

but, without fanfare or declamation, his long-formed resolution to destroy the cause of this pointless and painful
destruction reforged itself even as he laid the distress
aside.

Rachyl finished fiddling with her pack and drew a hand
across her flushed forehead as if she were hot. 'Why are
you helping us when you'd prefer to be without us?' she
asked without warning, though there was no reproach in
her voice.

The Traveller jumped down from the rock and set off
again. The others followed him. 'I told you before. I'm as
much like you as I'm unlike you. Knowing what I know,
I can't walk away and expect my life to be unsullied by
the neglect.' Suddenly he was walking quickly and waving
his arms. His voice rose. 'The average folly of the average
individual brings enough inadvertent pain into this world,
but that's part of our lot. Somehow, we need it. But wilful
sources of evil like your Gevethen . . .' he growled ferociously and clenched his fist. It was not the comic sight it
should have been from so small a figure and both Ibryen
and Rachyl winced at the passion in his words '. . . should
be rooted out and destroyed utterly. They are diseased.'
He twisted his foot as he spoke, as though crushing something under his heel.

No one spoke for some while after this. Nothing but
time could follow such a declaration and each was content
to let the sunlit valley open before them as they walked
along over the yielding mountain turf. Eventually, as they
moved steadily downwards, the many streams tumbling
from the slopes on either side merged into a single ener-
getic and noisy flow and the vegetation began to thicken.
They stopped for a rest by the bubbling river. It was
becoming warmer and the breeze had dropped, and from
where they were sitting they could see the river twisting,

white and silver, down into a forest which spread across the entire valley floor.

Ibryen frowned as he looked at the way ahead. 'That's going to present problems,' he said.

'It's going to offer food and shelter. And warmth if we need it,' the Traveller said, as to an ungrateful pupil.

'Not pressing needs at the moment,' Ibryen rebutted. 'I was thinking about our progress. It's so easy to get lost in dense woodland.'

The Traveller chuckled. 'How can you get lost when you don't know where you're going?'

'You know what I meant,' Ibryen said sternly. 'In trees like that we could travel in circles for hours, if not days, without realizing it. And marking the track's going to be laborious, to say the least.'

The Traveller tapped the side of his nose. 'I follow this,' he said. 'It rarely goes round in circles.' Ibryen's eyes narrowed.

'I thought you followed your ears,' Rachyl intervened caustically, then to Ibryen: 'As for going round in circles, why the sudden concern? I've no idea what you've been following but you seem happy enough with it so far, so you might as well carry on doing the same. And I'll just carry on doing what I've been doing – following the two of you. However . . .' she looked from one to the other significantly, then waved a small book at them, '. . . at our great leader's behest, I'm having to write this lot down, as well as mark the track, and I'm with him; I've no desire to plunge into a forest that could reach from here to your precious Girnlant unless it's absolutely necessary. Are you both sure we're going the right way – whatever that is?'

The small outburst silenced the two men for a moment. 'Your kin,' the Traveller said to Ibryen eventually, with a disclaiming wave and a humorous challenge in his eyes.

Ibryen smiled and shook his head in resignation. 'It *is* the way,' he said to Rachyl, looking down towards the forest. 'But whatever's reaching out is changing. It's getting weaker, but it's getting clearer as well. And it seems to be pulling the whole of me in some way. It's diffferent. It's going beyond.'

The Traveller was serious now. 'It's not easy so close to this river, but what I can hear still is just weaker, nothing else, no other changes. That's the second time you've said that. What do you mean?'

Ibryen gave a pained shrug. 'I don't know. I've told you before, the whole thing is beyond any words I can find. It's as though the ... call ... is beginning to come from some other place – or part of it is. And ...'

He hesitated.

'And?' the Traveller prompted.

Ibryen blew two noisy breaths as if to force the words out. 'And it's as though part of me ... the part that's hearing this call ... is somewhere else as well.'

Rachyl's face became anxious. Survivor of scores of savage encounters, and heroine of many a daring raid on the Gevethen's forces, she felt as though she were beginning to slide down some perilous slope at the end of which lay a terrible drop as she listened to her cousin and leader struggling so futilely with his strange inner vision. The Traveller reached out and touched them both. He spoke to Rachyl first.

'When you're lying in ambush, silent and still and in the darkness for endless, aching hours, strange images flicker past your eyes, strange sounds buzz and clatter in your ears. Sometimes up becomes down and down up. But you've learned that it's only your body, your own weaker nature, rebelling against the dictates of your will. You don't confuse it with that feeling which brings you fully alert and says, "danger", do you? Yet when you feel this, you've heard nothing, seen nothing. You've no idea what mysterious reaches of time and distance this feeling comes to you across.' Rachyl watched him uncertainly but intently. 'So it is with your cousin. He's as lost at the moment as you were on your first night attacks. He needs the assurance, the support, that someone probably gave you once, but there's no one here can do it except us. You with your loyalty and affection, me with my limited knowledge.' His grip tightened about her shoulder. 'And you have a touch of this gift yourself, I'm certain. Deep inside you understand. You can bear him when he leans on you. And I *have* heard of this thing often enough, and from intellects sceptical enough, to know that it exists – this ability, this gift, to reach into places which our hands and ears and eyes and all our commonsense tell us cannot be. Song forbid that we should be so arrogant as to think that what we can't sense or imagine doesn't exist! We, who can't even see what the owl sees, hear what the bat hears. We, who can't burrow beneath the ground, fly over the peaks or even move over the land faster than the merest trot without all manner of clanking devices to help us.'

He turned to Ibryen. 'Your gift is profound and very rare. You're disturbed because you're like an unborn child just becoming aware that it's time to leave the womb.'

Ibryen did not appear to be comforted. 'It's not unknown for babies to die on the journey to their new world,' he said sourly.

The Traveller gave a guilt-stricken grimace. 'My mistake. Bad analogy,' he pleaded, patting Ibryen's shoulder. 'But you understand my meaning. It'll do you no more hurt than any other natural gift. If any hurt comes from it, it'll be because of what you've chosen to do with it.'

His voice fell, as though he were afraid of being over-heard. 'From what you tell me, I suspect that your Gevethen too have this gift, but that's by the bye. Whether they have it or not, every fibre of me tells me that following this call to its roots will bring you to a new vision of your predicament.'

Neither Ibryen nor Rachyl seemed inclined to question him, or to pursue the matter further. For a while they sat silent, watching the river in its noisy dash down the valley. Eventually Ibryen stood up and adjusted his pack. He lobbed a pebble into the water. It arced white in the sunlight then disappeared into the cold mountain stream. The sound of its entry could not be heard and the water closed about it with scarcely a ripple. A few bubbles congregated on the surface then, after a hesitant start, scattered hurriedly like guilty witnesses, to join the flood.

'Eddies and waves,' Ibryen said, to no one in particular. He bent down and reached into the water. It trickled between his fingers as he lifted his hand out. 'Goes its own way, can't be moulded and bent like wood and iron, yet before our eyes it shapes itself into ridges and hummocks like rolling hills. Always changing, always the same. What power forms those, Traveller?'

'The same that forms us all, Count,' the Traveller replied.

Rachyl pulled a wry face and stood up. 'Come on, you two. We've a journey to make and a war to fight. You can philosophize later when we've got the Gevethen's heads on a pole. It'll be nightfall by the time we reach that forest as it is.' Her brusque command galvanized the others who found themselves having to scurry after her as she strode off.

It was indeed past sunset when they came to the edge of the forest. As they reached the first trees, the Traveller laid his hands against the trunks of some of them and, gazing up into the branches above, smiled. It brought him one of Rachyl's suspicious looks, but she said nothing. Catching the frown, he raised a finger to his lips, then, tongue protruding slightly, he bent down and picked up a stone. There was a brief pause while he looked around, then a sudden economic flourish and the stone was thrown, with a force that surprised Rachyl. The Traveller vanished into the trees after it, to return a few moments later carrying a dead rabbit.

'Shouldn't have stayed out so late, should you?' he was saying to it. He held it out to Rachyl. 'It'll save you eating your supplies tonight,' he said. She could not forbear a look of admiration as she took it.

'Not without more mundane resources, I see,' she said, taking the gift.

'Oh, you'd be surprised at what I can do,' he retorted, winking.

Rachyl ignored the challenge. She drew her knife and began skinning the rabbit. 'Impressive throwing, that. I could have used you on some of our raids,' she said, soldier to soldier, as her knife deftly laid open the animal. 'We're all good archers, but arrows are precious out here. Stones, on the other hand . . . plenty of those.' Ibryen was nodding in agreement. 'There!' The task was done. Wiping the knife on the grass, Rachyl looked at the Traveller. 'Why didn't you just . . .' she offered two fingers to her mouth vaguely '. . . whistle it down?'

The Traveller met her gaze. 'Amongst other things, it was entitled to a chance,' he said.

The answer seemed to appeal to her. She made to discard the skin. The Traveller frowned and held out his hand. 'Give me that,' he said with a hint of irritation. 'Have you no manners, no respect for the creature? I'll find a use for it. And don't forget to thank it for giving its life so that you could eat.'

'Y . . . yes,' Rachyl stammered, taken aback by this rebuke. She glanced at Ibryen for help but found none. 'I . . . we will.' The Traveller was walking away. 'Aren't you going to eat with us?' she called after him.

'No, thank you,' came the reply. 'I don't eat much and I had plenty at the camp. I'll be back in a little while.'

Ibryen shrugged helplessly as the little figure retreated. 'I'll get some kindling,' he said.

'Well-dried,' Rachyl reminded him absently, still watching the Traveller. 'We want no smoke.'

Ibryen did not dispute the point. They might be far from the eyes of the Gevethen here, but there was nothing to be gained by letting slip the habits that had kept them safe for years and which they would need again within weeks, whatever the outcome of this journey.

It was dark when the Traveller returned to a low, glowing fire and two replete companions. He seemed more cheerful than when he had left. 'That was a happy gift,' Ibryen said to him. 'We've saved you some.'

The Traveller smiled appreciatively but shook his head. He sat down. 'Finish it between you.' Then he looked at them both. 'You did thank it?' he demanded.

'Yes,' they replied simultaneously and uncomfortably.

'Good,' the Traveller said, though with some doubt in his voice. 'I can see it's something you're not used to.' He became stern. 'Understand this. You can kill your own kind however you fancy. That's between you, them, and your consciences. But while you're with me, have some respect when you kill something else. Where've you left the remains?'

Rachyl, wide-eyed, pointed with a bone she was chewing on.

'Did you offer them to the forest?'

Rachyl stopped chewing and looked at him like a child aware that an offence had been committed but not knowing what. The Traveller clicked his tongue reproachfully and stood up. 'I'll do it for you,' he said wearily. 'You young folk, you've no idea.'

As he marched off, Rachyl bit fiercely into the bone, teeth white and feral. She muttered under her breath. 'I don't know what to make of that little—' She stopped and then wilted. 'I think that's me in my place,' she whispered to Ibryen.

'I think it's both of us,' Ibryen whispered in reply, coming to the aid of a beleaguered ally. 'I've heard of rituals like that in primitive peoples, long ago, but . . .'

'Primitive is as primitive does,' the Traveller called back, making them both start guiltily. 'Just because we're alive and they're dead doesn't make us any wiser, you know. Still less, superior.'

Ibryen held up his hands in surrender. 'Peace,' he said. He was about to say, 'It was only a rabbit,' but quickly changed his mind. 'Thank you for the gift and for the instruction. We'll try to remember in future.'

The Traveller returned. 'Just be aware, Count,' he said, as he sat down again. 'That way you won't need to remember.' As sometimes happened when the Traveller spoke, Ibryen felt meanings in his voice far beyond the apparent content of the words. There was no outward indication of anything of great significance having been intended however, and the Traveller was now beaming at Rachyl, his face glowing in the soft firelight. It forced a smile out of her.

Though the night promised to be cold, there was no sign of rain pending so Rachyl and Ibryen lay down in their blankets rather than pitch the small shelter they had brought. For a while there was some desultory conversation between them. It became more and more subdued and incoherent as they drifted off to sleep, until the only sound in the small camp was the Traveller humming softly to himself as he remained squatting on his haunches and staring into the fire.

Ibryen was overwhelmed with longing.

He screwed his eyes tight against the brightness.

Where was he?

His body felt different. It was alive with sensations that he had never known before. Yet, too, he had known them always. As the eyes gave sight and the ears sound, so subtle touches caressing him gave him another knowledge. A knowledge as familiar as sight and sound, and one that he needed . . .

For what?

Where was he? The question returned.

Wherever it was, there was no menace around him. He was at ease. But he could not see properly. After so long in the darkness, the brightness was pressing on his eyelids, allowing him only a blurred and barred vision.

The air was cold and fresh and he could read every nuance in its movement – a myriad eddies twisting, turning, spinning, folding in and through one another – countless linking and shifting movements – all bound to a whole, yet free, like the shivering ridges and valleys of water in the bustling river.

He turned. The eddies turned and danced with him, unhindering and unhindered. He could make out little of the landscape though it seemed to be covered with snow. Yet it wasn't, he knew. In the distance there were darker tints – the brightness made it difficult for him to differentiate individual colours, but he knew that it was the land beyond this place. Yet the perspective was strange. It was not the view of a landscape from a high, snowy peak.

His eyes began to adjust. As his vision was returning, bright coloured shapes began to drift into his flickering view. Hailing voices reached him, full of surprise and joy. He lifted his arm in greeting.

Such elation!

He had never expected to return here.

After so long.

He was home again!

The call was all about him, urging him forward.

Ibryen opened his eyes with a jolt.

Darkness filled them.

As he blinked, a redness slowly formed and the call began to fade. Gradually the redness brightened until eventually it was the small camp fire, sharp and clear, and the call was now faint and distant. By the dim light of the fire he could see the dark shape of Rachyl wrapped tight in her blankets, head submerged, and the still-crouching form of the Traveller. As if he had heard something, the Traveller turned towards him and, making a slight gesture of greeting with his hand, smiled.

Ibryen grunted by way of reply and the Traveller turned back to his reverie.

I must tell him about that in the morning, Ibryen thought, drowsily.

Ask him what it meant . . .

He'd know . . .

The soft hissing of the fire mingled with the murmuring of the leaves above and the lilting hum of the Traveller's tune to become the returning tide of the great ocean of sleep. Gently it lapped around Ibryen, lifted him, and carried away.

His next awakening was less gentle, more in the nature of a shipwreck. It was Rachyl's booted and prodding toe. 'Come on, Cousin. Food to make, camp to break, and a journey to finish.'

Despite the unceremonious waking and the heartiness in Rachyl's voice, Ibryen smiled. He felt refreshed. Not even as stiff as he might have anticipated, he realized, as he disentangled himself from his blankets. The morning cold struck through to him. Between the trees he could see faint hints of lingering ground mist. He glanced up at the sky.

'Nearly sunrise?' he asked.

Rachyl nodded, taking his blankets and shaking them vigorously. Dew sprayed white into the moist air.

'Where's the Traveller?'

'Gone for some water.'

Ibryen looked at the commander of his camp a little guiltily. Tasks had been allocated while he slept. He passed a hand over the mound of grey ashes. It was very warm. 'I'll fetch some more wood. Get the fire going. Make some—'

'He said to leave it,' Rachyl told him, throwing the blankets over a rope slung between two branches. 'You can fetch the water tomorrow.'

The Traveller returned before Ibryen could find an opportunity to feel too much remorse for his tardy start. He bent over the ashes, nose twitching, then he poked amongst them with a stick. 'Here, try these,' he said, flicking something out on to the grass and bouncing it quickly to Ibryen. It was a tuber. Ibryen caught it instinctively only to toss it hastily from one hand to the other. It was very hot. Another followed for Rachyl and finally the Traveller retrieved one for himself.

'What is it?' Ibryen asked, more rudely than he had intended.

'Delicious,' the Traveller replied, blowing on his and nibbling it gingerly. 'Not as evenly cooked as I'd have liked, and a touch of salt and a herb or two wouldn't go amiss, but, here and now – and in such company – delicious.'

Carefully emulating him, Rachyl and Ibryen were obliged to agree.

'Did you remember to thank the trees?' Rachyl said with heavy irony.

'Of course,' the Traveller replied, quite seriously. He looked up at her with wilful ingenuousness. 'You know, I'd have sworn you'd have forgotten about it.' He turned to Ibryen. 'It's nice to see young people paying heed, isn't it?'

Ibryen however, was coping with too large a mouthful of hot root and, gaping alarmingly, was only able to gesticulate. 'Be careful,' the Traveller said needlessly.

'Twice you've fed us now, Traveller,' Ibryen said when he had recovered.

'Not often I get a chance to look after people,' the Traveller replied, a little self-consciously. 'Especially people as hurt as you've been.'

Rachyl frowned. 'We *can* forage for ourselves, if we have to,' she said defensively.

'Don't know where to find these though, do you?' The Traveller held up his half-eaten root and issued a challenging smile. Caught between the challenge and ingratitude, Rachyl became fretful. She looked to Ibryen, but he was drinking hastily from a canteen of water. The Traveller released her. 'Indulge me,' he said. 'I'm enjoying your company much more than I thought I would, and I need to pull my weight. Besides, we might as well live off the land while we can. If we have to move upwards – and I suspect we will – we're going to need our supplies.'

Ibryen, wiping his mouth, smiled as he watched his warrior cousin being defeated again. She was learning however, and counter-attacked immediately. 'I'm sorry,' she said. 'It was a thoughtless remark. And you're right, I've never seen tubers like these.' She leaned forward and became massively courteous. 'I'd be most grateful if you'd show me where they're to be found.'

The Traveller inclined his head in acknowledgement, then, baring his teeth he bit slowly and deliberately into the root. 'I'd be delighted,' he said, with similar irony. 'There are plenty of things I can show you as we go.'

They broke camp.

'What did you hear in the night?' Ibryen asked the Traveller as they moved off. The little man raised a quizzical eyebrow. 'I saw you sitting by the fire when I woke once, and there's no sign that you've slept anywhere,' Ibryen explained. 'I presumed you were glad of the quiet.'

The Traveller chuckled. 'I can sleep standing up if I have to,' he said. 'But you're right, I was listening.' He moved closer to Ibryen. 'Though it's difficult with the river so near. I'm going to the limits and there are many strange things there which confuse and mislead. But it's still there, though it's growing weaker. It almost winked out at one point – just before you woke, as a matter of fact.'

The reminder brought some of Ibryen's strange vision back to him. He recounted it. 'Do you think it's of any significance?' he asked.

The Traveller was silent for a moment, then he shook his head. 'I'm not sure,' he said, but Ibryen sensed that he was disturbed by what he had just been told and was keeping his peace until he had had a chance to think about it fully.

269

They walked steadily on through the day, following the line of the river. For the most part, the forest floor was quite clear, the main obstacles they encountered being fast-moving streams dashing across the valley to join the river. A brisk breeze sprang up to shake the tops of the trees, but only spasmodic gusts of it reached down to blow amid the trunks and strike the walkers. It was as though someone, somewhere, opened a large door from time to time. Conversation too, was spasmodic: the walking being easier, the three were able to sink into their own preoccupations.

Despite all the discussion that had brought him to this point, Ibryen still found himself concerned about the rightness of what he was doing. His mood oscillated between absolute certainty and awful doubt, but it lingered at neither for long, and generally calmed down to leave him with just enough certainty to keep him moving forward, with the assurance that they would not be away from the village for long. Rachyl, for the most part more concerned about the known enemies behind them than what might lie ahead, played discreet rearguard, protecting the backs of her Commander and his guide. The Traveller was quiet, though occasionally he would become bubblingly loquacious. At one such time he showed his companions where to find the tubers he had served them that morning. At others he pointed out various herbs and fungi: what a shame, this would have gone splendidly with their rabbit; this one made a most refreshing drink infused with hot water; this one an excellent poultice; this with some of *that* and *that* would make a meal that a king couldn't better. Most of the culinary references he levelled at Rachyl, to her annoyance. Finally, he plunged into the undergrowth to emerge with a drab green leaf. He squeezed it delicately between his thumb and forefinger and, before she realized what was happening, dabbed them behind Rachyl's ears. 'And this just perfumes the night.' As her fist came up he held the leaf under her nose. It brought her retaliation to an immediate halt and she smiled. Taking the leaf gently she squeezed it as he had done and held her thumb and finger to her nose. Her smile broadened and, oblivious to her audience, she followed the Traveller's example and touched the perfume behind her ears. Then, suddenly aware of the two men watching her, she hastily stuffed the leaf into a pocket and, clearing her throat, motioned the party forward with a scowl. Later, the Traveller dropped back to join her and with a conspiratorial wink, surreptitiously folded some of the leaves into her hand.

During the latter part of the day, without any spoken agreement, they began to edge away from the river, gradually moving to higher ground. Rachyl noted the change, but made no comment.

It was early evening and they were contemplating stopping for the night when they came to a great swathe cut through the forest. Splintered and uprooted trees were scattered about as if they had been so much kindling and, here and there, boulders were visible. Somewhere underneath it all, a noisy stream could be heard. Though burgeoning spring foliage, long grasses, and creepers were seeking to repair the hurt, the cause of the damage was quite apparent.

'More of Marris's dust blowing in the wind,' Ibryen said as he surveyed the scene.

'Only a few years ago too,' the Traveller remarked.

Rachyl looked at it sourly. 'What a mess. It's going to be awkward to cross, to put it mildly.'

Ibryen nodded absently. He was looking around and frowning. Suddenly he stopped and pointed up towards

271

the peak that lay at the head of the damage. It looked ominous against the darkening sky.

'That way,' he said.

Chapter 19

Jeyan stared up at the gloomy ceiling. She was shaking. In so far as she was thinking at all, it seemed to her that she had been trembling continuously since she had killed Hagen and that there would be nothing but trembling for whatever the rest of her life was going to be.

Dryness in her mouth and throat forced its attention on her. Her legs unsteady and her head floating uneasily, she got up from the long, luxurious couch and carefully moved down three carpeted steps and over to a table at the far end of the room. On it was spread an array of ornate silver dishes and plates, each laden with food, together with several bottles, jugs and decanters. There was also a tray of elegant glass goblets, all either decorated with fine-lined etchings or engraved and elaborately chequered. They glittered even in the subdued lighting. She picked up a decanter of what she took to be water and lifted it to her mouth. A sharp, sweet smell struck her, making her grimace. She returned it to the tray. Amongst the many things that the Ennerhald had taught her, one was not to get drunk. That was for others – it made them easier to deceive and rob when need arose; for all that had happened to her, her wits were not so addled yet that she could not use them. She worked her way through the jugs until finally she found one containing water then, in a manner markedly at odds with the refinement implicit in everything around her, she drank from it directly. The water that spilled down her chin she wiped with the back of her hand as she carried the jug back to the couch.

She sat for a long time as she had been sitting since she was put in this room – shocked and vacant, her eyes barely registering what they saw, her mind numb with conflicting thoughts and emotions. The excursion to the table had been the first sign of conscious activity. It signalled the return of her faculties however, and slowly, coherent thoughts began to form. Not that coherence brought any understanding to what had happened, or offered her any indication of what was to follow.

Following the Gevethen's instruction, the mirror-bearers had surrounded her and ushered her from the Watching Chamber into a room occupied by a group of what she presumed were the Gevethen's personal servants. These had been as silent and blank-faced as the mirror-bearers, but they had treated her with great deference as they had escorted her through parts of the Citadel that were apparently the personal quarters of high-ranking Citadel officers. Deference or no, she noted that their careful attendance left her no opportunity to attempt an escape.

Then had followed a bizarre humiliation. The servants, some male, some female, had stripped and bathed her. The instant hands had been laid on her ragged clothes she had feared the worst and reacted with massive ferocity, struggling, screaming and shouting. All to no avail. The hands that held her were at once gentle and immovable. And the only harm that came to her was the physical discomfort she had suffered in trying to break free from their grip. The bathing had proceeded as if she had been a small and unwilling child. She was far from certain which was the worst, her naked indignity or the seeming indifference of the stone-faced servants, performing their duties regardless of anything she did, pinioning her arms, her legs, her head as circumstances dictated, and oblivious to her abuse. Eventually she had stopped resisting and lapsed into sullen lassitude. She had had to fight too, against the reaction of her body which, after so long in the cold squalor of the Ennerhald, had eventually started to revel in the warm and scented water.

Then, to her horror, the Gevethen had been there, examining her, a circling reflected throng of them staring down at her. Watery, indifferent eyes had scanned her as they might a piece of furniture and, though nothing was said, full red mouths worked to and fro as if they were holding their own silent conversation.

And the floating white hands had touched her!

She shuddered and drew herself along the couch as she had tried again to edge away from the advancing hands. Water spilled from the jug still clutched in her hand. Yet, though the sight of the hands had been repellent, their touch was alive and vibrant, and they were laid only on those parts of her that had been injured: her face, her wrists, her ankles. She touched her face – it was less painful now, as were her wrists and ankles, though it was as if the pain had been driven from her rather than gently healed. Then the Gevethen were gone and she was being dried and dressed in the formal clothes she now wore. Men's clothes – a formal livery such as Hagen had worn. When she had realized what it was, she had tried to tear it off, but a hand had stopped her and, for a fleeting instant, she had looked into the eyes of one of the servants and seen a human being, trapped and terrified. Then, with a movement so swift and slight that it was barely

perceptible, the woman shook her head and, with a terrifying vividness, Jeyan understood her – *was* her. The intensity of the fear and the plea that swept over her snatched
Jeyan's breath away. Whatever she did that was not
acceptable to the Gevethen would redound manyfold on
these servants. And who could conjecture what torments
they were already suffering behind those blank faces? The
woman's fearful glance had been perhaps the first real
human contact Jeyan had known since her early friends
in the Ennerhald had been slaughtered and the impact of
it shook her severely. She had offered no further resistance and was eventually led to the room she was now in.
There she was shown the table of food and drink and sat
down on the couch like some large, stiff-jointed doll. The
servants had then silently slipped away, bowing as they
went.

As she began to think, so the events of the recent past
re-enacted themselves and she was afraid once again. She
looked about the room. Her father had been rich by
the normal standards of Nesdiryn and her life had been
comparatively privileged and protected, yet she had never
experienced anything which compared with the luxury
that was all around her in this room. The clothes she was
wearing, this awful mockery of Hagen's hated uniform,
were made of materials of the finest quality. The perfumes
which clung about her from the water she had been bathed
in, were more subtle and delicate than anything she had
ever known. Even the food on the table bespoke great
care and attention in its preparation.

And then, without a vestige of warning, she was weeping. Not in many years had she wept, but now nothing
could have stopped the torrent of tears. She had scarcely
cried out once during the ordeal of her pursuit and capture, and it is probable that she would have suffered much

more before she would have allowed her tormentors such satisfaction, but the softness all around her struck her with a greater force than the cruellest torturer's iron.

She did not rant and scream as her life poured from her eyes, but sat bolt upright and, save for her heaving shoulders, motionless, on the edge of the couch. Memories overwhelmed her. Memories of her parents, of what she had once been and what she might have become, of Dirynhald and Nesdiryn as they had been, of old friends slaughtered or turned craven by fear. And, not least, she wept for fear of what was going to happen to her. For everything that had occurred since she had been taken from the dungeon this morning must surely be part of some scheme of the Gevethen's to punish her for the murder of Hagen. It was not possible that she could do such a thing and fall into their hands and not be treated with appalling cruelty. That was how the Gevethen maintained their power over the land. Ostensibly there was freedom, but to disobey, to speak against, was to risk dying unpleasantly: perhaps publicly, perhaps secretly. It was hard to say which struck the greater fear into the people, the public executions or the nightmare uncertainty of the silent disappearance and the fearful speculation about what went on in the Citadel's dungeons – for everyone knew about the death pits beyond the city.

Eventually the tears slowed then stopped and she sat, still unmoving, staring bleakly at the richness all around her. It could not have contrasted more with everything she had known since she fled into the Ennerhald, and yet there was an emptiness, a deadness, about the room that she had not felt even in the most ancient and decayed parts of the Ennerhald. The workmanship in the furniture and the many artefacts placed about the room was exquisite, as it was in the carvings and paintings that decorated the walls and ceiling. Only great love for the work could have made it so. But the whole seemed to be incomplete. Worse than that, it was barren. Some vital ingredient was missing. It came to her that the room was not an expression of love or delight, but a shield, an accumulation, a barricade, to protect the occupant.

But from what?

From his own dark and dead soul. The answer followed without pause.

This must have been Hagen's room, she realized with a start. She stood up and began to walk round it. As she gazed about her, she found it impossible to imagine the brutal Hagen seeing what she saw and delicately selecting this, rejecting that. How could such a man attend to the slaughter and sadistic persecution of his fellows and then display the sensitivity necessary for the selection of such works?

He could not, of course. A man who did what he did could only be dead to such matters. That was why the whole was flawed. It reflected his true nature. It was incomplete, just as he was. He had gathered it together not from an inner response to beauty but out of some bizarre vanity, as if it could redeem him in some way. And as each item was a reflection of some other person's taste, so the whole was a reflection of him. Her thoughts darkened. How many of these items had been thoughtfully selected from the home of one of his murdered victims? The thought sickened her and her hand flinched convulsively away from a small statuette she was about to touch.

Reflections, reflections.

As the word echoed through her mind, she caught sight of her own in a long mirror. She stepped back in alarm, before realizing what she was looking at. For a moment, her thoughts full of him, she had taken the figure to be

Hagen himself, returned from the dead full of youth and suppleness and seeking retribution. She seized the front of the tunic to tear it off, but even as she gripped the soft fabric, she saw again the terror that had flickered briefly into the servant's eyes. It occurred to her that she knew absolutely nothing about the underworld of this place: who these servants were, where they came from, how they came to be here, and what bound them so. Who, for example, had prepared that bath, made this food, and, not least, made sure that these clothes fitted? For fit they did, and she was shorter and slighter than Hagen by far. Who could say what consequences might flow from anything she did in this place? And for whom? Her hand fell away.

The reflection gazed out at her, frowning slightly. It was vastly different from the ragged scarecrow that had formed the heart of her escort from the dungeons, but it was still slouching a little and its hands were hanging limply by its side. Instinctively Jeyan straightened as a long-silent paternal voice reached out of the past to reproach her. A movement beyond her reflection caught her attention and she turned quickly. There was nothing there. Nothing except another mirror. And another. And another. There were mirrors everywhere, large and small, all reflecting images from one another. Most of them were encased in elaborately decorated frames but one was conspicuous by its simplicity. She went to it.

Mounted on a wheeled stand, it had what appeared to be a plain wooden frame, though it was blacker than any wood or varnish that she had ever seen. Indeed, it had an unsettling quality about it. As though it were the deepest part of the night made solid. The mirror, by contrast, reflected the room about her so flawlessly that she felt she would be able to reach into it and take things from

279

the reflection of a nearby table. She remembered the fragment of mirror that she had found in one of the buildings in the Ennerhald and that was now lying in her erstwhile home. It must have been very old, yet that too had reflected with such clarity, despite the dirt and grime of her existence there. An old habit reached up and adjusted her hair. Then, drawn in some way, she reached out to the mirror. As she touched the fingertips of her reflection it was almost as if she had touched not a cold smooth surface, but another hand and the reflection pulled back from her, startled. As it did, the mirror moved slightly and, gathered from the other mirrors, an array of young Hagens swung in to surround the confrontation between herself and her mirrored half, all with hands extended accusingly.

She pushed the mirror away hurriedly. She had seen enough fantastic, mirror-formed images that day taunting her to judge what was and what was not real. And she could not forget them. They lingered in her mind, mocking her from the edges of her sanity.

Why did the Gevethen move always with this eerie entourage? Even more than with the servants the questions as to who the mirror-bearers were and where they came from, seemed unanswerable. As for how they had become what they had become, or why, these were questions whose answers were beyond even conjecture.

She drifted back to the long couch, her mind beginning to flounder. Not that she allowed herself too much time pursuing these strange questions; her education in the Ennerhald had made her deeply pragmatic. She would watch and listen constantly and if answers existed, then doubtless she would learn them in time. She managed to hold fear at bay by clinging to the resolutions she had made in the Watching Chamber. She must survive moment by moment until an opportunity to escape appeared, and she must find a weapon with which to destroy herself if the need arose. The thought of weapons took Jeyan's hand to her belt, but her knife had gone, along with her old clothes, and this new livery sported no weapons. Hagen had had no need for weapons, his reputation was armour enough. Jeyan was darkly amused. Until he met her, that is. Whatever else happened, that had been a deed well done. She must cling to that as well.

But she must find a weapon. She must not be left defenceless. The tray of goblets caught her eye, glittering in the dull light. She ran to it and seized one with the intention of breaking it and secreting a shard about her somewhere. But even as she picked it up she saw the futility of her action. If the Gevethen were merely taunting her, luring her with softness and hope, with the intention of tearing it away from her, then these fine clothes would be the first thing to go. She put the glass back on the tray and sat down in a chair opposite the plain mirror. It was difficult to watch moment by moment when nothing was happening.

Into the silence came, for the first time, the Gevethen's pronouncement: 'Take the Lord Counsellor to her chambers.'

Lord Counsellor!

What had they meant?

Their words tumbled after this question.

'We have known of you always.'

'You are kin.'

'You are chosen.'

And, of Hagen, 'He was flawed.'

'He served his turn.'

'One more fitting dispatched him.'

The implications were as chilling as they were

unbelievable. She ran her hand over the tunic. It was ridiculous. Indeed, if it had not been so grimly awful, it would have been laughable. How could she be anyone's Counsellor? She was well-educated but she had no training in matters of state, or the administration of public affairs. And surely they could not imagine that she would replace the monster she had just killed? Surely even they could not imagine that she would do *anything* to assist their vile regime?

'You seem uncertain, Lord Counsellor . . .'

'. . . Lord Counsellor.'

Jeyan and her reflection leapt from their seats as the voices grated into the room. The Gevethen were standing at the head of the three steps. Reflections of them flanked a widening path down the steps towards Jeyan. Despite herself, a snarl formed inside her. It never reached her throat however. Instead she felt one leg drawing back and the other bending in obeisance. Then her head was lowered. She could do nothing about either.

'This will become unnecessary in due time,' said the two voices. 'Soon you will learn the correct way to behave before your Liege Lords.'

Jeyan could feel them moving towards her. She was unable to move.

'You have eaten?'

'No . . . Excellencies.' She had to force the word out.

'Ah. Overwhelmed by the honour we have bestowed upon you. It is understandable in one so young, but you must eat. The position of Lord Counsellor is peculiarly taxing. It seeks out the frailties in its officers.'

The almost maternalistic expression of concern filled Jeyan with disgust and brought rage, thick and bitter, to her throat, though she could utter none of it.

'Still, hunger will sharpen your awareness.'

'And you are strong. Your body will sustain you well enough until you've grown accustomed to your new life. You may rise and look on us.'

Jeyan was released. Slowly she stood up. Part of her wanted to seize the glass she had just been holding, and slash it across the throats of her two tormentors, but memories of the speed and strength of the Gevethen's servants held her in check. Whatever grim game was being played here, a reckless display like that could bring it to a premature end.

She raised her head and met their gaze. The many Gevethen stared back. Abruptly, and without any signal being given that she could perceive, the mirror-bearers were moving frantically. The crowd milled and jostled as if exchanging views about what they had just seen. Red lips opened and closed silently, white hands fluttered like trapped doves. Then there was stillness again.

'You have such rage in you, Jeyan Dyalith . . .'
                                        '. . . Jeyan Dyalith.'

'Soon you will be able to give it full rein against those who brought your beloved country to this pitch.'

Jeyan clenched her fists and tried to keep all emotion from her face. They were laughing at her, mocking her. She would give them nothing. *Nothing!* She would be as stone-faced as their precious servants.

A tremor of amusement passed through the watching eyes, then hands beckoned.

'Darkness closes about the city. You must stand with us while we perform our Night Vigil.'

'And be shown the Ways.'

They turned and vanished as the mirror-bearers swirled down the steps and enclosed Jeyan as they had done on the journey from the dungeon. Once again she found herself in the train of the Gevethen. Now however, where there had been a straggling train of scarecrow attendants flanking her, there was line upon line of youthful Hagens, resplendent in formal attire. Unexpectedly, a hint of pride came into the lines as she drew herself up.

Helsarn was pacing the floor outside the Watching Chamber.

'Relax, Commander,' Gidlon said, smiling knowingly and laying heavy emphasis on Helsarn's new rank. 'Waiting is something you have to become very good at in the service of their Excellencies. It's not given to us senior officers to be able to ease the burden of our tasks by riding out into the city and cracking a few heads.' He gave Helsarn a slap on the back.

There was enough force in it for Helsarn to feel the pent-up anger and frustration in the man. To receive promotion as he had was virtually unknown and would obviously add a wild, complicating factor to the general jockeying for position amongst the Guards that had started as soon as Hagen's death became common knowledge. What companies would Helsarn be given, now that the five commanders had become six? What status would he be given amongst the existing Commanders, for the corps of Commanders, though small, was responsible for administering the policies laid down by the Gevethen and wielded considerable power within the city. Most importantly, what ambitions did Helsarn have? For though internal squabbling occupied much of the Commanders' time, they battled constantly too with their counterparts in the army with the intention of extending the limits of their authority ultimately to include the army. It was no secret that the Gevethen's ambitions lay far beyond the control of Nesdiryn and, to those intimately acquainted with the way they worked, there was little doubt that they would meet with success in whatever venture they undertook. Their coming to power in Nesdiryn had been a leisurely affair, but their consolidation and expansion of it in the last few years had been breathtaking. It was only a matter of time before the Count, persistent irritant though he was, was destroyed, then eyes could be turned firmly outward from the mountains and there would be substantial prizes to be gained by whoever rose high in the command of what would surely be a greatly expanded military force.

Helsarn's ambitions however, were not something to which any of them were privy. Progress through the ranks of the Guards was not made by publicly airing such matters and Helsarn with his previous murky history in the Count's Guards was particularly tight-lipped. Gidlon for one had concluded that it would be foolish to make an enemy of him. He might be the most junior Commander, but he *had* found Hagen's assassin – a measure either of his ability or his luck, but not to be ignored, whichever it was – and he *had* been appointed by the Gevethen themselves. Perhaps that had been only a whim, but no one could read the actions of the Gevethen, and who could say what plans they had for him?

Helsarn laid a hand heavily on Gidlon's shoulder in imitation of friendship. 'I'm beginning to realize that,' he said. 'And I appreciate you staying with me on my first duty watch as Commander.'

'Their Excellencies may well have ended their vigil and left the Watching Chamber,' Gidlon said, testing the new Commander for his response.

'They have,' Helsarn replied, tightening his grip on the smaller man's shoulder. 'They left by the Throne Door some time ago.'

Servants running to curry favour with this new star that

the Gevethen have hoisted into their constellation, Gidlon thought. Or have they been in his service all along? Perhaps he would be wiser to leave Helsarn to his watch and start questioning his own contacts amongst the servants.

'They took the assassin with them,' Helsarn added, after a significant pause. 'She's currently in Lord Counsellor Hagen's quarters.'

'*She!*' Gidlon broke free from Helsarn's grip and turned to face him, his expression disbelieving.

'She,' confirmed Helsarn with some relish. 'The Lord Counsellor was done to death by a woman. Compared to you and I, a slip of a girl almost.'

Gidlon made no attempt to disguise his surprise. 'But who?' he managed after a while.

Helsarn shrugged. 'Some creature out of the Ennerhald. A wild creature, I might add. Hagen's not the only one she and her dogs killed.'

Helsarn's pacing had carried them some way from the door to the Watching Chamber and the Guards. Unexpectedly, Gidlon smirked. 'The puritanical old devil must have been prescient,' he said, very softly. 'No wonder he never went near women. He must've known one of them would be the end of him.' He gave a brief, strangled chuckle then, as he turned Helsarn about and began strolling back to the door, his face became alarmed.

'You left their Excellencies alone with an assassin?' he exclaimed.

'Their Excellencies ordered it,' Helsarn replied, slightly unsettled by Gidlon's brief display of mirth. 'Just like they ordered me to wait here. I doubt they're in any danger from her. She made a dash for it on the way up from the dungeons, but those mirror-bearers ...'

'I know about the mirror-bearers,' Gidlon interrupted uneasily. He gave a hasty disclaiming wave as if anxious to get away from the subject. 'Well, if their Excellencies ordered you to wait, then wait you must. Many privileges come to a Commander, but disobeying orders isn't one of them.' He laid a hand on Helsarn's arm, genuinely friendly this time. 'It's nearly time for their Night Vigil, the normal duty Guards will take over then.' His voice fell. 'When you're free, come to my quarters. There's a lot we need to talk about.'

The sound of a door closing echoed along the passage before Helsarn could reply. 'They're coming back,' he said, signalling quickly to the Guards who came immediately to attention.

'I wonder what they've done to her,' Gidlon said out of the corner of his mouth. The question had been occurring to Helsarn continually since the Gevethen and Jeyan had disappeared into the Watching Chamber, but he kept his eyes firmly fixed on the bend in the passage and remained silent.

Then the passage was suddenly much longer and the Gevethen, surrounded by the fluttering attentions of the mirror-bearers, were approaching along its narrow perspective. Slowly, Helsarn and Gidlon sank to their knees and lowered their heads. The procession halted as it drew alongside them.

The two voices spoke. 'Commander Helsarn you are one of the blessed few, for He has chosen to smile upon you. To you He gave the honour of seeking out and bringing forth our new Lord Counsellor.'

Helsarn's mind raced. What were they talking about? He resorted to a time-proven formula. 'It is honour enough that I serve your Excellencies,' he said.

'Your humility becomes you, Commander, and your service is recognized, but know that we are all here to do only His will.'

Helsarn's every instinct was to remain silent, but there was a quality in their voices that seemed to be demanding a reply. He resorted to the truth.

'Forgive me, Excellencies. I'm just a simple soldier, I don't understand.'

'Nor should you seek to, Commander. Obedience is all . . .'

'. . . Obedience is all.'

'Remain here . . .'

'. . . Remain here.'

'Commander Gidlon, dismiss these men. Commander Helsarn will guard our Vigil.'

And they were gone.

As the procession passed through the doors of the Watching Chamber, both Helsarn and Gidlon looked up. For an instant they saw a row of slim figures, each like a young Hagen, then the image was gone and they were looking at a wavering row of themselves receding into the distance, gaping.

Jeyan cast about her. She had been too bewildered and frightened to pay any great heed to the Watching Chamber when she first entered, but now she must try to stay calm and look for doors, windows, anything that might prove useful should an opportunity for flight present itself. Despite the uncertain impression she had had of the place however, with its eerie lighting and innumerable shadows and reflections, it seemed to her that it was different now. Its intrinsic confusion was different though she could not have said in what way. Surely these precarious towers of mirrors could not have been moved? Nor the twisted lantern trees that seemed to be rooted deep into the floor? She tried to recall the Hall as it had been when it was the Count's Audience Chamber but she had only been there once or twice when she was young and the memories did not help. Nor was she given much time in which to make her survey, for the mirror-bearers were hustling her forward urgently, moving now to the left, to the right, turning about.

Finally they stopped, somewhere near the middle of the Hall, Jeyan judged, looking up into the lantern-tinged gloom above. Nothing was to be gained by looking around, for the mirror-bearers were all about her surrounding her with a bizarre assembly of the Gevethen and herself.

The crowd stirred uneasily then parted. Two mirrors moved through the gap. They were larger than the largest of those carried by the mirror-bearers and were being held in such a way that they reflected only the high lanterns that lit the Chamber. It was as though night itself, black and starlit, was intruding into the gathering. Jeyan did not move, curiosity briefly setting aside the fear and anger that was sustaining her.

The mirrors stopped in front of two of the many Gevethen and as their reflections appeared, so all the others slowly turned away and were gone. Jeyan screwed up her eyes. Was this the first time she had seen so few of her captors?

All movement stopped, save for the two mirrors, which came together until they touched. The line of their joining, sharp and black, slowly shrank and disappeared.

The two pairs of figures stood like a quartet of statues, staring fixedly at one another for what seemed to Jeyan to be an interminable time. Their stillness seeped into her and though her mind told her she might now be able to flee, she knew that her body would not respond.

'Lord Counsellor.' The voices raked through her. She stepped forward, feeling peculiarly exposed without the crowd of her own likenesses to support her. Tentatively her reflection emerged from behind the two motionless images of the Gevethen. For a moment she faltered, as she saw again a youthful Hagen arising sternly out of the darkness to stand by the side of his masters. The figure grimaced at her as she forced the thought from her mind. She was who she was. The image of Hagen had been that of the uniform not the face and it had burned into her mind with such intensity as she had steeled herself for the assassination that she could not now easily dissociate the clothes from the wearer.

The Gevethen moved apart and motioned her forward so that she stood between and slightly in front of them. Hands touched the broken rings which hung about the Gevethen's necks then floated up to come to rest on Jeyan's shoulders. There was a fearful symmetry about the three figures that stood in front of her. Though she could not see it, she sensed that the edge of the two mirrors passed vertically through her image and a momentary panic ran through her that should the mirrors move apart, she would be split in two.

There was another long silence, then: 'What do you see, Lord Counsellor?'

The young Hagen swallowed. Its throat was dry.

'I see reflections of myself and your Excellencies,' Jeyan replied. 'And the lights behind.'

'Reflections.'

'Ah!'

The Gevethen moved forward, easing Jeyan ahead of them until she was so close to her reflection that she could see little more than its eyes. Still she could see no sign of the line where the two mirrors joined and, still with her, was the fear of what would happen if they moved apart. Warm breath struck her face. It must be her own, she reasoned, standing so close to the mirror. But there was not even a hint of mistiness on the smooth surface. There was only Jeyan, staring at herself.

'What do you see, Lord Counsellor?' The question came again.

Despite her every endeavour, Jeyan began to tremble again. The hands tightened about her shoulders, coldly supporting her. The trembling ceased. 'I see myself, Excellencies,' she managed to say. 'My reflection.'

'Ah!'

'But which is yourself and which the reflection, Lord Counsellor?'

'I don't understand, Excellencies.'

'Close your eyes, child.'

'But . . .'

'Close your eyes.'

Briefly the idea of struggling free returned to her, but the hands on her shoulders forbade all movement. She closed her eyes.

Alone in the darkness she waited for some awful impact. Some punishment at last for what she had done – some pain, some torment. But nothing happened. There was only the weight of the hands on her shoulders and the warm breath striking her face, a little more frequently now.

Her ears began to fill with the sound of her breathing. The pressure on her shoulders began to pulse to its hastening rhythm. Then, before she realized what was happening, she was being moved forward.

A soft hissing filled the Watching Chamber, like the release of a long-held breath, as the mirror-bearers moved forward to form a protective circle about the two mirrors made one. None gazed into it, but had they done so they would have seen the reflections of the Hall's many lanterns and, faintly, fading like ripples in water, the retreating backs of the Gevethen and their new Lord Counsellor.

Chapter 20

'That way.'

There was urgency in Ibryen's voice and, without reference to his companions, he set off up the hill. Rachyl and the Traveller watched him for a moment, then, when it seemed he had no intention of slowing down, they hurried after him.

'What's the matter? Where are you going?' Rachyl asked when she finally caught up with him.

'This way,' Ibryen said, pointing, but not stopping.

Rachyl frowned. 'We can't go much further,' she protested. 'This ground's treacherous enough. There's no saying what it'll be like up there. And the light'll be gone soon. We should camp here. Tackle this fresh in the morning.'

Ibryen did not reply. Rachyl looked at the Traveller. He in his turn looked at Ibryen.

'What have you heard, Count?' he asked.

'I don't know,' Ibryen replied edgily, still ploughing forward. 'But something's changing. Something's . . .' he shook his head '. . . either beginning or ending, I don't know. But we mustn't delay. We must—'

'Must what?' Rachyl burst out, seizing his arm and forcing him to a halt. 'Break our necks going headlong up this slope in the dark?' She started to shout. 'Not that

293

we need anyone to break a neck – an ankle will do out here. And it'll be me who has to carry you back to camp. What in pity's name are you doing?'

For a moment, Ibryen seemed set to tear free from her grip and start off again, then he looked from Rachyl's angry face to the Traveller. 'Can't you hear it?' he asked, almost plaintively.

The Traveller shook his head. 'It's getting fainter and fainter. Whatever it is, it *is* this way, but I doubt I'd have found it so easily if you hadn't pointed it out.' He gave Rachyl an apologetic glance. 'Something *is* happening. I don't think we have time on our side.'

'We don't have light on our side either,' Rachyl announced, through clenched teeth. 'Nor terrain.' She took Ibryen's other arm and only just stopped herself from shaking him violently. Without releasing him, she paused to calm herself. 'Listen, Cousin,' she said eventually, and speaking with great deliberation. 'I don't know what's driving you, but I trust you and I'll back you up, you know that. But unless you're absolutely sure a dangerous night scramble up this mountainside is going to give us a definite strategic advantage against the Gevethen, then we should camp here, now.'

She spoke not as to her Liege Lord and Commander, but as to an obdurate child. Her manner reached Ibryen. He cast an anxious look up towards the darkening mountain then sagged. 'Yes,' he said fretfully. 'I suppose you're right.'

'*Suppose* doesn't come into it,' Rachyl retorted, her anger slipping through.

The Traveller intervened. 'That's settled then. Let's find somewhere to camp before it's completely dark.' He did not wait for any discussion but motioned his companions away from the broken edge of the forest. Ibryen moved after him and Rachyl followed, watching Ibryen warily.

Within minutes the Traveller had found a small clearing and was busy lighting a fire. It flared up quickly and, with much noise crackling, shrank the world to a flickering dome. The Traveller produced a pan from somewhere and was soon heating up a stew made out of the remains of the rabbit, some of the tubers on which they had break-fasted, and a variety of odds and ends that he had collected during their journey that day. The savoury smell that filled the firelit clearing took all minds away from their present concerns. 'Tree-scented mountain air, fine walking, and the subtle blending of nature's gifts. What more could one want?' the Traveller said, lifting a small spoonful to his lips with relish. 'Here's to refined and discerning appetites.'

Rachyl gave him a puzzled look, then delved into her pack and produced a small loaf of bread. She tore it up and thrust the mutilated portions at her companions. 'Here's to greed,' she said, holding a plate out impatiently. The Traveller gave a little sigh and looked sorrowfully at the stew before giving it a final stir and ladling it out.

'I'm sorry,' Ibryen said, as they ate. 'I don't know what happened to me just then. Something seemed to take hold of me and demand . . .' He paused.

'Demand what?' the Traveller asked.

'I'm not sure,' Ibryen said vaguely. 'That I go to it . . . listen to it . . .' He shrugged.

'Is it still there?'

'Yes. But I seem to have more control over it. Over what I . . . feel. While I have you two to hold me here.'

'You don't sound too sure,' Rachyl said, wiping out her dish with the remains of her bread. She crammed it into her mouth.

'Did you enjoy that, my dear?' the Traveller asked caustically.

Rachyl smacked her stomach. 'Excellent,' she declared, leaning back against a tree. She peered into the pan. 'All gone, has it? Pity. We must take some of these herbs back to the camp. In fact, I think I'll suggest we make you duty cook when we get back.'

'I've rarely been so honoured,' the Traveller replied in the same acid vein.

Rachyl grinned, then looked at Ibryen, still eating thoughtfully. 'What's the matter, Cousin?' she said, her heartiness turned to concern. 'Explain. What do you mean, *we* hold you here?'

Ibryen replied to the Traveller. 'It's almost as if there are two parts to me. One, here, now. The other, wandering somewhere, lost.' He held up a cautionary hand to Rachyl. 'It's all right. I'm neither crazy, nor sick. I've thought perhaps I might be over the last few days, but it's like when you're wandering the ridges in the mist and you see a vague light, in the sky, as you think. And as you get closer to it, it gets clearer until, without you noticing the change, it's not a light in the sky any more, it's a lake shining in the valley below. Now I'm closer, things are clearer, less disorienting.'

It was an analogy that Rachyl appreciated. Ibryen's brow furrowed. 'Not as clear as a mountain lake, unfortunately. It's still a strange light in the sky, but it *is* there. It isn't my eyes or my imagination playing tricks.'

The Traveller leaned forward earnestly, the firelight deepening the lines on his face and throwing his eyes into deep shadow. 'Tell us what you can of this other place you're in.'

Ibryen smiled broadly. 'Still misty,' he said. 'And that's the best I can do.' The Traveller looked inclined to pursue the matter but decided against it. 'But we must leave early and press on urgently,' Ibryen added. 'Something is slipping away. Moving from here and disappearing now into the mist. And it mustn't. We *must* find it. And soon.'

Ibryen was troubled with strange visions again that night. He was alone in the mist, greyness all about him. And the Gevethen were there too, somewhere, as lost as he was. He looked around, but nothing was to be seen. Yet there were voices all about him. Briefly, two of them became Rachyl and the Traveller talking soft and low – tenderly? The campfire was in front of him, glowing through the haze. Then a haunting music floated out of nowhere and swept up the orange glow of the fire and, wrapping it all about him, carried him into places beyond. Places between the pulse of all things, where he debated with learned men, and where great truths were revealed to him, from the Great Heat at the Beginning of All Things to the dancing creation of the mountains and the seas, and all the life that dwelt in them, some seen, some not.

It was so simple, so clear.

And flawed!

He was suddenly wide awake. And the thoughts that were not his were going ... were gone. They slithered from his memory and vanished like smoke in a breeze as he strove to grasp them.

He was merely himself again: Ibryen, deposed Count of Nesdiryn, with his Cousin Rachyl and the strange Traveller trekking through long-untrodden mountains.

And too old to be sleeping out like this, he mused ruefully as his shoulder told him he had rolled on to a stone during the night. Gingerly he levered himself up on

297

one elbow and cast a pained eye at the sky. It was dull, but clear. Not yet sunrise, but the fine weather looked as though it might still be with them. That was good. At the moment, he didn't want to think too closely about the consequences of continuing this journey if the weather turned bad. They must make as much progress as they could today.

Even as the thought formed, the call was about him again, urging him forward.

'We are coming,' he replied inwardly, not knowing how he did it.

The call quivered and a rush of familiar emotions ran through him.

'We are coming,' he said again. Then he drew himself back to the cold dawn mountainside and stood up, shivering. Stretching himself elaborately to ease the stiffness out of his limbs, he glanced around the little camp. He was alone. Rachyl's blanket was draped across a branch, but neither she nor the Traveller were to be seen. He reached down and checked the fire. The grey ashes had been carefully raked and it was still hot underneath. He was touched by the thought that they had awoken early and once again left him undisturbed while they went about preparing breakfast. However, the Commander in him determined not to let it happen again. He was not the invalid of the party; he must pull his weight.

'Ah, you're awake.' It was Rachyl. She was smiling and looked very happy. She held up two partly plucked birds. 'Caught these myself,' she said proudly, brushing feathers off her tunic. 'Still got the knack. Can't have him doing everything for us, can we?' She winked. 'Finish these and draw them, will you?'

Taken aback by both her demeanour and the two still-warm birds thrust into his hands, Ibryen answered the questions the wrong way round. 'Yes. No.' Then he managed to gather a little authority into his voice. 'And by the same token, you must stop letting me lie asleep after wake-up.'

'Yes, sir!' Rachyl replied with the heavy respect of complete insincerity.

A jaunty whistling speared into the little clearing before Ibryen could assert himself further. 'A fine day ahead of us,' the Traveller said, clapping his hands together and smiling.

'Everyone's extremely cheerful this morning,' Ibryen said, almost churlishly.

'A good night's sleep, Count, that's all. An appreciation of . . . simple pleasures.' The Traveller patted him on the back and chuckled to himself. When he saw Ibryen fumbling with the birds his manner became quieter. 'How does he cook?' he asked Rachyl.

'Badly,' Rachyl replied without giving the question any thought. 'Don't worry, I'll do them. You brighten that fire up.'

'You'll have to make the most of this meal,' the Traveller said as he bent over the ashes. 'I've picked a few more roots and bits and pieces, but once we get above the trees you'll have to start using your supplies.'

'We?' queried Ibryen. 'You too, I presume.'

The Traveller was dismissive. 'Yes, but I need a lot less than you. And I can live on grasses and mosses if I have to. I belong here, don't forget, just like those birds and the rabbit.'

Rachyl shot him a glance. 'I thanked the birds,' she said.

The fire blazed up and the Traveller nodded with genuine appreciation. 'I know you did,' he said. 'I heard you.' Then, imitating the fire, mischief flared into his eyes.

'As I heard you catching them. Thought it was another avalanche.'

Rachyl contented herself with a scowl as she snatched the birds back from Ibryen's unhappy fingers.

Though the breakfast was relaxed and pleasant, there was an undertow of restlessness and they did not linger unduly. The sun was just beginning to strike the tops of some of the higher peaks when they broke camp and they were soon moving steadily uphill. For most of the way they kept to the edge of the forest to avoid the chaotic disturbance that marked the passage of the avalanche. Ibryen however, found himself increasingly drawn towards the lower shoulder of the mountain and as they drew nearer to the treeline, he directed them across the damaged swathe. It was slow, unpleasant walking, across loose mildewed rocks and over rotting tree trunks and dead undergrowth tangled about with creepers and new foliage. Progress was not helped by a series of fast-moving but wide and shallow streams still uncertain about the route they should be taking through this comparatively new landscape.

Eventually reaching the other side they began moving up the rocky shoulder without pause. It was steep and craggy but still negotiable with care. For the first time, Ibryen gained a small insight into the Traveller's climbing abilities as the little man clambered effortlessly from rock to rock while he and Rachyl laboured along behind. Further, he had an uncanny eye for routes which made the climb much easier than it might have been. Nevertheless, despite the guidance he was giving, he was constantly having to stop and wait for them although he showed no impatience at their relative sluggishness. The sun was high when they reached the top of the shoulder and the view of the surrounding peaks and valleys was breathtaking. Despite the cold wind that was blowing over the ridge, they stood for some time gazing around before taking a brief rest in the lee of a small outcrop.

Ibryen took the opportunity to examine the record that Rachyl had been keeping of the route they had followed so far, then they went over it together verbally, to ensure that it was clear in their minds. 'We're moving generally south-east,' Rachyl announced. Then, with a hint of irony: 'How much longer before we reach this Girnlant of yours, Traveller?'

'Quite a time,' the Traveller replied, tilting his head back as though he were scenting the air. 'It's more south, south-west from here. If we carry on long enough in this direction we'll come to the ocean.'

Rachyl looked impressed. 'I've never seen the ocean. Have you?'

'Yes.'

'What's it like?'

The Traveller raised an eyebrow. 'Very flat,' he replied. 'And wet.'

Rachyl's eyebrows came together. 'Very droll. What's it really like?'

The Traveller thought for a moment. 'It's not my place,' he said. 'I find it beautiful but very frightening. It's like and unlike the mountains. Where the mountains are sheer and immobile, the ocean's flat and full of movement. But they're both powerful and indifferent, full of grim chances that can sweep you aside like—' he pulled a stray feather clinging to his sleeve and released it into the wind; it leapt away from him, flying high, twisting and turning, then it was gone. '—like the merest feather. And too, if you don't pay heed, forget who and where you are . . .' He drew a finger across his throat. Then he became agitated. 'And not a foothold to be found anywhere. How people can get into boats and go wobbling across it defies me. The merest thickness of timber between them and those dark cold depths.' He concluded with a violent shudder.

Rachyl, who could swim and who had rafted on mountain lakes, was about to allow herself a touch of disdain but the Traveller forestalled her. 'It's not like the puddles you find round here. Even the largest are as nothing. I've stood high above where the mountains and the sea meet. Eavesdropped on their mighty discourse. Heard the rumbling belly of the water and the creaking roots of the mountains. Listened to the whispering chatter of the air and the spuming spray. Watched waves many times the height of your Council Hall storming in like crazed horses and smashing into cliffs, time after time, then fuming up them as if they were trying to bring the peaks themselves down.'

Both Rachyl and Ibryen were listening enthralled by the Traveller's passionate description. 'Will we see it?' Rachyl asked.

The Traveller smiled and shook his head. 'Wherever we're going, it's much nearer here than the ocean.' When Rachyl looked disappointed, he raised a hand for silence, and tilted his head to one side. 'Close your eyes and listen. Both of you. There's enough material here for me to bring the sea to you.'

Ibryen was reluctant. 'We should be pressing on,' he said, making to stand up.

'The merest moment, Count,' the Traveller protested. 'Close your eyes. Listen.'

Seeing Rachyl's eyes already closed. Ibryen gave the Traveller a reproachful look then closed his own. For a few seconds there was only the sound of the wind buffet-

ing around their shelter, then, changing almost imperceptibly, it became the sound of pounding breakers and the
hiss of swirling spray. At its height, the din of the waves
was counter-pointed by the high-pitched cries of squabbling gulls. Neither Ibryen nor Rachyl could have said
how long they listened to the Traveller's strange creation,
but, as mysteriously as it came, so it faded, until there was
only the sound of the wind again.

When they opened their eyes, the Traveller was looking
at them expectantly. 'Only a rough outline,' he said.

Ibryen smiled appreciatively and Rachyl applauded.
'How did you *do* that?' she asked.

The Traveller stood up, laughing. 'Not an answerable
question,' he replied, then, to Ibryen: 'Which way now?'

Ibryen levered himself to his feet and cast about briefly
before pointing. 'Clearer now by far, and still urgent,' he
said.

'You're sure it's that way?' Rachyl asked.

'Yes.'

'Pity,' Rachyl muttered. For Ibryen was pointing away
from the peak they were standing on, and towards its
neighbour which was higher by far and snow-capped. 'We
can't get up there,' she said. 'There's too few of us and
we've not enough equipment.'

'Oh, I don't know . . .' the Traveller began.

'I do,' Rachyl said unequivocally. 'There are limits to
this venture, and going to the top of that is one of them.
Perhaps you can make it on your own, I don't know. If
you crossed the Hummock, then I suppose it's possible.
Maybe *I* could make it, with a team.' She flicked a thumb
at Ibryen. 'But he couldn't.'

Ibryen had too accurate a knowledge of his own climbing skills to be offended by this seemingly casual judgement. He stepped away from his companions and stared

up at the mountain. Rachyl and the Traveller watched him in silence.

The need of whatever was calling, filled him.

'You're right,' he said eventually. 'It *is* too dangerous. But this is the way we have to go.' He looked at the Traveller. 'What do you hear?' he asked.

'Precious little,' the Traveller replied. 'It's been fading steadily since we set out.'

'But this way?'

The Traveller nodded. Ibryen turned to Rachyl. 'We'll go as far as we can,' he said. 'If the conditions become too difficult . . .' He pulled a sour face and shrugged. 'We'll just have to turn back.'

'Go back with nothing?'

More reproach came through in her voice than she had intended. Ibryen felt the weight of his responsibilities return redoubled. 'Go back with nothing,' he confirmed coldly, straightening up. 'At the worst, that's what it'll have to be. This has always been little more than a scouting trip.'

'I think we left higher expectations than that behind us,' Rachyl said, the reproach continuing.

Ibryen scowled. 'This isn't the time for this debate,' he said. 'More than ever I know there's something very strange out there.' He pointed. 'Something powerful and something that needs help. If we can't reach it, or if we reach it and it's of no value to us against the Gevethen, then so be it. *I* can't leave its . . . call . . . unanswered. We take back to the village what we take back, and deal with what we find there as we find it. *Now* we continue until circumstances bring about a conclusion. All else is needless speculation.'

He swung his pack on to his back and strode off. Rachyl hesitated for a moment as if she had something further to say, then she set off after him in silence. The Traveller watched them both for a while then extended his hands into the air. 'Go now, be free again. And take my thanks with you,' he said softly, and once more the air was filled with the sound of breaking waves and screeching gulls. It soared high above its creator, twisting and turning, until it was gone – dispersed into the myriad other tiny sounds from which it had been woven.

The three travellers walked on in silence for some considerable time, Ibryen carrying his dark mood like a shield. Though the call that was drawing him onward was clearer than it had ever been, so the call of his duty to his people seemed to grow relentlessly as he moved steadily away from them. It brought doubt and anxiety with it, weighing him down. Rachyl too was withdrawn. It troubled her she had aired her concerns and thus burdened her cousin when she had intended only to support him. But many things had changed for her since the arrival of the Traveller, and the prospect of returning to life in the embattled village with its grim, albeit necessary routines, disturbed her in ways she could not define. Even the Traveller was quieter than usual, walking at the rear, head lowered, perhaps regretting the fact that he could not give freedom to his companions as easily as he had to the nebulous components of his seascape.

And the mountain they were approaching seemed to mock them all with its cold and hulking indifference. As the day passed, it took on an element of their darkness as clouds began to form about its summit and, though the weather about them remained fine and sunny, the three walkers found themselves moving steadily further underneath this grey canopy.

Ironically, and despite the mountain's dark welcome, once they started to climb again their various moods began to lighten. The Traveller's nimbler gait carried him back into the lead as he sought out the easiest ways forward while Rachyl and Ibryen came together to share a common bond of mild envy at the little man's agility and seemingly boundless energy.

After a while, the sunnier regions of the mountains moving further away from them, and their height up the mountain having increased considerably, the wind became both stronger and colder and they were obliged to stop and change into warmer clothes. Nothing was said of the sullen silence they had spent much of the day sharing.

'Another hour and we'll be almost on the snowline,' Rachyl said.

'And in need of somewhere to camp,' Ibryen added.

It was an accurate estimate. When they stopped an hour later, streaks of snow were to be seen in hollows here and there, and a low, brilliant sun was flooding in under the mountain's cloud, washing out such colour as there was in the rocks and throwing long, fantastic shadows. It seemed to wash out also the remains of the inner gloom that had darkened the day for the three companions as they gazed around at the transformed landscape. It would have been possible for them to climb a little higher with the help of the fading light, but they decided against it. Once the sun was gone, the clouds overhead would darken the mountain quickly and the going would become very difficult, not least because of the thickening snow they could see ahead.

They found an area out of the wind, and Ibryen produced the small tent that he had been carrying. 'It's a touch intimate, but it'll take the three of us,' he said.

The Traveller looked at it critically and then tested the fabric between his forefinger and thumb. 'Not bad,' he conceded. 'But I'll decline your offer, Count, if you don't mind.' He patted his pack. 'I have my own protection against the elements, and I tend not to sleep very much anyway. I'm afraid you'd find me a restless bedfellow.' He winked at Rachyl who turned away from Ibryen and, shielding her eyes with her hand, began peering towards the sun. The Traveller laughed. 'And I doubt I'd be able to resist doing something with your snores.'

Rachyl turned round, indignant. 'I do not snore,' she proclaimed forcefully.

The Traveller retreated, waving a self-reproaching finger. 'Ah! Of course. My mistake. I meant your susurrant breathing, my dear, with its many subtle textures, like gossamer tinged with the innocent peace of sleep . . .'

'*Nor* am I your dear,' Rachyl added grimly, cutting across his laudation. 'Come on,' to Ibryen. 'Let's get this tent up and some food inside us.'

They ate well enough, having with them the remains of the two birds, some tubers and herbs and enough kindling to light a small fire. It lacked the relaxed quality of their previous meals however, not for want of either geniality or decent food, but because of the wind. Now resolute and full of the remains of winter it kept buffeting round into the lee of the rocks where they had set up camp, shaking them all like an unwelcome guest. The fire, encased in an impromptu oven the Traveller had made from stones, snarled and roared at it for some time, like an ill-tempered guard dog, though eventually it sank back, spent, and became a dull red glow. Such light as they had came mainly from a small lantern that Ibryen had lit as the daylight finally faded.

No one seemed disposed to talk a great deal, each being rapt in their own thoughts. Rachyl drew her sword and examined it. The blade was dull except for the edge which glinted brightly in the lanternlight. She tested it carefully with her thumb, then took a neatly folded cloth from a leather bag on her belt and began wiping the blade with it. A pungent, oily smell filled the tiny camp.

'You anticipate needing that?' the Traveller asked after watching her for some time, his expression unreadable.

'Oh yes,' Rachyl replied, sheathing the sword and delicately folding the cleaning rag. She looked up and met the Traveller's gaze. 'Perhaps not within the next few minutes, or even on this whole journey, but yes, I anticipate using it again – many times until the Gevethen are defeated.'

'Or you're dead.'

Rachyl nodded. 'Or I'm dead,' she agreed without emotion.

'A waste,' the Traveller said.

Rachyl closed her eyes briefly then opened them and held him with a relentless stare. 'No. Not so. I'd have preferred another direction for my life, but who could say where and what I might be now if things hadn't gone the way they did. We all of us do what we do because of where we are, and nothing's to be served by howling to the moon about it. It would have been worse than a waste for me to sit idly by while the Gevethen destroyed everything I'd ever cared for.' She spoke quietly and without either the passion or bitterness that often coloured her speech when she talked of the Gevethen.

The Traveller held her gaze gently for a little while then lowered his eyes and looked into the dying fire. 'It was an insensitive remark. I'm sorry. I live a simple and selfish life. I'm still not fully used to being amongst people again. It's so complicated.'

Ibryen watched and listened to the exchange, sensing a deeper meaning in it than just the words. But he was too

308

troubled with his own concerns to give it too much heed. Though he had somehow learned to set himself apart from the call that had drawn him here, it was not easy and the need within the call was becoming more intense, more disturbing.

'Enough,' he said, forcing it aside again. 'We'll tell you when you're causing offence, Traveller. Why don't you . . .' he waved his arms vaguely, in search of an idea '. . . teach us that whistling language of yours?'

'Yes,' Rachyl agreed, abruptly enthusiastic.

Her enthusiasm was not shared by the Traveller however, who looked at the supplicants rather as if they had asked him to teach a rock how to swim.

'It's very difficult,' he claimed uncomfortably. 'I wouldn't know where to start.'

'Yes, you would. Go on.' Rachyl's arm reached across the fire and pushed him, uncharacteristically girlish. It was not an argument that could be withstood and for some time thereafter the mountain rang to a mixture of penetrating whistles and laughter.

'It's no good,' Rachyl conceded finally, wiping tears from her eyes. 'I'm out of breath, sweating like a bull, and my jaw's aching.'

Ibryen was little better, rubbing his face and laughing. He nodded in earnest agreement. The Traveller was looking as much bemused as amused. 'I don't see what the problem is,' he said. 'This is very elementary. All you have to do is—'

'No more, no more!' Ibryen protested, still laughing. 'We'll be foaming at the mouth if we carry on. I'm afraid we'll have to admit defeat and stick to our crude signalling language.'

'It goes against the grain to give up on you so soon,' the Traveller said, 'but at least you've fulfilled one requirement of the language already – you're enjoying yourselves. I think you'll make good progress if you give it a few hours' practice a day for a year or so.' This brought on a further spasm of laughter.

When it died down, the Traveller smiled broadly. 'A good sound,' he said, looking around as if watching the laughter on its journey through the darkness. Then he started whistling, if whistling is the word for the full, deep sound that he made. A bouncing jig of a tune emerged which defied hands and feet to remain still and, for a few minutes, Ibryen and Rachyl could have been sat about a comfortable hearth celebrating some happy occasion, two people far removed from any form of conflict. The tune finished with a loud, high-pitched note which, as it faded, was lost under the applause of the audience.

'You're a writer of tunes as well as a Sound Carver, then?' Rachyl said.

The Traveller affected modesty. 'I'm no Sound Carver, I'm afraid – a passing fair apprentice, perhaps, but a mere shadow of a true Carver. And even the song isn't mine.' He leaned forward confidentially. 'I learned it not long ago, from a man in a dream.' He cocked his head on one side. 'At least I think it was a dream. As I remember, he was very insistent that it was *his* dream. Quite a disturbing experience in many ways.' He shrugged. 'Still, I'm here and he isn't, so he was probably wrong – I think. And it's an excellent tune, isn't it?' He whistled the last few measures again.

This time, as the sound died away, a gust of wind swept into their shelter, bringing a brief brightness to the dying fire and reminding them that they would be best advised to retire and let the night become dawn in the wink of an eye.

But it brought other news as well. Both the Traveller

and Ibryen started, and Rachyl reached for her sword again. For in the wind, faint but quite unmistakable, was the sound of someone whistling.

Chapter 21

Fearful of being pushed painfully against the mirror, Jeyan stiffened and prepared to resist the Gevethen's urging grip. A sudden wash of biting coldness passed over and through her, taking her breath, and she had been thrust a pace forward before her mind began to register what was happening. She had been almost touching the mirror yet there had been no impact! Nothing! Nothing except the coldness which seemed to be lingering inside her. She shivered and, unbidden, opened her eyes. At first she thought she was in absolute darkness. Then she saw, or sensed, the reflected lights of the Watching Chamber. But they were not immediately in front of her like fixed stars, they were all about her, seemingly hovering in mid-air. And they were vague and unclear, as though she were looking at them through sleep-misted eyes. Her hand had come up instinctively as she had been pushed forward and she saw it now, lit by some unseen light and with a quality about it that made it feel like someone else's. When she moved it, the strange reflections passed through it. She blinked desperately to clear her vision, but it made no difference.

And where was her own reflection?

She tried to turn round to see what had happened to the Hall, but the Gevethen's grip tightened and held her head to the front. 'You are passing through the portal that will bring you to the Gateways and thence to the Ways. You must not look back. Not yet. There is deep and awful madness here for those who are unprepared.'

Their voices were subtly changed. Was it fear she could hear in them? The prospect of there being something here of which the Gevethen were afraid was not something she wanted to think too closely about.

'What's happened?' she said. 'Where are we?'

'Near the Gateways . . .'

'. . . the Gateways.'

'Where's the Hall gone?'

There was cold amusement.

'Nowhere.'

'It is here.'

'All about us.'

'But . . .?'

'Rather you should ask, why are you here?'

She tried to drag her feet, to resist the inexorable movement forward, but nothing happened. Was she actually moving? She had the feeling of movement, but she could see nothing that could give her that impression other than the blurred images of the lanterns that hung all about her. And *they* were motionless.

Yet there were other things in this darkness. Wisps of sound, hints of voices. Voices that were speaking in many languages. Flickering lights which vanished as her eyes turned towards them.

Panic began to rise up inside her. This could not be happening. Her mind scrabbled frantically for something on which to gain a purchase other than the sustaining grip of the Gevethen. Somehow she was still standing in front of that wretched mirror. Some trick had been – was being – played on her. As a child she had seen street performers do amazing and impossible tricks, often, contrary to knowing but benign parental advice, losing money to them in the process of expounding her childish certainty. The panic subsided a little. That must be what was happening here. She must follow the advice she had eventually come to listen to – she must look to see things as they are and, in those circumstances in particular, mistrust everything she saw even then. The latter in particular presented no new problems for her.

But there had been no blandishing words here, no deceiving flourishes. Merely, 'Close your eyes,' and then that eerie coldness.

Again she blinked her eyes in an attempt to bring this place into focus, but again nothing changed. The blurred images of the lanterns still hung about her. She was still moving – or not moving – in a place which was pitch dark and yet in which there was light enough for things to be seen. Another alternative came to her. Perhaps she had simply gone mad and her mind had wandered into this place while her body was still standing in front of the mirror and gazing vacantly into it. This however, had the least ring of truth about it, not least, she reasoned, because if she had sought refuge in madness, she presumably wouldn't have brought the Gevethen with her.

'Care.'

The voices drew her back from her rambling.

'One is near.'

There was definitely fear in their voices. It occurred to her momentarily that something the Gevethen were afraid of might well prove to be her ally, but she relinquished the idea almost immediately. With Assh and Frey gone, she had no allies.

Then, without warning, she was in a world of light. Shapes of all colours were moving about her, some swift like flitting birds, some like slowly changing clouds, some like cascading, tangling ribbons. How near or far she could not have said, for there was nothing against which size could be judged. She reached out, but, like the images of the lanterns, the shapes seemed to pass through her. And with the shapes there came also sounds. The fleeting hints she had heard previously rose to become a great clamour. Sometimes it was a babbling chorus, sometimes a single voice, though she could make out no words. And, rising and falling in the background, was a noise that was perhaps thunder, perhaps a great crowd cheering, perhaps a roaring wind, perhaps something the like of which she had never even imagined.

The suddenness of the transformation made her start violently.

The Gevethen answered her question before she asked it. 'We are at the Gateway to the Ways, Lord Counsellor. Beyond here are all the things that can be, and that cannot be. The myriad worlds that lie between the worlds.' The shapes and colours about her danced to the rhythm of their words.

'I don't understand, Excellencies,' she said. 'I can see nothing but—'

'Confusion . . .'

'. . . Confusion.'

'You stand at the edges of the worlds beyond. They echo here.'

'Escape.'

'Exude.'

'But pass beyond and . . .'

The sentence remained unfinished, but fear and doubt coloured all about Jeyan.

She became aware of the Gevethen reaching out. The shapes and sounds changed in response to their movement. For an instant, Jeyan felt herself standing in a bright summer field, then at the edge of a great lake, then at the heart of a great city, but then the impressions were gone and she was gazing down what appeared to be a vast tunnel. It tapered into an unseeable distance.

'Ah.'

It was a soft exclamation of gratified desire. But even as it formed, the tunnel began to twist and convulse, as if it were the tail of some monstrous animal. Jeyan could feel the Gevethen struggling to stop this wayward movement, but the greater the effort they put forward, the more the paroxysms of the tunnel increased until finally, with a soul-wrenching screech it whirled into a giddying vortex and was gone.

Jeyan felt the Gevethen stop whatever it was they had been doing and through the tumult she heard them whispering to one another.

'This place is ours.' Petulant.

'But He tests us yet.' Fearful and resigned.

The brief exchange wrapped a cloak of human concerns about the Gevethen which unexpectedly fired Jeyan. She stood very still and made no response, sensing somehow that to acknowledge having heard it would be to die instantly in this eerie place. As it was, she felt a decision being made.

'Hold firm to us, Lord Counsellor.'

Without knowing why she did it, Jeyan brought her hands up to seize the Gevethen's hands holding her shoulders, for fear she might suddenly be relinquished. And, though she felt no change, she was in another place.

It was dark and cold.

'Where . . .?'

'Many eyes the glasses give us, to watch our foolish subjects. And many chambers they have.'

317

The answer was meaningless but it did not matter for, slowly, she was becoming aware of a brooding presence all around her. It was not that of the Gevethen, though – she still clung to their hands fearfully – yet it was familiar. There was a quality about it that she had sensed only recently. A bizarre mixture of malevolence and vanity, of weakness bolstered and shielded by great power.

It was Hagen! The Hagen whose overweening spirit she had measured as she gazed about his room. But it couldn't be! He was dead, and by her hand. She had seen him die. Exulted in it. Been captured and bound for it. The presence touched her. It *was* Hagen. She recoiled in horror, grasping desperately at the hands holding her shoulders, imploring them, but they would allow her no movement. What was this place?

'You are the misbegotten creature who brought me to this?' The words formed in Jeyan's mind. They were full of blistering hatred. Most would have quailed before such an onslaught, but, like flint to sparking flint, it served only to bring back to Jeyan her own hatred for the man she had killed. In full force, it flared up through the clamouring demands of her tottering reason and brushed aside the cautious acquiescence she had carefully nurtured before the Gevethen. It reached out through the darkness, clawing, gathering strength as she felt Hagen's presence retreat before it. But, abruptly, she was restrained. Hagen's presence began to close about her horrifically.

'You shall be the vessel of my return to the world. Within you I shall complete the work that you so sacrilegiously cut short.'

'That cannot be.' The Gevethen's icy voices cut through Hagen's ranting venom and tore him away effortlessly. 'Your place in that world is ended. Your task is completed. There can be no return for you. Perhaps when the Ways are opened again may a place be found for you as you were.' Then they were full of rage. 'And talk not of sacrilege. You are a mere servant of servants. It was an honour given to few to be allowed to serve Him as you did. That His blessing is with you is shown by your being here instead of being scattered, howling, between the worlds. You are here now to instruct the child. She is kin else she could not have come here. She will continue your work.'

'I have been betrayed.' Bitterness and rancour filled the voice.

It met only disdain. 'You are beneath such effort. Mysterious are His ways. You were the first. You were flawed. The child is less so. And still less so will be those who follow her. When there is one who can truly stand in our place, then will the Ways be opened again and then shall we be at His left hand when the great righting of the Beginning is begun.'

The words were portentous, but there was no reply. Only a sullen silence.

'Instruct well.'

And, to Jeyan, 'Learn well.'

The hands that were holding her, and to which she was clinging, were gone. Hagen wrapped all about her, she was falling. Faster and faster she fell, the darkness passing through her, possessing her. She screamed in terror, but she could hear no sound. Yet, as the touch of Hagen had rekindled her deep hatred for him, so, in the wake of her scream came the hatred she had for the Gevethen. Fuelled by the awful revelation of the continued existence of Hagen, albeit in some place that seemed to be beyond the world in which Nesdiryn lay, it drove out the darkness, and Hagen's presence shivered. She screamed again, a scream of primeval rage.

A fine tapering line of light, bright and unbearable, split

319

into the rushing darkness, like a stabbing needle. Her scream continued, though still she could hear no sound. The line widened and penetrated further and others formed at its root, spreading and spreading, tearing apart the darkness like slowly shattering glass.

She could feel consciousness slipping from her. The frenzy of the pursuit and the fighting in the Ennerhald flashed into her mind; Assh and Frey, blood-stained muzzles and wild eyes. Glinting blades. Abruptly her scream became the shrill whistle that she used to summon the dogs. The lightning-flash cracks spread and shattered the lingering fabric of the darkness that bound her. She felt herself staggering backwards.

The hands were holding her again. She was gasping desperately for breath and shaking violently. And she was gazing at her reflection in the mirror, the red-lipped moon faces of the Gevethen on either side of her, watery eyes fixed on her. For a moment, the images rippled, as though they were reflections in a disturbed pool. Then they were still, perfect again. And the Gevethen were talking.

'She is kin.'

Uncertainty. 'She is flawed.'

'She will learn.'

'Return to your quarters, Lord Counsellor.'

'Rest.'

'Ponder.'

'You will have duties soon . . .'

                     '. . . soon.'

'Much to learn . . .'

            '. . . to learn.'

Dark amusement.

The mirror-bearers folded around her and, almost oblivious to what was happening, Jeyan found herself marching from the Watching Chamber and through the Citadel amid a crowd of haunted likenesses. They accompanied her to Hagen's quarters and as before the servants had bathed and dressed her, so now they removed her uniform, dressed her in night-clothes and placed her in Hagen's bed. This time she was too shocked to resist, though she managed to stop one of the servants from extinguishing all the lanterns before they left. She needed no more darkness.

The bed was comfort such as she had not known in years, but she was scarcely aware of it. Her mind was filled totally with what had just happened. But what *had* happened? Had it all been some strange sleight of hand by the Gevethen? Were they after all no more than street entertainers who had tricked their way into power? The very foolishness of the idea was not without attraction, but it could not be thus, she knew. It was no idle trick that had taken charge of her limbs as she had knelt at their feet in the dungeons, contemplating a desperate slashing attack upon them. Nor was there any deception in the power that had marched her much of the way to the Watching Chamber. As for the force that had threatened to crush her when she had asked about the mysterious person before whom the Gevethen seemed to quail – she put a hand on her chest and took a deep breath at the memory – she did not want to think about that too closely. No, whatever else they were, the Gevethen were not charlatans. They possessed real and awful power the like of which she could not begin to understand. Power that she had never even heard of save in old tales and myths. Impossible though it seemed, she must accept that she had been carried through the two mirrors become one, and into a place that was ... where?

It did not matter. It had existed, she was certain, though her hands gripped the soft sheet she was lying on for support in the face of such a thought. It had been too solid to have the quality of a piece of trickery. And too, she had felt the Gevethen's reactions. They would not willingly have exposed their fears to her as they came to that mysterious turmoil they called the Gateway to the Ways, for the sake of a petty trick. Nor would they have shown their excitement at the opening of the great tunnel and their frustrated anger as it had vanished despite their efforts. Their whispered exchange, with its all too human quality, and the further revelation of a power beyond even them, returned to her suddenly and hung in her mind like a clarion call. Not only did it reinforce her acceptance of the alarming reality of what had happened, it also revealed to her that the Gevethen were as lost in that strange world as she was. The realization thrilled through her, turning her from fearful prey to cautious predator again. The thoughts of suicide she had been nurturing faded to be replaced by others, older and more familiar. *I'll kill you both, yet. I'll lay you dead at the feet of this . . . master . . . of yours, whoever He is.*

As for Hagen, her first reaction to realizing that he still existed had been one of horror. But so many perspectives had changed since her capture and the close contact she had had with the Gevethen, that the shock was already fading. For what was Hagen now? A misshapen spirit growling in the darkness. Further, she was protected from him in some way, perhaps even by the Gevethen themselves. She smiled at the irony into the shadowy gloom of Hagen's own room. It was fitting that such a man should come to such an end. 'May you remain there for all eternity and may the spirits of your victims rise up to torment you,' she whispered. It was the kind of dark and bloody vision that had often warmed her twilight thoughts when she was in the Ennerhald.

As she slipped finally into sleep, her last thoughts were not of Hagen, or the Gevethen. They were of something she had heard – felt – as she had splintered through the falling darkness to return to the Watching Chamber. She had grasped it tight to herself breathlessly and had hardly dared think about it since for fear that in some way the Gevethen might sense it. But, faint and distant, yet quite distinct, she had heard Assh and Frey baying, hunting.

Despite the comfort of her bed, she woke the next day as she invariably did, alert and watchful. Though the only light in the room was that of the solitary lantern, she knew that it would be just past sunrise. She lay still as the chaotic and disturbing events of the past three days rushed in upon her. For some time she tried to bring some order to them, but in vain. She could do no other than accept the reality of what had happened, but it made no more sense now than it had before, and despite her optimism of the previous night, or perhaps because of it, the future still seemed to be dark and fearful – suicide and murder sharing it equally.

Eventually, reaching no new conclusions, she managed to let her thoughts go and made to get out of bed. No sooner had she thrown the blankets back however, than the servants glided into the room. Her first reaction was to oppose them as she had the previous day, but sensing that this would be just as futile, she abandoned the idea. What followed was nevertheless as disconcerting as before, as she was undressed and bathed and then dressed in her uniform. To take her mind off the indignity of the proceedings she took the opportunity to study these strange people. She felt no need to gain friends in this place – her time in Ennerhald had taught her that no one was to be trusted, and these people were probably here as much to spy on her as help her – but she did need to learn what hierarchy existed – who did what, and for whom, who was weak or inept, who strong, who corruptible, who not.

So she co-operated, helping where she could, and constantly looking into their eyes. And she was rewarded, for there were signs to be read there. Slight, admittedly, but sufficient for a predator such as she was, made acutely sensitive by her hunger for freedom. Mainly they were signs only of fear, but there were hesitant hints of gratitude from time to time. And then there were small tasks that she was allowed to do for herself.

When the servants had finished with her they set about laying a table. Jeyan went to one of the windows and lifted the corner of a heavy curtain a little. Sunlight flooded in. She felt an agitated stir behind her and turned. The bright beam had dulled the lanternlight and the servants were standing motionless like vague shadows in a dun, unreal twilight. For a moment, Jeyan thought she was looking at an old and soiled picture, then, without knowing why, she said, 'Sorry,' and slowly closed the curtain. As the lanterns repossessed the room, the servants became real again and continued their tasks as though nothing had happened. Jeyan watched them. 'Don't you like the light?' she asked. There was no reply, though one of them turned to her briefly. For a moment, a snarling urge took hold of her to fling the curtains wide and flood these half-creatures with cleansing daylight, but she resisted it. Nothing was to be gained from such a gratuitously disturbing act and perhaps potential allies were to be lost. 'I didn't mean to upset you,' she said, making a deliberate decision to talk to them as much as possible to see what response she would get.

'I'm not Lord Counsellor Hagen, you know,' she went on. 'If it was he who insisted on your staying silent and on your dancing attendance on him at every moment like the Gevethen's mirror-bearers, this is not something I wish.' The servants stopped moving and stared at her. Their silent observation threatened to release the anger she had just stilled. It emerged in a different form. She *would* get a response! Moving to the table she picked up a knife then looked round at the still-watching servants. She spoke slowly and very deliberately. 'Lord Hagen, your erstwhile master, is dead. I killed him. Killed him with a knife that's probably lying about somewhere in this place. My dogs overturned his carriage and I jumped on to it and stabbed him as he stood in the doorway.' She pushed the knife into a loaf of bread forcefully. 'Stuck him like a pig. He was as mortal as you or I. Now he's no more. And I'm in his place.' Her announcement did not have the effect she envisaged. The servants just continued to watch her in silence. She gazed at them for some considerable time but still there was no reaction. It came to her, frighteningly, that perhaps they were used to seeing violence and remaining silent in its presence. She tried another, gentler approach. 'Many of the things you did for me, yesterday and just now, I should prefer to do for myself. It is *my* will that you speak to me and ask what I require. Do you understand?'

Again, briefly, Jeyan felt that she was staring at a picture as the servants gazed back at her blankly. Then, as if they had never stopped, they were about their tasks again.

Jeyan snatched the knife from the loaf and stabbed it twice, violently. 'Do you understand?' she shouted. At the second blow, the knife passed through the loaf and struck the plate underneath. The point screeched unpleasantly, and the servants became motionless again 'Do you understand?' she said again, more softly.

She was aware of a flicker of communication between them. One of them, a woman, turned to her. 'Lord Counsellor, it is not approved of, speaking,' she said.

Jeyan looked at her. It was the woman whose gaze had told her so much when she had recognized Hagen's uniform and tried to tear it off. Jeyan waited, but the woman did not elaborate.

'Who doesn't approve?' Jeyan asked finally.

'Their Excellencies.'

'Why?'

There was a subtle stir amongst the still-motionless group. 'Their Excellencies are not to be questioned, Lord Counsellor.'

Jeyan remembered again the weight that had threatened to crush the life out of her when she had questioned them. She nodded. 'Are you servants to their Excellencies?' she asked after some thought.

'We are not worthy. We lack the perfection for the way that will be.'

Jeyan frowned. 'What way is that?' she asked.

There was a faint hint of surprise in the woman's voice as she replied, 'The way that will come to pass. The way that their Excellencies prepare us for – when all that is imperfect in this world will be destroyed and no flaws shall exist.'

Jeyan was almost inclined to laugh at the intensity in the woman's voice when the Gevethen's words returned to her. 'We shall be at His left hand when the great righting of the Beginning is begun.' The words meant nothing to her but their utterance had been ominous and, for the few moments before she had been plunged into the darkness, grim images of purging and cleansing had possessed her. Some instinct told her to avoid the subject. It lay too near the heart of the Gevethen's true intent and to venture there recklessly could only be hazardous. She returned to the mundane. 'Are you my servants then?' she asked.

'We are the Lord Counsellor's servants,' came the reply.

Subtle difference, Jeyan noted.

'Then I should prefer that you ask me before you perform . . . intimate . . . services for me,' she said.

'Speaking is not approved of.'

Back once again at the beginning of the conversation, Jeyan put a hand to her head. Whatever authority she had over these people, she must not abuse it, she told herself sternly. 'I understand,' she said. 'I shall speak to you, then, when you are doing something I do not wish. Is that acceptable?'

She sensed another bat-wing flitter of communication between the motionless figures. The woman slowly nodded her head but there was a hint of distress in her eyes. Without knowing why, Jeyan stepped closer towards her. Scarcely moving her mouth, the woman whispered very softly, 'But commit no rashness, Jeyan Dyalith; we are theirs, not yours. We are without choice.' The exposure of this touch of humanity seemed to cause her great pain and, for some reason she could not have explained, the mention of her own name shook Jeyan like a blow. She had difficulty in keeping her emotions from her face as she moved away.

What binds these creatures? she thought. Wringing out the message had cost the woman in some way, and it told Jeyan that she must be more careful here than she ever was in the Ennerhald. Here, powers were being used which were quite beyond her comprehension. Here, a

327

patient ambush, a sudden blow and flight were of no value to her. She must start again, learn the ways of this new, far more dangerous Ennerhald. It was no joyous prospect. Try as she might, she could still see nothing in the future other than the Gevethen slain, or herself.

It was not easy to force the images from her mind. Then, like a blast of icy wind, came the realization that these two alternatives were not the only destinations at the end of the path she was on. They were merely a measure of her inability to see the future, and that could hardly be called a failing. We are without choice, the woman had said. Perhaps *they*, the servants, were, but *she* wasn't. Only a few days before, not the wildest conjecturing would have led her to imagine that after the slaughter of Hagen she would be his replacement. And it would not even have hinted at all the other things that had happened. From where she was, for all that two bloody endings dominated her thinking, the reality was that an infinite number of futures lay ahead. And if she was good at anything, it was at adapting to changing circumstances.

The insight almost made her gasp.

'What's your name?' she asked abruptly, turning back to the woman.

'It was Meirah,' the woman replied. 'But names . . .'

'. . . Are not approved of.' Jeyan finished the sentence for her acidly. Meirah did not respond and Jeyan decided against asking anything further.

The servants finished their work and left as silently as they had entered. Jeyan returned to the window and tried to draw one of the curtains fully. After a brief struggle she realized that the two curtains had been sewn together. Swearing, she thrust them upwards, but they flopped down, releasing a tumbling mist of grey dust. She was loath to eat by lanternlight when the sun was shining brightly outside and, in the end, she propped them up on a large branched candle-holder. It was a bizarrely unsuccessful experiment: the sunlight was too confined to illuminate the room and merely turned it into a dusky cave that was neither sunlit nor lanternlit.

The food that had been laid out for her was excellent though she tasted everything tentatively at first, despite the fact that she realized the Gevethen were unlikely to resort to poisoning if they wished to be rid of her.

When she had finished, the servants appeared again and cleared the table. One of them moved to the window to remove the candle-holder.

'No!' she said as he took hold of it.

He released it, but it was patently an effort and Jeyan sensed it disturbing the others. 'Thank you,' she said gently and, on an impulse, she lifted the curtain off the candle-holder, snuffing out the sunlight. It occurred to her even as she did this, to ask if the curtains might be separated so that they could be fully drawn, but she recalled Meirah's soft caution and decided against it. She *must* remember that this place was more dangerous than the Ennerhald and that she was at the absolute mercy of her captors. Little games with the servants and petty restraints would serve no real purpose other than to amuse, or give her momentary reassurance that she had some control over events. In the end, this was the Gevethen's place, and these their people – willing or coerced. If need arose, she must be prepared to sacrifice them.

After the servants had gone she tried the door. It was locked and nothing was to be seen through the keyhole. A quick search told her that there were also no windows through which an escape could be effected.

Full of resolve not to plan ahead, she was nevertheless disturbed by what happened during the rest of the day.

329

Nothing. Used to being constantly on the move and invariably in the open air, this was more of an ordeal than she would have imagined and she became gradually more restless and irritable as that day wore on. For a little while she gazed out of the window but the room was not high enough for her to see over the Citadel wall and across the city, and it was too high for her to see the courtyard below. Then she began prowling to and fro about the room, at first studying it in detail and later quite oblivious to it, her mind buzzing with plans and daydreams involving the destruction of the Gevethen. Her mood oscillated between elation and black despondency. Only her Ennerhald discipline kept her from giving voice to these changes or pounding an angry tattoo on the locked door.

When the servants arrived with her evening meal she was feeling comparatively calm. As they went about their business she watched them with an outward display of cold indifference. Internally however, she was calculating. It was purely fortuitous that the servants had found her thus. Had they arrived at some other time they might have been greeted by a Lord Counsellor either sobbing and plaintive or manically hearty. She must not risk that again. She must be in control of herself at all times no matter what the circumstances. And if she disintegrated merely because she was left alone in a room, what might she do in more testing circumstances? A lesson well-learned, she decided. She must remember her basic resolve – to be like Assh and Frey – endlessly patient, waiting for that movement, that mistake, and then pouncing.

Had she really heard Assh and Frey in the darkness?

It had seemed real.

It had *been* real. As real as anything else in the eerie world beyond this one to which she had been carried. Just as Hagen's lingering spirit was bound in the darkness so, somewhere, were the spirits of Assh and Frey. But they were not bound, they had been hunting, there was no mistaking that. She did not know what any of it meant, but the memory felt good.

The servants left as silently as they had arrived and, for a while, Jeyan picked at the food they had brought. Silently she reiterated her new creed to herself. I am confined here but there is no need for me to roam, because here I am fed. What I must not do is plan, that is merely to push my mind into the future and fasten it to things that cannot possibly be known about. It is to rely on whims and fancies when I need stark reality above all. Nor must I fret about things that I don't understand. What I must do is watch, listen, wait. Moment by moment, heartbeat by heartbeat.

The servants came and went again when she had finished but she ignored them. She sat on the long couch and leaned back.

Some hours later she was still sitting thus when the Gevethen entered the room, the mirror-bearers weaving about them. She stood up and turned to face them, then sank slowly down on to one knee and lowered her head. 'What is your will, Excellencies?' she said.

There was a long silence, then:

'Tomorrow, you will sit in judgement.'

'And as you judge, so shall you be judged.'

'Prepare yourself.'

Chapter 22

'Douse that fire, quickly!' Rachyl hissed, drawing her sword as she jumped to her feet. She placed herself in front of Ibryen, one hand extending the sword horizontally, the other held down by her side in a peculiarly protective attitude by the Traveller's head.

'No, leave it,' the Traveller said urgently, before Ibryen could respond. He reached across the fire, seized the lantern and turned it up.

'What are you doing?' Rachyl mouthed furiously, snatching at the lantern with her free hand. 'We'll be seen!'

'Precisely,' the Traveller said, taking hold of Rachyl's wrist and lifting the lantern high.

'What?' She yanked her hand free and for a moment seemed set to knock the little man to the ground. Ibryen came between them, his own sword drawn.

'Who is it?' he demanded of the Traveller.

'I don't know, Count,' the Traveller replied. 'But not your Gevethen, for sure. Nor anyone native to this part of the world.' His face looked suddenly pained in the flaring lanternlight. 'Or even to this time,' he said softly, as if to himself.

'No riddles, Traveller,' Rachyl said grimly, brushing wind-blown hair from her face. 'Any stranger in these mountains is an enemy.'

The Traveller waved an irritable hand at her then uttered a piercing, elaborate whistle. It vanished into the booming wind and he craned forward intently after it. Rachyl looked quickly and significantly at Ibryen, but he shook his head in reply and raised a finger to his lips. Rachyl scowled and returned to her search of the darkness with occasional glances at the Traveller.

'Can you hear anything?' Ibryen asked.

'Can you?' the Traveller replied, unexpectedly. Ibryen felt the voice penetrating deep into him, asking him many other questions than that in the words alone. Involuntarily, his eyes closed and almost immediately a desperate longing swept over him.

'It's here,' he heard himself saying, hoarsely.

'What?' Rachyl's voice seemed to be an unimaginable distance away.

'Come back, Count.'

Ibryen staggered as though he had suddenly been snatched back to the blustering camp from some other place by the Traveller's command. Rachyl seized his arm and held him firm, though her sword was still moving steadily through the darkness. 'What the devil's—'

'Put your sword away, Rachyl,' the Traveller said, cutting across her oath. 'Are you all right, Ibryen?'

'Yes,' Ibryen replied, gently removing Rachyl's hand. 'But what's happening?'

'Journey's end, I suspect,' the Traveller said, though his tone was anxious and his manner uncharacteristically fretful. He turned back to the night and whistled again; this time it was so loud that Ibryen and Rachyl put their fingers to their ears. Again there was no reply that they could hear.

'We'll have to search for whoever it is,' the Traveller said. He answered Rachyl's protest before she made it. 'I told you, it's no enemy. No one lives in these mountains, and the Gevethen couldn't have come here, could they?' He looked at Ibryen for confirmation. 'I think it's who we've been looking for, but I fear he's very weak. There was great desperation in that call we heard.'

'What I just felt was more powerful than anything I've felt before,' Ibryen said, uncertain about the implications of what he was saying.

'Yes,' the Traveller said, without elaborating, though the news seemed to make him more agitated.

Rachyl looked at the two of them. 'You're sure about this?' she said to the Traveller sternly.

'Yes,' he said again, shifting his weight from foot to foot as if having difficulty in restraining himself from plunging off into the darkness.

Reluctantly, and after a confirming glance at Ibryen, Rachyl sheathed her sword. 'Turn that lantern down, then,' she said, bluntly practical. 'It won't last much longer burning so high, and it's destroying what night vision we've got. And it's no use as a signal if whoever's out there can't get to it.' She looked concerned. 'I suppose we'll have to leave one as it is, to mark the camp.'

The Traveller handed her the lantern. 'You lower this, I'll mark the camp,' he said. While Rachyl adjusted the lantern and Ibryen sealed the tent, the Traveller stood looking at the rock in whose lee they had been sheltering. He seemed to be weighing alternatives for a little while, then he opened his mouth slightly and a sound like a distant bell filled the tiny camp. It lingered apparently unaffected by the noise all about them. 'Remember this,' he said, tapping his ear as he joined the others. 'It'll guide us back better than a light, and it should see the night out.'

Before anyone could question him, his fidgeting legs

finally took charge of him and he was striding into the gloom.

'Come back, damn you,' Rachyl shouted after him. 'We must stay together.'

He stopped with patent impatience.

'I suppose you move in the dark like a bat, do you?' Rachyl snapped as she and Ibryen reached him.

The Traveller grimaced. 'Well, as a matter of fact . . .'

But Rachyl was not listening. She flicked an angry thumb towards Ibryen. 'You might be lighter than he is, Mountain Man, but I've still got no desire to haul you back to the village over my shoulder just because you've gone sprawling. We go together, we go slowly and we go carefully. That way perhaps we might find this benighted whistler and be in a condition to help him. Do you understand?'

The Traveller bridled.

'You go first, Traveller. *Slowly*. We *must* stay together,' Ibryen said quickly, in a commanding but more conciliatory vein. 'I'll follow and, Rachyl, you take the rear with the lantern.'

Maintaining this file order they moved steadily up the mountain. The terrain became steeper and rockier but it was still negotiable without resorting to climbing. Once again, the Traveller demonstrated his uncanny knack of finding the easiest routes, though, on more than one occasion, Ibryen had to call out to him as he went too far ahead. Despite the fact that they were moving relentlessly away from their camp, both Ibryen and Rachyl found that the sound the Traveller had made was lingering with them. From time to time, Rachyl put a hand to her ear and looked over her shoulder with an expression of mild disbelief on her face.

As they moved higher, so the occasional patches of

snow became more frequent until eventually, everywhere was covered. Visibility improved a little as the snow caught the faint lantern-light, but progress slowed markedly.

'I'm not sure this is wise,' Rachyl said, as they paused briefly after a particularly treacherous scramble.

'It's very unwise,' the Traveller replied. 'But I don't think we've any choice. I can hear only the faintest signs now.' He turned away and whistled again, an unnaturally loud and penetrating sound that seemed to make the wind fall silent momentarily. Neither Rachyl nor Ibryen heard any reply, but the Traveller nodded urgently. 'We must press on as fast as we can. I don't think it's much further now.'

'Wait a moment,' Ibryen said, leaning back against a rock and putting a hand to his forehead. 'Something's wrong.' Rachyl held up the lantern to see his face. It was haggard.

'For mercy's sake, what's the matter?' she gasped.

Ibryen shook his head. 'I don't know,' he said. 'I feel as if I'm in two places at once. I'm having to force my arms and legs to move, and my eyes to watch where I'm going. Even talking now, you keep slipping away from me.' He gritted his teeth as if he were struggling with a great weight. 'Everything is taking so much effort.'

Rachyl turned to the Traveller, her face a mixture of anger and fear. 'What's happening?' she demanded.

Her anxiety mirrored itself in the Traveller's face as he looked out into the darkness before replying. 'What is there in this other place, Ibryen?' he asked, with forced patience.

Ibryen gave a long, laboured shrug. 'Only hurt. A feeling of failure – no, worse – a trust betrayed, an obligation abandoned.' Recognition came into his face. 'It's grief –

terrible grief.' His eyes became distant.

'Do something, for pity's sake,' Rachyl burst out.

'Listen to me, Ibryen,' the Traveller said, his voice soft but very powerful. 'Hold to my words – their meaning and their sound. Tell me where you are now.'

There was a long pause. Rachyl took the Traveller's arm anxiously. He patted her hand, though more as if he needed her support than in reassurance. Ibryen's eyes cleared.

'I'm here,' he said. 'On this mountain with you and Rachyl, and in this freezing wind.'

'And?'

'In the middle of the pain. Somewhere else. Somewhere that's near here and yet impossibly far away.'

The Traveller took a deep breath. 'You are whole, Ibryen. Don't be afraid of your fear. The part of you that belongs here *is* here, and only here. That part of you that belongs elsewhere is untutored and unskilled but not without strength. Say to that which is in pain, what you would say to a grieving soldier who fought to his limit, back to back, but lived where his companion died. "You have not betrayed, you have not failed. You have done well and could not have done more. Go your way in peace and without reproach. Help for your companion in this place is coming. You . . ." ' He hesitated. ' "You must . . . return . . . to your own. Perhaps guide his true kin to us for his future needs".' He took Ibryen's arms and moved very close to him. 'Say, "In this way you will serve as you have always served, but release me now or you will be a burden".'

A violent gust of wind swept out of the night and buffeted the tiny group. At its height, Ibryen gave a slight cry. His hands jerked up to touch his face, shaking off the Traveller, who stepped back a few paces.

'It's gone,' he said, his face clearing. Then, 'Most of it, anyway.' He looked at the Traveller. 'A small part is still there, lingering. What the devil's happening, Traveller? What was that?'

Untypically, the Traveller looked anxious and lost for an answer. 'I think it was what I said. A grieving companion.' He became urgent. 'No more questions, not now. We must move on, quickly.'

'Now, wait a minute—' Rachyl began, seizing his arm.

'No!' the Traveller said with a force that made Rachyl start away from him. 'Come now, or I go alone.'

'You can't . . .'

'We've no choice now. Move.' The Traveller hesitated. 'If I go too fast, follow the sound I'll leave you. Do you understand?' He was clambering over the rocks before either Rachyl or Ibryen could reply. Rachyl started after him then stopped in angry frustration and turned back to Ibryen. 'Are you all right?'

Ibryen motioned her forward after the retreating figure. 'Yes,' he said, as convincingly as he could manage. 'It seems to have gone, truly. My head's clearer than it's been for days. Come on. Quickly. We mustn't let him get too far ahead.'

They had gone scarcely twenty paces however before the Traveller had disappeared from view. Rachyl swore and promised him a violent end under her breath.

'He wouldn't have left us for any slight reason,' Ibryen said. 'Listen.'

From all around them, twisting and echoing in the wind came more whistling. 'We're supposed to follow that?' Rachyl snarled.

'No,' Ibryen replied. 'I think that's for whoever's out there. At least we can follow his footsteps now.'

They pressed on, moving carefully over the snow-covered rocks, following the Traveller's footprints. 'Ye gods, he's running,' Rachyl said after a little way. 'This isn't a walking stride.'

Ibryen could do no other than agree. 'I've not seen him breathless since we left the village and you can see it's a strain for him to move at our speed. And he came across the Hummock, don't forget. There's far more to him than meets the eye.'

'Oh yes,' Rachyl replied quietly, in a tone that made Ibryen look at her strangely.

They continued in silence, following the lightly impressed footprints. 'Well, at least we'll have no difficulty in following our own footsteps back,' Ibryen growled angrily as he slithered for the second time down a short rocky slope, throwing up a spray of snow.

Then, the faint bell-like tone that had been hovering about them since they left the camp, changed suddenly, becoming louder and more resolute. And it was ahead of them now, inviting them to follow it. They stopped and looked at one another uncertainly. Rachyl's response was unexpected. 'Under other circumstances, I could be very afraid of such a person,' she said.

'Under other circumstances, one can fear anything,' Ibryen said tersely. 'I think all we have to fear here is our own carelessness.'

They moved on again, heads bowed against the increasing wind, the Traveller's strange beacon guiding them and Rachyl's faint lantern bobbing in the stormy darkness to show the way. They did not speak.

Then they were at the entrance to a narrow cleft in the rock. The sound came from it with the purposefulness of an arrow. 'Traveller!' Ibryen called. There was no reply, but the sound quivered impatiently. Cautiously they

340

moved forward into the cleft. It was scarcely wide enough for them to walk side by side.

Almost immediately, the noise of the wind faded and as they made their way carefully over the uneven ground, it became an echoing moan, a resonant summation of the clattering din outside, rising and falling to a rhythm of its own, now a soft whistling, now an ominous tolling, sometimes an angry clamour. Disconcerting as the change was, the comparative stillness in the cleft was a marked improvement on the battering they had been struggling against since they left the camp, and both of them straightened up with some relief. The absence of the wind also made them feel much warmer.

The Traveller's guiding note wound through the uneasy soughing like a silver thread, drawing them steadily on, and their progress was helped by the fact that there was very little snow underfoot. They had been walking for some time when Rachyl took Ibryen's arm and pointed. There was a faint light ahead of them. As they drew nearer they saw that it was coming from the mouth of a cave. No sooner had they reached it, than the sound faded. Ibryen was about to step inside when Rachyl, sword drawn and lantern extended, moved in front of him.

'I'm sorry I got so far ahead.' The Traveller's apology greeted them. He was kneeling some way from the entrance. Balanced on a rock nearby was what appeared to be a small lantern, giving off a light which caused both Rachyl and Ibryen to shield their eyes. The Traveller reached out and the light became dimmer. Lying on the ground beside him was a figure, wrapped in a white blanket.

'Who is it?' Rachyl asked, wide-eyed as she sheathed her sword and knelt by the Traveller. The blanket shrouding the figure was wrapped tightly, leaving only a lean, pale face exposed. A curved nose and prominent cheek-bones gave the face a birdlike, but stern appearance.

'Is he dead?' Ibryen asked.

The Traveller shook his head. 'It's who we've been looking for,' he said. 'And no, he's not dead, but he's very weak. He was mumbling a moment ago, then he drifted off.'

'But who is he?' Rachyl was testing the material wrapping the man between her thumb and forefinger. 'I've never seen cloth like this,' she digressed. 'It's very soft but it's got an odd feel to it. And how's it been wrapped around him like this? He couldn't have done it himself.'

'Did you hear what he said?' The question came out arbitrarily from the bewildering flood that was swirling through Ibryen's thoughts. At the same time, his hand was pursuing Rachyl's inquiry. As he took hold of the fabric, the Traveller seized his wrist with great urgency.

'No!'

But even as it was spoken, the word was distant and faint and all about him was whiteness and longing. Like old memories, faint images of panoramas flickered into his mind; images made strange by the vantage from which he could see them, though they did not linger long enough for him to be able to identify them. Yet they were not just *like* old memories, they *were* old memories. But whose? And of what?

The whiteness trembled. From deep within, a know-ledge told him he should not be here so totally, that to be here thus was to bring extinction to that part of him which was Ibryen. Familiar but forgotten, white woven threads drifted down to him, but he could not grasp them.

'Let me go,' he heard himself calling silently, then he spoke as the Traveller had told him to previously. 'You've done all that you could do. You've neither failed nor betrayed. Go to your own now and rest as you deserve. Find his true kin. We will tend him here.'

Doubt filled him.

Then, with an authority he did not understand he commanded, 'Go. Release him. And release me also.'

The doubt wavered and the elusive dancing threads twisted and turned about him. As he reached for them he found that they were sounds – voices.

'Ibryen, Ibryen!'

He was kneeling by the strange figure again, the fabric slipping from his fingers and the Traveller's unexpectedly powerful grip about his wrist. The Traveller's voice was echoing around the cave, calling his name. What drew his attention however, was the stark fear in the little man's face. 'I was right,' he said breathlessly. 'You are . . .' He did not finish the sentence. Instead, he released Ibryen and took hold of the material and spoke to both his companions. 'This is Culmaren,' he said, his voice soft and full of awe. 'The material, the plant, the . . . creature . . . that's the very substance of the cloud-lands that the Dry-envolk dwell in. That lives both here and in the worlds beyond. That is many parts and a whole. And, if I'm any judge, this is dead, or almost so. I've never heard of such a thing.' He stared at Ibryen. 'How did you come back?' he asked.

Ibryen stammered. 'You . . . you . . . called me,' he said.

The Traveller shook his head. The fear had been replaced by bewilderment. 'Yes, but that wasn't what brought . . .'

'Be quiet!' Rachyl's command cut across the faltering reply, making the Traveller start. She was bending over the motionless figure, her hand raised for silence. 'He's trying to say something.'

The Traveller placed a hand on her shoulder and leaned

343

forward, bringing his head next to hers. The figure muttered something then fell silent. Rachyl shook her head, but the Traveller sat back and leaned against the cave wall.

'Well?' Ibryen asked.

'I only caught a couple of words,' the Traveller said. 'They didn't mean anything, but he *is* Dryenvolk. Give me a moment.' He closed his eyes and turned his face away to compose himself. Ibryen watched him unhappily. It was some time before he spoke and then there was an undertow of agitation in his voice. 'He couldn't ever have been anything other than Dryenvolk. Everything pointed to it. But it's still a shock to find him here. Conjecturing in your Council Hall is one thing. Even growing more certain as we drew nearer . . .' He puffed out his cheeks and shook his head. 'But actually seeing him . . . how can it be? How can a Dryenwr be down here, in the middle depths? And wrapped in Culmaren.'

'Whatever he is and however he came here, doesn't really matter, does it?' Rachyl said, impatiently practical. 'We'd better decide what we're going to do to help him.' She looked at the Traveller. 'My healing skill's confined to stopping gashes from bleeding and strapping up damaged limbs well enough to get people safely back to the village. And Ibryen's precious little better. Do you know what's wrong with him? Can you help him?'

The Traveller grimaced. 'I don't know,' he said. 'I didn't dare unwrap the Culmaren, it seems to be almost part of him. I could only check some of his pulses, and they're weak.'

'We can't just stand by and do nothing if he's ill,' Rachyl insisted. 'And we can't take him back to the tent in the dark without some kind of a stretcher. Still less back to the village.'

344

'There'd be no point taking him back to the tent, anyway,' Ibryen said. 'There's scarcely room for us and he's not small. At least he's out of the wind here and it's fairly dry.' His hand hovered uncertainly over the white fabric, then pulled away. 'Why didn't you unwrap this . . . blanket?'

'I told you,' the Traveller replied. 'The Dryenvolk have a strange bond with the Culmaren. And it has healing properties, I think. I've heard it said that the Dryenvolk use it with weave and voice to cure all manner of ailments.'

'Well, we're not Dryenvolk, are we?' Ibryen said. 'Nor are we likely to come across any. *He's* the centre of all the strangeness that's drawn us here. You said his pulses are weak. If you know *anything* about healing, you must do something. He might be dying. We can't just sit around and watch.'

'But . . .'

'Traveller, we came on this journey for answers – each of us. But there are only questions here. We must . . .' He stopped, and his hand hovered hesitantly over the fabric again. A pattern was beginning to form. 'What you've been hearing has been growing weaker, what I've been . . . feeling . . . has been growing stronger – almost taking possession of me at times.' He frowned as the pattern became a realization. 'If this exists here and beyond – wherever beyond is – then its existence here must be finished. It's just clinging on. Lost, bewildered.'

His jawline stiffened as if he were preparing for a clash of arms, and, eyes wide, he reached out and gripped a handful of the fabric resolutely. The whiteness and the longing closed about him again and he felt its seductive power trying to draw him to its heart. There was no malice in it but he knew that to succumb would be to lose himself for ever. With a grim effort he forced his eyes to stay

345

open, focusing them on the lean face of the Dryenwr. Then he took hold of the fabric with his other hand also and spoke into the whiteness as he had before.

'Release him. Your work is done. You hinder us in ours and he may die. We will tend him while you seek out his kin. Go now!'

The longing increased, but Ibryen kept his gaze fixed on the Dryenwr's face. No more could be said, no more would be said. Then the longing and the whiteness and everything about it was gone. Ibryen was aware of something vast fading into an unknowable distance, a haunting cry tailing after it. For a long moment, though he knew himself to be in a mountain cave with his companions, feeling the coldness on his face and hands, and the rocky ground hard on his knees, with the moaning wind echoing around him, he was also alone in another place, alone in a ringing emptiness. The one he knew, the other was strange beyond anything he had ever imagined. Yet he belonged to both.

He released the fabric; then, though he could not have said how, brought himself to the world he knew, as simply and easily as if he were passing over a friend's threshold. The Traveller took his arm anxiously.

'I'm fine,' he said anticipating the question. 'We'll talk later. Look after the Dryenwr.' He stood up and moved away.

Tentatively, the Traveller eased part of the fabric from the man's face, then he nodded to Rachyl to help him. Carefully they began unwinding the blanket. As they removed it, a tall and muscular figure was revealed, clad in what was obviously a uniform, pale grey in colour with various ornate markings about the breast and on the arms. In his hand was a sword. Where the man's uniform was immaculate, the sword was polished and bright but its edge was hacked and scarred. The Traveller turned up his lantern. Its light flickered brilliantly from the sword to dance about the cave.

'Warrior caste,' he said, running a finger across one of the markings. 'And a high-ranking officer at that, I'd say.'

Rachyl looked at the Dryenwr critically for a moment. 'A fighter for sure,' she said flatly, 'if it was he who did the damage to the edge of that sword.' Cautiously she took it from his hand and placed it on the ground, then she briskly folded the blanket and, kneeling down, laid it gently back over him with an oddly maternal gesture.

The Dryenwr's eyes opened.

Chapter 23

'Carver's Song. I heard the Carver's Song.'

Rachyl jumped backwards with a cry of alarm which became an oath as she tumbled over to land gracelessly on her behind.

The voice, deep and with an unfamiliar accent, was that of the Dryenwr. It was weak, but there were clear notes of authority in it. Dark, unfocused eyes moved around the trio of watchers as he levered himself up into a sitting position.

'Through the mists I heard it. In a dream? It seems so long since I heard such, yet it can scarcely be a moon since I heard of their coming together again.' The Dryenwr frowned and put a hand to his head. 'Then I was walking in the darkness over land hard and without life, Culmaren cape about my shoulders and Svara's will all about me, cold and angry, tearing at me. I answered the Song.' He whistled faintly and smiled. 'Never had the true skill – warrior caste is warrior caste – but the Culmaren fired me. I sounded a measure or two such as I couldn't begin to do if I were awake. Then . . .' He frowned again. 'I was so weak. I was drawn back again, I think. Drawn into the waiting, into the mists . . .'

His eyes were clearing. 'Is this a dream, too? Is this the fate of the dead? An eternity of dreams?'

'You ask questions that none can answer, Dryenwr,' the Traveller said. 'But this is no dream, as far as I know, nor are we shadows in your imagining. This is Rachyl, this is Ibryen, Count of Nesdiryn, and I'm just a traveller, each of us as real as yourself. How you came here I can't say, nor how long you've been here, but you're in the middle depths, and I suspect your Culmaren has sustained you for some considerable time.'

The Dryenwr looked at him intently, then at the Culmaren draped over him. As he fingered the material, his eyes opened in horror and cried out, 'Nightmare! Not a dream. Nightmare.' He brought the Culmaren close to his face. 'No, this cannot be.'

Ibryen eased Rachyl and the Traveller to one side and knelt down by the suddenly distraught figure. 'Neither dream nor nightmare, warrior,' he said. 'But perhaps something stranger than you'd find in either. I doubt we can answer many of the questions you must be asking, but you're truly awake and in the real world, albeit perhaps in a place that's as profoundly alien to you as one of your high-flying cloud lands would be to us.'

The Dryenwr stared at him, his hands rolling the Culmaren and his face full of confusion. Unsteadily he ran a hand over his tunic then over the rocky ground. He turned from Ibryen to look at Rachyl and then at the Traveller. 'The middle depths?' he said. The Traveller nodded.

'Here.' Rachyl offered the cap of her water bottle. The Dryenwr reached out then hesitated. Rachyl smiled then drank a little of the water and offered it again. The Dryenwr took it. 'Careful, it's cold,' Rachyl said as he took a first cautious sip. 'And I'm afraid we've no food with us. It's all down with the tent.' The Dryenwr closed his eyes as he drank the contents of the small cap then he held it out for more. Rachyl filled it again. 'That's enough,' she said.

'The middle depths,' the Dryenwr said softly to himself. 'The middle depths. I *am* here. Svara protect me.' His hand circled over his heart. He took hold of the Culmaren again and his face became pained. 'But how could such a thing happen? How could the Culmaren die? This must be a fearful place.'

Ibryen's own face reflected the man's distress. 'We know nothing of your ways, Dryenwr. In fact, only a few days ago I'd have laughed to scorn even the idea that cloud lands existed. But change is the way of things and I'm learning to bend to it or break as never before. So, I suspect, must you, now.' He paused, uncertain how to continue. 'This land of ours may be strange to you and, indeed, it can be a fearful place, but we mean you no harm and will not wittingly hurt or even offend you. Here, as a token of this . . .' He took the Dryenwr's sword from Rachyl and held it out to him, hilt first. Ibryen heard Rachyl shifting behind him as the Dryenwr took the sword and he held out a hand to restrain her. 'I see from this hacked edge that there are terrors in your own lands also,' he said.

The Dryenwr did not reply, but stared fixedly at the sword. Then there was a long and painful silence as the three spectators could do nothing other than watch the manifest return of awful memories – at first slowly and then, like water through a shattered dam, in a single engulfing flood. The sword began to tremble and, for a moment, it seemed that the Dryenwr was going to unleash a great howl of anguish. No such sound emerged, however. Instead, the sword wilted and his head dropped forward.

'My people, where are you? What happened?' He looked at Ibryen and began a desperate plea. 'We debated,

351

agonized, even at the heart of the battle. Then the Carvers' messenger, the sword-bearer, pressed in battle himself, spoke to me in my extremity. We'd sought no conflict, he said. We'd the right to be. All creatures have that. *He* and his corrupted flights had to be defeated or, with his foul brothers assailing the middle depths, sky, land and sea would have fallen to the Great Corrupter. We could do no other, could we?' Ibryen made no reply. The Dryenwr looked up to the shadowed roof of the cave. 'So I sent the word and we did as *he* did.' He was almost whispering. 'Moved the land against the will of Svara, hiding it high within the clouds. Then my Soarers re-doubled their attack, flight upon flight of us, a desperate venture now, to draw his attention away. Such a sight we were. The sky alive with glittering wings. Such discipline, such courage.' He gripped Ibryen's arm, full of warrior pride. 'And we held them. Despite their numbers. We held them. His corruption had taken more from them than it had given and their will was weak.' He bared his teeth and both hands took the sword. 'Then *he* was among us. He could not resist the victory he saw falling to him, so blood-crazed was he. At the height of the conflict he came forth. On his dreadful screaming mount. Cutting through our ranks as though we were mere fledglings. But I faced him.' He shuddered. 'Stopped his bloody progress. Stared into those dead, white eyes. Fear racking every part of me but freeing me of all restraints and burdens save one – that he must die even as he slew me. His creature shrieked in my face, but I saw only *him*.' Ibryen could feel the Dry-enwr trembling, his eyes focused on something far beyond the confines of the cave. 'He raised his sword. Then he faltered. And I looked up. There was my land, emerging from the clouds, descending on to the land that this abomination had made his own.'

He closed his eyes and shook his head. 'A blasphemy, yet magnificent... and who would judge us?' He fell silent. No one spoke, there had been such intensity in his telling. When he began again, his voice was distant. 'I remember him turning with a fearsome cry. I remember feeling the great power of his true self being exerted. Then... such a noise... and the sky was torn apart, ablaze with a terrible fire. And I was being hurled downwards, ripped from my wings, helpless amid the forces that had been unleashed. Then there was only darkness, and dreams... strange dreams.' He put a hand to his eyes. 'My people, my people. What became of you? What could have withstood that burning?'

Grief rose up to fill Ibryen. He had understood little of what the man had said, but his pain was all too familiar. Was this to be *his* destiny? Lost and despairing in a strange land, all loved ones gone, their fate unknown?

'You must rest,' he said hoarsely. 'You're weak and shouldn't tax yourself thus. In the morning we can go down to our camp and eat, and perhaps talk a little more. Then you can come back to our village. It's only a couple of days away and you'll be welcome to stay there for as long as you wish.'

But the Dryenwr did not seem to be listening. 'The middle depths,' he said again, his voice a mixture of awe and disbelief, as he gazed about the cave. Many emotions were obviously struggling for primacy within him but even as Ibryen watched, he saw a powerful will taking control of the man's features. 'Forgive me,' he said, grasping Ibryen's arm and looking at Rachyl and the Traveller in turn. 'I burden you with my concerns, matters about which perhaps nothing can be done. As you say, change is the way of things, and at least I am alive, however mysteriously.' He became suddenly agitated. 'What of your own battle? I feel none of His taint about you. Is it over? Are you part of the sword-bearer's army? Can you use another blade?' He shook his head and his expression became grim. 'What bond brought us together in that way I don't know, but it grieves me deeply that there were mighty forces ranged against him on that snow-covered shore, and he was sorely taxed when it happened. I hope it did him no hurt.'

Ibryen looked at the Traveller, who shrugged.

'We *are* at war,' Ibryen said hesitantly, 'but there've been no great battles here in many generations, nor in any of the lands hereabouts. And we're far from any shoreline.'

The Dryenwr frowned in bewilderment. 'But . . . the return of the Great Corrupter must surely have sounded about the whole of the middle depths?' he said. He pointed upwards and his voice cracked. 'And the destruction of His lieutenant's land – and perhaps my own – could hardly have gone unnoticed. It tore open the very fabric of the heavens.'

Ibryen did not reply immediately, there was regret in his voice when he did. 'There's been nothing such as you describe,' he said. 'No uproar in the heavens, nor even rumour of a . . . Great Corrupter.' He hesitated. 'The name itself has only the ring of something out of myth and legend.'

The Traveller laid a hand on his shoulder. 'Perhaps not,' he said, unexpectedly sombre. 'It's a name that I heard in the carvings on the Great Gate. And there were rumours in Girnlant of an evil having arisen in the north.' He spoke to the Dryenwr. 'When was this battle that you fought?'

The Dryenwr looked surprised. 'A few . . .' He faltered. 'I don't know exactly. A few hours ago, I suppose. Perhaps a day or so. How long have I been here? It's still the second moon, isn't it?'

'I never had cause to learn the ordering of your months,' the Traveller said.

'It's the second moon measured from the solstice,' the Dryenwr said, with a hint of impatience. 'The second moon of Ravenyarr.'

The Traveller pulled a wry face. 'The year of the Raven. That leaves us none the wiser, I'm afraid, for the same reason.' The Dryenwr seemed about to lose his temper. The Traveller took the edge of the white Culmaren thoughtfully. 'How long would it take for this to die?' he asked forcefully, looking squarely at the Dryenwr.

The Dryenwr started slightly then grimaced. 'Culmaren doesn't die,' he said. 'It's not possible . . .' His voice faded.

'How long?' the Traveller insisted.

'Perhaps it was hurt thus in the destruction of the land.'

The Traveller shook his head. 'I've been thinking since I found you. Isn't it possible that as you were thrown from the battle, this sought you out – as would be its way? Sought you out and protected you. Carried you to the only safe place it could find – your own land having moved on. Then couldn't it have sustained you? Kept you alive with its own life essence. That is its nature, isn't it?'

The Dryenwr lay back on one elbow and looked down at the Culmaren without replying. 'It mended your injuries, even mended your soiled and bloody uniform – mended everything, save the damage done to your sword, which is not Culmaren, is it?' The Traveller paused. 'Perhaps even changed you so that you could live here more easily – the middle depths are no comfortable place for the Dryenvolk as I remember. It kept you alive until it could do no more. That *would* be the way of Culmaren, wouldn't it?'

'That's the lore,' the Dryenwr replied uncomfortably.

'That's the *fact*, warrior,' the Traveller said. 'That's what would have happened; that's what *did* happen, I'll wager.' He lifted up the white fabric. 'Just as the whole sustains your entire people, so this fragment sustained you alone. Until it was utterly spent. Then it cried out. Both here and in its other home beyond.' He paused again, watching the Dryenwr carefully. 'I heard the one.' He indicated Ibryen. 'He, the other.'

The Dryenwr looked up sharply. 'No!' he said, though the denial was strained.

'Yes,' the Traveller said categorically. 'This is a lonely place, Dryenwr, as you'll see when morning comes. We haven't stumbled upon you by chance. We were drawn here by its calls. I, thanks to my ancestry. He...' He shrugged. 'Who can say?'

'It can't be,' the Dryenwr said weakly.

'Why not?'

'You're not a Carver, nor he...'

The tune that the Traveller had been whistling at the camp suddenly filled the cave with rich, elaborate sound. It stopped abruptly. 'That was what you heard. My Song. You're right, true Carver I'm not, but their line is strong in me. As for him,' he pointed to Ibryen, 'what is he not? Not Hearer caste, is he? How could he be? He isn't Dryenvolk. But even amongst yourselves, your castes are hardly clearly marked, are they? Don't you all have some aptitude for Hearing, for Shaping, for the poetry and music of the Versers? Don't you sometimes move from one caste to the other as you grow older? And would you presume that such gifts are confined only to the Dryenvolk?'

The Dryenwr looked from side to side as though he were being trapped. Then he held out his hand to silence

356

the Traveller, and turned to Ibryen. 'I am Arnar Isgyrn, leader of the Soarers Tahren of Endra Hornath. I'm fresh from a battle and far adrift in every sense. Perhaps now without a land or people.' He nodded towards the Traveller. 'That he has the gift of the Carvers is beyond doubt, but do you truly have the gift of Hearing the voice of the Culmaren?' The question was blunt but not discourteous, and his voice shook with the control he was exerting.

Ibryen replied in similar vein. 'I am Ibryen, Count of Nesdiryn, as the Traveller told you. My land still exists, but I too am adrift, dispossessed by usurpers, my own people divided, one against the other. I have a gift that I do not understand.' He reached out and touched the Culmaren. 'A gift that leaves me both here and elsewhere, in a place full of strange longing. It was I who let the spirit of this go free. I commended it for a duty well done, and asked that it seek out your kin.' He closed his eyes. 'I hear it now. Faint and very distant, across the void, singing, calling.' He opened his eyes and met the Dryenwr's gaze. 'It drew me here when perhaps my wiser judgement would have left me with my followers to continue the fight for my people.'

Isgyrn looked at him earnestly for a moment, then seemed to reach a decision. He glanced round at all three. 'A Carver who is not a Carver. A Hearer who is not a Hearer.' He finished his examination with Rachyl.

She shrugged. 'Warrior Caste, I suppose,' she said, with acid knowingness. 'I certainly wouldn't have given you your sword back so quickly.'

Isgyrn smiled ruefully and gave an appreciative nod. 'Very wise. Rooted well in the lowest depths like all women. Though, in fact, I doubt I could stand, let alone wield this,' he said, laying a hand on the hilt of his sword.

'And your doubts about us?' the Traveller asked.

'You'll allow me a little bewilderment, Carver?' Isgyrn replied sternly. 'A little time to gather my wits fully?'

'I'm sorry.'

Isgyrn fell silent. He fingered the Culmaren pensively. 'It's true we all have a touch of each other's gifts, but I've precious little of the Shaper in me to judge the fate of this.' He closed his eyes and continued manipulating the Culmaren. Then his face became hard and when he opened his eyes he looked at no one. 'This *is* a nightmare,' he said softly, rubbing his hands over the white blanket in a peculiarly childlike gesture. 'But my head must agree with such meagre talent as I have. This was part of the wing that bore me, only days ago it seems. Young and strong. Full of the love of Svara's will, responding to my least touch. How we flew.' He looked again at the three watchers and almost whispered. 'To become as it is now, may have taken . . .' he forced the words out '. . . ten, perhaps twenty years.' He held up his hand and looked at it, turning it over slowly. 'But this is the hand I had only hours ago in my mind as I faced the abomination.'

There was a long silence. Isgyrn stared bleakly ahead. Ibryen looked at the Traveller who gave a helpless shrug.

'Is such a thing possible?' he asked hesitantly.

Isgyrn turned to him and smiled sadly. 'In myth and legend,' he said, echoing Ibryen's own words though without any mockery. 'But also now. The Seekers understand the Culmaren enough in this age to know it could be so. Though we would not treat it thus.'

Ibryen could not meet his gaze. 'I've no words to comfort you, Arnar Isgyrn,' he said, after an uncomfortable silence. 'Other than to say that we've gone to some pains to find you and will give you what help we can. I think now you should rest. We're all tired and little's to be gained fretting the night away. Let's talk again when there's daylight around us.'

Isgyrn grasped his arm purposefully. 'Ten, twenty years ago. Was there a battle then?'

Ibryen shook his head and repeated his earlier answer. 'Not in generations, Isgyrn. Not in generations.'

The Dryenwr looked at the Traveller. 'This evil that arose in the north. How far was it? How long ago?'

'I don't know. And it was only a rumour. It could even have been a lie invented by those who were seeking to gain power, for their own ends.'

'But it had the feel of truth about it, Carver?'

The Traveller nodded.

Isgyrn ran his hands over the Culmaren again. 'Everything is so vivid in my mind. Yet too, there's a sense of a long and fitful sleep also. Of stumbling wakings that I can't fully recall. It's possible that my confrontation with that demon has plunged me into madness – into a crazed dream, though everything about me seems real enough for all its strangeness. For the time, I suppose I must accept things as being what they appear to be, and, given that, my reason tells me beyond doubt that my memories of a few hours ago are indeed ten or more years old.'

Despite himself, Ibryen repeated his earlier remark. 'There've been no great battles in this land . . .'

'. . . in generations.' Isgyrn finished the sentence, laying a hand on Ibryen's arm again, though this time almost as if to comfort him. 'I understand. If I'm to accept that I've been sustained by the Culmaren . . . asleep . . . for so long, then I can readily accept that the battle I fought in was far from here. Simple logic brings me to that. My wing wouldn't lightly have come down to the middle depths. It's possible that I've been in this place only a short time.

And who can say how far Svara's will has carried us before we came here?'

For a moment, a spasm of rage and frustration distorted his face and he laid a hand on his sword again. Rachyl's eyes narrowed dangerously, but the anger was gone as quickly as it had arrived and he merely moved the sword to one side. 'If you have it to spare, may I have some more water?' he asked.

Rachyl's hand moved from her knife to her water bottle and she handed it to him. 'Be careful,' she said. 'It's no warmer than it was a few minutes since and you'll find stomach cramps just as pleasant now as they were ten years ago.'

The Dryenwr smiled weakly and took only a small drink before handing the bottle back. His stomach rumbled. He apologized.

'Think nothing of it,' the Traveller said, his head cocked attentively on one side. 'I can do great things with that.'

Isgyrn looked at him blankly. Ibryen repeated his earlier advice. 'Rest, Isgyrn,' he said. 'He who sleeps, dines, they say. At least, the well-fed say it to the hungry. We'll go down to our camp in the morning. We've not got a great deal to offer, but we won't die of starvation between here and home.'

'I cannot burden you,' Isgyrn said.

Ibryen waved the comment away airily. 'Sleep,' he ordered, paternally.

Rachyl frowned and glanced around the cave. Then she leaned forward. 'All debts are paid in full if you share your blanket with us. It's big enough,' she said. 'We might be out of the wind but it's none too warm in here.'

Isgyrn looked a little taken aback. 'Yes . . . yes, of course. I'll . . . I'll put my sword between us,' he stammered.

Rachyl's frown became puzzled for a moment, then her eyebrows rose. 'Don't worry, I'll put my cousin between us,' she said. 'And this.' She offered him a clenched fist.

Both Ibryen and Rachyl woke at the same time the next morning. There was a hint of greyness about them, and their breaths misted the air. They rose stoically, carefully stretching stiffened joints and massaging where the rocky floor of the cave had made its mark.

'Well, at least we weren't cold,' Rachyl said. She examined the Culmaren closely. 'It's a very strange material, like animal fur and the finest of weaves, and yet like neither. I've never seen anything like it.' She was holding it against her cheek with conspicuous pleasure. Then, clearing her throat self-consciously, she looked round. Isgyrn was still asleep. She cast a glance at Ibryen, who shook his head.

'Let him sleep until we're ready to leave. The sooner he wakes the longer he's going to have to wait to eat.'

She clamped a hand to her stomach. 'Don't mention it,' she said. 'Thinking about him not eating for ten years had me dreaming about food half the night and I'd swear I could smell cooking even now.'

'Ah, you're back.' It was the Traveller, silhouetted in the greying entrance. 'I thought you were *all* going to try for a ten-year sleep the way you were snoring.' Rachyl glowered but he pressed on. 'Sun'll be up soon. Come on, there's food here.'

'Food?' Ibryen queried. Rachyl sniffed noisily.

'It's only your supplies, I'm afraid. Nothing lavish,' the Traveller said. 'There's nothing up here that *you'd* want to eat unless you were really hungry. I went down for it. Didn't feel like sleeping and I thought perhaps it was a little churlish of me to make free with the poor man's stomach rumblings, even though they were interesting.'

'You're a man of rare sensibility,' Ibryen conceded.

'It's been noticed before,' the Traveller said blandly. He motioned them outside. The smell of cooking was stronger here but, looking round, they saw no sign of a fire. The Traveller lifted a flat slab to reveal slices of meat crackling on a softly glowing bed in a hollow between two boulders. He flicked them over gingerly and, after blowing on his fingers, dropped the slab back. 'Wake our guest,' he said.

Ibryen went back into the cave.

'That's a peculiar fire,' Rachyl said. 'Where did you get the firewood from?'

The Traveller gave her a long look. 'I wasn't going to go that far down the mountain,' he said, mildly indignant. He eased the slab up again and peered under it. 'These are just a couple of my sunstones. I don't normally use them for cooking, but I thought it was a bit unkind to ask our guest to trek back to the camp before—'

'Sunstones?'

He smiled reassuringly. 'Don't worry,' he said. 'They won't lose much with this slab over them.'

'But what . . .?'

Ibryen emerged with Isgyrn before she could pursue her inquiry. The Dryenwr had folded the Culmaren in an elaborate fashion and it was draped about his shoulders like a cape. He was about the same height as Ibryen but, in so far as could be judged under the Culmaren, bulkier, although he seemed to be very light on his feet.

He looked up at the steep walls of the cleft uneasily. 'This is a disturbing place,' he said.

The Traveller followed his gaze. 'We'll be away in a moment,' he said sympathetically. 'You'll soon have open sky above you. Do you have a knife to go with that sword?' He held out his hand. Isgyrn checked about

362

himself uncertainly then produced a long knife that he handed, hilt first, to the Traveller. Like his sword, the edge was hacked.

Nimbly, the Traveller skewered three pieces of the meat and handed the knife back to him. 'Your first meal in the middle depths, Arnar Isgyrn. Simple, I'm afraid, but sufficient to carry you as far as your next one. Take care, it's hot.'

The Dryenwr seized the knife hastily then, with a conspicuous effort, paused. 'Thank you,' he said apologetically, glancing significantly at Rachyl and Ibryen.

'Eat,' the Traveller said airily, handing the others the rest of the meat. 'There's plenty for everyone.' As Rachyl and Ibryen were struggling to control the hot food, he produced a cloth and, reaching down between the two boulders with it, picked up the four glowing rocks that formed the bed on which the meat had been cooking. Unhurriedly, but with practised deftness he wrapped them in the cloth and put them in his pack. Rachyl, her mouth full, waved her arms in alarm.

'Don't concern yourself, my dear,' the Traveller said, catching the gesture. 'They're good stones. Cooking these bits and pieces used hardly anything. They've got days left in them.'

'You could've burned yourself. And you'll burn your pack,' she spluttered.

The Traveller looked at her uncertainly then turned to Ibryen with a look of mildly surprised realization. 'You don't use sunstones round here, do you?' he said. 'I thought you were just being thrifty with your oil lantern and the firewood – perhaps a bit low at the end of winter – having to eke out your resources.' He shook his head. 'I should have realized, they didn't use them in Girnlant either. Sorry to be so obtuse – I misunderstood. Anyway,

363

we can talk about that later. Come on, there's no point delaying, this place is upsetting Isgyrn more than he's prepared to say. Let's get back to your tent and below the snow before we decide what to do next.'

He was moving away before anyone could question him further.

Ibryen took Isgyrn's arm. 'Follow me,' he said. 'Rachyl will follow you. I can't imagine what this place is like for you, and I've no knowledge of the ways of your people, but the only danger we face here is injury caused by our own carelessness. If you want to rest or feel the need for support, speak. If you don't, you may endanger us all.'

'I understand,' Isgyrn said. 'There are wild places in my lands also. I'll do as you say.'

The journey back to the tent took them some time. Isgyrn did not seem to be disturbed by the wind, which was still blowing strongly, but he found the snow-covered terrain very difficult, frequently slipping and having to be caught by Rachyl. On two occasions he called the party to a halt while he recovered his breath. When they stopped for the second time, Rachyl looked at him then voiced his complaint for him. 'You may curse and swear, if you wish,' she said. 'There's nothing more frustrating for a fighter than to be made dependent on others because of physical weakness.'

Isgyrn, leaning back against a rock, smiled grimly. 'I don't think it would a wise idea,' he said, addressing them all. 'Your kindness and patience remind me constantly that, for all we come from such different worlds, we've many things in common. But my mind's awash with such confusion and questioning I don't know what I might plunge into if I gave it free flight.' He patted his chest. 'That I can even breathe comfortably down here raises questions that I suspect would tax our finest Seekers.

364

Perhaps indeed the Culmaren . . .' He waved his arm dismissively then frowned. 'Not the time or the place,' he declared, adding with a nod of acknowledgement to Rachyl, 'though I'll concede I'm finding it difficult to stay calm when simply lifting my arm requires a deliberate effort.'

He looked up. Light mist filled the valley below them but the sun was rising in a sky which was clear of clouds save for a few trailing wisps drawn out by the wind from some of the higher peaks. It needed little sensitivity on the part of his companions to understand his thoughts as he gazed around the empty sky.

'First thing in the morning's not my strongest time either, Isgyrn,' Rachyl said, good-humouredly. 'How I'd feel after a ten-year sleep I can't imagine.' She held out her arm. 'Warrior's way,' she said. 'All we need concern ourselves with is putting one foot in front of the other.' Isgyrn took it gratefully to pull himself upright and they set off again.

When they eventually reached the tent they rested for some time and ate again before breaking camp and beginning the descent back down to the forest. Away from the snow, Isgyrn became more sure-footed and, following the meal and the rest, he seemed a little stronger. Ibryen nonetheless made the Traveller maintain a leisurely pace and it was early evening by the time they reached the upper reaches of the forest and made camp.

They spoke very little as they sat around the fire. Isgyrn kept dozing off until, at the prompting of the others, he made his excuses and, wrapping the Culmaren about him, lay down. 'Is that going to be warm enough?' Rachyl asked.

'More than enough,' Isgyrn said. There was a suggestion of both surprise and sadness in his voice. 'Even dead, it would seem that the Culmaren has many . . . worthwhile attributes. Do you wish to share again?' She smiled and shook her head. Isgyrn fell silent. Then, unexpectedly, as the others were turning back to the fire, 'I did a little calculating on our way down, to keep my mind focused. It wasn't easy, I haven't the flair that makes a good Seeker but my head serves well enough.' He was drifting in and out of sleep. 'Perhaps fifteen years since . . . fifteen years . . . my family . . . people . . .'

He was asleep. Ibryen watched him for a little while then turned to gaze into the fire.

'Are you easier with yourself now?' It was the Traveller. Ibryen understood the question.

'Yes and no,' he replied. 'I've no doubts about my sanity now. Though I'd be lying if I said I was anything other than bewildered by what's happening.' His voice fell. 'And something's happened to me.' Both Rachyl and the Traveller watched him intently. He was almost talking to himself. 'It's nothing bad,' he went on. 'Just strange – very strange. Almost as if I'd just discovered I could hear like you do, or see things vast distances away. But it's neither of those, nor anything like them.' He frowned as he struggled to find the words. 'A talent's been awakened in me – a gift. But I don't know what it is, or what it's for.' He was silent for a moment then shrugged and became prosaic. 'But I'm no easier about the future. Now that the lure that pulled me out here has gone, my thoughts are turning back to the Gevethen and the problems we face back in the village. Part of me is sorely tempted to uproot everything and take our people further south. There must be other valleys where we can live in peace.'

Rachyl's head jerked up. He held out a reassuring hand. 'Don't worry,' he said. 'It was just an idle thought. It's probably because we've been so free to move these last

366

few days. We forget the values of such simple things. I know well enough that enemies like the Gevethen have to be faced in the end and the only thing that keeps us all together as a community is our opposition to them.'

'But how's he going to be able to help us?' Rachyl flicked a thumb towards the sleeping Dryenwr. The question crystallized Ibryen's concerns.

'He offered us his blade,' he said.

Rachyl pursed her lips. 'One more's better than nothing, I suppose. Even though he's weak, he's obviously been a commander of some kind and, judging from the state of his sword, he commands from the front. But tactically we're still back where we started.'

'Too premature a judgement,' Ibryen said firmly, straightening up. 'Who can say what kind of an avalanche might come of the dust that's been stirred up these past few days?'

Rachyl gave him an arch look. 'I'd prefer dispositions and logistics to Marris's poetry,' she said caustically.

'What happened fifteen years ago?' The Traveller's voice cut through their dying debate.

Ibryen leaned back and yawned. 'Nothing special, as far as I can recall,' he said after a little thought. 'The Gevethen were here. Very powerful already, though we didn't realize it, as they'd wormed their way into the workings of the court so quietly. They weren't as openly crazed in their manner as they became later, with their mirror-bearers and everything, but they were beginning to become conspicuously odd.'

The Traveller turned to Rachyl . 'Fifteen years,' she said pensively. 'Such a long time ago. Several lifetimes at least.' She smiled at some long-forgotten memory. 'I was a burgeoning woman,' she announced with heavy irony.

'You were a ruffian,' Ibryen interjected. 'The terror of

the Citadel. You were always up to some devilment.'

'Probably as well,' Rachyl said, briefly more sober, though the weight of happy memories made her smile again, almost immediately. 'Do you remember those wretched little brown birds?' she said. 'Creepy little things with yellow eyes. They used to be all over the city. And they were always buzzing about inside the Citadel. There seemed to be more and more every year.' She nodded to the Traveller. 'We could've used your stone-throwing in those days. We tried all sorts to catch one but never managed it. And they flew so fast! We never even found where they nested. What was it we called them?' Her teeth glinted in the firelight as she bared them.

' "Gevethen's eyes",' Ibryen said coldly. For some reason, the memory of the birds made him feel uncomfortable.

Rachyl snapped her fingers. 'They vanished suddenly, didn't they? All of them.'

Ibryen nodded. 'Some change in the wind brought them and some change in the wind probably took them away,' he said off-handedly. Even as he spoke however, the memory came to him again that he had had as he lay in the sun on the ridge before his encounter with the Traveller. It seemed to drop into place as part of a pattern that he could not fully identify. He voiced it. 'It was about then that the Gevethen became more ... exposed ... for what they truly were. More open, or more clumsy in their manipulations, less subtly knowledgeable of events than they had been.' The memory brought him no enlightenment, however.

The Traveller rested his chin on his hands. 'Birds, eh? Doesn't seem to be of any great significance, does it?' He shook his head slowly. 'I wish I'd read that Gate more carefully. There was something about birds on that, I'm sure.'

Their conversation faded and shortly afterwards Rachyl and Ibryen emulated the Dryenwr and lay down to sleep. The Traveller sat staring into the fire for some time, then stood up and walked off into the forest.

There was only the faintest hint of light in the eastern sky when an insistent hand shook Ibryen awake roughly. It was the Traveller.

'Wake up,' he was saying. 'Isgyrn's gone!'

Chapter 24

Jeyan did not sleep well that night. She had achieved a degree of inner quietness by her resolution to watch, listen and wait, and to take her strange new life moment by moment, heartbeat by heartbeat, but the Gevethen's brief visit had shaken her badly. There had been such menace in the words.

'As you judge, so shall you be judged. Prepare yourself.'

What did they mean?

Was she to come to trial after all? Had the past two days been only the beginning of a punishment? Were they only taunting her with luxury and the promise of power? Raising her high so that her fall might be the harder?

It did not help that her body made no demands upon her for rest. She had spent the day in enforced idleness where normally she would have been wandering the Ennerhald and the city, preoccupied with her next meal and the avoidance of the Citadel Guards. Thus she woke many times, each time forgetting the sleep she had just had.

At one point, during the deepest part of the night, she found Meirah by her bedside; a dimmed lantern in one hand, a glass goblet in the other. She started violently, causing the woman to step back.

'This will help you to sleep,' Meirah said, offering the drink.

Jeyan nearly knocked it from her hand in a spasm of anger, but she caught herself in time. 'Did I wake you?' she asked. Meirah shook her head and offered the goblet again. Jeyan thought for a moment. Was this a kindness or some kind of trick? Who could say what was in that drink, what consequences might flow from addling her brain with it?

'Put it on the table,' she said. 'I may take it later.'

And Meirah was gone.

The visit did little to ease Jeyan's mood. How had the woman come so close without waking her? No dogs, of course, came the sad answer immediately. She set it aside with a small moue of pain and the question was replaced with others. How did these servants know what she was doing all the time? Were they spying on her even now? She made a promise to herself to search the room carefully tomorrow for spy-holes. The thought of tomorrow however, merely served to remind her of the Gevethen's words and she was soon tossing and turning fretfully again.

She was thus jaded and weary when the servants woke her in the morning, at one stage even making a slight resistance to their endeavours. The ineffectiveness of this gesture brought her to her senses and she implemented the policy she had determined the previous day of saying what she did and did not want doing. It ensured her a marginally more private ablution, and made her feel that she had some semblance of control over events. It was the *merest* semblance however, she knew, and though her head relished the fine food that was placed before her, her stomach nervously protested otherwise.

'What's to happen today?' she said casually, as though

372

she had a whirl of social events before her. There was no reply. 'You may speak,' she added. 'I should prefer it if you would.' She risked a little menace, to test her authority. 'I do not like to be ignored when I ask questions.'

There was a flutter of unease amongst the servants, but still no one answered. 'What's to happen today?' she asked again.

Silence.

She caught Meirah's eye but received no acknowledgement. She let the matter lie. The question had indeed given her a measure of her authority. She had very little. Speaking was not approved of by the Gevethen, and that was that.

She forced herself to eat something.

Jeyan was not the only nervous person that morning. Helsarn had been given the task of escorting the new Lord Counsellor. The euphoria following his sudden promotion was gradually beginning to wear off. Though no hint had been given, it must have caused considerable concern to the other Commanders, with its implications for the reduction of their own power, and to give the Commanders concern was to court mysterious and silent disappearance.

Of course, the very suddenness of the promotion gave him the Gevethen's implicit protection, but that could not be relied upon indefinitely: they were notoriously indifferent to the jockeying for position that went on in the Guards, providing that it did not impair their effectiveness. It was important that he did not appear as a threat to his new peers. He must make himself useful and relatively inconspicuous, at least until such time as he had increased the size of his loyal following amongst the men. He had little anxiety about those from his own company: he knew their various ambitions and characters well enough by now, and he had already taken the precaution of raising them up along with himself. They would thus have enhanced status as and when other companies were brought under his command.

More pressing concerns were troubling him that morning, as he stood before the mirror and checked his uniform for the fourth time. He it was who had hauled the prisoner in and thrown her in the dungeon, and that was hardly likely to endear him to her now that she had become Lord Counsellor. He thanked his good fortune that that oaf of an Under Questioner hadn't realized she was a woman, with all that would have meant, but the thanks dwindled into insignificance against his railing at the fate that had prompted the Gevethen to do such a thing. He had long ago learned that little was to be gained by trying to anticipate the Gevethen's actions, but replacing Hagen with his murderer was unbelievable even by the standards of seeming arbitrariness that they set.

Who was this woman? What did they know about her? What qualities had they seen in her that would make her a substitute for a sadistic fanatic like Hagen? It was a chilling thought even for him, and it brought back vividly the sight of her face as she struggled to choke the life out of the wounded soldier who had captured her. And there were the others. The patrol that her dogs had savaged, and the other two soldiers who had been left on guard. Where were they now? Doubtless rotting somewhere in the Ennerhald with knife wounds as the marks of her benediction. He struggled to contain a shudder. The depths in a woman were far more fearful than in a man once they were plumbed. It was no new insight, but it did little to calm him and he set about checking his uniform yet again.

He had prepared one or two excuses – explanations – for his conduct in case the need might arise. 'Only doing my duty, ma'am.'

Ma'am? He tested the word and wrinkled his nose. Lord Counsellor, he decided. That was, after all, what the Gevethen called her. 'Only doing my duty, Lord Counsellor.' That was better.

Then there was, 'Very dangerous characters in the Ennerhald – safety of my men – not got the vision of their Excellencies, didn't recognize who you were.' Quite a good one, that last, he thought, though he wanted to say none of them. Nor would he, if opportunity allowed. It would be better by far if he could confine himself to the clipped courtesies of his office as official escort. Behave as though they had not shared such an unfortunate history. As though she had always been Lord Counsellor. Yes, he decided, that was what he would do.

He turned away from the mirror angrily as he caught himself fiddling yet again with his uniform.

Jeyan waited before the door. She had been dressed in the familiar replica of Hagen's uniform when she woke, but after her breakfast the servants placed a cape about her shoulders. It glistened golden even in the subdued lighting, and it was decorated with a single silver star. 'What is this for?' she had asked, but as usual, had received no reply. Then she had been stood in front of the door.

Almost immediately it opened, both leaves swinging wide to reveal Helsarn, immaculate and standing stiffly to attention. Behind him were two ranks of Citadel Guards in equally formal uniform. The servants closed behind and to the side of her and her stomach lurched. Was this the moment? Had they come to take her for punishment? To strip her of all this finery before destroying her?

But Helsarn was saluting. 'Commander Helsarn, Lord Counsellor. I have the honour to present your escort for the day.'

She recognized him. It was the one who had captured her. Whatever game was being played here she would give no one the satisfaction of seeing her fear. She fixed him with a cold gaze. Unexpectedly she caught a flicker of nervousness in him.

'Their Excellencies have asked me to take you to the Judgement Hall, Lord Counsellor,' he said.

'Why?' Fear, and the control of it, made her response sharp and commanding.

Helsarn hesitated. The Gevethen's orders were to be obeyed immediately, not debated, but he couldn't remain silent in the face of a direct question. 'Many have been arrested in the purging, Lord Counsellor,' he said. 'They are to be brought before the law for trial and judgement.'

What do I know about the law? Jeyan screamed inwardly. And I'll be no one's judge.

As you judge, so shall you be judged.

The memory of the Gevethen's words strangled any response and held her rigid. Helsarn, anxious to avoid any further questioning, saluted again then turned about. The Guards turned with him. A soft drumbeat behind her startled Jeyan, but before she could turn to see what it signified the servants hedged about her, obliging her to move after Helsarn and the Guards who had set off at a slow march.

The procession wound its way through the Citadel's interminable corridors, the drumbeat relentlessly setting its pace and marking its progress. Eventually they came to the part that, in the Count's time, had often been open to the people of Dirynhald who would come to marvel at both its high arches and ornate architecture, and the magnificent paintings and statues that decorated it – some of the finest works of art to be found in the whole of Nesdiryn. Then, the place had been made to seem even more spacious and open by the light which came from innumerable, subtly crafted mirrorways. Now, with the paintings and statues either removed or replaced by mocking pastiches, and the mirrorways sealed, it had been transformed into an echoing, gloomy cavern, full of concealing shadows, their darkness increased by the occasional shafts of mote-filled light that escaped the sealing of the mirrorways to shine through the interlaced woodwork of the ceiling.

Jeyan had been there as a child and vaguely recognized where she was. The contrast with her childhood memory weighed down on her and the grotesque events of the past few days became almost unbearable. For a moment, she thought her legs were going to buckle and she staggered slightly. Hands discreetly supported her but she was herself again almost immediately.

They moved into a wide entrance hall which led to what had once been the Banqueting Hall. Along the sides, shadows amongst shadows, were rows of people. The drumbeat pulsed on, unforgiving, shrivelling with its touch the faint murmur of voices that had preceded the arrival of the Lord Counsellor. Jeyan, at once curious, fearful and full of anger, looked from side to side as she passed by. It was not easy to make out details in the gloom but she could see that heads were bowed. As she peered more intently, those onlookers who felt the weight of her examination sank to their knees, like grass before a withering flame. It took her a little time to associate the two events and when she did she felt first shame, then elation, then shame again.

She became aware of more Guards falling in behind her and then the crowd itself. The sound of shuffling feet and rustling clothes rose up to fill the shadows with dark whisperings that scurried to and fro at the goading of the unyielding drum.

Then they were at the Gevethen's grim Judgement Hall – the Count's once glorious Banqueting Hall – another example of the Gevethen's wilful corruption of the richness that had preceded them, their brutal fist replacing the Count's open-handedness.

Towering doors, already opened, led to a wide aisle that ran straight down the centre of the Hall between the tiers of banked seats that now filled the place. Clusters of sallow lanterns hung from the ceiling and walls, replacing the glittering chandeliers and mirrorways that had brought light to innumerable past celebrations. Now, as though lit by a jaundiced moon, the Hall was pervaded by cold pallor and deep, concealing shadows.

Jeyan saw there were already a great many people present. Faces, rendered corpse-like by the light, turned to greet her entrance, then faded into the shadows as they bowed. Those following the procession drifted silently sideways up stairs and along walkways to fill the standing galleries at the rear and sides of the hall.

The tone of the drum became sharper and more jagged, attenuated by the shape of the Hall and the number of people occupying it.

As they reached the end of the Hall, Helsarn and his Guards moved to each side to form a line between the people and a dais on which was mounted a wide judicial bench. It had two levels. Behind the lower, standing motionless, was a group of people whose dark robes identified them to Jeyan as scribes and clerks. Like many officers of the Gevethen's regime, they looked little different from those who had served the Count. Indeed, many of them *were* those who had once served Ibryen, their new leaders keenly appreciating that there is no better device for the working of human cruelty than the belief that service to another or to an institution in some way absolves individuals from personal responsibility for their actions. But Jeyan noted these clean-handed toilers in the Gevethen's charnel-house only in passing, as her attention was drawn inexorably to the bench itself. Unlike the clerk's, this was markedly different from the one that had served the Count. That had been simple, elegant and workmanlike in its design: a symbol of the clarity and honesty that the Count strove for as he dispensed Nesdiryn's law. The bench now facing Jeyan however, was a tangled mass of intricate carving: elaborately woven branches, full of barbed thorns and sinister blooms, formed recesses and shadows from which sharp-featured faces peered and tiny mirrors glittered like predatory night-eyes. The whole was obsessively symmetrical, patterns unfolding within patterns and all seeming to grow from a golden escutcheon at the centre which, like Jeyan's cloak, bore the symbol of a single silver star. Unlike Jeyan's cloak however, the star was surrounded by two sections of a ring, broken in the same manner as those which hung about the Gevethen's necks. The bench was obviously the work of a considerable craftsman – a considerable, but tormented craftsman.

Jeyan hesitated as the Guards parted, but she was allowed no uncertainty about where she was to go as the servants manoeuvred her up on to the dais and thence to a chair behind the bench. Even when she sat down, the servants remained close to her, two of them flanking her, standing slightly behind. The chair was the centre of three and a partner to the bench, its straight, carved spine unwelcoming as she leaned back against it. Someone had placed a deep cushion on the seat. Presumably to allow for the difference in height between herself and Hagen, she decided, but the impromptu character of the adjustment heartened her a little – it was a peculiar flaw in the fearful perfection that surrounded the Gevethen, the perfection that had made the copy of Hagen's uniform for her, that had turned servants almost into automata, that had turned the mirror-bearers into who could say what . . . and that reflected itself, perhaps above all, in their meticulous, symmetrical movements. She squeezed the cushion as if it might give her some kind of reassurance as she stared out at the moonlit rows of watching faces. It did not, though she valued the effort if only because it smacked of secret personal independence. Such small benefits as accrued from this rebellion however, were set at naught by the intensity of the focus she could feel boring through her.

Let me faint, she thought. Let me sink into darkness and wake up somewhere far from this. The thought had a pathetic, childlike quality to it such as she had not experienced in many years, and it brought a snarling scorn in its train. Let them stare. Cravens! Lickspittles! Sustaining this grotesque pair with their fawning cowardice. Her long hatred flared up suddenly, almost snatching her breath away. The Gevethen had murdered her parents and many of her friends and, whatever game they were playing with her, she would play it too, until eventually some further flaw in the seeming perfection of their rule would give her that one opportunity that would bring her revenge. She was not aware of any of this showing on her face, but the atmosphere in the hall changed perceptibly.

Her gaze drifted from the watchers to the bench in

front of her. Save for a part of the top which was smooth and level and on which various papers were laid, the rest of the bench was a continuation of the elaborate carving that formed the front. It was as though the entire bench was a world of its own, a solid mass of labyrinthine weavings housing a myriad strange populations, all darkness and hidden movement. It added to her unease.

She had little time to ponder about the desk however, as a fluttering disturbance caught her eye. She did not need to look to know that it was the mirror-bearers presaging the entrance of their masters.

No drums to herald them, no guards to protect them, she thought. Fear announced them and the enigmatic mirror-bearers shielded them. There was a rustling from the assembled people as they slipped from their seats to kneel. The clerks below her bowed also. Presuming that she was expected to do the same, Jeyan made to move from her chair. However, though the servants on either side of her scarcely seemed to move, purposeful hands took her elbow and motioned her to stand. She had already felt the intent in such hands too often to dispute with them though she was half-expecting a further hand to push her head down into a respectful bow. None came however, and in its absence, she kept her gaze on the approaching group.

It was the first time she had looked at the Gevethen clearly from a distance, but it gave her no insight. The mirror-bearers moved about them with a precision and deftness that was chillingly unnatural. And even though she was aware of what she was looking at, it became difficult for her to differentiate the two principals from the images that hovered about them. Now a throng, now ordered rank and file, now a twisting line of pilgrims vanishing into an infinite distance . . . The movement and constantly changing perspectives made her feel dizzy. Focus on *them*, she demanded fiercely of herself. On *them*. Everything else is transient. Whatever purpose this endless reproducing of themselves served, whatever need it fulfilled, she could not begin to imagine, save that it was diseased, but any killing stroke she had to deliver eventually would have to be to the heart, and that is all she must see. *Nothing* must distract her.

Then, glowing inside her, came the revelation that she need only destroy the one to unbalance the other beyond recovery.

Only the one!

The Gevethen had reached the end of the aisle and were directly in front of her. A long row of dead, watery eyes stared up at her. No prompting came from the servants and she did not move. Instead, she looked at one of the two figures at the centre of the row.

Imbalance. The word came in the wake of her revelation. What it implied she could not hazard, but it was important, she knew.

Then, alarmingly, the two figures were moving apart, walking towards steps on either side of the dais. Though it was only a few paces, she sensed a tension growing as they moved further away from one another. As if to calm it, the mirror-bearers glided to and fro so that the diverging figures became merely the vanguard of two striding columns emerging from a busy cluster of their own kind at the centre, immediately before their Lord Counsellor.

Despite her new resolve Jeyan found herself still staring at this oddly shifting crowd when it abruptly disappeared, and the two Gevethen were at the chairs on either side of her. Hands took Jeyan's elbows again and eased her down on to her seat. Only when she was sitting did the Gevethen sit, and only then did the audience rise from its

382

knees. Though she did not look, she was aware of mirror-bearers seeping into the edge of her vision, as they began to hover at the ends of the bench. Others she could just hear moving behind her. Then merely by turning her eyes she saw more of them at the ends of the bench. What ghastly display was she part of for the benefit of this audience? she wondered.

Without any hint of an introduction, the Gevethen suddenly began speaking. Their harsh, simultaneous tones rasped across the Hall.

'The Lord Counsellor Hagen has been translated from this place. It was his time. He has been taken so that he might better serve He who is to come. No greater honour can be granted. Yet too, he serves us as faithfully and diligently as ever, for his spirit remains with us still, in the body of his successor, Lord Counsellor Jeyan Dyalith.'

The power that had carried Jeyan from the dungeons now straightened her legs and slowly brought her to her feet. She reached forward and rested her hands on the bench to catch her balance. The force that had lifted her from her seat took her arms also then held her solid and leaning slightly forward in a posture of silent menace. Although she was a little calmer now than she had been when she first encountered the Gevethen, the complete absence of control over her own limbs was nevertheless terrifying. She could not begin to imagine what ghastly power it was that these creatures possessed, that enabled them to manipulate her thus, but it was overwhelming. The thought of disputing with it did not even occur to her. The part of her mind that was still thinking coherently tried to tell her that it was just something else about the Gevethen she would need to study, quietly and carefully, but it was the merest whisper of rationality in the tumult of panic that was suddenly clamouring inside her and she barely heard it.

It seemed that only her eyes could move and as they searched through the coldly lit assembly, she became aware of a movement rippling through them. It was like a wind blowing across a field of tall, dark grasses. They were standing and bowing. When the wind had passed and there was stillness, Jeyan's head inclined forward a little as if in acknowledgement of this obeisance. Then she was seated again and released, and the dark grasses were swaying as the audience too, resumed their seats.

'The forms must be observed, Lord Counsellor,' came the voices from either side of her, soft and sibilant. 'Remember this well. Without them, all is disorder and chaos, and His way is the bringing of order, of perfection, in all things.'

The question, 'Who is this person you serve?' formed and despite herself, was almost spoken, but the voices turned from her and raked out across the Hall.

'Bring forward the first accused.'

There was a brief flurry of activity from the clerks just beneath her, then heavy rhythmic footsteps heralded the arrival of a solitary individual escorted by two Guards. He was barely capable of standing and his swollen face gave testimony to a severe beating. Bloodstains were seeping through his torn shirt even as Jeyan looked at him.

One of the clerks intoned the man's name, to which, after a none too gentle prod from one of the Guards, he nodded. The clerk continued: 'You are charged with fomenting disorder and with the preaching of rebellion against the will of the people and to the detriment of the peace, in that you did aid and abet the followers of the outlaw Ibryen.'

The man gazed at the clerk blankly.

'Serious charges,' the Gevethen said, their voices even more acid than normal. The sound seemed to bring the man to his senses. 'Who is Pleading Voice for this man?'

'I am, your Excellencies.' It was another of the clerks. He stood up, turned to face the Gevethen and bowed. Jeyan noted that his robes were of a different style to those worn by the others and of a conspicuously better quality. Further, his voice indicated a superior education. Anger began to curl inside her. A lawyer of some kind, she surmised. Are you one of those on whom my father leaned for support only to be abandoned? she thought viciously, memories flooding back to her.

'Have you anything to say that will prove your innocence . . .?'

'. . . your innocence?'

The voices, addressed directly to the prisoner, brought Jeyan sharply back to the present.

Fear filled the man's face. He looked towards the lawyer who had stood up on his behalf but the man was apparently engrossed in some papers.

There being no help from this quarter, the man spoke for himself, though with difficulty through his swollen mouth. 'I've not done anything, Excellencies,' he pleaded. 'I've always supported you. I helped in the riots . . . the liberation . . . when the Count . . . the outlaw Ibryen . . . was exposed and driven from the city.'

'How are you here, then?'

The man shot another glance at his Pleading Voice, again to no avail. 'I don't know, your Excellencies. I was nowhere near the place where Lord Counsellor Hagen was . . .' he faltered, obviously searching desperately for the word that had been used '. . . where he was translated. I kept the curfew that followed. I was sitting peacefully in my house when, for no reason, the Guards broke down

385

my door and started smashing everything and beating me and my family.'

The Gevethen leaned forward. 'If this is so, then it may be that you have indeed been brought here unjustly. Order is our way, citizen. We cannot tolerate random and arbitrary behaviour by our servants . . .'

'. . . our servants.'

Jeyan started and glanced quickly from one to the other. Their harsh tones were suddenly avuncular and concerned. The man became pathetically grateful. 'Thank you, your Excellencies. Your justice is legendary. I knew you'd see that a mistake had been made when it was explained.'

A reassuring wave from the Gevethen silenced him and their voices became harsh again. 'Bring the Commander responsible for this man's arrest before us so that these accusations can be put to him.'

There was a short pause, then Commander Gidlon appeared from somewhere at the side of the Hall. He moved hurriedly to the side of the prisoner and bowed deeply to the Gevethen.

'You have the official account of this man's arrest, Commander?'

'I have, Excellencies.' He held up a thick file of papers.

'Read it then. In full. Omit nothing. Serious allegations have been made against the men in your command and they must be answered . . .'

'. . . be answered.'

Their voices bore down on Gidlon powerfully and he began to look decidedly uncomfortable. The prisoner however, was brightening at each word, looking from the Gevethen to Gidlon in growing triumph.

Jeyan, orphaned by the Gevethen and moulded by the Ennerhald, watched the man in disbelief. Surely he couldn't be taking this black charade at its face value? She did not know exactly what was happening, but she wanted to scream out to him, 'Don't listen to them, they're taunting you. There's no justice here, only treachery and death. Spit in their faces.' But she knew that if she moved, either the hands of the servants or the Gevethen's strange power would pinion her to the chair before she could utter a word. Yet, something else was restraining her. Then, from the darkness within her, where murder had hatched, it came. It was unexpected but not unfamiliar. It was a withering contempt. The man was a fool. He deserved whatever was going to happen to him. He'd been stupid enough to get himself arrested and he'd grovelled before the Gevethen and now he would see the measure of their gratitude. Watching him learn would be amusing.

Gidlon began to read. 'The prisoner refused to open the door to your Guards, making it necessary for them to force an entry. He then assaulted them, injuring two before being over-powered. On searching this house, extensive evidence of his support for the outlaw Ibryen was found. Subsequent to his arrest, freed from the fear of his dangerous presence, witnesses have testified that on numerous occasions he has actively tried to persuade them to join him in plotting for the overthrowing of your Excellencies and the reinstatement of the outlaw Ibryen.'

His voice was brisk and formal and he stood smartly to attention when he had finished.

As Gidlon spoke, the prisoner's face registered first disbelief and then indignation. Still having difficulty in speaking, he spluttered, 'Lies! All lies! That wasn't what happened. I never refused to open the door. I didn't even know they were in the street until they smashed the door in. And they set about me – and my family – without

387

any provocation.' He turned to Gidlon. 'You lying—' He stopped himself and after a struggle to regain some composure, looked up in hopeful appeal to the Gevethen. 'Your Excellencies. The officer is mistaken. Perhaps he's confused my name with someone else's. There was a great deal of confusion following Lord Counsellor Hagen's . . . translation.'

'Indeed,' the Gevethen agreed with sympathetic nods. They motioned to one of the clerks. There was a brief exchange between the prisoner, the clerk and Gidlon followed by a comparing of documents, then the announcement, 'There is no error, Excellencies. All the papers are in order. Commander Gidlon's report refers to this particular accused.'

The prisoner burst out, 'Your Excellencies, you must believe me. This man is lying to protect himself. His men looted my house, beat me and my wife and son. And you can ask anyone who's ever known me – my neighbours – my friends – I've never spoken against you, ever. You have no more loyal subject . . .'

But the little game was over. Jeyan sensed the mirror-bearers moving behind her. The Gevethen were themselves again, and the man's words were frozen in his throat by whatever it was he was now looking up at.

'Be silent. You add to your offences by continuing to lie thus and by impugning the integrity of our officers.'

'We have already spoken to many of your friends and neighbours.'

'They have denounced you.'

'As a liar.'

'As a follower of the outlaw Ibryen.'

The prisoner's mouth dropped open as his gaze swung between the two Gevethen, then he turned to the lawyer. The Gevethen followed his lead.

'Pleading Voice, is anything to be said to mitigate the guilt of this man . . .?'

'. . . this man?'

'I'm guilty of nothing, Excellencies,' the prisoner protested.

He was immediately the focus of the Gevethen's attention.

'You are perfect? Without flaw?'

The question was spat out, its vicious tone striking the man like a spear. He opened his mouth to speak but no sound came. Not that the Gevethen were waiting for an answer.

'All are flawed, thus all are guilty. All that is to be determined here is the extent of your guilt.'

'That is the law.'

'Pleading Voice, what is to be said for this man?'

The lawyer slowly stood up and turned to the Gevethen. 'Excellencies, the prisoner begs forgiveness and throws himself upon your mercy,' he said portentously.

Jeyan suddenly found herself being addressed on either side by the Gevethen.

'Thus it is, Lord Counsellor.'

'Such are the imperfections that we have to deal with.'

'Flawed.'

'Flawed.'

Their tone was confiding, encouraging, and hung about with the pains that the responsibilities of office brought. It told her that she was one of them now – or soon could be. One of those who held the power. But there was a question there also.

Jeyan looked down at the prisoner; his battered face was a mixture of anger and fear which gave it a sulky appearance. His manner invoked no sympathy. The man shouldn't have got himself in this predicament. Her mind was racing. What was she being asked? She knew nothing of such proceedings, still less what she was doing here. What grotesque farce was being played out as part of her punishment?

'He betrayed the usurper Count.'

'Now he betrays us.'

'He is on the verge of betraying those same neighbours and friends whose goodwill he just referred us to.'

'What is the worth of such?'

'He and his kind betrayed your father.'

'Sentenced you to the Ennerhald.'

'Denied you your place at our side.'

'Should not the stable be cleansed, Lord Counsellor?'

'Made pure?'

The disdain in their voices chimed with the contempt that, despite her own fear and confusion, was still dominating her thoughts. They were right, she knew. It was the likes of the man before her who had rallied fearfully behind the Gevethen when they had seized power. Had they shown some spirit, some determination, some loyalty to the Count, then perhaps the Gevethen's coup would have foundered. But they hadn't. They had run before the sight of the disloyal Guards, then they had bent the knee, and the Gevethen, having once taken hold, assiduously tightened their grip daily.

What did it matter if this wretch was disposed of? Left to linger in a dungeon somewhere. He was not the first, nor would he be the last, whether she was there, masquerading as Lord Counsellor, or not. The thought of the death pits passed suddenly through her mind, but she turned away from it. It wasn't relevant. Whatever she said, this man had done nothing that would warrant execution, surely?

Her thoughts hardened and her contempt for the

390

prisoner merged into that which she had for the Gevethen. Whatever else happened, she must keep the privileged position that they in their arrogance, or folly, or rank madness, had thrust her into. Sooner or later, an opportunity would present itself for her to destroy them.

The Gevethen were leaning towards her, staring intently. Once again their words returned to Jeyan. 'As you judge, so shall you be judged.'

'What is your will, Lord Counsellor . . .?'

'. . . Lord Counsellor?'

Jeyan hesitated, uncertain what she should say, then, almost as if someone else were speaking, she said coldly, 'Betrayal cannot go unpunished, Excellencies. Nor can defiance.'

'Ah!'

'Ah!'

The two moon faces swam away from her as the Gevethen sat back in their chairs again.

'Guilty,' they said. 'Send him to the Questioners to discover the extent of his betrayal then bring him before us again.'

Jeyan felt a coldness inside her at the word 'Questioners' but she steeled herself. The Gevethen would do what they wanted to do and nothing she said or did would make any difference except to cost her her new-found advantage.

The two Guards closed about the man and marched him away. Just as they passed out of sight, Jeyan saw him stumble and to the sound of the marching was added that of feet being dragged over the close-timbered floor. She closed her ears to it.

Several hours later, Jeyan was back in her room sitting dully in front of a lavishly spread table. The Gevethen

391

had accompanied her there in a formal train.

'You have learned much, Lord Counsellor.'

'You will be a worthy successor.'

'Eat.'

'Rest.'

'More are to be judged tomorrow.'

As she sat motionless, the happenings of the day passed relentlessly through her mind, over and over. An endless line of prisoners paraded before her. She could feel their eyes on her still: expectant, contemptuous, angry, a few full of hatred, most full of fear. As for her own part in the proceedings, she was still no wiser. There had been some sadistic toying with each prisoner by the Gevethen, ably assisted by the clerks and the Guards, then she had been turned to for 'her will'. Each time she had intoned to herself, 'As you judge, so shall you be judged,' and then uttered the condemnation that she knew was expected. And each time the Gevethen had passed sentence as though they had been enlightened by her in some way.

Alone in the silence of her room, other thoughts came to trouble her, for, more than once that day, she had found herself enjoying the tormenting of the prisoners, enjoying the revenge she was taking on the people who had betrayed her and her family and the old Nesdiryn, and who now found the new Nesdiryn betraying them in their turn. She could not avoid relishing the idea that from where she now was, vengeance could be taken on more than the Gevethen.

Nevertheless, though she drank a little water, she ate nothing and she spent a restless night.

The following day was no different, though this time several of the prisoners had been to the Questioners and were being returned for sentencing. They were in an appalling physical condition and Jeyan wilfully gazed past many of them rather than risk meeting their gaze. Each one however, freely admitted a raft of crimes against the Gevethen and bowed when they were sentenced.

It came to Jeyan during that second day that whatever else they were doing, the Gevethen were showing her one of her own possible destinies. It strengthened her resolve to retain her present position at any cost.

That night she ate, and she slept more quietly.

It was before dawn when she was awakened. The servants were moving about the room with unusual urgency and she was dressed before she was fully awake.

'What's happening?' she managed to ask eventually.

Even as she asked the question however, the Gevethen were in the room. Though their round, pale faces were expressionless, there was an agitation about them that she had not seen before, and indeed, the mirror-bearers were transforming them into a trembling crowd.

Fearfully she dropped on to one knee and bowed her head.

'Lord Counsellor, you have judged well . . .'

                '. . . judged well.'

'But there is a lack.'

'A vision is missing.'

'Hagen has not taught you well enough.'

Memories returned of falling through the darkness with Hagen's spirit all about her. But what were they talking about? Though Hagen's presence had undeniably been there, he had communicated nothing to her. He had simply been there.

And so too, in whatever passed for distance in that strange world, had been Assh and Frey – hunting. Though she could not understand what had happened, the idea began to form that in some way the Gevethen's intentions in taking her into the world beyond had been thwarted, and they were not aware of it.

Not yet! The realization brought her fully awake.

'Excellencies, have I failed you?' she asked. 'My wish is only to serve.'

There was an agonizing pause during which Jeyan saw herself being dragged to the Questioners and returning to confess in the Judgement Hall, looking up at the Gevethen and admitting to any crimes that were put to her.

'Hagen must complete his work. We will hold Vigil, now. Come, rise.'

As Jeyan stood, the Gevethen moved to her side, and the two large mirrors came together in front of her.

Chapter 25

'What do you mean, gone?' Ibryen growled bad-temperedly as he pushed the Traveller's hand away and made to roll over.

'Gone, as in "not here any more, left, departed",' the Traveller retorted, scarcely more sweetly. The words shook Ibryen fully conscious. As he reluctantly disentangled himself from his blanket the faint light enabled him to see the Traveller trying to waken Rachyl. This proved to be only marginally less hazardous than waking Ibryen for, with a throaty chuckle, she rolled over and, seizing him with a powerfully affectionate arm, pinned him down by her side.

It took him some effort to free himself, during which time Rachyl came to full and dangerously indignant wakefulness. Holding her at arm's length he blurted out his news very quickly.

Then, with the aid of a lantern, the three of them were examining where the Dryenwr had lain and speculating as to why he had chosen to leave silently.

'It'll be for some honourable reason,' the Traveller told them. 'He's Warrior Caste, and a Soarer.'

'He's also in a world he knows nothing about,' Ibryen said. 'Warrior or not, honourable or not, he'll not survive long without our help. We must find him.'

The Traveller agreed. Rachyl, stretching and rubbing her eyes, looked up at the sky. 'We might as well wait until the light's better,' she said. 'The terrain's difficult for him. He won't have gone very far.'

Though it was the correct decision, neither Ibryen nor the Traveller found the waiting particularly easy.

'Sit down, the pair of you,' Rachyl ordered eventually. 'Pacing about like that you'll destroy whatever tracks he's left.' She looked pointedly at the Traveller and flicked her ears. 'Wouldn't you be better employed listening for him?'

'I've done that,' he said testily. 'There's nothing to be heard.'

'Which means?' Ibryen asked.

The Traveller thought for a moment, then frowned. 'Which means he's either a long way away or . . .'

'He's not moving.' Rachyl finished his reply. She levered herself to her feet and swore. 'I *knew* I'd end up carrying someone back off this trip. Well, poor light or not, we'd better start looking for him. You two stay where you are until I pick up his track. Pass me the lantern.'

'I'm not exactly without experience in tracking, you know,' Ibryen said, mildly irritated by Rachyl's manner.

'True, but you're not as good as I am, and you're still half-asleep or you wouldn't be debating the point with me,' Rachyl replied brutally as she began slowly and steadily circling the place where Isgyrn had slept. 'Here,' she said after a little while, though her face was puzzled. 'He seems to be very light on his feet for someone his size.' Then she shrugged and became practical. 'It looks as though he's gone uphill. We might as well break camp, take everything with us. I'll go first. Ibryen, will you keep close behind and confirm sign with me? I don't want to go lumbering past anything.'

'I'll stay at the back and keep listening,' the Traveller said, anticipating his orders.

Progress was very slow at first, Rachyl moving with great caution in the poor light. As the sky brightened, they began to move more quickly.

'At least he's made no attempt to disguise his tracks,' Rachyl said.

'I doubt he'd know how to down here,' Ibryen replied. 'It must be as strange for him as being underwater would be for us.'

'I told you. He's not gone for any dishonourable reason. It wouldn't occur to him to hide,' the Traveller said. 'He probably thinks he's a burden to us. Being independent and self-sufficient is important to the Dryenvolk.'

Isgyrn's trail led them steadily upwards through the forest and they pressed on in silence for some time. It was fully daylight when they came to the upper edge of the forest, but the sky was grey and overcast and threatening rain. Rachyl stopped and looked at the Traveller expectantly. He shook his head. 'Nothing,' he said. 'Wherever he is, he isn't moving.'

Rachyl grimaced. 'His tracks are faint enough here,' she said. 'Once we get to the rocks it's going to be *really* hard to find them. Not to say impossible.' She cast a sour look upwards. 'And if it starts to rain . . .' She left the conclusion unspoken. They set off again.

After a while they left the forest completely and all sign of the Dryenwr's tracks disappeared as they found themselves facing sheets of tumbled boulders and the choice of routes they had faced two days previously – a mountain on either side. The Traveller was about to speak when Rachyl raised a hand for silence. Ibryen nodded a confirmation to him. Rachyl stood for a long time, slowly looking from side to side, like an animal wary of a hiding

397

predator. It started to rain, but still Rachyl did not move. Then she pointed. 'This way, I think,' she said. The Traveller looked at Ibryen for an explanation but received none.

A few minutes later Rachyl, with a combination of triumph and relief, showed them a small skidmark in the moss lining a boulder. 'He's heading back up towards where we found him,' she announced.

'Why would he do that?' Ibryen asked the Traveller.

The Traveller shook his head. 'I doubt he is,' he replied. 'I doubt he'd want to go into that cleft again. He's probably just looking for a high place. Somewhere where there's more sky than land.'

Shortly after that they came to the ridge and, quite unspectacularly, found him. As the Traveller had said, he had made no attempt to conceal himself and he was visible for some time before they reached him. Indeed, he had not even made any attempt to shelter from the wind that was sweeping the rain horizontally over the ridge, and he was kneeling on the rocky ground, relaxed, but very straight, with the Culmaren about his shoulders.

'Isgyrn.' Rachyl announced herself softly before she reached him, for fear of provoking a violent response with too hasty an approach. The Dryenwr did not reply however, and as she drew nearer she saw that his eyes were closed. Rain was running in wind-blown streams down his face. She spoke his name again, a little more loudly, tentatively laying a hand on his arm. Still he did not respond.

Ibryen and the Traveller reached her. 'What's the matter with him?' she asked anxiously.

Ibryen looked at the Dryenwr, then shook him gently. This had no effect either. He crouched down and touched Isgyrn's throat and forehead, then carefully checked his head. 'His pulse is slow, but it's strong enough,' he said. 'And he's not feverish. He seems to be in some kind of a trance, but I can't find any sign of head injury.'

Rachyl lifted the Culmaren from Isgyrn's shoulders and draped it protectively over his head. 'He might be fine now but if we leave him like this he won't be in a few hours,' she said sternly. 'We'll have to get him to some kind of shelter while you two debate what's wrong with him.'

It was not a conclusion that could be denied. Ibryen moved to lift him.

'No!'

The Dryenwr's voice was resolute but distant, as if he were having to turn from some other task to speak. Ibryen started violently. But there was no other response from Isgyrn. His face remained impassive, his eyes closed, and his posture unbent.

The Traveller took Ibryen's arm. 'Leave him,' he said, then, to Rachyl: 'See if you can rig up your tent to give him some shelter.'

He led Ibryen a few paces away down-wind. 'How do *you* feel?' he asked.

'Fine,' Ibryen replied with some surprise. He patted himself, then, concerned, asked, 'He hasn't got something catching, has he?'

The Traveller shook his head. 'No, no, nothing like that. But how do *you* feel? The part of you that's . . . somewhere else.'

'That's a bizarre question.'

'Answer it nevertheless.'

Ibryen hunched his shoulders against the blowing rain. 'I'm not sure I can. The discomforts of this world are dominating my thoughts at the moment. Why the sudden interest?'

The Traveller bared his teeth impatiently then patently rebuked himself. 'The Dryenwr aren't arbitrarily separated into their castes by birth as in some societies, they're separated by their aptitudes and abilities. But it's not a rigid separation . . .'

'I've gathered that from our talk the other night,' Ibryen interrupted. 'It's an odd way to do things if you ask me, but what's it got to do with what's happened to Isgyrn?'

'It suits them,' the Traveller declared, irritably dismissing Ibryen's digression. 'Just listen. Not only is it not a rigid separation, they each tend to take a pride in whatever skills they have that lie outside those of their own caste.'

Ibryen fidgeted with the hood of his cape, which was flapping in the wind, and turned to Rachyl wrestling darkly with the tent. The Traveller drew him back. 'One of the Dryenwr castes is that of the Hearers. Those who, like you, can reach into the worlds beyond – or at least that world in which the Culmaren's true nature lies.' He glanced towards the still motionless form of Isgyrn. 'I think perhaps Isgyrn has drawn on whatever Hearing skills he has and is trying to reach out to contact the Culmaren.'

'Why?'

'He's lost, man!' the Traveller exclaimed heatedly. 'Lost in time, lost in place. From what he told us, he doesn't even know whether his homeland even exists today or whether it, and presumably his friends and kin, were destroyed fifteen, sixteen years ago in the cataclysm that threw him here, down to the middle depths.'

Ibryen held up his hands both to apologize and to subdue. 'Why shouldn't he try to seek out the Culmaren, if he can?' he asked.

'Because it's *dangerous*,' the Traveller said with a heavy

400

emphasis. 'The gift of the Hearer is no light thing. Guides and Mentors are needed. Their lore is full of stories of Hearers who have gone beyond and never returned.'

Ibryen's eyes widened. 'Dangerous! You never told me anything about that.'

The Traveller's reply held little comfort. 'It wouldn't have made any difference, would it? There was nothing I could do about your . . . talent. I've neither the knowledge nor the ability to help. You came, you went, all to some inner need of your own. Had you gone and not returned – just left a comatose shell behind you,' he nodded towards Isgyrn, 'I'd not have been able to do anything for you.' He seemed discomfited by this apparently ruthless abandonment of his companion. 'You're part of my journey back to the Great Gate, Ibryen,' he went on. 'I'd no choice but to follow you. And you're much more.' His voice fell and became almost awe-stricken. 'Some deep instinct protects you. You are guarded by a great and ancient strength. Don't ask me what, because I've no measure of it, but it *is* so. I doubt even the finest of the Dryenvolk's Hearers move into the worlds beyond with the ease with which you do, still less carry a waking awareness of them as you seem to do.'

Ibryen looked at him unhappily. 'All of which means what?'

The Traveller waved the question aside. 'I don't know. Just tell me how . . . *what* . . . you feel in that other part of you now, Ibryen?' he asked again.

There was an intensity in his voice that forbade any more questions. Ibryen closed his eyes. A gust of wind shook him. He felt the Traveller taking his arm to steady him. Danger, he thought nervously. Bewilderment he'd felt almost constantly at the strangeness of all that was happening. And fear, certainly, though that had been fear for his sanity and an inevitable fear of the unknown, not the skin-crawling fear of a silent night attack against greater odds, or the heart-pounding terror of pitched battle against an equally terrified foe intent on killing you. But he had never had any feeling that the very act of moving into these strange other worlds was intrinsically dangerous. Perhaps he was indeed protected by some great and ancient strength as the Traveller had said, for the change that had come upon him over these last few days did not have the character of a wrenching metamorphosis, but had been more like a simple opening of the eyes and a raising of the head to see for the first time what had been there all his life.

Even as he pondered these ideas, the blustering mountainside slipped into the echoing distance and he became aware of the floating emptiness that he had entered when he separated the spirit of the Culmaren from Isgyrn. But this time there was a rippling disturbance moving through it – something calling, thrashing helplessly, like a drowning man. It jerked him back to the cold mountain. He opened his eyes and spun round to look towards Isgyrn. The tent had been crudely rigged and Rachyl was approaching.

'Thanks for the help,' she said caustically, but she did not pursue the observation when she saw the look on Ibryen's face as he strode past her. He crawled into the tent, motioning the others to follow. Rachyl and the Traveller could not enter the tent with Isgyrn kneeling in it and Ibryen settling himself on the rocky ground as comfortably as he could, but they were able to squat in the entrance out of the worst of the wind and rain.

'Tell Rachyl what you just told me,' Ibryen said to the Traveller. 'I understand none of it, but I think you're right – no, I *know* you're right. I can't leave him there, he's utterly lost. I'll try to fetch him back. I don't know how long it'll take, or what you can do. Just keep us both warm, I suppose.'

'What's he doing?' Rachyl demanded of the Traveller fiercely, but the little man lifted his hands in a plea for silence, as did Ibryen.

Then, with no more thought than he would give to the taking of a single step, Ibryen was in both the cramped, rattling tent and the world beyond.

Though he knew that Isgyrn was immediately beside him in the tent, the emanations of panic that Ibryen could feel in the world beyond were elsewhere – distant from him, in so far as distance existed in this place. The fear that he felt in them chilled him, so primitive and awful was it and he had to steel himself before he could move towards the disturbance.

'Isgyrn,' he called, though he had neither body nor voice – such things had no meaning here. 'Isgyrn. Be calm. There's no danger here except what your fear makes.'

The fear shifted and changed but did not diminish. Ibryen moved steadily towards it, though even as he did so he could feel it infecting him. He repeated the call, this time as much for his own benefit as for Isgyrn's. 'There's no danger here except what you make for yourself.'

Then he was proved correct, for the danger that Isgyrn had brought was all about him. Tales flooded into him of men drowned as they had sought to rescue others, weaker by far, but given an adamantine embrace by primordial fear. Such was his position now. Isgyrn's fear clung about him, thrashing and clawing, beating out a battering rhythm which echoed that of the wind shaking the tent in the world where Rachyl and the Traveller sat watching, as helpless as they were unaware of what was happening.

Ibryen found himself resisting with weapons and skills he did not know he possessed. He reached into the very

403

heart of Isgyrn's terror, for he knew that the Dryenwr was no coward. He was a man, already desolated by events beyond his understanding, who had woken to find himself in one alien world and had now entered another, even stranger. A world that was vast and empty and dead and at the same time teeming with life and circumscribed by the merest mote. A world in which time did not exist yet in which it also flickered and was different in all directions. He was a man too, burdened by the lore of his people and by a lack of the sight that, even as Ibryen wrestled both with him and, worse, the corrosive contagion of his terror, he realized he possessed. For he saw this world with a strangely cold eye, and he knew that Isgyrn could see it only as through a cracked and distorted lens.

Yet still Isgyrn was whole. That which had made him Warrior Caste and had made him stand fearful but unflinching before his greatest and most feared foe, high amid the clouds, sustained him even now, though it was failing rapidly.

Ibryen spoke, imbuing that which served for his voice here with such calm as he could muster, though Isgyrn's struggling was taxing him grievously. 'Isgyrn. Hold to me. There is nothing to fear here. Nothing can harm. What you see are but shadows.'

'Who . . .?'

'I am Ibryen. The Traveller tells me your people would call me a Hearer. I see this place more clearly than you, and I see your pain. Hold to me, I'll take you back to the world where you properly belong.'

Denial washed over him and, for a moment, Isgyrn's fear threatened to sweep them both away. 'It is so, Dryenwr!' Ibryen shouted. 'Even now, Rachyl and the Traveller are watching our bodies, waiting for our return.'

But Isgyrn was barely listening. Then, for the first time,

Ibryen began to feel a fear which was other than that which was rising in response to the Dryenwr's. He had no words for the knowledge, but he knew that Isgyrn's wild thrashing must be contained or harm would be done that could destroy them both. Such as time was in this place, it was moving against them. Bounds were being strained which could tolerate little more. The very fabric of this world seemed to be groaning under Isgyrn's onslaught.

For a moment, Ibryen teetered on the edge of panic himself, then, the ancient legacy of the battle-hardened transmuted his fear into anger. He blasted contempt into the Dryenwr's frantic spirit.

'Is this the Warrior who led his Soarers against over-whelming odds and prevailed? Is this the Warrior who faced your white-eyed usurper and his screaming mount? Or is it some mewling child, fearful of the dark?'

Briefly his mind was filled with a vision of Isgyrn's Soarers Tahren carried beneath their arching, many-coloured wings, as they swooped and dived upon the black ranks of their enemy, like great fighting birds. Though the vision was fleeting he saw the order and discipline and courage which sustained the fighters. He saw the long-trusted tactics of this extraordinary arena forged anew by vision and desperate imagination to turn the hitherto irresistible tide of the enemy. His heart both soared and cried out in pain as he saw too, and heard, the all-too-familiar consequences of battle as the sky rang with war cries and death screams, and was streaked with skeins of blood and gore. And he felt the deep injustice of the insult he had just offered. Then, the vision was swept away – his baiting had proved as effective as it had been crude and it was an unknown reflex that protected him from the first flush of Isgyrn's anger.

It came to Ibryen that perhaps he had made a mistake.

Isgyrn might not have understood the nature of the place where he now found himself, but he understood honour and insult, and he understood fighting. And now, as Ibryen's fear had become anger, so did his – an awful, berserker anger – the anger of a man who has only death before him and who, with no further fear left, will carry as large an entourage of his enemy with him as escort into the shades as his strength will allow. It was also an anger re-doubled by shame for what he perceived as his previous cowardice and it seized Ibryen with a crushing power, threatening to extinguish him with a single monstrous effort.

But just as Isgyrn's fear had threatened to infect Ibryen so now did his fighting frenzy, for Ibryen was no stranger to wild and desperate combat. Further, this was *his* world. Defeat was unthinkable.

Thus, while Rachyl and the Traveller sat in the mouth of the tent huddled against the driving rain, and nervously watched the silent, apparently sleeping men, that part of them which existed in the world beyond wrestled in a manner that neither of them truly understood.

Ibryen, the more aware of the two, defended himself while he sought for a way to overwhelm Isgyrn, though it was no easy task against the Dryenwr's primitive but battering attacks. 'No, Isgyrn,' he shouted, over and over. 'Stop fighting. You'll destroy us both.' Then a small inspiration floated into the mayhem. 'Think Warrior, think. The Hearer in you has failed, the Warrior in you brings only pain here. Be a Seeker. Think. Think of your land, of your kin. Think of the Culmaren that died to bring you this far and keep you alive until help came for you. Is this a fitting reward for its sacrifice?'

The onslaught faltered, though whether because of Ibryen's challenge or Isgyrn's exhaustion was not apparent. Part of Ibryen tensed instinctively, scenting victory and preparing to leap and seize the advantage. But the part of him that was a leader of his people, reined the urge back and waited. Twice, in the ensuing silence, Isgyrn seemed set to renew the conflict, but twice he hesitated and twice Ibryen remained still, carrying only the thought of the dead Culmaren in his mind.

Then came a hesitant and bewildered voice. 'Ibryen, is this truly you? How have you come after me? Where is this place? What has happened to me?'

Ibryen winced as an acrid mixture of fear and shame touched him. He did not allow the Dryenwr to speak further, but reached out in reassurance and silent, unconditional forgiveness. 'More questions than I can answer, Isgyrn,' he said. 'But I am Ibryen here just as I am Ibryen elsewhere. As to how I came here, I don't know, but I can take no more pride in it than in my black hair and black eyes, as it seems I was born with the skill to travel thus for all I've only just come to know of it.'

Understanding suddenly washed over Ibryen. 'I remember,' Isgyrn gasped out. 'I came here to call the Culmaren. To see if I could touch them and learn about my kin, my land.'

There was such an aching loneliness in his voice that Ibryen could do no other than reach out to him again. 'This *is* the place where the Culmaren dwell, but it's also a place where you do not belong,' he said. 'That you're still sane is perhaps a tribute to the Hearer's blood you carry within you.'

There was a brief stab of sharp and fierce resentment that he, a Dryenvolk Warrior, should be addressed thus by this dweller in the middle depths, but it was gone almost before Ibryen could respond to it, though he felt a flicker of resentment of his own that he should be drawn

407

into this predicament when his people were placing their trust in him to find a way of bringing down their own enemy. And, whatever else was happening on this strange journey, that prospect was as far from him as ever. He felt suddenly burdened.

Though both remained silent, Ibryen sensed their combined anger coiling and twisting and shifting something fundamental in this world. No, he realized suddenly, not in this world, which was beyond disturbance by such trivia, but in his grip upon it . . .

And in his grip upon his form that sat on the mountainside.

He seized Isgyrn protectively, uttering again the injunction, 'Hold to me.'

A soft, haunting call echoed through the vast emptiness that was Ibryen's perception of the world of the Culmaren. Another followed it.

But neither of the flickering consciousnesses that were Ibryen and Isgyrn heard it.

They were gone.

Chapter 26

Jeyan's second passage through the mirrors was no less frightening than her first, though this time it was quicker. The Gevethen moved to either side of her and led her forward as before. Despite the pressure of their grip, she could do no other than close her eyes and flinch away as her reflection strode towards her. The wash of bitter coldness passing through her made her gasp, then she opened her eyes to find herself once more in darkness. Vague reflections of the dimly lit room she had just left hung about her.

There was little time for pondering these matters however, for the Gevethen's grip about her shoulders was urgent. Once or twice she felt them hesitate, and she caught the faint whisper, 'Gateways', passing between the two unseen figures.

Fearful that the Gevethen might learn that Hagen had in some way failed to perform whatever task it was they had set him, Jeyan searched frantically for some means of postponing what was presumably an imminent meeting. Escape was impossible. Even if she could break away from the Gevethen's grip – which felt very unlikely – where could she go in this place? She was not even sure that she would exist here without the presence of the Gevethen.

Wisps of light began to appear. And hints of sounds.

'What is this place, Excellencies?' she asked, snatching at the first coherent idea to form.

There was a short stillness as though everything about her was holding its breath.

'This is the place between the worlds, Jeyan Dyalith.'

'The place of the Gateways.'

Jeyan risked again. 'Forgive my foolishness, Excellencies, but I don't understand. What worlds? How can there be—?'

The grip about her shoulders tightened painfully.

'Seek not to understand.'

'Obey.'

Jeyan gritted her teeth against the pain. 'If I understand, will I not be better able to serve you, Excellencies?'

There was another stillness. Longer this time, and tense. There was a strange quality in the Gevethen's voice when they replied, as if they were reluctant to discuss the matter.

'Obedience to His will is all, Jeyan Dyalith.'

'What is needed, you will be shown.'

'Understanding is His and His alone.'

Jeyan bit back her inquiry about who He might be. Instinct told her that pain, even death or worse, lay down that road if she persisted.

Though the vague reflections of her room were unchanged, the shifting patterns of light and the eerie chorus of sounds had been growing in intensity. And something was hovering in her mind, something small, but important.

Suddenly, she knew what it was. It was the Gevethen's voices: there was fear in them! There had been a hint of it when she had been brought here before, but she had been too shocked and afraid to think about what it meant. It was taking the edge off that cold harshness in their voices. It was making them into ordinary men. Brothers. Wretched twins. Loving and hating one another at the same time, inextricably bound together.

'The strange passageway you showed me when you brought me here before, Excellencies, was that one of the Gateways to the other worlds?'

'No, that is . . .'

'*Hush!*'

The word, with its urgent sibilance, echoed into the movement about her, and arrowed off into some unknowable distance, all shapes and sounds drawn after it, twisting and dancing in its wake.

Conflict! Her question had caused a conflict between the Gevethen! Even the hint of such a thing had never manifested itself in the time she had been with them. Had she thought about creating such, she would have deemed it impossible. Yet Jeyan allowed herself no triumph: there was no saying what she might have released. She braced herself for whatever might follow, becoming suddenly desperately fearful, and resolving to break away from the Gevethen if opportunity presented itself, regardless of the consequences. Better to wander lost in this mysterious place than to suffer what might come to pass at their hands.

Then she became aware of a whispered dispute being carried on behind her. It was reflected in a quivering of the arms about her shoulders. For a fleeting instant she had the impression that the two men were pummelling one another, like spoilt children, but she wilfully tore her attention away by focusing intensely on what appeared to be a pale yellow mist that had floated into her view. Like everything else about her, the mist shifted and changed, both in shape and colour. And, she noted, the sounds that were hovering about it changed also.

'We *must* try.' The soft voice floated into her awareness. She tried not to listen.

'It will fail again.'

'We *must* try. He tests us ever. We must open the Way to come to His presence again.'

'I am afraid of His anger. We have been so long.'

'But the merest moment in His endless patience. We have much to tell Him. His will is being done in this place.'

Then, very softly, and so full of fear, that despite her own cruel hatred of the Gevethen, Jeyan felt stirrings of pity.

'What if He is no more.'

All about Jeyan froze. The endless moving stopped as if it had never been. She was alone in a frozen landscape. The voice continued and the landscape moved again.

'The birds – our eyes – went. Vanished overnight. No warning, no message. Then the Way to His fastness closed against us and could not be opened.'

Jeyan waited, terrified lest her heart beat again and reveal her as an eavesdropper.

'You blaspheme, brother.' There was naked terror in the answer. 'He is the One True Light. He is eternal. He will come again to right that which was flawed in the Beginning.' Then there was venomous fury. 'It is your lack of faith that has brought this about.'

'No.'

'Yes. Have you forgotten so soon the great powers He gave us?'

'No. I . . .'

'Curse you.'

The voice began to cringe and plead. It lost all semblance of the cold, grating harshness that marked the Gevethen's voice. 'No. I was just . . . He is testing us, as you say. Many Citadels He was building to prepare the world for His coming, and ours was to be the finest and strongest. Remember? I use the power better than you – you've always said that. It's not my fault, truly. We'll discover how to open the Way eventually. I'll try harder. See, see!'

'Wait!'

But the injunction came too late and Jeyan could feel something reaching out into the disorder. Almost immediately, another power joined it. The Gevethen were one again, she sensed. As had happened before, she felt herself briefly touching a myriad other worlds, each one vivid and real, but gone almost before she could register it. Then she was standing before the long tunnel again. Its walls glowed and shimmered uneasily, and in the far distance, it seemed to waver as if searching for something.

'It is done.' There was triumph in the voice. 'Further than ever before. My power is stronger than ever.'

'*Our* power.'

'Our power.'

'Soon we shall come to His presence again.'

But as well as the triumph, there was strain also, and the distant unsteadiness began to move nearer.

'No!'

'Hold firm!'

Jeyan felt the trembling of their effort pass through her. But the wavering grew wilder and closer, gathering speed as it drew nearer. Then the walls of the tunnel immediately before her began to grow diffuse and to twist and turn until finally they were spinning giddily. An ear-rending screech began to grow out of the collapsing confusion.

The Gevethen's effort grew increasingly frantic, but she could feel it worsening the disintegration. It became a hypnotic maelstrom. Only when the onrush was nearly

413

upon her did Jeyan manage to tear her gaze from it. With a cry she pushed backwards. But the Gevethen held her still, their grip firmer than ever, despite the battle they were waging for control of the shrieking vortex the tunnel had now become.

Then, with the noise so intense as to be almost tangible, the mysterious Way that the Gevethen had opened came to its crashing end, drawing into it all the shapes and patterns that were floating around Jeyan and crushing them at its heart into nothingness. Jeyan knew that her mouth was open and that she was screaming, but she could hear nothing above the awful din. For an instant it seemed that every part of her was being drawn into the terrible destruction and that soon would be nothing more than a tiny glittering part of the whirling kaleidoscope.

Then there was darkness, and silence, save for her own piercing shriek.

And the grip of the Gevethen about her shoulders was no more. She was alone.

Where there had been a vast echoing emptiness, there was now milling confusion and colour and a cacophony of many voices and sounds. And floating amid this was Ibryen. There and not there. An awareness that was diamond-hard in its clarity yet tenuous as an idle summer breeze.

I should be afraid. The thought drifted through him. But he was not. He had had doubts about his sanity many times during these past few days, and this place, this state he was in, was so far beyond anything he could have imagined that those doubts should have become a screaming clamour. Yet they had not. For though he was not of this place, he knew that he was no intruder and that it was neither an unnatural rending of the fabric of reality

414

nor the collapse of his mind that had carried him here. Strangely he felt less disturbed here than he had in the world of the Culmaren. That had been profoundly alien. It was as though he belonged here, albeit rather as he would belong as a guest in the domain of a neighbouring Lord.

Though there was no scrabbling fear however, there was concern. He was not a guest, nor was there any host. Rather he had wandered here inadvertently – an aimless traveller, and one deeply ignorant of the ways of the land to which he had now come. And he was lost, though that seemed to be inherent in the nature of this place. But his real concern was for the other awareness that was with him, held at once free and bound, like a planet by a more massive neighbour. And Isgyrn indeed now seemed to be teetering on the edge of insanity.

Ibryen reached out to him. 'Hold firm to me, Warrior,' he said, repeating the injunction he had given before they had found themselves transported here. 'This has little more substance than our thoughts. Our bodies are safe, guarded by Rachyl and the Traveller on the mountain.'

The authority in his manner surprised him in that it did not surprise him. For while *he* might perhaps belong here, he knew that Isgyrn definitely did not, and that he was responsible for bringing him here.

Yearning images suddenly flooded into his mind: clouds, bright against a blue, all-encompassing sky; spires and domes glittering silver and gold, and lesser buildings, many-hued, nestling amongst them. And beyond, a strange undulating landscape, and vast cloudscapes. And everywhere, people. People walking broad highways that soared like rainbows from building to building, and people gliding beneath many-coloured wings like great birds . . .

'Hold to *me*,' Ibryen said again, powerfully, intruding,

with some regret, into the vision. 'You need no lessons from me, Warrior, to know that to survive you must see things as they are. Neither solace nor safety is to be found in such memories. They will sustain you in other ways. *Hold to me.* I will guide us from this place.'

Fear and panic replaced the longing memories, but at their heart Ibryen could feel Isgyrn's stern will struggling with them. He sought for something to say that would help the Dryenwr, but no inspiration came, only the knowledge that Isgyrn's inner battle was his alone, and beyond any helping. Whether at the end he would be returned to his body whole and wiser, or a gibbering shadow, was now his choice. All that Ibryen could do was wait and be there.

'Helplessness does not sit well with me either.'

Isgyrn's words startled Ibryen. The Dryenwr was suddenly in command of himself again. 'I think I'd rather face that white-eyed demon and his shrieking mount than another such ordeal again,' he went on. Then he answered Ibryen's question before it was asked. 'Of my various aptitudes the most modest is that of Verser – I haven't the imagination to create a place like this. My friends . . .' he faltered briefly '. . . my friends often rebuke me for being stern – too logical. It causes . . . *caused* . . . great amusement. Maybe I've been driven mad, maybe I've perished and am in some hellish limbo, but for the time being, I'll consider myself and you, whatever we are here, and all this around us, however strange, to be real simply because it seems to be so and because I remember setting off on this journey of my own free will knowing that places beyond our ordinary worlds existed and that I ventured thus without a guide at no small risk.' There was a pause, then, 'Though, warrior to warrior, and logic not withstanding, I confess I'm mightily afraid. You sit easier

416

here than I do – do you know what this place is, or what's happened to us?'

'I've no answers, Isgyrn,' Ibryen replied. 'I think we must await events.'

Even as he spoke however, Ibryen felt a pattern in the shifting shapes and sounds about him. A feeling of hopefulness rose inside him, like the sun over the mountain tops. He took Isgyrn and moved into it.

And they were whole again.

Though they were not cramped in a noisy tent on top of a rainswept ridge. They were standing on a small grassy hummock in a forest. Sunlight danced through the swaying tree-tops, sending dappling shadows everywhere, birdsong filled the air, counterpointing the rustling of the trees, and forest scents pervaded everything.

The two men stood for some time carefully testing hands and arms, then gazing at one another, before finally examining their new surroundings. Isgyrn's eyes were wide with inquiry, but Ibryen shook his head.

Tentatively he stepped forward, as though too sudden a movement might cause the whole scene to vanish. Soft woodland sward yielded under his foot. Isgyrn followed him. 'This is a forest, isn't it?' he said as they walked slowly down the hummock. 'It's so beautiful. Such colours, such perfumes. How—?'

Ibryen shook his head again. 'This is a forest, yes,' he said. 'But I've no more answers now than I had a few moments ago, only a great many more questions.'

Isgyrn rubbed a hand down his arm unhappily.

'Don't worry. You're still here,' Ibryen said. 'We're both here, though where *here* is belongs to that list of questions.'

'This is nowhere that you recognize then?' Isgyrn said. 'No part of your land?'

Ibryen chuckled softly. 'I wouldn't pretend to be familiar with every tree and field of Nesdiryn, but no, I don't think it is. And it's summer, judging by the state of the trees and the temperature.'

Isgyrn nodded. 'What shall we do?' he asked simply.

'Await events still, I fear,' Ibryen replied. 'But we might as well try to answer your other question – where are we – while we're waiting.'

They selected a direction at random and set off. As they disappeared into the trees, a figure emerged moving in the opposite direction. It was a youth mounted on a well-groomed horse and leading a sturdy pack pony. His head was bowed and his face lowering, and unlike the two newcomers he seemed to be angrily oblivious to the beauty of his surroundings.

The echoes of her scream faded, but a greater terror threatened to take possession of Jeyan as she stood blinking in the darkness. Carefully she extended her trembling arms forward. They touched nothing. Then, softly, she said, 'Excellencies?'

There was no answer. She repeated the call, but still there was no reply.

And she could not feel their presence!

What had happened? It occurred to her that all this had been an elaborate trick so that she would be left abandoned in this dark world within the mirrors as her final punishment. But even as the idea formed, she dismissed it. The hissed quarrel she had overheard had been no act, nor the effort she had felt being exerted as their strange creation had slipped from their control. The terrifying memory of that onrushing power was still vivid in her mind. It seemed inconceivable that anything could have survived it.

Were they dead? Had that monstrous tunnel and its destruction destroyed *them*? Yet she was alive. But then, she had been a mere bystander – while *they* had been at the heart of it. And now there was not even a hint of their cloying presence about her. She felt a flicker of exhilaration. Maybe they were dead, maybe not, but they were gone from her. She was free!

True, she was utterly lost, and surrounded by darkness, but though she was afraid of many things, darkness was not one of them. Perhaps she was its creature, perhaps it was simply that as a hunter she knew that what she could not see, could not see her.

She was about to turn around when she remembered what the Gevethen had said when they first carried her through the mirrors. 'You must not look back. Not yet. There is a deep and awful madness here for those who are unprepared.'

She paused for a moment, then sneered and turned around.

Nothing happened. The darkness was all about her.

Arms extended she began to walk slowly forward. Then she became aware of a familiar presence.

'Hagen?'

There was a shifting in the presence, as of something waking, or pulling itself away from a deep reverie.

'The new Lord Counsellor again, I presume.'

The voice was full of sour weariness. Gall rose in Jeyan's throat at the sound of it. 'Indeed,' she snarled. 'The new Lord Counsellor. And your judge and executioner. I trust that whatever passes for your soul is burning endlessly here.'

There was a long silence.

'It seems you are to share this place with me, upstart. Sent here without their protection for me to dispose of.

Have they discovered the flaw in you already?'

The presence closed about Jeyan. For an instant, fear threatened to flare up inside her but it was transformed into anger and hate almost immediately. The presence faltered. 'You've no terrors to offer anyone, Hagen,' Jeyan rasped. 'Least of all me. I opened your veins. Sent you to this place. I've slept in your bed, eaten from your plates, sat in your grand seat of judgement, *seen into your worthless soul*. Whatever you are here, you are nothing in the real world. A mouldering corpse somewhere. Probably dumped in the death pits, where my dogs used to play, your precious limbs mingling with those of your victims, while this dried and shrivelled remnant lingers howling in the dark.'

'You'll see how dried and shrivelled a remnant I am when you look into your own worthless soul, Jeyan Dyalith.' Hagen's voice was full of taunting rage. 'Already I can feel the joy inside you that comes from the power of the Judgement Chair.'

A dreadful chill closed around Jeyan's stomach as memories returned of the relish she had taken at times as she had sat in Hagen's chair during the last two days. 'No!' she cried out. That had been in revenge for the betrayal of the Count, she wanted to say but dared not. As it was, there was grim disdain in the response.

'Too loud, Lord Counsellor. Too loud. Too shrill a protest. If you lift the veil that hides your true self, you'll see me looking out at you. We are one and the same.'

The taunting continued. 'How do you think I came here? Even after death I was to serve them. My body was committed to the Ways. They needed me to find the truth of them, but all I found was that those who come here without the gift or a true guide can look to be trapped in Ways of their own making. Like you, *Lord Counsellor*.

Ask me why you're trapped in the Way that is mine and mine alone if you are not me?'

Jeyan found herself almost choking. 'You're rambling, dead man. The Gevethen bound you here. They need nothing from you; they have the mirrors to bring them here and guide them.'

Black amusement and scorn washed about her. 'Here is nowhere, child. A rough-hewn ante-chamber, crude and ill-formed, at best a window of bent and crooked glass.' Then incongruously confidential, 'Great knowledge. Knowledge beyond our imagining made the mirrors, but they are as nothing to the gift. And they are dangerous. So dangerous. This I know now.'

'*This you know*,' Jeyan echoed witheringly, recovering herself. 'You know nothing. Leave me. You contaminate even the darkness with your bleating.'

The response was almost childishly petulant. 'They needed me to find the truth of the Ways, to open again that which would bring them to—'

It stopped abruptly and Jeyan felt the presence withdrawing. Suddenly suspicious, she seized it. 'To where?' she demanded, then, savagely: 'To whom?'

There was no reply. 'To Him, of course,' she said slowly, testing the idea. 'This Master of theirs.' She felt Hagen's presence squirming. 'Who is He, Hagen?' she said, driving the words into the growing distress like stilettos. Still there was no reply. 'Who is He, damn you!' she blasted, suddenly furious. 'Who is this creature that the Gevethen grovel before? Tell me!' The darkness quivered with her rage, wringing a reply that was the merest of whispers.

'He is the One who gave them their powers. Gave them the mirrors to enter the Ways. Sent them here to prepare for His Coming, for the time when the Righting of the Beginning shall begin.'

421

Jeyan's anger became contempt once more. 'You're parroting their words, Hagen. I've heard them. And they're as meaningless from you as they were from them. If you know anything worth knowing, tell me who He is and *where* He is, so that when I've finished with the Gevethen I can stick a knife in His throat like I did in yours. Avenge us all.' Hagen's presence began to flail and gibber in terror. Jeyan's rage grew in proportion. 'Tell me why this all-powerful Master has abandoned His servants.' Hagen finally tore himself away. Jeyan screamed after him, 'He has, hasn't He? Abandoned them? TELL ME WHERE HE IS, DAMN YOU! I'll spill His blood like I spilled yours! I'll drown His every follower in a flood of it!'

Her scream dwindled into the empty darkness.

Then it was echoing back, ragged and broken, bringing with it shards of sound and light, glittering and shining. They hovered about her, merging imperceptibly into the chaos of movement and noise of where she had been with the Gevethen before her casual question to them had wrought such havoc. And, to her horror, in front of her, silhouetted against a brilliant, whirling maelstrom of light, were the Gevethen.

What had they heard?

Hastily she tried to calm herself, pushing from her mind the murderous frenzy into which she had wound herself. Should she turn and flee while she was still free?

But there was something strange about the Gevethen that held her there. It took her some time to realize what it was. They were motionless. Even the drifting birdlike hands were still. And they were leaning against one another, like two once-proud statues, now tilted with age. But the real strangeness lay in the fact that she could see only two of them. There were no mirror-bearers flowing about them making milling moon-faced crowds and marching ranks and files. There were just two men.

If she had a knife she could kill them both, she knew. But she had not!

Rage and frustration flooded through her, threatening to bring back the screaming passion with which she had just blessed Hagen. Mirror-imaged, the two figures started apart slightly, then slowly began to turn to face her. Quickly she dropped to her knees and bowed her head.

'Ah!'

'Ah!'

She waited, holding her breath, still and silent. Had they heard?

There was a faint whispering, but she could not catch any of it through the all-pervading clamour. Well, knife or not, if she was threatened here she would rend at least one of these creatures with her bare hands! Mar their precious perfection!

'Ah!'

'Ah!'

'You have learned . . .'

'. . . learned.'

'We feel the spirit of Lord Hagen about you.'

'I have been in his presence, Excellencies,' she said, choosing the truth in the absence of any other inspiration. It brought its own. 'Seeking the benefits of his wisdom, the better to serve you.'

'How did you come there, Lord Counsellor?' There was uncertainty in the question and she could not avoid a hint of surprise in her answer.

'By your will, Excellencies.'

There was more whispering, then, 'Rise.'

As she stood up, the Gevethen's grip closed about her shoulders again. It was different, however. There was a hint of a tremor in it and a weight which told her that they were leaning on her as they had just been leaning on one another. Vulnerable, vulnerable, she thought. She had hurt them with the least of questions. She must seize the initiative again. Who could say what might follow?

She looked at the whirling confusion of lights in front of her.

'What is that, Excellencies?' she asked, affecting a nervousness she did not truly feel.

There was a pause and the grip on her shoulders shifted.

'Beyond your understanding, Lord Counsellor.'

'A wonder few have seen.'

Liars! It's the wreckage left from your attempt to reach your precious Master, isn't it?

Oh for a knife, she could surely slay them both now!

Perhaps she could pitch them into this swirling violence? But while the Gevethen were obviously weakened in some way, they were not leaning so heavily on her that she could hope to unbalance them without throwing herself in as well. And too, what end would it serve even if she could? Would that maelstrom destroy them? She had no answer. Besides, she realized starkly, not only did she not know what it was, she did not even know where it was, so disorienting was this place. True, it was in front of her. But was it a dozen paces away, or ten dozen, or half a day's walk? She could not tell, nor was there anything nearby that could help her.

The Gevethen were drawing her firmly backwards. Reluctantly, she offered no resistance, trying to take solace in the thought that having tried to create the tunnel twice within the last few days, the Gevethen would undoubtedly try again and probably have no greater success. But, despite herself, a raging frustration at the loss of this opportunity swept aside any consolation.

The Gevethen hesitated.

'The Lord Hagen has truly inspired you, Lord . . .'

The single voice stopped. An urgency was suddenly patterning the shapes and sounds that filled this world. And moving with it, as though it had been there for an eternity, was the sound of Assh and Frey, baying in full cry.

Chapter 27

Ibryen and Isgyrn walked slowly through the forest. With
no destination in prospect they seemed tacitly to have
agreed that nothing was to be gained by moving quickly.
Ibryen's gait however, was markedly at odds with his
racing thoughts. What had happened? Where were they?
How were they to return? *Could* they return? But worst
of all, clutching coldly and tightly at his stomach, his many
and long-carried responsibilities returned with unusual
force. What would happen to his beleaguered people if
he could not return? He tried desperately to keep the
speculations that cascaded frantically from this question
from overwhelming him with guilt and shame, but with
little success.

Unexpectedly, and despite his many other dark
thoughts, he also found himself burdened with an acute
sense of responsibility for Isgyrn, though the latter, now
that he was whole again, seemed to be accepting this
further inexplicable and bewildering change in his circumstances with remarkable equanimity. Ibryen glanced
around at the sunlit forest. Stern and logical was he, this
man? he mused bitterly. *I wonder how calm he would be
if our surroundings were not so idyllic?* Then he grimaced
and inwardly apologized.

'We must try to find a high place,' he said. 'See if we

can get some idea of where we are.'

Isgyrn agreed readily. 'The higher the better,' he said.

They talked as they strolled. Ibryen told Isgyrn of his land and of the Gevethen who had treacherously ousted him and now held the people in thrall with brutality and terror. And he told too, of the strange call that had carried him alone up on to the ridge to meet the Traveller. The story of the Gevethen seemed to disturb Isgyrn disproportionately and though he seemed reluctant to discuss his own concerns, either from fear of further burdening his host, or because the memories and uncertainties were too recent, he told enough to show a common bond between their fates. For the evil that had usurped some of the Culmadryen lands had also come at first in the guise of good will offering betterment to the people.

'It seems that for all our many differences, our peoples are tragically alike in their folly,' he concluded.

Ibryen was less harsh. 'Alike in our willingness to trust and reluctance to see evil in others.'

They had not pursued the debate. 'It doesn't matter,' Isgyrn said. 'We warriors have no excuse. We must bear the guilt. It's our task above all to see things as they are, even when we can't see *why* they are, and to defend those less able when the need arises.' Ibryen nodded. *That* could not be disputed. They continued in silence.

Though their arbitrary path carried them over undulating ground, they came across no consistent inclines nor even any broad clearings that might give them an indication of the land beyond the forest. And it was with mixed feelings that they encountered signs that others frequented this place. One was a broad grassy track, obviously used by horses. Another was a carving of a face ingeniously worked so that it was peering out between the branches of a tree.

Ibryen looked at the mischievous face. 'This is not my land,' he said unequivocally. 'Nor any that I know of.'

The possible implications, both bad and good, of meeting strangers in this forest flooded into a mind already awash with doubts and fears, and, despite himself, he sat down on a nearby embankment and put his head in his hands. He could not think any more.

Isgyrn looked at him for some time then crouched down in front of him. 'At the height of my people's despair, I found myself in two places at once. Speaking with a man, himself fighting an awful battle. A strange man who, like you, had had a great and unwanted responsibility thrust upon him. I spoke to him as I speak to you now, at one with him in the middle depths and yet, at the same time, soaring above my land.'

Ibryen looked up and met his gaze. 'I remember,' he said flatly. 'You told me. The sword bearer, you called him.'

Isgyrn nodded. 'Who he is ... was ... is of no great import here. What is important is that without any witting action on my part, such a thing happened to *me* – a Warrior, frantic with battle fever. I had never heard of such a thing. Not even happening to Hearers, silent and secluded and at peace, surrounded by comfort and friends.'

He looked down guiltily. 'Whatever's troubling you, be as clear in your mind as I am that it's my fault we're here. I don't know why I left your camp secretly, like a thief. Perhaps it was because I didn't wish to burden you with my helpless presence when you had a war of your own to fight, perhaps it was just a quiet desperation to learn what had happened to my land. Perhaps I just wasn't thinking clearly.' He looked up again and met Ibryen's gaze. 'But even when I was floundering, maybe about to die, in the

Culmaren's world, a small part of me knew that it was real, that it was true, that it was not just a frenzy in my imagination. I was suffering because of my *ignorance* about where I was, not because I was suddenly crazed. I was untutored in the ways of the place, not insane.' He gave a rueful smile. 'Not that the knowledge served me much, but it *was* there.'

Ibryen frowned a little and made to speak but Isgyrn waved him silent. 'You and I have strange skills – you more so than me – skills that we're barely aware of and certainly don't know how to use. Wherever this place is, and whatever people live in it, it's real and so are we. Yet we're also still on that cold mountainside where the Culmaren brought me and tended me.'

'You seem suddenly very knowledgeable,' Ibryen said acidly.

Isgyrn took no offence but shook his head. 'No,' he admitted. 'I'm guessing, but guessing with a part of me that I trust – a part that I trust in battle. Knowledge deep and long-learned. Some things come only with time.'

The remark struck Ibryen like a winding blow and he started perceptibly. Despite the urgency of his immediate concerns, the phrase carried him across the years to bring him again to the feet of his old instructor and he felt a lightness spreading through him. He clapped his hands softly and smiled. 'Let's go. Only dead things are rigid, and rigid things shatter,' he said.

Isgyrn eased back a little, nervously. 'Are you all right?' he asked.

Ibryen stood up. 'Yes,' he said. 'Just remembering an old lesson.'

Isgyrn's eyebrows rose, but he opted for a pragmatic response. 'Has it told you where we are?'

'I'm afraid not. It just reminded me not to worry about things I can't change.'

'We're to continue awaiting events, then?' Isgyrn said with some irony, though his face remained serious. 'Still, not worrying about the unavoidable isn't as easy as it sounds.' He levered himself up. 'I'll confess I don't know what I said to remind you of such a valuable lesson, but shall we continue?' He indicated the grassy track.

They had not walked far along it before the sound of running water reached them.

'Well, at least we'll not perish of thirst in this place,' Ibryen said.

When they reached the river however, they encountered another reminder that they were not alone in this land. It was a timber bridge, built with considerable skill and decorated with bright colours and many carvings. They stood for some time admiring it and Ibryen took some consolation from the fact that a people who spent time on such work were perhaps not given to spending time on excessive warring and feuding. Nevertheless, he reminded himself, he must still be very cautious in approaching anyone they might meet.

They decided not to cross the bridge, but moved instead upstream, Isgyrn seeming to have a strong natural inclination to move always upwards. After a little while they came to a clearing where the river meandered quietly between shallow banks. They sat down.

Ibryen looked around and frowned. 'There's an unease about this place,' he said, answering Isgyrn's unspoken question. 'Like a thunderstorm coming.'

Isgyrn cast a glance up at the sky. It was cloudless. 'There's no thunder about,' he said confidently. 'And I sense no ambush being laid for us. But this is even less my land than yours so I don't know to what extent my instincts can be trusted here.'

'It's not a feeling of threat,' Ibryen said uncertainly. 'It's just . . .' He gave a shrug and left the sentence unfinished. Then he leaned over the bank and looked down into the water. Isgyrn joined him. The water, eddying slowly, sent back their reflections, sharp and clear.

Jeyan froze as the sound of the dogs rolled over her. The hovering lights became angular and jagged, and began to dance to the hunting rhythm being sounded. Then she could feel the spirit of the dogs bounding all about her, wild and savage, yet bursting with affection and joy at finding her again. She wanted to cry out to them, to embrace them, but her brief time with the Gevethen had already taught her to judge her every action carefully, and even as she recognized the dogs, she knew she must force herself to affect an ignorance of what was happening until the Gevethen responded.

She did not have long to wait. Their response was swift and alarming.

And full of fear.

They began to tremble and, to her considerable surprise, Jeyan could feel flight building up in them. Their fear seeped through into her. Who could say what the consequences would be, should they abandon her in panic and flee screaming through this bizarre world with the spirits of the dead hounds pursuing them? Already she could sense an instability around her that she had not felt even when the ill-fated tunnel had crashed to its end. Then she noted that the faint images of her room which lingered at all times, were wavering. What was happening to the mirrors there?

'Don't move!' she cried out, ignoring caution. 'They'll

pursue you. It's their nature.' She reached up and seized the hands gripping her shoulders.

'They're His creatures come for us!'

'We have failed!'

Jeyan tightened her grip malevolently on the faltering hands. It was good to know the Gevethen were feeling what they so readily subjected others to. But still she must not let them run amok.

'Whatever they are, if we run, they'll follow. They're hunters, I can feel it.'

It was to no avail however, for as the dogs continued their barking, the Gevethen suddenly tore themselves free and were gone. Jeyan spun round. The Gevethen were nowhere to be seen. There was only a disorienting confusion of lights and shapes swirling in their wake.

'Excellencies! Masters!' she shouted, but her voice fell dead in the twisting air and there was no reply. She swore. Then the spirits of her two dogs were clamouring about her again, demanding attention. She reached out and embraced them, though their enthusiasm did little to ease her alarm at what would be the outcome of the Gevethen's flight.

An inspiration came to her. Quickly she quietened the dogs then gave them the command that would set them hunting again, though this time silently. The dogs were away, Jeyan following them, attached to them in a manner that she could not determine, but which was quite different from the crude holding by which the Gevethen held her.

Sniffling, snuffling, twisting, turning, the two dogs moved through the unseen chambers and avenues of the world within the mirrors, their erstwhile mistress following, unseeing but trusting.

Then, in front of her, were the Gevethen. Silently

dismissing the dogs, she fell to her knees. 'Forgive me, Excellencies. I've not the skill to move as you do.'

'Are they gone?'

'They vanished just as they came, Excellencies,' Jeyan lied.

'It was your fault, trying to open the Way again,' one of the Gevethen hissed softly to the other.

As before, Jeyan kept her head lowered and gave no indication that she had heard this remark.

'No, it couldn't be.'

'The Way must be guarded by His creatures.'

'No!'

'Yes!'

'No!'

Once again, Jeyan felt that she was in the presence of squabbling children. She had scarcely registered the first occasion but now came the frightening revelation that the Gevethen's lust for power might be rooted not in the familiar arrogance of over-ambitious men but in childish vindictiveness – a trait quite without restraint. A cold shivering threatened to overwhelm her but she remained absolutely still and silent – it would take very little to end the quarrel and bring their combined anger down on her. Assh however, did not have this perception. Disturbed by the dispute in the immediate vicinity of his pack leader, he growled. The hissed exchange stopped immediately.

Jeyan's tight-gripped fear goaded her into action.

'Be still, Excellencies,' she whispered urgently. 'They're back.'

To her considerable relief, no reproach came for this brusque order. Instead, the Gevethen took her shoulders again, though this time the hands were conspicuously unsteady.

Petty in your viciousness, jealous of each other, and

afraid of dogs, eh? Jeyan found herself exulting in these continuing indications of the Gevethen's vulnerability, but she was sufficiently in control of herself not to allow any outward sign to manifest itself. She reached up and took the two hands firmly.

'Hold me, Excellencies,' she said, as if pleading. At the same time, she reached out to Assh. The dog growled again. The hands tightened and she felt another flight pending. 'Do not move, Excellencies,' she said. 'They haven't attacked. Perhaps they've been sent to warn us of something.' Her own viciousness took command. 'Do you know what they are?' she asked. 'Are they often in this place?'

The solitary voice that replied was almost trembling. 'Lord Counsellor, we must leave here quickly.'

'We must not flee,' Jeyan insisted. 'If we move or run then they'll follow and attack us for sure. It's the way of all hunting animals. I learned this in my exile in the Ennerhald.'

Tightening her own grip on the Gevethen's hands, she reached out to the dogs again. They both growled menacingly. As she had expected, the Gevethen's meagre control broke and they began to run. This time however, she clung to them, crying out, 'Excellencies, no, wait!' while bidding the dogs to continue their barking pursuit.

There followed a buffeting nightmare as she was dragged in the wake of the fleeing Gevethen. Every sensation in her body told her that she was moving at great speed, falling almost, yet she saw no sign of this in the colours and flitting shapes that moved endlessly about her, other than that they seemed to change in character, becoming pale and frayed. She knew nothing of this place, and must not be abandoned here. Who could say what happened when the mirror through which she had been carried

435

became two again? And what had Hagen said about the place? 'A rough-hewn ante-chamber, crude and ill-formed – and so dangerous.' No, she must return to the real world with these foul creatures, enhanced in their eyes perhaps by her conduct here, and wiser by far about them.

She made the dogs break off. It was not easy, either for them or for her. She could not conceive of where they were, or even what they were now, still less what journeying had brought them back to her, and leaving them again was almost unbearable. But they would be here again, she knew. She had heard them the first time she had been brought here and now they had found her. They would find her again, she was certain.

'Guard,' she cried out silently to them in the end. She might know nothing of this place, but that command would make some part of it hers irrevocably.

The dogs stopped their pursuit and their barking began to fade as the Gevethen's unseen flight bore them relentlessly away. Jeyan allowed it to continue for a little while, then she began to cry out, 'Excellencies, they are gone.' It was some time however, before her message penetrated their blind panic and when eventually all felt still again, she sensed a marked difference in the atmosphere about her.

'Excellencies, your courage and will defeated them, they are gone,' she gasped before either of them could speak, anxious to assure them that she had not noted their cowardice.

But to her surprise and alarm, though she could hear them breathing heavily, they did not respond.

'Excellencies?'

'Gateway.'

'Too close.'

The words, spoken very softly, seemed to take form in

the air and hang there. There was a fear in them that was even greater than their fear of the dogs.

'Something here . . .'

      '. . . here.'

'Drawing us . . .'

      '. . . Drawing us.'

They released Jeyan and moved to her side. They were staring at something. As she watched, Jeyan saw the lights about them forming a coherent pattern. It was blurred and vague, as though seen through sleep-filled eyes, but it was unlike anything that she had seen since entering the mirrors.

Then she gave a startled gasp, as the pattern came suddenly into focus. The Gevethen cried out and, arms extended, lunged forward.

The reflections broke and scattered as Isgyrn and Ibryen reached down into the water with cupped hands. The walk had made them hot and they drank noisily and with relish.

'Cold,' Ibryen said, wiping his hand across his mouth and then down his tunic. 'Perhaps not too far down from the mountains. Shall we go back to the bridge and the path or continue upstream a little further? See if we can get a view of this place.'

Isgyrn chuckled softly. 'I'm afraid my instinct down here seems to be always to move upwards. But I'll accept your judgement in such a decision.'

Ibryen leaned back over the bank and looked down into the water, now smooth again after the disturbance the two of them had made.

'Well, I suppose—' He stopped abruptly. Behind his reflection in the water was a great agitation, as though storm clouds had suddenly appeared in the sky. He cast a quick glance upwards for reassurance, but there was only the cloudless blue that there had been since they arrived. As he turned back, a sharp intake of breath from Isgyrn drew his attention. The Dryenwr was staring, wide-eyed, into the water.

Ibryen followed his gaze. Though the surface of the water was still smooth and untroubled, the turmoil in the reflected sky was growing, moving faster and faster. He started back in alarm, but his silhouetted reflection did not move. Disconcerted, he reached out a tentative hand to stir the water. A powerful grip seized his arm. It was Isgyrn.

'It's Him,' he said hoarsely. 'I can feel His presence. We must get away from here.' He made to stand but Ibryen resisted, staring fixedly into the water.

'For Svara's sake, Ibryen . . .'

Isgyrn's oath faded as the turbulence suddenly stopped and the reflection cleared. Except that where he and Ibryen had been staring up out of the gently rippling water, there were now the faces of the two Gevethen. He opened his mouth to cry out, but no sound came. His gaping mouth was mimicked by the two moon faces.

Ibryen's face was suddenly a mask of fear and rage. He reached for his sword but had scarcely begun to draw it when, like ghastly leaping fish, glittering and sparkling with what should have been cascading drops of water but which seemed more like a myriad shards of broken glass, four arms burst up through the water. The summer air filled with a terrible screeching. Ibryen's head jerked back violently to avoid them, but one of the clawing hands caught the loose front of his tunic. Unbalanced, and arms flailing, he lurched forward as it dragged him down. Only one hand just catching the edge of the bank prevented him from plunging immediately into the water. His other hand thrashed wildly at the remaining three, still clawing out to reach him, but balanced as he was, he could not resist the pull of even the single hand for more than a moment. The screeching intensified.

Then, Isgyrn had wrapped determined arms around him and, with a great cry, was hurling himself backwards. For an eternal moment, it seemed that this effort was going to drag the Gevethen themselves across the worlds, as a cracked, crazed and glittering dome swelled up out of the water. Isgyrn had a fleeting vision of the two faces, distorted and awful, at once frantic and triumphant. Then the grip on Ibryen was gone and he and Ibryen were tumbling backwards on the grass. On the instant their roles were reversed and it was Ibryen who was on his feet and dragging a stumbling and shocked Isgyrn along. 'This way! This way!' he was crying.

And they were gone.

As were the Gevethen.

Both the Traveller and Rachyl cried out in alarm as the two motionless figures of Ibryen and Isgyrn burst suddenly into life and lurched forward, arms flailing.

The Traveller held out a hand to restrain Rachyl as she made to move forward to help. He spoke powerfully to the two gasping men. 'You're safe now. You're back with us on the mountain.' He had to say it several times before recognition came into their eyes.

Isgyrn reached out and took hold of Ibryen, turning him so that he could peer into his face. 'It was a dream,' he said. 'A nightmare?'

Ibryen clutched the front of his tunic convulsively. 'A nightmare, yes,' he shuddered. 'But real. The Culmaren's world, the place of lights between, and the forest. All real.'

'And those creatures?'

439

'Real too. The Gevethen.'

Isgyrn tightened his grip on Ibryen's arm. '*His* creatures, Ibryen. They were His creatures. The war continues. I must find my land – any land.'

Arms raised to protect her head and eyes screwed tight shut, Jeyan spun round and offered her cowering back to the scene she had been watching as it shattered into a blizzard of brilliant, jagged edges. But these, like the awful noise that accompanied them, raked through even the darkness behind her eyes.

As the din faded she straightened up and turned round, shaking as she examined herself in the terrifying expectation of seeing great gaping wounds all over her body. But she had suffered no hurt. She gazed down at herself and, still shocked, her mind relived the last few moments for her – the sudden appearance of the Count and a companion staring down at her and the Gevethen – the Gevethen's frantic lunge and the brief, frenzied struggle – Ibryen's rescue by his companion and the startling vanishing of both of them as they turned and fled. Then there was the terrible noise and the shaking which had seemed to rack the entire world that was held in the mirrors. A noise and a shaking that were continuing, she realized, as senses long-developed in the Ennerhald gathered her wits together for her and roused her with urgent warning signals. Whatever had happened, had happened. Questions would have to wait. All that mattered was that she had survived, and survived uninjured. Now she must turn to the next danger. And danger there was, for much of the continuing noise was that of the Gevethen shouting and screaming a tirade of unbridled obscenity.

Though she was no delicate bloom, she nonetheless shied away from the horrific intensity of abuse that was pouring from them, addressed to each other and to Ibryen and to fate in general. Slowly, Jeyan sank to her knees and lowered her head.

'He has the gift! Our enemy has the gift!' was the dominant gist, though it was heavily larded with reproaches in the form of, 'You let him escape!' and, 'You were too slow!'

As before, a childish quality in the exchanges served only to heighten the horror of what she was hearing. And it seemed that they might continue thus for ever, each spiralling off the other into greater excess. She began to feel more afraid than at any time since she had been captured. If even the slightest portion of this mounting odium were directed to herself she would be snuffed out with less thought than a guttering candle.

Then, as if the thought itself had been sufficient, it happened. She was suddenly the focus of their attention.

'Ah. Lord Counsellor.'

Jeyan quailed. There was such hatred in the voice that it seemed as though the continuing buffeting shaking everything around them were merely a reflection of it. Death was heartbeats away, she knew. Gone was any pretence at subtle torment. Now there was only bloodlust, and though she was less than dust to them, she was nearby and would serve as a beginning.

In response, a choking knot of her own hatred formed within her and, almost unaware of what she was doing, she braced herself to make a final spring at her enemies with the intention of seriously harming, if not killing, one of them.

Yet she did not. Instead, without thinking, she prostrated herself and began shouting passionately, her inspiration scarcely two words ahead of her speech. 'Beyond our imagining are His ways, Excellencies. His hounds have led you here so that you might both know the secret of your enemy and find your guide to the Way.'

There was a long pause. Jeyan held her breath, bracing herself for a blow. Then she felt the fury about her alter. A whispered exchange began which she could not hear at first. It rose in intensity very quickly however.

'He has led us here. Ibryen is to be our guide through the Ways. Our enemy shall be our salvation and our slave. We shall come to Him once again. And in triumph.'

The manic fervour that had fired their anger returned, though now it was sustaining an excited and frantic elation. 'He must be found and brought to our service.' Over and over. '*He must be found.*'

No praise came down to the still-prostrated Jeyan, but she knew that she was safe for the time being.

Yet, despite this change in the mood of the Gevethen, the shocks and vibrations that were continuing to shake their strange world, were undiminished. In fact, just as they had seemingly resonated to their anger, so now they resonated to their excitement.

And they grew worse, though the Gevethen seemed to be oblivious to them.

Then, there was a sudden, jarring jolt and, for the briefest of moments, there was terrifying chaos. Jeyan felt as though she was being torn in half. She could hear herself screaming – screaming with two voices. And she could hear the Gevethen screaming too, though with countless numbers of voices. She had a fleeting vision of a line of Gevethen figures, arms thrashing frantically, disappearing into a distance that seemed to outreach the stars. Then the vision was gone, almost before she could register it, and at the same instant, she was whole again.

Slowly, the world within the mirrors reformed. The moving, intangible shapes and lights returned to pursue their own mysterious, bewildering paths, the sounds became again the rising and falling of a senseless chorus. And finally, she noted the faint reflected images of her room hovering about her.

For a moment she thought she was going to be violently sick. Then the hands of the Gevethen closed about her shoulders.

'We are served by flawed creatures, Lord Counsellor . . .'

'. . . Lord Counsellor.'

'The offenders must be punished for their weakness and folly . . .'

'. . . weakness and folly.'

Jeyan did not know what they meant, though she suspected, from their tone and their returning control, that it was associated with what had just happened rather than anything previously.

Then they were moving. Very quickly. Though not in flight, as before, but in furious excitement. It filled their voices when they spoke again. 'He shall be ours, Lord Counsellor. He shall be our guide. The traitor Ibryen shall bring us again to His feet.'

'He must be found. He must be found.'

Chapter 28

It was a considerable time before the clamour of voices in the wind and rain-battered tent began to reach any semblance of order. Rachyl's dogged insistence that, 'You never left here, you must have been dreaming,' proved to be not the least of the difficulties to be overcome. Ibryen knew better than to attempt to force her to silence by use of his authority and, in the end, it was only Isgyrn's description of the Gevethen that made her reluctantly concede that something more substantial than a dream had affected the two men.

But a more worrying plaint than the voicing of Rachyl's doubts was that of Isgyrn and his fretting that he must somehow contact his land. Ironically, where Ibryen had declined to use the authority he held over Rachyl to silence her, he used an authority that he did not possess to silence Isgyrn.

'You can't contact any of the Culmadryen, Isgyrn,' he said forcefully as the Dryenwr seemed set to circle through his concerns again. 'If only for the simple reason that none have been known over Nesdiryn in recorded memory. And I require your word, Warrior, that you'll not try to enter the world of the Culmaren again.'

'But—'

'Your word, Isgyrn,' Ibryen's tone was unequivocal.

'You said yourself you had no knowledge of how to survive in that place and, as far as I know, it was the purest chance that took me to you and brought us safely away. There's no guarantee that I'll be able to do it again. For all I know, we could easily have died there.'

'I'm of no value to you here,' Isgyrn protested. He pointed upwards. 'I belong among the clouds where I'm a leader and can truly serve.'

'I'll determine your value here, Isgyrn,' Ibryen said. 'And as you've already saved me from the Gevethen, I'll start it high. As for service, you must decide that for yourself. I think you'll provide far more than just another sword against the Gevethen, but in any case it'll be a sword against this enemy of yours.'

'Of ours, Count,' Isgyrn corrected. 'The Great Corrupter is the enemy of all living things. He's an evil from the very Heat of the Beginning, not some petty prince or warlord.'

The Traveller spoke before Ibryen could reply. 'I don't pretend to understand fully what you're talking about, Isgyrn,' he said. 'But I've seen enough strange things not to dispute with you too heatedly. Yet if this Great Corrupter is as you say, He must have been defeated. You said that others were fighting Him, down here, and you yourself saw His lieutenant's land destroyed even as you were thrown down into the middle depths. And although I heard some odd rumours in Girnlant, there's been no news of wars spreading out into the world as surely there must have been over the last fifteen years if He'd won.'

'It's fifteen years or so since those creepy little birds disappeared and since the Gevethen began to grow conspicuously strange.' It was Rachyl. She offered no conclusion.

For the first time Isgyrn faltered.

Ibryen laid a hand on Isgyrn's arm. 'None of us can say what strange forces are moving events, Isgyrn,' he said softly. 'Or what part each of us has to play.' He indicated the others. 'I'm not usually given to talking in such portentous terms, but we've not been from the village a week, and yet the world – my world, at least – is vastly different from what it was. I haven't begun to get a measure of what's happened and still less what it all means. I can't command you to do anything, but if you enter the world of the Culmaren again, I doubt I'll be able to abandon you, so I ask you not to try for both our sakes.' He straightened up. 'Let's you and me confine ourselves to simple practicalities. I will go into Culmaren's world for you and . . .' he shrugged helplessly '. . . call out, or send some kind of a message, whatever seems fitting. You, if you wish, can return with us and turn your fighting skills to helping us defeat the Gevethen. Whether this terrible leader you fear so much has been defeated or not – and it seems that He might have been – other of His lieutenants are perhaps still doing His work. You faced one in the air and defeated him, and we apparently have to face two of them down here in the middle depths.'

Rachyl looked anxiously at Ibryen. 'I don't think it's a good idea, you going off into a trance again, if half of what you've just told us is true,' she said.

Isgyrn too, was concerned. 'I can't ask you to do what I'm not prepared to do,' he said.

Ibryen smiled. 'But you *are* prepared,' he retorted. 'You're just not capable.'

Isgyrn lowered his head. 'Let me think for a little while,' he said. 'I need to be alone. I'll go outside.'

Ibryen looked at him uncertainly. 'I'll do nothing foolish,' Isgyrn promised sadly. 'So many strange things have happened in these last few hours. I just need to have the sky above me and to feel Svara's will about me.'

As he crawled out of the tent Ibryen offered him the Culmaren which had slipped from his shoulders. Isgyrn refused it. 'It has too many powerful memories,' he said. 'I need to be free for a while.'

He walked a little way from the tent and sat on a rock. The rain had stopped and the sky was less overcast, but the wind was still blowing strongly. Nearby mountains and valleys were beginning to appear.

'Will he be all right?' Rachyl asked.

'He might be from up in the clouds,' Ibryen said, idly fingering the Culmaren, 'but his feet are on the ground. He's no real choices. He'll die for sure if he goes searching for the Culmaren in their world again, and I think he knows it.'

'You didn't.'

'Part of me belongs there,' Ibryen replied. 'Perhaps part of all of us does, but only a few can reach it, and still fewer know what to do with it.' He held up a hand quickly as Rachyl made to speak again. 'Until I meet someone a great deal wiser, I've just got to accept things as they are, and without explanation. I doubt a young bird could tell you how it knows that it's safe to launch itself from a high ledge for the first time.'

Rachyl frowned. 'I've seen squashed fledglings before now,' she said.

'Another bad analogy,' Ibryen replied, laughter bursting out of him. 'But you understand my meaning well enough.' His laughter shook off much of the tension that had pervaded the group since he and Isgyrn had sprung so abruptly into consciousness.

A few minutes later, Rachyl walked over to join Isgyrn. The Dryenwr was staring thoughtfully out across a neighbouring valley. 'This is a mysterious and beautiful place,' he said. 'Everything felt dead to my touch and my tread when I first woke, but now I feel many subtle things – in the rocks and the plants – even Svara's will. It's so elaborate and full of tales down here, twisting and turning over the crooked surface of this vast land.'

'Your people don't come down here?' Rachyl asked.

'Culmaren has the need to touch the peaks at times, and the seas, to draw sustenance.' His eyes became distant. 'A splendid sight, that. The roots of the land reaching down into the depths, like a slow cascading mist, so that when it touches, the whole land seems to be precariously balanced on a mountain peak, or to be rising out of the ocean like a huge tree.' With some reluctance he left the scene and returned to Rachyl's question. 'But we ourselves rarely venture this low.' He placed his hand on his chest. 'I think my wing must indeed have changed me in some way to enable me to survive down here.'

A thought occurred to Rachyl. 'Does that mean you might not be able to go back even if you could contact one of your lands?' she asked. It was kindly put, but it was a stark question. Yet Isgyrn did not seem to be disturbed by it.

'I'm not sure,' he replied. 'In fact, I'm not even sure whether I've been changed or not. I feel no different. No one ever comes low without protection, but that could be no more than a tradition handed down through the years.'

Rachyl gazed at him quizzically. Isgyrn, in his turn, looked apologetic. 'There's very little interest in coming to the middle depths, so survival here's not a topic that's been studied extensively.'

'Funny attitude,' Rachyl said, mildly offended.

Isgyrn smiled. 'What do you know about the clouds?' he asked.

449

Rachyl gave a tight-lipped grunt to indicate an end to the debate.

'Your Count is a remarkable man,' Isgyrn said, moving both to the centre of his concerns and on to safer ground.

Rachyl nodded. 'It seems he's even more remarkable than we thought. I still find it hard to believe the tale you've both just told. Those other ... worlds ... you say you found yourselves in, and the Gevethen rising out of a river and actually seizing Ibryen. It's far beyond the bounds of my simple, sword-swinging commonsense. If I didn't know my cousin so well, and if he wasn't so patently sane, I'd have said he should be fed on calming gruels and given over to kindly relatives in the country.'

Isgyrn turned to her. 'It *is* true,' he said soberly. 'Although ordinary words don't really do justice to what we both experienced. And the Gevethen didn't come out of the river. It was as though they fractured their way into that forest world from somewhere else.' He looked up at the grey sky. 'It was a profound act of folly for me to do what I did. Even respected Hearers do not try to reach the Culmaren alone. Your Count saved my life and found his own at risk as a consequence.'

'We've all done foolish and dangerous things at times,' Rachyl said.

'Indeed,' Isgyrn agreed bitterly. 'But not at my age. I'm a Commander of others, not a young and reckless young man.'

'It's finished and everyone survived,' Rachyl said, abruptly dismissive, concerned by his tone. 'Great Corrupter or no, *we're* still at war, for all there's been no fighting of late. You can't afford the luxury of dwelling on such things excessively if you're going to be of use to yourself or anyone. If I can accept the wild tales I've just had to listen to, *you* can accept *that*. And, Commander or not, your circumstances are unusual to say the least. I presume you'll be taking Ibryen's advice and not trying to go into this other place again?'

Isgyrn frowned at Rachyl's forceful rebuke. 'I'm not *that* foolish. Some lessons even *I* can learn at one telling,' he replied caustically. 'I'm content to stay here and fight by your side, if Ibryen will have me. Especially as we seem to have a common enemy.' He began walking towards the tent. 'I'll take whatever oath of allegiance your people require, and without condition. But I can't allow Ibryen to seek out the Culmaren for me. That's too great an imposition.'

Rachyl took his arm and stopped him.

Ibryen drifted in the echoing vastness. Untroubled by the waves of fear that Isgyrn had created in his panic when he had come here before, Ibryen slowly realized that this world was stranger by far than either of the others he had found himself in. Stranger than the world of shifting lights and sounds where only his awareness existed, and more impossible than the wooded land which had allowed him a wholeness both there and on a windswept mountainside.

No words could compass a description of where he was. It was as though he was in a world that reached out through the stars yet touched none of them. That existed in directions that could not be – not up or down, not here or there. That existed in times that could not be – not past, not present, not future. A world in which each part touched all and all touched each part.

This was a place that was deeply alien. Even for someone with his mysterious gift he knew that the limitations of his very humanity meant that he could experience only a single, simple aspect of it. Though, to him, it had a wholeness, it had also a quality akin to that of a painting

451

– a picture of Now, lifted from its future and its past and fixed forever in the shifting Now of the observer. Whatever he perceived here, however rich and complex, it would be less than a shadow of its true reality.

The knowledge was frightening, but only because of the perspective it offered him of himself and the world he lived in.

Yet he felt no fear, no threat. He was both here and at ease in the crudely rigged tent with the Traveller watching him and Isgyrn's carefully folded Culmaren in his hands. Nothing would wilfully harm him here except his own fear.

As before he felt both a great emptiness and a teeming bustle of life pervading the place. Somewhere there would be that aspect of the Culmaren which his inadequate senses could detect but it would be pointless for him to search for it. He knew that all of this world was already aware of his presence, and accepted it, and that his call would be heard even if it was not understood.

He could feel the softness of the Culmaren in his hands. He allowed the sensation to permeate him and he spoke into it the essence of the words he had spoken before. 'Your charge is safe again. Your duties more than fulfilled. But he is as I am – in a place that is not truly his – and the pain diminishes him. Come to him if you are able. Bring him his true kin.'

Very faintly, he thought he heard a long sighing call, plaintive and beautiful, but it slipped from him even as he turned his attention to it.

He had done all that he could.

Isgyrn was crouching at the entrance to the tent. Rachyl was standing behind him and he was being gently restrained by the Traveller as Ibryen opened his eyes.

'What have you done?' he asked breathlessly.

'The best I could,' Ibryen replied, almost apologetically.

Isgyrn grimaced with self-reproach and shook his head. 'No, I meant what risk have you taken for me?'

'None.' Ibryen smiled. He held out the Culmaren. Isgyrn took hold of it. As he did so, Ibryen held it for a moment.

'This is he,' he said silently into the world beyond.

Something touched him in the timeless moment that did not exist in the tent.

Isgyrn let go of the Culmaren with one hand and reached up as if to brush something from his face. 'You put me under an obligation I can see no way of repaying,' he said.

'Nonsense,' Ibryen said gently. 'I saved you when you were lost. You tore me from the grip of my enemy. Obligations can't exist between us. All I've just done for you is simple courtesy such as I hope I'd offer any stranger – an unusual one, I'll grant – but nothing more, for all that. You're a free man. You may come back to our village, our besieged camp, and fight against the Gevethen, if you wish, or you may go wherever your fancy takes you, with my blessing, and never to be forgotten.' He looked at the Traveller. 'Would you take him with you to find this Great Gate of yours?'

'If he wants to come, yes,' the Traveller replied without hesitation. 'I'm getting quite used to company, and I've questions to ask him that should last us the entire journey and more.'

Isgyrn waved his hand impatiently and dropped on to one knee. 'I pledge you my sword, Ibryen, Count of Nesdiryn. I have few fighting skills suitable to this place but they are yours if you would have them.'

Taken aback by this sudden formality, Ibryen did not reply at once.

'I will lay down my life for you,' Isgyrn pressed on.

Rachyl's eyebrows rose in amusement and expectation. Ibryen recovered himself and looked at Isgyrn sharply. 'If you fight for me you'll fight by me, and you'll lay *other* people's lives down, Soarer, not your own. As many as are needed to end this business.'

Isgyrn gaped at him uncertainly. Rachyl laughed and put a hand on his shoulder. 'Come on, let's get this tent down and make our way back to the village.'

A little later they were ready to leave. Rachyl, swinging her pack on to her back and hitching it to and fro until it was comfortable, looked at Ibryen.

'What are we going to tell them when we get back?' she asked unhappily. One man and his blanket and a plethora of strange tales, her manner said, though she spoke none of it.

'Let's see if we can get back down to the forest and make camp before the light goes,' Ibryen said, avoiding the question, then, 'What we always tell them,' he said. 'The truth, as far as we're able. I set out on this journey on little more than a whim. Perhaps a desperate whim, I don't know. I'd no clear expectations and if I'd had any I doubt very much whether they'd have matched the reality of what's happened. We go back with an extra sword and changed from what we were. Perhaps that'll show us the way.'

'Lead us to the Gevethen from a direction they don't even know exists?' Rachyl said, echoing the reassurance they had left behind them.

Ibryen's expression suddenly became pained and he put his hand to his head. 'What is the greatest danger that winter offers us, Rachyl?' he catechized.

'It makes us forget,' she responded, surprised but without pause. The exchange, and variations of it were common fare in the village during winter.

'It does indeed. We stop thinking,' Ibryen said. 'And not least myself.'

'What's the matter?'

'I had the Gevethen within dagger's reach,' Ibryen said angrily. 'Not that I could've used it, but it's only just occurred to me that this was the way to which I was being directed. The way to come upon them unseen and unheard. And not only does it take me half a day to grasp that, it's only just come to me that it was *they* who attacked *me*! They who came unseen and unheard on me. They know of these strange worlds beyond. They too can travel between them.' His voice was full of despair.

'No!' Isgyrn's firm voice cut through Ibryen's distress. 'They were neither unseen, nor unheard, if you recall. In fact they made a fearful din. And I saw their faces more clearly than you. However they came there, they were shocked to see you. And afraid, for all they seized you.' Ibryen looked at him, his eyes doubting. 'Think, Ibryen. If they knew the secret of these other worlds so well that they could move where they wanted, when they wanted, why haven't they discovered your secret village and sent their army against it? Or, for that matter, why haven't they come to your room and killed you while you slept? It's not only you who's been changed by this journey. You *touched* them. Their enemy came upon them unexpectedly and *touched* them. Whatever they were, they're different now. Whatever they thought, they're thinking differently now. Change has been set in motion. Incalculable change. And where there's change, there's opportunity.'

Ibryen clenched his teeth. 'You're right, I suppose,' he said. 'Forgive me. It was just a momentary—'

Rachyl slapped him on the back. 'Come on,' she said heartily. 'Enough talk. Let's get down the hill and make ourselves a decent camp. I'm starving.'

Jeyan hesitantly moved to the door of her room. It had been left slightly open. Cautiously she pulled it wide and peered out into the dimly lit corridor beyond. There was no one about. Almost to her own surprise she stepped backwards away from the door, then sat on a nearby chair and stared at this unexpected invitation to freedom.

What had happened? She had been asking the question continuously since, with a rush of piercing cold that had chilled her to the core, and which still lingered, she found herself staggering uncontrollably across her room. Two servants caught her and she held on to them as though they might offer her protection when she turned round.

As the Gevethen had screamed abuse at one another when Ibryen had escaped from them, so now, transformed into an arm-waving multitude, they were screaming abuse at the mirror-bearers. She could not see those who were supporting the two great mirrors that became one, but she could see the mirrors shaking. With each tremor, the Gevethen's screaming became worse. The moon-faced multitude milled about wildly. Yet something was wrong. The endless dancing movements of the mirror-bearers were stilted and jerky, and some of the images of the Gevethen flickered unevenly, appearing and disappearing.

Jeyan could feel the two servants beside her trembling. Gradually the two mirrors became still. Then they parted. As a black shadow cut between them, Jeyan briefly felt again as though she were being torn in half. She gasped and shuddered. Is part of me still in there? she thought, without knowing what she meant.

As she recovered, she noticed the state of the room.

456

Chairs and tables had been knocked over, ornaments and crockery broken, rugs and carpets scattered. It was almost as though the servants and the mirror-bearers had been brawling and rampaging while their masters were away. She had barely taken in the scene however, when the mirror-bearers washed to one side of the room like an incoming wave up a beach. She stepped back involuntarily, then there was a sudden whirl of activity and the still-screaming Gevethen rushed from the room, escorted by a furious mob of their own kind. Jeyan stood still for a moment, as shocked by the sudden silence and stillness as she had been by the frenzied movement and noise. What she took to be another piece of upturned furniture caught her eye in the half-light. She looked at it curiously then took a lantern and moved to examine it further.

She stopped as the light from the lantern fell on two bodies. Their simple dress identified them as mirror-bearers, and what she had taken to be the ornamental legs of a small table jutting into the air proved to be their arms reaching up, fingers bent into claws.

She turned up the lantern and stepped forward uncertainly. The floor became alive with glittering lights and there was a noisy unsteadiness beneath her feet. She paused and crouched down carefully. The floor about the two mirror-bearers was covered with countless fragments of glass. She picked up one of them. Her face, tiny, drawn and fearful in the light of the lantern, looked up at her. About her feet, other images of her stirred as she moved. For a moment she thought she was going to sink into them. The fragments were the remains of their mirrors, she realized as she shook off the impression. But what could have broken them so totally? And what had killed the mirror-bearers? For she needed to check no pulse to know that they were dead. Even if their rigid postures had not told her, their gaping eyes and mouths would have.

She shivered. What had happened in the Gevethen's 'crude and ill-formed ante-chamber' to bring this about? What had been the consequences in this room of the buffeting and vibrating that had shaken the mirrors' inner world? And which was cause, which effect?

She remembered that as Ibryen had disappeared and the Gevethen had staggered back, the scene had fragmented into a storm of jagged and frightening lights. Lights which passed clear through her. As she looked down at the dead figures she felt an unexpected twinge of pity. What terrible burdens did these wretched people carry in addition to their mirrors? What hideous bargain had they stuck to bring them to this?

She became aware of the servants gathering around her, hands raised to protect their eyes from the brightened lantern. She dimmed it.

'What's happened here?' she demanded, though more from want of something to say than from any hope of receiving an answer. There was no reply. Briefly she considered pressing the question but she knew that it would be to no effect.

'Get help,' she said quietly, standing up. 'Get . . . your friends . . . taken away and tended to properly, and get this mess cleaned up.'

She had scarcely finished speaking when she was surrounded by hectic but disturbingly silent activity as the servants began to do what she had asked, though whether this was because of her order or in response to some other command she had no idea. As the bodies were carried out she noticed that they were as rigid as their arm positions suggested. It was as if they had been dead for some time. Then the fragments of the mirrors were removed. As

Jeyan watched, this began to assume the quality of nightmare, so obsessively meticulous was the behaviour of the servants as they crawled about picking up first the large pieces and then bending closer and closer to the floor in search of ever smaller pieces.

At one point, she was sorely tempted to scream at them as the Gevethen had done, but again a sense of the futility of the action deterred her.

Now they were gone. And they had left the door ajar. A strange final flaw in the chaotic and frightening events of the day. No wiser for her further review of what had happened, she stood up and moved purposefully out into the corridor.

Chapter 29

Jeyan was far from clear about what it was she intended to do. She was also fearful about the consequences that this impromptu exploring might bring down upon her.

'I was anxious to follow your Excellencies but I'm unfamiliar with the Citadel and I became lost.'

Like a child she had prepared this excuse when barely a dozen paces from her room in the event of her encountering the Gevethen or being challenged. After all, the door had been left not only unlocked, but open, hadn't it? Initially she included an account of the time spent removing the two bodies and the remains of the shattered mirrors, but some more reflective instinct told her to make no reference to these unless they were mentioned first.

Her heart was thumping painfully as she moved cautiously through the corridors of the Citadel. Not only was she afraid of meeting anyone who might call her to account but she had little or no idea where she was and still less about where she was going. During her trips to and from the Judgement Hall she had been surrounded by Guards and mirror-bearers and, more significantly, she had been too preoccupied to pay much attention to her whereabouts. Soon however, meeting no one, she grew calmer and old Ennerhald habits returned, slipping her silently into darker shadows at the least sound or sign of movement. Several times she caught herself glancing rapidly from side to side to assure herself that Assh and Frey were keeping station. The involuntary action made her grimace, reminding her as it did, brutally, of the deaths of the two dogs and of the wound that their absence left in her life – a wound she was struggling to ignore. It gave her little consolation that in some way they were still alive. They were a hunting trio – she needed the touch, the sight, the smell and the sound of them, the look in the eye, the whine. And she needed them in this world, now, not in some strange other world to which access could be made only through the mirrors and, as far as she knew, at the behest of the Gevethen.

Finally she made a determined effort to force the anger and distress from her mind. They weren't here and that was an end to it!

'Lord Counsellor?'

Jeyan spun round, hand reaching for a knife that was no longer there. In front of her stood one of the Citadel officials – an ordinary clerk of some kind, she registered, from his livery. His eyes were lowered and he was just dropping awkwardly to his knees. Jeyan recalled how those watching her as she was paraded to the Judgement Hall had knelt when she looked at them.

Relief followed the initial shock of the encounter and lingering remains of her old life prompted her to tell the man to rise. She should confide in him, ask him where she was, how she might escape from the Citadel. The thoughts caught her unawares and mingled confusingly with a frisson of elation at the power that the man's obeisance invested in her. Then came anger again that she should even think such foolishness after all she had learned in the Ennerhald.

Without knowing why, she laid a hand on the man's

head. He flinched and she felt him trembling as he struggled to remain still. This time the confusion of emotions effectively paralysed her.

It was the Ennerhald that released her. Be silent, she thought. Within the Citadel at least, it could be that the Lord Counsellor's uniform was as effective as any shield wall, but the place was still unbelievably dangerous. She must say nothing – to anyone. She must watch and listen and learn.

Besides, she realized, she was far from certain that she wanted to escape from the Citadel. Where would she go? To the Ennerhald again? A bleak and unlovely prospect after even these few days of luxury, and how empty it would be without Assh and Frey. She could always try to reach the Count in the mountains but, the practicalities of the journey aside, what purpose would that serve? No more now than it had ever done. In the Ennerhald she had been near the source of all her distress – *now* she was within dagger's reach.

The last thought brought a sudden purpose into her meandering. She must use this freedom, whatever its cause, to obtain a weapon for use against either herself or her enemy, as circumstances dictated.

She abandoned the kneeling figure and also her stealthy progress through the shadows, and continued along the corridor. When she reached the corner she slipped behind a shrouded statue and looked back. After a moment, the clerk glanced about nervously, then clambered to his feet and scurried off, one hand stroking his hair repeatedly as if trying to dispel her touch.

Not minutes before, Jeyan had considered seeking his help, now she watched him leaving with scorn. It was these cravens and their ilk that sustained the Gevethen in power; they deserved no pity.

Turning from the retreating clerk she made to set off again. Closed doors lined the short gloomy corridor that she had turned into and a panelled wall sealed it. She hesitated. Guilt and painful memory filled her as, for a moment, she was back in the blind alley where she had been captured and the dogs slain. She was about to turn around and return the way she had come when a dark vertical line split the centre of the panelled wall and it began to move. The image made her catch her breath and threatened to disorient her until she realized that the end of the corridor was not in fact a wall, but a pair of doors, and that one of them was being opened. She edged back into the shadows again. Then someone was walking towards her. It was another clerk and he was engrossed in a sheaf of papers, holding them close to his face in an attempt to read them in the poor light. She let him pass unhindered and waited until he had gone from view before walking quickly to the double doors.

Pushing one of them open, she found herself in a broad hallway, and the silent stillness of the corridors she had been walking along vanished instantly. Servants, messengers, clerks, officials of all kinds were bustling around in great agitation.

Briefly she considered closing the door and fleeing back to her room, then the anger that had begun with the kneeling clerk, boiled up to fill her. Dancing attendance on your masters, are you? she thought bitterly as she looked out over the scene. Scurrying about like ants, keeping them secure in their power. Fearful for your little lives. I'll teach you fear. I'll grind your nest into dust.

She straightened up and entered the hallway.

The weaving streams and tides shifted and changed sharply as she entered, and the rumbling hubbub became sibilant with the whispered hiss of her name.

'The Lord Counsellor!'

Those farthest away quickened their pace while those nearby stopped and fell to their knees. None met her gaze, which was as well, for they would have seen their worst fears reflected in it. Jeyan drew in the effect she was causing as though it were air to a drowning man. It fed her condemnation of these people and she relished it.

As her initial exultation faded however, she began to feel concerned by all the activity. It was not normal, she was sure. Even allowing for her presence, there was an unusual alarm and urgency in almost every face she looked at. And, excitement, she decided, puzzled. It must have something to do with the Gevethen's encounter with Ibryen and their precipitate departure from her room – but what? She cast about for some semblance of a pattern in the movement, but nothing was immediately apparent, though she noted that a table at the far side of the hallway seemed to be some kind of a focal point. Slowly, and with wilful casualness, she moved towards it. It was manned by four obviously senior officials and, as she drew nearer, she noticed with pleasure the signs of discomfiture amongst them. They were all abandoning their work and about to start pushing back their chairs prior to kneeling when a door behind them opened and a Guards' officer emerged. It was Helsarn.

Jeyan recognized him immediately. The murderous killing fever that had been in full flow when she was captured rose undiminished, like hot bile, to mingle with the anger already swirling within her. Though she managed to keep her features motionless, her eyes betrayed her feelings and the officials dropped to their knees in an undignified scramble. Helsarn's insides tightened into a freezing knot as Jeyan's gaze struck him, but training and long-established habit carried him through the moment. He saluted smartly, then dropped down on to one knee and lowered his head in the formal obeisance adopted by the Guards.

It was some time before Jeyan could trust herself to speak. The upsurge of violent emotion had taken her completely unawares and she knew she must control it. Nothing was to be gained by going for the throat of this man in a blind fury.

'Stand up, Commander,' she said.

Helsarn rose up before her, standing stiff as a board. Being considerably taller it was an easy matter for him to keep his gaze from hers. He was glad of it for he was genuinely afraid. He had seen Jeyan at the heart of a terrible death struggle when he first encountered her and the subsequent knowledge that she had been a woman had frozen the memory in his mind. In common with anyone appointed to maintain civil order he knew that women, pushed beyond a certain point, were far more dangerous than men.

'My knife, Commander,' she said. 'Return it.' She spoke softly because her throat was so dry she was afraid her voice would crack. The effect however, was to make her presence even more menacing.

A memory of the gaping wound she had inflicted on the soldier who had captured her returned vividly to Helsarn. Others, ill-formed and vague, featuring the soldier's lost companions hovered about it but he refused to pursue them. He clung to the simplest. What did she want her knife for? Hagen had never carried one, nor any personal weapon for that matter. The one answered the other. Hagen had died at her hands in front of hundreds of witnesses and she had been rewarded with his office; she obviously had no intention of suffering the same fate herself. But there were other problems. She had access to

466

the Gevethen and she was patently unhinged. What if she turned the knife against them and it became known that he had given it to her? Yet he could not disobey a direct order. He prevaricated.

'As you command, Lord Counsellor,' he said. 'But the mobilization? I can't leave my post here. Their Excellencies have ordered that nothing is to impede the full levying of the army and the Guards – not even our sleep.' He risked a rapid but significant movement of his eyes towards the officials cringing behind the table.

Full levying of the army and the Guards! The news struck her like a plunge into cold water, and the fiery rage that had carried her this far vanished to become a renewed concern for the Count. This surely boded no good for him. She had to force herself not to respond. Change was afoot. Rapid change, full of opportunity. She must find out what was happening, and as quickly as possible before the leash she was stretching pulled her back.

She deliberately ignored Helsarn's mute appeal on behalf of the officials but silently motioned him back to the door through which he had just come. He held it open for her. It revealed a scene not very different from the one in the hallway, though the room was smaller and here the scurrying figures were all army and Guards officers except for a few who were obviously messengers. She hesitated, her faith in the new-found power of her office faltering before the experience of years of avoiding soldiers and Guards on the streets of Dirynhald when she was scavenging for food. The room had become suddenly still, as everyone present stopped their work and saluted.

Helsarn's words came back to her. 'Nothing is to impede . . .' She had a vision of the Gevethen suddenly

467

appearing and striking her down for this interference with their orders.

'Continue,' she said brusquely, as if annoyed that they had stopped.

There was a momentary hesitation then the room was bustling again. She turned to Helsarn. 'My knife, Commander. Send an underling – *now*. Then return to your duties.'

Helsarn saluted again then sought out one of the messengers and spoke to him urgently. The man cast a quick glance at Jeyan before running from the room at great speed.

Jeyan looked around coldly. Unusually for the Citadel, the room was quite well-lit, the light coming from lanterns placed on tables and hung about in an obviously makeshift fashion. It awoke ambivalent feelings in her. The light would protect her from the Gevethen, but too, it might expose her for what she was.

She moved from table to table. On some, documents were being received and studied and dispatched – sometimes out of the room, sometimes just to another table. Around others, groups of men were poring over maps and plans. These meant little to her though she caught occasional phrases which confirmed for her the general feeling of alarm which seemed to be pervading the room as it had the hallway outside.

'They can't all be brought together so quickly . . .'

'They'll be too exhausted for anything . . .'

'They'll be strung out from here to the mountains . . .'

'The logistics are impossible . . .'

Even once, the word 'Suicide . . .' though this was hastily curtailed as Jeyan turned round to see who had said it.

'A bold and imaginative stroke,' she said to Helsarn,

moving to his side as he bent over a table studying something.

'Indeed, Lord Counsellor,' Helsarn replied. It unsettled him to have her singling him out. Not only did he not want to become conspicuous to the other Commanders as a possible favourite, he was far from certain about what manic thoughts lay behind that stern face. It seemed to him that she was even beginning to look like Hagen. Still, it was pointless hoping to avoid her, and it would be folly to do anything that might be construed as a rebuff. His safest course would probably be to ingratiate himself somehow. He expanded his terse acknowledgement.

'It'll be costly in lives, but the outlaw Ibryen's been a thorn in their Excellencies' side for too long. The men will be glad to die gloriously for the greater good.'

Not most of the men I ever knew, Jeyan thought, though she confined herself to a clipped 'Yes,' as she peered at what Helsarn had been studying. It was a model of the mountains. She recognized the river and some of the larger peaks.

'Where is the outlaw Ibryen believed to be?' she asked.

Helsarn waved a hand vaguely over the model, encompassing several valleys. 'We don't know exactly,' he said. 'We have look-outs here, and here, but they rarely see anything and they're frequently murdered. I've often thought that a major offensive such as this, however costly, is the only way to deal with the problem. Their Excellencies must be freed to lead us out beyond the confines of this land.'

There was an uncertain inflection in his voice. 'But?' Jeyan prompted.

Helsarn looked at her awkwardly then turned away, still reluctant to meet her gaze. 'It concerns me that their Excellencies themselves intend to come with the army.'

'You fear for them?'

'Ibryen's people know the terrain intimately and use it well. They're ambushers to a man. And there are places where only narrow columns can pass, where only a small group of men can be brought to bear. Even closely guarded I fear they could be in great danger.' He shrugged anxiously. 'Ibryen will surely strike at them if he discovers they're with us.'

Opportunities indeed, Jeyan thought. The Gevethen had brought her to the heart of their world, now they were exposing themselves to Ibryen. They must surely be destroyed by one or the other. Even as the thought occurred to her however, so did its dark converse. If they were not destroyed now, then perhaps they would never be. She felt suddenly afraid. What had that evil pair learned when they had come so strangely upon Ibryen and his companion? Without intending to, she spoke her thoughts. 'The Gevethen see ways which are denied to others.'

Helsarn stiffened, misunderstanding the remark and taking it as a rebuke. 'I meant no disrespect, Lord Counsellor,' he said hurriedly. 'I merely voiced a concern for their Excellencies.'

He was spared any further awkwardness by the arrival of the messenger with Jeyan's knife. The man was kneeling beside her and holding out the knife, still in its crude leather sheath. His face was flushed and he was breathing heavily. 'My apologies for the delay, Lord Counsellor,' he panted. 'The Under Questioner had taken it for his own use.'

Jeyan took the knife without comment, drew it, tested the edge, then re-sheathing it, pushed it into her belt inside her tunic. As she turned her attention back to the model, Helsarn saw again the face he had seen trying to strangle the life out of the bleeding soldier in the

470

Ennerhald. He was wise to be afraid of this one, he thought. The Gevethen had an uncanny knack of picking their own kind.

'Where will you attack first?' Jeyan was asking.

Helsarn showed her. It needed no military training on Jeyan's part to see that large numbers of men would be required to mount an attack on so many valleys simultaneously, though she was careful to avoid asking direct questions.

'At least that's what the army Commanders have decided so far,' Helsarn elaborated, risking a little disdain. 'Though they keep changing it as information about troop arrivals comes in.'

Jeyan snatched at a phrase she had heard earlier. 'The logistics are difficult,' she said.

'They are, Lord Counsellor,' Helsarn agreed. 'Ordering virtually every army unit back to Dirynhald at the double *and* moving them to the mountains almost immediately presents serious problems. But we all regard their Excellencies' commands as a great challenge which it is our honour to meet. Even now, units are marching to establish a base camp.'

To his relief however, Jeyan was already walking away. She had heard and seen enough. The Gevethen were going to throw their entire resources against Ibryen.

Now she must be with them!

Chapter 30

'After the Great Heat, in the timeless time, the Shapers rejoiced at being and, in the dance and song of their rejoicing, formed all that is today: Theward shaping the mountains and the lands; Enastrion weaving the rivers and the lakes and the great oceans; Svara, the finest and most subtle Shaper of them all, soaring above all to make the boundless, shifting Ways that cannot be seen. Yet all were as one and their many talents were not separate, but resided one in another, bound together inextricably by the will of the greatest of the Shapers, Astrith. He it was who made all living things as they now are, though some say that their essence too came from the Great Heat and that he merely tended and guided. But that is beyond our knowing.

'And as they surveyed their work and found it good, Svara said to Astrith, "Theward's mountains and rich lands are a delight for all to behold, in their magnificence. As too are Enastrion's silver, tumbling rivers and thundering oceans. But it saddens me that only we have the vision to know the Ways that I have woven, and that only we may take joy from them."

'And the Shapers looked again at their work and saw that it was so. For while living things walked and rejoiced on Theward's lands, and swam and rejoiced in Enastrion's waters, few could follow Svara's Ways and none could follow those that rose beyond the highest of Theward's peaks.

'Then Astrith thought on this, and, as in a dream, his greatest creation came to him. Waking, he travelled the dreamways between the heartbeats of the worlds until he came to that which was before and beyond all things. And in this, he willed the Culmaren to be, breathing life into it and drawing it forth so that alone amongst his creations it could be known in this world and beyond. And he said to it, "You are the greatest and most mysterious of all my works. Rejoice that you now are, and tend the needs of those I shall bring you to." '

Isgyrn smiled, almost mischievously. 'Then Astrith chose the very finest of his people and gave them the sight to know the Ways of Svara and the skills to use the Culmaren. And he sent them forth to move along Svara's Ways, high above the lands and the waters, so that *all* the works of the Shapers should be known by men and rejoiced in.'

He leaned forward and his face became thoughtful. 'And as the Culmadryen rose into the high clouds, he pondered the ways and the destiny of men saying, as to himself, "I have found in this creation, that which I did not put there, and their nature is deep and strange and many-leaved and clouds all future knowing." And he went from the world to think on this.'

The tent became silent.

'Ah,' the Traveller said. 'A sombre and mysterious note on which to end. How splendid.'

'You tell a tale well, Isgyrn,' Ibryen said.

'A tale, Count? You'd deny the truth of our most ancient history?' Isgyrn said, though his manner was easy and he put no challenge in the words.

'A deep question,' Ibryen replied, in like vein. 'But who could deny or affirm the truth of a story so rooted in the mists of times gone and so well told?'

Rachyl leaned over and peered out of the crowded tent. 'It's raining as heavily as ever,' she announced, glancing upwards. 'And it's definitely in for the day.'

Ibryen confirmed the decision they had made earlier. Being caught in such weather while travelling was one thing, but setting out in it was another. There was, after all, no urgency about their journey now. They were not expected back so soon and they had more than enough supplies to serve them for the two days or so that it would take them to get back to the village. More seriously, for Ibryen, though he made no mention of it, he was glad of an excuse to spend some time doing nothing so that he could think quietly about all that had happened and its implications for the future. Though he had affected an optimism about the changes they had all experienced, it concerned him greatly that he was indeed returning to the village with 'only one more sword'. An awful foreboding was beginning to grow within him.

What he had learned over the past few days was obviously of profound significance, but how it related to the immediate needs of his conflict with the Gevethen he could not begin to see. The message that he had given to Iscar that he would come on them from a direction which they did not even know existed returned to reproach him constantly. Particularly so as it had proved to be almost prophetic. Strange Ways *did* exist. He could even enter them, though with little conscious knowledge of what he did or how he did it. But what were they? Where were they? How could he use them? Was there a way in which he could travel them that would bring him to a known destination? He had answers to none of these, nor any of

475

the many other questions that kept arising to disturb him.

Not that he was given a great deal of time for meditation as it transpired. The small tent was very full and, in the absence of anything to do, conversation ranged over many and varied topics. Ibryen told Isgyrn and the Traveller more fully about his land and the rise to power of the Gevethen and their subsequent depredations. Isgyrn told his own similar tale, though he was reticent about the cause and the telling distressed him. The Traveller yarned of many places and deeds, and Rachyl just asked questions and, as the youngest there, allowed herself at times an air of mildly smug tolerance as her elders rambled on.

It was one of the tales that the Traveller had told that prompted Isgyrn to tell the Dryenvolk's story of the creation of the Culmadryen. His stern face had come alive as he spoke and his manner had held the others spellbound. The Traveller in particular leaned forward and listened intently.

'I've heard many such tales,' the Traveller said, taking up Ibryen's rhetorical question. 'All with too many things in common to allow them to be lightly set aside as mere myths.'

'I'm not inclined to dismiss *any* tale, however fanciful, after everything that's happened since I met you on the ridge,' Ibryen said. He pulled a rueful face. 'I wish I could see to a time when we'd all have the leisure to pursue such matters further. Scholarship is infinitely preferable to swordsmanship.'

'To neglect either is a serious mistake, although I'm as guilty of the latter as many another.' The Traveller's tone was unexpectedly dark. He clapped his hands straight away to dispel the effect. 'But let's pursue just one small piece of scholarship while we've the chance.' He turned to Isgyrn. 'Tell us how the joyous world of the Shapers

476

became the flawed world of today,' he said.

Isgyrn grimaced. 'I'm rather as Ibryen now,' he said. 'The story of Astrith has always been regarded as significant but allegorical, and the story of the Coming of Samral even more so. "Red and baleful, He too came from the Great Heat, with lesser figures at His heels, carrying an ancient corruption with Him from what had gone before . . ." '

Isgyrn stopped with an unhappy wave of his hand. 'I can't speak it any more. It's a tale of treachery and deceit, of the seduction of people by fair words and seemingly fair deeds into dark folly while the Shapers slept. It was a tale to make fledglings shiver with delight and fear, and curl up in warmth and security, knowing that in truth, all was well. But now . . .' He fell silent. No one spoke. 'Now,' he went on after a long interval, 'I must accept that it was not an allegory, but perhaps an historical truth.' He looked round at the others, his eyes pained. 'Samral came again. It was His agent, one of the three Ahriel, who racked our lands, while the others racked the middle depths. I felt His very presence in His white-eyed agent.' He shivered. 'I saw deeds done, powers used, beyond anything we've ever known.' He looked at Ibryen. 'Yet He must indeed have been defeated or sorely wounded in the war that brought me here, or He'd surely have swept out across the world in these last fifteen years, and all would have known of Him. All. His purpose knows no bounds.'

'I can't doubt that you believe what you say,' Ibryen said uncomfortably. 'But it's a difficult tale to accept. We've many stories ourselves of giants and ogres in days long gone. And tales of how the world was made, but—'

Isgyrn levelled a warning finger at him. 'I understand your doubts. They're the doubts of any rational man, and the Dryenvolk are nothing if not a rational people. But had we thought and researched more and wallowed in doubt less, perhaps matters would have been greatly different and many lives spared. Trust me in this, Ibryen. Whether He has been defeated or not, I *felt* Samral in your Gevethen. Powerful and awful. They are not Ahriel, but it's said that He always had many human servants, equally as foul. The Gevethen are His, I'm sure. From what you've said, they possess the kind of power He bestows, albeit they use it rarely. They do His work, and they'll not stop with the enslavement of your land alone. We must never sleep again.' His tone was grim, but Ibryen could not keep the doubts from his face. 'I've stood where you stand, Ibryen,' Isgyrn went on. 'And I take no offence at your doubts. But whether you believe me or not, base your actions on the assumption that I'm correct.'

A gust of wind buffeted the tent, dispelling the dark mood that Isgyrn's story had created.

The conversation moved on.

From time to time the Traveller brought bouncing, whistling tunes into the damp twilight of the tent which allowed no foot to remain still. Isgyrn made no further reference to his tale and no one questioned him about it and, gradually, the debate settled on to Ibryen's immediate problems. Here, Isgyrn proved to be a determined inquisitor as he sought out knowledge of the fighting techniques that armies could use in this strange world where all battles had to be fought on one plane. He found it difficult, though he proved to be a perceptive listener, more than once making both Ibryen and Rachyl retreat into earnest thought with questions which obliged them to look at some long-established practice from an unusual perspective.

Eventually however, Ibryen's darker concerns about what was to be done on their return to the village began to surface and he could do no other than voice them. Isgyrn tried to reassure him as he had when they were preparing to leave the ridge the previous day. He had touched his enemy, change had been set in motion, who could say what would ensue? But practicalities were closing about Ibryen, binding him.

'Each step from now, takes me nearer to my people,' he said. 'They'll need to hear how we intend to attack and defeat the Gevethen. As Rachyl said – dispositions, logistics. My people fight well because we not only have a common purpose, we think alike. Each is as much a leader as follower. If we here have come to accept the inevitability of our decline if we continue as we are, then it's only a matter of time before the entire village reaches the same conclusion. I can't allow that to happen: we'll all perish for sure.'

But Isgyrn persisted. 'You mustn't encumber yourself thus,' he urged. 'Many changes *will* have happened and you can only deal with them as you find them. You can foresee none of them.'

'Go blindly and with faith?' Ibryen said ironically.

'I'm afraid so,' Isgyrn replied.

'It's no comfort.'

'It wasn't meant to be, but it's all you'll get. It's simply a statement of the reality of your position. The warrior's way, the warrior's burden. Dealing with the now, whatever it is, because others cannot.'

That night, Ibryen slipped silently from the tent. The rain had stopped and the darkness was alive with rich, fresh-washed forest perfumes. A chorus of tiny insect sounds and dripping water seemed like an earthly echo of the brilliant array of stars that covered the sharp, clear sky and peered down through the forest canopy.

He was uncertain why he had left the tent, other than that his circling thoughts and the idle day had left him unable to sleep; the tossing and turning that threatened to take him over would be too much for the others in such narrow confines.

Yet it was more than that, surely, and more even than the leaden foreboding that had been weighing on him all day. It wasn't the awful tension of pending battle – that, he was familiar with. It wasn't even guilt at the deception he had left behind as an excuse for this strange journey, although this would have to be accounted for soon, and he did not relish the prospect. It occurred to him that in fact he had told no lie. The very abandoning of the old procedures within the village could only lead to a new destiny, a way which none could have imagined. Perhaps what was disturbing him was no more than as Isgyrn had said, a reluctance to accept that all ahead was unknowable.

But none of these carefully crafted arguments could bring him any peace, and he stood for a long time in the cool darkness, leaning against a tree, pondering the unease that tugged at him. He could not believe the story that Isgyrn had told, yet neither could he casually discount it. Isgyrn clearly believed it and even during the short time he had known him he judged the Dryenwr to be clear-thinking, lucid and logical. And his conclusion had been open and honest – base your actions on the assumption that I'm correct. He could not argue with that. And it *was* as though his concerns came from beyond himself, as though he were the unknowing focus of events which were moving in ways beyond his control. And too, he was vastly different from the man who had been the Count of Nesdiryn scarcely a week ago. But what value was this change that had come over him?

He had no answer.

He had answers for nothing.

Weary, he let all questions slip away.

At the edges of his consciousness he could sense the Ways that would lead him into the worlds beyond. For a moment it came to him that he could simply slip from here and search out a place where horrors such as the Gevethen did not exist, where men might look at a sword and think it a farm implement. Was there such a place? He found it hard to imagine. Perhaps that sunlit forest had been one such? But it might simply have been somewhere else in *this* world. Nothing there had been disturbingly different, not the trees and the vegetation, not even the unusual carvings, and certainly not the fine bridge. And even there, the Gevethen had come. Or worse, he had drawn them there. That brought a coldly awful thought – that he should be the herald of the evil in some untrammelled new world. It laid a dead hand on his brief flight of fancy and carried him to the conclusion that he had known was always there: how could he live any kind of a life elsewhere, knowing what he had left behind?

There was no escape. There never had been. Whatever was afoot, and whatever his part in it, it could not be resolved by flight. Sooner or later – he corrected the thought – *soon*, he would have to confront and destroy the Gevethen or die in the attempt.

Knowing he could not leave, he closed his eyes and slipped into the place of lights and sounds where only his awareness existed. The confusion about him was beyond any describing, but it no longer disturbed him. He could feel Ways all about him that would leave his sleeping form here and carry him to places far beyond this rain-scented forest. And too, he suddenly sensed, there were still other worlds. Worlds that were ill-formed and vague. Ephemera

481

that did not truly exist yet were there for him to enter.

Are these dreams? he thought. Other people's dreams?

He had never dreamed.

A cry stirred within him. He did not want to hear it, but it could not be stilled.

I should be free to roam these worlds.

I should not have to die in battle, in fear and pain.

I should not have this burden to carry.

LET ME GO!

The cry echoed into an unknown distance, tailing off slowly into a sigh which became the stirring of the trees about him.

'Are you all right?'

Briefly he was once more at the door of his quarters in the village, being startled by Marris's enquiry out of the chilly night. Then he was in the forest, identifying the voice as that of the Traveller.

'Are you all right?' The question came again, and a slight movement showed him the deeper shadow within shadow that was the inquirer.

'Yes, I'm fine,' he replied, keeping his voice low to avoid disturbing Rachyl and Isgyrn.

'I thought I heard you calling out,' the Traveller said. 'But it was far away.' He sounded puzzled.

Ibryen smiled, a faint whiteness greying the gloom. 'Your hearing goes further than you realize.' He did not elaborate. 'Couldn't you sleep either?'

'I don't sleep much,' the Traveller replied. 'I've just been playing with the sounds of the forest. There's such a richness about us.'

There were resonances in his last sentence that brought Ibryen almost to tears. 'Indeed there is,' he said. Though he did not know why, his mind was clearer. Slowly he drew his sword. Resting it on the palms of his two hands he held it out at arm's length, as if offering it to the darkness. Stars were reflected faintly in the blade. 'I pledge myself again to my people,' he said quietly. The Traveller remained silent.

Jeyan leaned on the parapet of the balcony. In the distance, stark against the evening sky, like the fingers of a dead, warning hand, she could see the towers in the Ennerhald from which she had spied on the city to see the effects of her murder of Hagen. The train of events that had led her from there to where she now was, passed through her mind many times. There was a grim irony in them which she savoured, together with rich veins of self-justification. She had been right to stay in the Ennerhald for all those years. Had she fled to the Count, she would not now have been in a position to strike such a blow for him. She pressed a hand against the knife beneath her tunic. Or for her slaughtered parents. She pressed the knife harder until the pommel dug into her painfully. Or for herself. Yet, too, another irony was dogging her that day, for she had been unable to find the Gevethen. It did not help that she was quite unfamiliar with the rambling intricacies of the ancient and much added-to Citadel, and that the cold exterior she felt the need to maintain prevented her from flitting quickly about the place and, still less, from asking help of anyone. All she had been able to do was watch and listen. She had however, relished the effect that her presence had wherever she went. Any questioning glances directed her way had been inadvertent and had, without exception, been rapidly lowered as knees had hastily buckled. She had moved through crowds like a scythe through a field of tall corn. It was good. It was fitting that these people who sustained the Gevethen should bend before her.

You've done your work well, Hagen, she thought. The very terror of your office strips all protection away from those it was intended to guard.

But the Gevethen eluded her all that day, though the effects of their presence could be seen vividly all around. The activity she had first encountered as she emerged from the silent corridors into the hallway was as nothing to what developed as the entire administration of the Citadel was marshalled to implement the Gevethen's order for the committal of every resource to the immediate capture of the Count. Only one senior Army officer, it transpired, had suggested that the proposal was perhaps unwise and that not only would the cost in lives be appalling, but control across the whole of Nesdiryn and its borders might be dangerously loosened. The Gevethen had watched him coldly, then turned away with a casual gesture. The man had collapsed, writhing in pain. It had taken him an hour to die and he had died screaming such that even the hardest of the men around him were troubled in their dreams for long after. It had been a considerable time since the Gevethen had demonstrated their own frightening power, and news of it spread through the Citadel and to every army outpost faster than any other message delivered that day. All reservations about what was happening were subsequently spoken with the softest of voices and only in the presence of the most trusted of friends. Better to take your chance in the mountains than face certain death here. Catching the tale in transit, Jeyan stored it away as a reminder that the Gevethen were not without personal resource and that when finally she struck she must strike quickly, for there would be no second chance.

The net effect of the Gevethen's order however, was confusion and disorder, for there were no procedures established for undertaking such a venture. Even those like Helsarn who managed to keep their minds clearly focused on the Gevethen's intentions spent most of their time explaining to bewildered underlings and civilian officials, confirming messages to exhausted gallopers, and countermanding the orders of his more confused fellow officers. Nevertheless, the Gevethen's will gradually took shape and soon, albeit raggedly, men and matériel were following in the wake of those who had been sent immediately to establish a base camp.

Jeyan remained on the balcony for a long time after the Ennerhald towers had faded into the night. Raised voices, the clatter of hooves and the rattle of carts rose in an incessant clamour from the courtyard below, and the city streets were alive with moving lights. As the darkness deepened, she began to see a faint glow in the sky beyond the city as a transit camp for the incoming forces grew ever larger.

Eventually, the night cold made itself felt and she was shivering when she retreated inside. The gloomy corridors seemed almost welcoming after peering so long into the darkness. Uncertain about what she should do, she decided to return to her room. If the Gevethen wanted her they would presumably look there first. It took a great deal of finding as, even after wandering the Citadel for several hours, she was far from familiar with the place. On her rambling way there, an opportunity presented itself to satisfy a simpler appetite and her Ennerhald habits had her steal some food when she found herself in the kitchens.

She was still eating when she finally located her room. Nothing had been changed since she left it. What had happened to her ever-watchful servants? she wondered. She stepped back out of the room and looked up and down the corridor. There were several doors each set back in a deep alcove. After a brief hesitation she went to the nearest and boldly seized the handle. The door opened silently to reveal a darkened room. She took a lantern from the corridor and turned up the light. The room was completely empty. She stopped after a couple of paces as her footsteps bounced back hollowly. Moving to the next door she found the same, and so it proved with all the other rooms, though some were furnished and some looked as if they might have been offices at one time.

After the milling confusion in the rest of the Citadel, the echoing emptiness unnerved her slightly. Then, she thought, it was understandable. Few would wish to be neighbours to the Lord Counsellor. But where were the servants?

She shrugged. It was hardly a matter for great concern. She was glad to be rid of their overwhelming presence. Not least because had they set about preparing her for bed again, they would have discovered the knife and she knew she would have been unable to stop them taking it from her. Worse, the news that she had been carrying one would certainly have reached the Gevethen – with who could say what consequences? She turned over one or two excuses, but none of them felt particularly convincing.

Tugging the knife from her belt she moved to the bed and slipped it under the pillow. Then, taking off her tunic, she lay down. She wanted to think about everything that had happened since the Gevethen had come for her that morning. Was it only *that* morning – the sudden awakening in the pre-dawn darkness and the almost hasty dash through the mirrors? The memory brought back the penetrating coldness that marked her passage into that eerie world within, and she clamped her hands to her face, shuddering violently. If only she could be away from here – somewhere safe. Her eyes began to close as she went through again the Gevethen's frightening, childlike quarrelling – the mysterious whirling tunnel and its collapse – Hagen – Assh and Frey. Then Ibryen in the sunlit forest – a world within a world? And who was the man with him, the one who had torn him free from the Gevethen's grasp? Strange powerful face, with piercing eyes. And strange clothes too. She had never seen the like of him before.

And, above all, what had the Gevethen seen, or learned, in the brief scuffle with Ibryen?

'He has the gift,' they had screamed at one another in the midst of their rage. What gift? Had they not said to Hagen's spirit that *she* had the gift? No, she remembered, they had said that she was kin, whatever that meant.

She started awake. She mustn't doze off. She must remain awake and alert, ready to move as circumstances dictated. They might suddenly be in her room again. Then she rolled on to one side. Her hand slipped under the pillow and touched the knife as once she might have touched a cherished toy replete with the love of her parents.

What was Ibryen's gift? The question returned. What had the Gevethen seen that had led to this frantic activity, this overturning of every ordered procedure in their administration? For though she knew little of the detailed workings of the Gevethen's regime, she recognized well enough the near-panic that was pervading the Citadel and that it was markedly at odds with all that had gone before. And too, from remarks that she had overheard, she was beginning to realize the political implications of withdrawing the army from all the major towns and cities. The

Gevethen were risking losing their grip on the entire country. And moving forces from the borders could well embolden neighbours who, peaceful in Ibryen's time, had become increasingly alarmed by the Gevethen's growing army.

What could possibly be so important to them?

What was Ibryen's gift?

She forced her heavy eyes open.

What was Ibryen's gift? What was so precious?

She fell asleep, her hand still touching the knife.

As ever, she woke abruptly and lay motionless. The lanterns were still lit, but there was more light in the room than they were making. She swung off the bed and went to the window. Daylight was seeping around the edges of the curtain. She returned to the bed and took the knife from under the pillow. A few deft cuts severed the stitching holding the curtains together and the morning light flooded in like fresh air. The sky was overcast though quite bright, but the distant mountains were lost under a lowering sky that reached right down to the ground. Though she could not see the sun, she judged that it was quite late in the morning. Her stomach confirmed the conclusion. This was unusual, for she did not normally sleep much after dawn. She looked around the room. It looked peculiarly small and dingy in the daylight. And it was unchanged from the previous night. Still the servants were missing.

Good, she thought, quickly throwing on her tunic and sticking the knife back in her belt. A little more familiar with the Citadel now and the authority that her uniform carried, she would spend as much of the day as she could learning more about what was happening. Then she would seek them out. Rested, armed again, and free of the cloying presence of the servants, Jeyan felt more her old self. The disorder that the Gevethen had left in their wake renewed and fed her long hatred. Whatever their reasons, whatever their intentions, they were of no concern to her now. It was sufficient that events were swirling in disorder and that opportunities would arise that might never come again. She must strike the Gevethen at the first chance she had. For a fleeting moment, her elation plummeted into awful fear, then sprang back again.

'No choice,' she said to the silent room, and the words echoed over and over through her mind. *No choice.*

She preened herself for some time in front of the tall, black-edged mirror. The Lord Counsellor's uniform must be without flaw; it was both her sword and her shield. Her reflection stared back at her disdainfully.

Checking that her knife was held securely and secretly in her belt, she opened the door. Helsarn was framed in it, his hand raised.

Chapter 31

'My apologies, Lord Counsellor,' Helsarn stammered, lowering his hand awkwardly and bowing as he stepped back. 'I was about to knock. Their Excellencies ask that you attend on them in the Watching Hall.'

Helsarn's momentary confusion prevented him from noticing Jeyan's.

Her stomach became leaden. What did they want? Had they been searching for her yesterday?

'There are no servants to carry such errands, Commander?' she asked sternly, forcing herself to remain at least outwardly calm.

Helsarn misunderstood the question at first, but provided the answer to one she was reluctant to ask. 'Your body servants have been called to the mirrors, Lord Counsellor,' he said hurriedly. 'And it was not fitting that a lesser person carry such a message.'

Jeyan nodded and motioned him to lead the way. She noticed that he was dressed for travel, and was carrying a helmet under his arm. 'The mobilization goes well?' she asked as they walked along.

'It does, Lord Counsellor. It has gathered pace through the night and new units are arriving by the hour. Such a levying will enter Nesdiryn history as a truly great military achievement. A force is being gathered that will crush the

491

outlaw Ibryen's rag-tag followers once and for all, and bring him back to Dirynhald in chains.' He took the opportunity to associate his own name with this glory. 'It's been a great honour for me to play my small part in such a venture.'

'Indeed,' Jeyan said coldly. The news added to the darkness growing within her. It wasn't possible that Ibryen could stand against the forces being marshalled. More and more it was becoming apparent that she was the only one who could put an end to the Gevethen. 'Ibryen will prove no easy prey,' she said. 'What is the condition of the men?'

Helsarn half-turned towards her. The question was unexpected and he started answering without thinking. 'Those from the city and nearby are fresh. Others . . .' He hesitated, realizing that he was on the verge of casting doubts on what was happening. This creature was beginning to unsettle him as much as Hagen had.

'Yes?' Jeyan pressed.

Cornered, Helsarn resorted to the truth for inspiration. 'Others are sore and weary with the hard marching when they arrive, but the very nearness of their Excellencies sweeps all fatigue away.' He began to walk a little more quickly, his body reflecting his anxiety to be away from this topic. In reality, the men in some of the units could barely stand and were on the verge of mutiny. The news was being kept from the Gevethen as their response was already known: 'Execute one in ten.' Helsarn wanted no part of that. Not that he suffered from any problem with his conscience in taking such an action, but what might be expedient in a single, isolated unit was another matter altogether when so many were being held in such close proximity to one another and in so disorganized a manner. He also had sufficient foresight to see that in the difficult mountain-fighting that was to come, opportunities for the discreet removal of unpopular officers would abound. They continued in silence, Jeyan preoccupied with what the Gevethen might want, Helsarn relieved not to have compounded his error.

As on the previous day, the Citadel was alive with activity, though to Jeyan it seemed to be a little more ordered. When they reached the Watching Hall, the Guards opened the doors without command and Helsarn entered as well. It took Jeyan a moment to orient herself amid the scattered lights and the crooked, dully glittering towers that rose, tree-like, into the dusty gloom. She was sure that these had been moved, but it did not seem possible, some of them were so large. Her eyes went first to the high throne platform at the far end, but it was empty. Then they were drawn to the only movement in the place. Turned into a milling crowd by the surrounding mirror-bearers, the Gevethen were standing at the centre of the hall, in what could almost be called a clearing in this strange forest. For a fleeting instant Jeyan felt the urge to turn and flee but her legs were already obeying the command she had given them, and were carrying her resolutely towards the waiting throng. She was aware that it was Helsarn who was now following.

As she drew nearer, the mirror-bearers continued moving. There were more of them than before, Jeyan thought, though it was difficult to tell, they moved so quickly and with such eerie precision. The Gevethen became a circle, then there were just six of them, and Jeyan became aware of converging lines of marchers on either side of her. She was approaching the Gevethen flanked by lines of herself. The marchers glanced at her surreptitiously.

A thought came to her, sudden and vivid. Should she strike now? Should she spring forward instead of kneeling, and drive her knife into the throat of one of them? The answer crashed upon her with such force that she almost stumbled. Yes! *This* was the moment. Another might never come. Who could say what they wanted her for, or when she might come so close to them alone and armed again? She embraced the resolve. This day in Nesdiryn history was going to be very different from the one that Helsarn imagined, though he would indeed be mentioned in it – if he lived, for she was steeling herself for a frenzy of killing that would not stop until she was exhausted or dead.

She straightened up and ran a hand casually down her tunic as if smoothing it. The actions brought her hand close to her knife. Her heart began to race. Soon it would be over. She wished Assh and Frey were with her. What an end to these creatures they'd make together!

Then something seemed to be wrapping itself about her legs. It was as though she was wading through water or deep soft sand. The resistance increased with each forward movement and within a single pace she was completely halted. She recognized the force that had possessed her on the march from the dungeons. She was powerless against it. Her tight-wound intent twisted and screamed within her at this unseen and unexpected frustration and turned instantly to terror. Did they know about the knife? Had they sensed her intention? She did the only thing she could. She dropped to her knees and bowed her head.

'Rise, Lord Counsellor,' the two voices grated out. 'We are to the battlefield today. The worm eating at the heart of our new order is soon to be torn out.'

It took a moment for the words to register, so prepared for an assault was she, and then it was a strange excitement in them that reached her first.

'I go where you will, Excellencies, though I am no

soldier,' she managed to say, though she remained kneeling. The excitement filled with a repellent amusement.

'You are a life-taker, it is sufficient.'

Jeyan felt naked, exposed and suddenly sick. For a moment she could neither speak nor move. Then relief swept over her – she had not been discovered! In its wake, her hatred returned to make her wholly herself again. Let them take the consequences of bringing a life-taker so close to their scrawny throats then, she blazed silently. But it could not be now, for all about her she could feel the force that was keeping her from moving closer, like a glutinous expression of their will.

As she was about to stand, Helsarn said, 'May I speak, Excellencies?'

'Commander.'

'Excellencies, I'm concerned for your safety in the mountains,' he began. 'Several of your servants within the city have returned with the same rumour. It's said that the outlaw Ibryen has left his secret camp and that he plans to come upon you from a direction that cannot be guarded against.'

The amusement grew. 'Your concern is unnecessary, Commander. We are guarded in all Ways.'

Helsarn persisted. 'I have never known so widespread a rumour before, Excellencies. It is most unusual. And there are many narrow and dangerous places in the mountains.'

Jeyan sensed the mood about her changing towards one of impatience, then abruptly there was stillness and silence.

'Leave us, Commander.'

The command was like the snapping of dried twigs under a soft and long-feared footfall. Jeyan heard Helsarn leaving. The silence remained. Then a soft hissing filled it. The Gevethen were whispering – it was like the wind across a graveyard. She strained forward. The power that was holding her at bay had eased, but it was still there. She made no further effort. She was too far away, and, besides, could do nothing from her knees. She remembered too well how quickly the mirror-bearers had moved when she was being escorted from the dungeons. She caught snatches of the conversation.

'He is coming through the Ways.' The wind rose and fell, punctuated by gusts of panic but gradually changing to an uneasy confidence.

'He fled from us . . .'

'But he was there. And with a strange companion.'

'Could his army come thus?'

'Let him come.'

'We are guarded.'

'Yes.'

'Yes.'

The whispering faded and she was the focus of their attention again. 'Rise, Lord Counsellor. And follow. The hand of our law must be seen to reach into all places.'

Then there was confusion and movement, and while, the previous day, she had floated idle and neglected at the edge of the Gevethen's great enterprise, now she stood near its centre, as they moved through the Citadel. She watched, fascinated and scornful, as senior army and Guards' officers, and high-ranking officials, came and went seeking advice about this, bringing news about that, wanting to know 'their Excellencies' will'. And all were afraid. It was good.

Yet, though she was by the Gevethen's side, still she could come no nearer to them; still their mysterious power held her away.

And always, the mirror-bearers were about them,

moving relentlessly to their own unheard tune. There *were* more than there had been before, she decided, for she noticed several if not all of her own servants amongst them, including Meirah, the only one with whom she had spoken. Twice she deliberately caught her eye, but there was no response. The woman's face was as blank and cold as all the other mirror-bearers. Somehow their behaviour was almost more frightening than any of the overt menace of the Gevethen. Was this what was in store for her? Was this what was in store for everyone? An eerie, pointless perfection? The question tugged at her incessantly even though she knew she would never know the answer. By one means or another she would be dead before such a thing could come about.

Then, at the front of a crowd of officials she was witnessing the departure of the Gevethen. It was an event without formal ceremony, though there was a large escort of Citadel Guards, armoured and carrying short, axe-headed pikes which gleamed viciously even in the grey light. Apart from the group behind her, such onlookers as there were did not linger, for fear that their dawdling would be taken as a lack of enthusiasm for the Gevethen's grand design. There were however, many discreet glances made from the safety of the Citadel's curtained windows. For the most part these were to satisfy the watchers that their beloved masters were indeed leaving – it was a rare occurrence – but there was also great curiosity about the Gevethen's strange carriage. Not that 'carriage' was a particularly fitting word for the contrivance that was to carry them to the mountains, except in so far as it resembled a funeral carriage. Black and huge, and in two articulated sections, it was pulled by six horses. Its sides flared up and out, curling over at the eaves into ornate carvings like a tangle of thorns from which wild-eyed faces gaped down at passers-by. There were apparently no windows in it though there was a platform at each end large enough to carry the Gevethen and several of the mirror-bearers had they so desired. Toiling figures decorated the rims of the wheels and the spokes and hubs were carved into angles and barbed spikes. The whole was covered in intricate carvings, though, being black on black they could be examined only by standing very close. The only relief to the dark complexity was a single silver star set on each side. They were identical to that which adorned Jeyan's judicial bench, though here there were no gold escutcheons nor broken rings. The effect was stark and frightening.

A row of more conventional carriages waited behind it.

Jeyan watched as the Gevethen moved down the stone steps and into the back of their menacing vehicle which opened silently at their approach. The mirror-bearers moved round them as ever, only much closer than usual and in such a way that they could not be seen. Nor did any of their confusing images emerge into the dull daylight. Jeyan was reminded again of some soft-shelled creature scuttling for the darkness of its lair. Many of the enlarged contingent of mirror-bearers did not enter the carriage but moved alongside it, standing between it and the Guards. As the carriage moved off, the mirrors began to move again, making it seem that the carriage was being carried on many legs. It was an unsettling sight.

Jeyan turned away from it and looked back up the steps to the door through which the Gevethen had come. It occurred to her that before the mirror-bearers had closed about them they had seemed so much smaller, so much more fragile, so much more easy to kill. The recollection brought with it a sudden sense of incongruity about the Gevethen's great black carriage. What use would that thing be in the mountains? she thought. There was many a street in Dirynhald that it couldn't negotiate, let alone the terrain they would encounter once over the river. How were they going to cope then? She remembered Helsarn's concern about the narrow passes. She shared it. The Gevethen were hers, they mustn't fall to some nameless ambusher.

Then Helsarn was discreetly ushering her into a carriage of her own. As she was entering it she saw the Citadel officials who had been standing behind her dashing with unseemly haste for the other carriages. It was not until she had been inside it for some time and it was rattling out of the courtyard that she realized it was the one in which she had murdered Hagen. The thought amused her greatly and, leaning back, away from the window, she laughed silently to herself and laid her hand on her knife.

The journey through the city was uneventful, news of the Gevethen's passage having sped ahead and emptied the streets more effectively than a sudden thunderstorm. Such people as were about were kneeling, heads bowed by the time Jeyan's carriage passed them. That added to her amusement though her main interest lay in the familiar buildings passing by. This had been her territory once, or, more correctly, it had been the rich neighbour to her territory upon which she was free to prey for whatever needs she had. At one point they came near to the edge of the Ennerhald and several times it occurred to her that a bold leap from the carriage and a few strides would lead her into the confusion of alleys, cellars and derelict buildings that had long served as a protective labyrinth to her land. But it would indeed have to be a bold leap for it would have to carry her through two lines of Guards, and Helsarn and other senior officers were also moving up and down the columns on horseback. And what would be the point? Now that the possibility of escape was nearer than it had been at any time since she had been captured, she realized its futility. The Ennerhald held nothing for her now. It had served its turn. It had trained her in the skills she needed and carried her to the heart of her enemy.

When they came to the outskirts of the city, the carriage began to slow and Jeyan had to fight back an urge to lean out of the window to see what was happening. It soon became apparent as they began to pass ragged lines of soldiers moving in the same direction. Travel-stained and obviously exhausted, they contrasted markedly with the immaculate Guards escorting the Gevethen's train. To Jeyan it seemed not that they were about to fight a battle, but that they had already fought one and were in retreat. What condition would these people be in by the time they reached the mountains? Briefly and somewhat to her surprise, she was torn. How many of these people would die needlessly in the Gevethen's sudden manic need to capture Ibryen? How many of them had wives and families dependent on them, fretting for them? Visions of sad faces and weeping eyes began to come to her. She crushed them as violently as if they had been so many snakes. These people had betrayed their lawful lord and chosen to follow the Gevethen, now they could suffer the consequences, now they could feel the weight of the Gevethen's justice. Had anyone seen her face at that moment they would indeed have believed that Lord Counsellor Hagen had returned to possess her.

The informal escort to the train grew as they continued, more incoming troops joining at every crossroads they came to. Not all were in the same sorry state as the first group they had encountered, but all were obviously tired.

Then there was cheering ahead and into Jeyan's view

500

came the transit camp whose fires and lanterns she had seen lighting the sky on the previous night. It was an inglorious sight. Bedraggled tents had been thrown up, to all appearances at random, to stand like decaying fungi on what had been rich meadow-land, but which was now an expanse of brown earth, churned into mud by foot, hoof and wheel. It seemed to Jeyan that there were hundreds of men involved in almost as many activities. More tents were being erected, carts were being wrenched through the clinging mud, equipment was being carried hither and thither, put down, picked up and carried somewhere else, reluctant horses and mules were being sworn at and whipped, reluctant soldiers were being sworn at and threatened with whipping. Harassed officers and officials were stumbling through the disorder watching the confusion increase with each step they took to bring order. Men were walking, running, marching, standing on guard, standing around fires, or just wandering aimlessly.

The cheering was coming from groups of soldiers lining the road, though there was little enthusiasm in the sound and still less in the faces that Jeyan saw as her carriage moved past them. She noticed officers standing at the rear, obviously there to ensure that this spontaneous burst of loyalty to the Gevethen and their entourage went as planned.

She glanced towards the mountains. The grey mistiness hiding them was nearer. Rain was coming. Good, she thought. The camp would be like a swamp before the day was out.

It took the Gevethen's train some time to pass the camp, then it was moving along the road that would carry it to the mountains. Once this had been little more than a winding track used by local farmers, leading eventually to a modest bridge which served the few people who

501

chose to live on the other side of the river. It had been adequate. It was, after all, a road to nowhere.

Now, to facilitate the regular campaigns into the mountains, the bridge, hitherto capable of carrying a few cows, had been replaced by one which could carry columns of marching men, provided they had the wit to break step. The track too, bore the marks of progress. It had been widened and straightened and metalled, so that in parts it was the equal of some of the finest avenues within the city itself. It was still a road to nowhere, however.

And it could not cope with the traffic that was passing along it now. From time to time the carriages stopped. Jeyan gave little thought to such interludes though the causes often made themselves known as she passed carts with shattered wheels and broken shafts languishing by the roadside, their contents tipped out haphazardly and their escorts struggling to make temporary repairs or standing round staring vacantly at the damage. What price your great army, Gevethen, halted for lack of a wheelwright? she thought darkly, though her amusement was tempered by the knowledge that the halts were only temporary and that the many soldiers walking alongside, never stopped. The army, though weary, was making relentless progress.

Then it was raining. Steady, vertical rain. It rattled on the top of her carriage, splashed on the close-paved roadway, and drenched the escorting Guards. She leaned back into the comfort of the well-upholstered seat and imagined the rain making its leisurely way along to the camp, ignoring the prayers and curses of the occupants as they saw it approaching. It would take very little to turn the camp into a quagmire and, she judged from the sky, this would continue all day. It was all very satisfying.

Eventually they were moving over the bridge. The river

was high with water from the melting snows. Like a panicking crowd fleeing from a great terror, waves rose and fell, grey and spuming white, as they shouldered one another aside to force their way through the constricting arches of the bridge. The sight made Jeyan thankful that she had not attempted the journey to the mountains. At some point she would have had to cross this and even at its least turbulent, during the summer, it would still have been very dangerous.

She did not dwell on the thought. All such conjecturing had been taken from her now. The bridge, however, caught her attention. It was the first time since they had passed the camp that she realized the changes that had been made to the road. How far did it go? she wondered. She tried to remember the model that she had seen Helsarn studying, but without success. Almost without thinking what she was doing she began raking through long-buried memories of childhood when she had occasionally been brought here by her parents. A vague picture of a wide cart-track winding through the increasingly hilly countryside came to her. It passed by a few farmhouses, then became narrower and narrower until it just petered out. A flood of other memories came in the wake of this, all of them painful, and she shied away from them violently, pressing herself tight into the corner of the seat as if to hide there. From here she found that she could peer through the window without being seen from the outside. The road was turning slightly and she could just make out one side of the Gevethen's black, lumbering carriage. The discovery availed her little however, for the mist and the rain obscured not only the mountains but everything beyond a hundred paces or so.

The carriages rolled on. The escorting Guards marched on. The army trudged on.

And Jeyan learned the answer to her question: how far did the road go? It was: a long way – and she soon stopped searching into the mist ahead. By the time the carriage came to a final stop, it was late afternoon and the overcast sky was bringing night early. Despite the comfort of the carriage, Jeyan found she was stiff and tired when she tried to move. As a consequence, she had no difficulty in maintaining the stern expression that she had chosen to affect when Helsarn opened the door. He was soaked.

'This is our base camp, Lord Counsellor,' he said. 'Quarters have been prepared for you.'

As Jeyan stepped from the carriage she found herself under an awning supported by four Citadel servants. She took a deep breath. Unexpectedly, the damp coldness of the mountain air rushed into her like a bright morning wakening and she felt her every muscle and joint crying out to be stretched so that this would fill her entire body. She forced herself to stillness. She must show as few signs of her humanity as possible. It took her some effort and it showed.

'Is anything wrong, Lord Counsellor?' Helsarn asked, a small cascade of rainwater running from his helmet as he leaned forward.

Jeyan slowly glanced back along the line of carriages. Servants carrying awnings were also protecting the contents currently being disgorged, and the grey mountain light was spreading a demeaning hand over the cream of the Gevethen's administrators and officials. It reduced them to creaking, arm-waving, bent-backed shadows, floundering pathetically now they were away from the musty twilight of their normal environment. Jeyan was glad that she had forced herself not to respond to her natural instinct after leaving her carriage. Helsarn surreptitiously followed her gaze. Seeing themselves so exam-

504

ined, the nearest officials stopped their fussing and bowed respectfully. Jeyan allowed her mouth a small twist of contempt as she turned away to look at the Gevethen's great carriage. By contrast with the others, there was no activity about it at all save for the steam that was rising from the motionless horses.

'Their Excellencies' quarters could not be prepared until they arrived, Lord Counsellor,' Helsarn said, anticipating her question.

The remark meant nothing to Jeyan. 'Take me to mine,' she said curtly.

As they moved off, the servants carrying the awning moved with them, like a poor imitation of the Gevethen's mirror-bearers. The carriages had stopped on an area just to one side of the road along which the army was still passing. It was covered with crushed stones. They were loose underfoot and obviously had not long been laid for only a few small puddles had gathered. Around the area was an array of tents. They were black and rectangular and, to Jeyan, looked like so many rotten teeth set in pallid gums. Helsarn led Jeyan to the largest. As she stepped inside it was as though she had been transported back to the Citadel. Not because of the furnishings which, though similar to those in her room, were simpler and more sparse, but because of the gloomy lighting and the general atmosphere. How could that clinging heaviness have survived the journey and the rain-sodden erection? she thought. Perhaps it was the low sloping ceiling that heightened the sense of oppression, perhaps the black walls, perhaps the many mirrors. She did not dwell on the question. All she knew was that she did not want to stay here one moment longer than was necessary. She needed to be out in the fresh clean air. 'Get me a cape and hood,' she said as she took in the scene again.

Helsarn, who was standing at the entrance, dripping respectfully, looked uncertain.

Receiving no reply, Jeyan turned and repeated her request with an edge to her voice. 'I wish to inspect the camp and the men,' she added.

Helsarn started. 'Lord Counsellor, this section is for their Excellencies' staff,' he said uncomfortably. 'The main camp is further up the valley. It's . . .' He was about to say 'very disorganized', but caught himself in time. 'There's a great deal of activity going on up there – men, equipment, animals, moving everywhere. And the weather's made the ground very treacherous. We've had several serious accidents already . . .'

'A cape and hood,' Jeyan repeated coldly, cutting across his explanation. Helsarn hesitated, then saluted and strode off. Jeyan looked around her new quarters again, and she had to fight down an urge to lay about her, to smash this wretched remnant of Hagen's personality, to shatter all these mirrors, to tear down the walls and let an honest light into the place.

Helsarn was not long and when he returned, Commander Gidlon was with him. Helsarn was carrying a cape, but both men looked decidedly uneasy. They had had a swift and uncomfortable conference. Even Helsarn's unspoken remark that the camp proper was very disorganized had been a euphemism. It was a little way short of complete chaos and it was only ruthless action by the army and Guards' officers that was bringing any sense of order to it. It was true there had been several serious accidents. There had also been a far larger number of summary executions, for offences ranging from the questioning of orders to preaching mutiny and actually attacking officers. It was no brave-hearted soldiery that was going boldly to face the outlaw Count and free their land.

For the most part it was a bedraggled and conscript army whose only choice was to move forward and take their chance against the Count's followers, or risk the swords of their officers if they retreated.

For Gidlon and the other Commanders, the idea that the Lord Counsellor should see any of this and thence confide it to the Gevethen was unthinkable, not to mention the fact that they might not be able to guarantee her safety, so uncertain were conditions there.

'Lord Counsellor,' Gidlon said, saluting, then dropping to one knee. 'I've brought the cape as you asked, but may I respectfully request that you remain here. As Commander Helsarn has doubtless told you, so much is being done so quickly to implement their Excellencies' orders and conditions are so bad that the camp is very dangerous.'

For a moment Jeyan considered debating with him. As Helsarn had gone running for help, it was obvious that there was something they did not wish her to see. Instead however, she decided on silence and, walking past him, she took the cape from Helsarn.

Gidlon rose and tried again. 'Lord Counsellor, please allow me a little time to select an appropriate escort of Guards for you . . .' He stopped. As did Jeyan.

She was standing with the cape draped over one shoulder, staring at the activity now filling the area centred by the Gevethen's carriage. Silent figures were rapidly erecting a further tent, though it was very different from the ones already built. Black canvases were already spanning from the high eaves of the Gevethen's carriage to those of Jeyan's tent and those of her immediate neighbours, and others were being run out even as Jeyan and the two Commanders watched. An unnatural nightfall was descending ahead of the premature one being brought by the weather. Jeyan felt as though she were watching the building of a great spider's web. She felt also, the oppression within her tent slowly growing around her, threatening to enclose the entire area. And the smooth efficiency of the silent builders was deeply unnerving. It was as though they were part of a machine rather than the people they appeared to be.

Gidlon recovered his composure first. He did not know what was happening but, in his time, he had seen many strange things happen around the Gevethen and he had schooled himself to accept them without comment. 'Lord Counsellor,' he said, after a while, lowering his voice as though he were in a holy place. 'Any danger aside, should their Excellencies wish to seek your advice it will be difficult for us to find you quickly if you're wandering about the main camp.' Receiving no immediate rebuff he risked embroidering his tale. 'I will tell the men of your wish to visit them. They'll find it heartening.'

Dull lanterns were being hung from the ceiling. The hiss of the rain striking the stones was becoming a low drumming note. Jeyan motioned the two Commanders to leave her.

She stood as if unable to move, until the great dark tent was completed. Then, head bowed, she turned and went back into her own tent.

Chapter 32

Marris cast a sour glance across the valley. He could not see the far side. In fact, he could barely see to the far side of the village through the steadily streaming rain. The sole consolation he could find in the weather was that it was at least not windy. Still, whatever the conditions, he'd still have to do his rounds – visit the outer perimeter guards and exchange a grumble or two about the rain while ensuring they were all still alert. Not that there should be anything to be particularly alert about at the moment. True, the passes were clearing rapidly, but the Gevethen had never sent anything against them so early in the year, and Iscar had brought no hint of unusual army activity. And the death of Hagen would surely have caused the Gevethen a great many problems. In his brighter moments, Marris even toyed with the notion that this unexpected assassination would cause such difficulties that perhaps no expedition would be made against them at all, this year. He did not toy with it for long however, and never spoke it out loud, even in ironic jest. It was equally probable, as Ibryen had said before he left, that the Gevethen might mount an early campaign to draw attention away from the problems caused by Hagen's death.

And, for all the assurances he rehearsed, he still felt the unease he always felt when the weather closed in like this. At times it was an invaluable ally, enabling his people to move quickly about the mountains with much less fear of discovery, and to launch sudden ambushes and vanish almost immediately. But that was when the enemy's position was known. The danger when it was not known was that it could be they who were laying the ambush. On the whole, Marris preferred to see what was happening, despite the problems it brought to moving safely about the mountains.

'Are you ready?' Hynard came out of the Council Hall still fastening his cape. He gave the valley a glance similar to the one Marris had given it, then, at Marris's nod, the two of them set off. They did not speak as they walked through the silent village. This was partly due to the mountain discipline that was always with them, but also due to the fact that they had little to say to one another. Whether it was just the absence of Ibryen and Rachyl or the strange reasons that had been given for their going it was not possible to say, but the whole community had been subtly unsettled and the two men were not immune. Both of them had set their faces resolutely against worrying and while both succeeded in looking unconcerned, both actually failed. The net result was an alternation of awkward silences and bursts of forced heartiness.

Not that either had any serious concerns, yet. Those they would have given voice to immediately. After all, Ibryen had said he would be away for a month at the most and what was to be served by fretting after only a few days? Yet the two absences dragged – made looking forward difficult – introduced too many unresolvable 'What if?'s.

They walked on through the rain in silence and were challenged successfully at each of the outer perimeter guard posts.

Hynard smiled as they left the last one. 'I wonder if this alertness is due to Ibryen's, "Vigilance must be redoubled", or your suddenly doing three times as many tours of inspection?'

But Marris did not respond. He was staring into the mist, preoccupied.

'I said—'

Marris raised a hand.

'What's the matter?' Hynard asked softly, abandoning his light-hearted taunt.

Marris curled up his nose in irritation. 'Something feels bad,' he said looking from side to side as if that might help him see better through the mist. Hynard did not ask for clarification. He sensed nothing himself, but Ibryen's followers trusted one another's instincts and he stayed silent.

The two of them stood for some time, then Marris shook his head, though his expression was more concerned than ever. 'I can't hear anything,' Hynard whispered, to prompt him.

'Nor I,' Marris said after a long pause. Then he shrugged. 'Probably imagination,' he decided, though without conviction.

Hynard looked at him doubtfully. For a moment he considered offering Marris another taunt, about his lack of imagination, but Marris's mood was contagious. Instead, he opted for action. 'Let's check the north end ridge-post while we're here,' he said. 'This rain's in for the day, there's no chance of us being seen.'

It would probably be dark when they returned, making the journey difficult, but Marris nodded his head and moved off without further debate.

Despite the poor visibility and the unlikelihood of there being any Gevethen troops or spies in the area, the two men moved with increasing caution as they neared their destination. They stopped from time to time and listened, but nothing was to be heard except the sound of the rain and the many streams that tumbled down the valley sides. Each time Hynard glanced at Marris however, the older man still looked uneasy.

They both stopped suddenly. Hynard pointed as the movement which had caught their attention occurred again. It appeared to be a solitary figure. Both of them crouched down slowly and edged their way to the shelter of some nearby rocks. The figure continued towards them.

'It's no stranger, moving so quickly and using the cover like that,' Hynard whispered.

'It's a runner from one of the ridge look-outs then,' Marris replied. 'What the devil's he playing at?'

He was about to stand up and hail the figure when Hynard seized his arm and pointed frantically. Coming into view were other figures. There were four of them altogether and they too were moving quickly, though not in the manner of one of Ibryen's people. And they were noisy. Not that they were shouting, but to the ever-sensitive ears of Marris and Hynard, the clatter of their weapons stood out above the murmur of the valley as clearly as if they had been ringing hand-bells.

'Ye gods, they're army,' Hynard hissed as they drew closer. The two of them became very still, making themselves indistinguishable from the rocks they were sheltering amongst. Marris glanced after the fleeing look-out, his mind racing. Ibryen's conjecturing had been right then, the Gevethen *were* launching an early attack to draw attention away from problems in the city. But patrols had never ventured into this inconspicuous little valley before. And what was that idiot of a runner doing leaving his post when they were about? Worse, what was he doing

512

leading his pursuers back towards the village? More immediate concerns pushed the questions aside. The man was passing them now and it looked as though he was going to pay a harsher price for his folly than any reproach he could have expected from his peers.

'They're going to catch him,' Marris said. 'He's hurt. He's limping.'

Hynard swore softly. It was the limit of their debate. They did not need to discuss the seriousness of what was happening. Having seen someone, the four soldiers would have to be killed, even though that would risk bringing others after them. Normally, in some distant valley, that was no great problem, but here, so close to the village . . .

Marris clenched his fists at the thought.

Yet what could he and Hynard do? For the two of them to attack four was out of the question. To stand any chance at all it would be essential to fall on the men suddenly and silently, and radically improve the odds before the attack was even suspected. Yet placed as they were, even that hazardous option was impossible. The soldiers were too far away and too spread out.

But to let them escape was unthinkable.

The look-out went sprawling. Both men involuntarily breathed in sharply. The man staggered to his feet but fell again. Then he was crawling. He was sitting with his back to a boulder and his sword drawn as the four soldiers closed on him. The first one to reach him casually kicked the sword aside and raised his own.

Marris felt Hynard's grip tightening about his arm.

The blow never fell however. One of the other soldiers seized the raised arm and took the sword. Angry voices drifted to Marris and Hynard, then the first soldier was knocked savagely to the ground and his sword thrown contemptuously after him. He lay still for a moment, then, shaking his head and using his sword for support, he clambered slowly to his feet. The look-out was dragged upright, but collapsed immediately with a cry of pain. There was another brief debate then two of the soldiers dragged him up again and, draping his arms around their shoulders, began carrying him.

This time it was Marris who swore. 'No choice now,' he said bitterly. 'If he's taken back to their base camp they'll torture the location of the village out of him.'

Hynard bared his teeth in an expression of grim but reluctant acknowledgement. There was no need to discuss tactics. Speed, silence and an unhesitating resolution to kill were all that were needed – dark attributes that their years resisting the Gevethen had enhanced in them all too well.

They neither spoke nor moved until the returning party had gone past them then, silently drawing their swords, they crept after them, hands trembling. The four soldiers were walking in a closer group now, two of them half-supporting, half-dragging the look-out while the other two walked behind. Their swords were sheathed but they were obviously anxious to be away now their chase was successfully concluded for they were talking very little and kept glancing up the rain-misted sides of the valley. Hynard and Marris drew steadily closer; at the nerve-wrenching last, matching them stride for step for some twenty or thirty paces for fear that too soon a final charge would announce their presence.

In the end, it was Hynard's victim who sensed danger to the rear rather than from the side. As he turned suddenly, his vision was filled with Hynard's eyes, wide and intense, coming rapidly closer. They were the last thing he saw, for an arm and a sword-length in front of this frightened and frightening gaze was the point which passed through his throat. As his companion spun round,

Marris's descending blade struck him on the side of the head.

The two soldiers supporting the look-out fell before a murderous knife and sword attack from Hynard as they tried to disentangle themselves from their burden and draw their swords. Marris had scarcely freed his own sword from the second soldier's split skull before they died.

Then there was silence.

Hynard, shaking violently and breathing heavily, pushed his sword into the thin turf then bent double and rested his head on the pommel. Slowly he sank to his knees. Winter and the peace it brought was over; spring had come again – and the killing.

Marris too, knelt.

'Commander Marris.' It was the look-out. Marris looked up sharply. His face became angry as he focused on the cause of this blood-letting. It was a young man whose face he knew but whose name he could not remember.

'What in thunder's name were you—'

The look-out was waving him silent desperately and pointing along the valley. 'Commander. The army's moving along the lower valley. Thousands of them. *Thousands*. I've never seen so many. And little patrols scouting everywhere.' He screwed up his face in pain and put a hand to his leg. 'I was coming to warn you when I missed my footing on some loose stones and . . .' he realized he was learning on one of the bloodied corpses and started back, wincing as the movement hurt him '. . . and this lot heard me. I'm sorry.'

Marris was in no mood for apologies. The whole incident had probably been caused by this hysterical youngster panicking at the sight of a routine army patrol. 'How many?' he demanded roughly.

515

'Thousands,' the look-out repeated. He sensed Marris's doubts and, regardless of the bodies, he dragged himself forward and took hold of Marris's arm. 'I counted,' he insisted. 'Like you told us. As well as I could, when the rain shifted. Ranks and files, in so far as they had any, I counted. Over five hundred that *I* saw, and there were as many already gone and more coming, a lot more.' His tone was full of pain and fear but he was coherent enough. Hynard looked up and stared hard at him.

'Who else was on duty with you?' he asked.

'My father and uncle,' came the reply. 'They sent me down to bring the news while they kept on watching. I gave no signal when I was being chased. I didn't want them to be—'

'It's all right,' Marris intervened, beginning to repent his earlier suspicions. He turned to Hynard. 'Are you all right?' he asked. Hynard had pushed the hood of his cape back and rain was running down his face. He looked down at the dead men. The rain had already washed most of the blood off them. He nodded slowly. 'Get up to the ridge-post and find out exactly what's happening,' Marris went on brusquely, to help him. 'I'll take this lad back and rouse the village.'

'What about these?' Hynard indicated the bodies.

'They'll have to stay here. We'll move them later if we can.'

Some hours later, a weary and stone-faced Hynard returned with confirmation of the young look-out's story. By then however, he was but one of several, for shortly after Marris's return to the village, frantic runners had started to come in from other distant look-out posts with the same news.

When Hynard arrived at the Council Hall it was filling

516

rapidly and the atmosphere told him immediately that his news had preceded him in some way. He went straight through to the room where he knew he would find Marris. The door was wide open. He made to close it as he entered.

'Leave it,' Marris said, looking up from the table. 'You saw those faces out there. Close that door and we'll have a panic on our hands.' He took in Hynard's appearance. 'The lad's story was right?' he asked, though his tone indicated that he already knew the answer.

Hynard nodded. 'They're still moving along the lower valley. And he wasn't exaggerating. There are thousands of them.' He dropped heavily into a chair opposite Marris and flicked a thumb towards the open door. 'Did you tell them?' he asked, almost in disbelief.

Marris ignored the implied reproach and prodded the map in front of him. 'Here, here, here and here,' he said. 'The same story. Hundreds, if not thousands of troops marching into the mountains, and scouting parties everywhere.' He put his hands to his head. 'They must have drawn every soldier and Guard in the land to raise a force of this size. It's incredible.' The hands came down and slapped the table. 'How could Iscar have missed something like this? They must have been planning it for months.' Hynard offered no reply and Marris grimaced guiltily. 'That's unfair of me,' he said softly. 'Iscar takes risks enough for us. This has obviously been kept very secret.' He paused. 'Though I can't think how.' He shook his head, then waved the puzzle aside. 'Still, I don't think advanced knowledge of an expedition this size would've been of much use. In fact, just waiting for it to come might have broken our morale. At least we've been spared that.'

'We need Ibryen,' Hynard said.

'We need the Dohrum Bell to fall on the Gevethen,'

Marris snapped angrily. 'Ibryen's not here, nor is he likely to be for perhaps two weeks or more. And without any disrespect, I doubt he'd know what to do any better than we do in the face of this. It's not something we ever seriously envisaged – not on this scale anyway.'

The untypical outburst shook Hynard and gave him a measure of Marris's anxiety. For a moment he felt a surge of anger in response but he restrained it. 'You know what I mean,' he replied. 'Ibryen's worth a hundred swords in morale alone.'

Marris nodded unhappily. 'Then we'll need several hundred Ibryens,' he said flatly. 'But I've already sent runners after him, for what it's worth. Rachyl will have marked their track. Maybe we can get him back within the week.' He glanced at the door and lowered his voice. 'At least that's what we can say, if necessary.'

'And in the meantime?' Hynard asked.

'In the meantime, we use our wits and survive,' Marris announced.

It was from Marris that Ibryen had learned much about dealing with his people but the old man's skill was tested to its limit as he faced the burgeoning panic of those who had gathered in the lantern-lit Council Hall.

'Ibryen's abandoned us ... betrayed us!'

There were not many such cries, but they were potentially disastrous. With difficulty Marris swallowed the anger that the remarks ignited within him and focused it into a quiet, but ruthless rebuttal which was many times more effective than any ranting denunciation. It was thanks to Ibryen they had survived so far at so little cost. It was Ibryen who worked while they rested, who lay awake planning while they slept, who carried the burden of responsibility for the whole community but who accepted no privileges for himself. Ibryen, who was even now searching for a way that would defeat the Gevethen. Larding his reply with personal reminiscences directed at the complaining individuals, the crushing of such comments proved to be comparatively easy. Less easy was the quietening of the concerns of the majority, not least because they were his own also. As he spoke, an almost offhand remark from one of the runners who had brought the news, returned to him. 'They look very tired.'

He leaned across to Hynard who was standing nearby. 'What state was this army in when you saw them?' he asked.

'Hard to say from the ridge-post,' Hynard replied. 'It's very high. But, thinking about it, they weren't moving quickly, and their lines were broken and disordered – more so than the terrain demanded. There was nothing text-book about them.'

'The ones I saw looked exhausted.' It was another of the runners, catching Marris's drift.

Marris laid a grateful hand on his shoulder and turned back to the gathering. 'I'm telling you nothing you don't know when I tell you that we had no forewarning of this attack. Not only is it earlier than usual, it's of unprecedented size. I thought at first that it had been kept very secret, though I couldn't think how. Now I'm coming to the view that something has made the Gevethen panic – has made them scrape together their entire army in just a few days and drive them into the mountains to find us. *Why else would they be exhausted and in bad order?*' He let the point sink in. 'Perhaps, unknown to us, Ibryen has already assailed them in some way. That *was* what he set off to do.'

'That doesn't help us,' came an immediate response. Other voices picked it up.

519

'You'd rather face that army when it was fresh and in good order?' Marris retorted fiercely. He pointed towards the invisible invaders and hardened his previous doubts into certainties. 'We'd have heard if they'd been preparing such a campaign,' he said. 'They couldn't possibly have kept it secret – we've too many friends left for such a thing to go unnoticed.'

'The Count said they might do something to distract the people from Hagen's death.'

Marris gave a conceding nod then rejected the idea. '*This* is no casual spectacle to distract gossip-mongers and those the Gevethen perceive as troublemakers. The Citadel Guards can handle almost anything that's liable to happen in Dirynhald. This *is* panic. Considerable panic.' He paused again, weighing the mood of his audience. Then, conspiratorially, 'What we have to be careful about is that we don't do the same.'

'Right now, panicking seems like a good idea.'

It was an acid observation from someone, but Marris seized it like a dog bringing down a hare. His sudden and unexpected laughter induced the same from much of the crowd and almost instantly the tension that had filled the Hall was gone. As the laughter faded, he spoke with a confidence that defied any disagreement.

'You've all done enough fighting to know that it's the one who stays calm – who keeps his nerve – that wins. We know the terrain: the mountains are ours. If the Gevethen want to pack them with tired and fearful soldiers, then that's to our advantage. When we catch them in the narrow passes and the first ranks turn and run – and they *will* – they'll crash into those following and the panic will run faster than any of them. The Gevethen could have made a mistake that will bring them down.' He did not pause to allow any debate. 'I want all the

Company Commanders here as soon as possible to plan our best response. We seem to be spoilt for choice. The rest of you go back to your normal duties, but be ready to move at a moment's notice. Send out extra runners – we need to know what's happening as soon as it happens.' He ended on a cautionary note. 'Runners, and anyone else who's moving about – be doubly careful. Look-outs and guards – be doubly watchful.'

Even as the people were dispersing, Marris felt a desperate and icy darkness closing about him. With an invasion of this size, they must surely be discovered... and though his people could do great harm to the army, they could not hope to resist a concerted attack by such numbers. Despite himself, he uttered two silent prayers. One simple and prosaic, that the bad weather should continue. The other, from the depths of his soul:

'*Ibryen, come back.*'

Chapter 33

Marris's first prayer was not answered. After a long night of desperate planning, his body had overcome the frantic workings of his mind and he had slumped, fully clothed, on to his bed and fallen asleep immediately. When he woke, only a little while later, it was to a bright spring day. For a brief moment he luxuriated in the warm sunshine washing into his room, then, with a sickening jolt, he remembered where he was and what was happening. Despair and bitter anger flooded through him and his hands rose to cover this face as if to hide him from the outside world for ever. It was but a fleeting gesture, and the momentum of years of service and responsibility carried him through it, distressed but unhurt.

Not that it brought any true solace – merely an element of objectivity. He could see the Gevethen's army drying out and resting under this same sun, recovering its morale. He could see mountain peaks clear and sharp to the farthest horizons. It was not good. He knew well enough that a solitary arrow hissing unseen out of a damp mist held far greater terrors than even a dozen arrows flying from distant but all-too-visible figures halfway up a hillside. And, just as the defenders would be clearly exposed, so too would the full extent of the attacking army, with all that implied for the defenders' morale.

At the touch of this joyous spring sun, most of the carefully considered plans of the previous night withered, and even as he rose from his bed, he saw that only one of the few remaining could be realistically implemented. He stood for a few moments breathing slowly and deeply. It was a wise act, for had he emerged immediately into the village, his reproachful thoughts would have been read from his face as clearly as if he had bellowed them at the top of his voice. Why had Ibryen abandoned him to face this horrific onslaught – their worst nightmare come true? Why had Ibryen not considered it more seriously as a probable occurrence and made plans accordingly? Who was that damned Traveller? Was he, after all, an agent of the Gevethen? These and many other questions tumbled uncontrollably through his mind, battering him brutally and, for a little while threatening to gain dominance.

Though it was difficult, he pursued none of them, nor wasted anything other than the smallest mental effort in arguing the injustice in them. He had lost enough good friends in his life to recognize his own responses when faced with that which could not be faced. Such thoughts must be allowed to escape, or, like swallowed vomit, they would wreak untold harm later. Like vomiting also, their passing left him trembling and a little light-headed and, as they gradually faded, he remained motionless, composing his features and filling the aching emptiness inside him with the resolve that he knew he must ruthlessly impose on the rest of the community today if they were to survive.

As he stepped through the door of his private quarters, he almost tripped over Hynard sitting across the threshold.

'Why didn't you wake me earlier?' he said sternly.

Hynard glared at him. 'You've only been asleep a couple of hours or so,' he replied bluntly. 'And you needed it. I'd have woken you fast enough if it'd been necessary.' He pointed at the bright, clear sky. 'What are we going to do?'

Marris strode forward, motioning Hynard to follow. 'Attack the army from the Greskilva Valley to draw them away, and evacuate the entire village to the south, along whatever route Ibryen's taken.'

Hynard halted. 'What?'

Marris ignored the exclamation and continued walking. 'What's the latest news from the look-outs?' he demanded, over his shoulder.

Hynard caught up with him. 'Mainly bad,' he said. This time it was Marris who stopped.

'*Mainly* bad?' he echoed inquiringly. 'You mean, there's some good?'

'Not much,' Hynard replied unhappily. 'Troops are pouring into the mountains. What we can see of the road is still choked with them. But a lot of them are in a bad way. And there seems to be virtually no organization.'

Marris's brow furrowed in bewilderment and frustration. 'What's happened?' he said, clenching his fists and looking up at the surrounding peaks as if the answer might come echoing back to him. 'It makes no sense. The Gevethen are nothing if not patient and cunning. Yet this has all the earmarks of the *entire* army being scratched together at a moment's notice. I wonder if Ibryen's . . .'

He left the question unasked. The answer to it could perhaps be vital, but as it was not available the question was irrelevant. He set off again, checking the obvious with Hynard.

'Even so, there are enough in good fettle and order to find and destroy us if they're prepared to pay the price?'

'Yes,' Hynard answered coldly. 'And they're prepared to pay the price. They're already paying it. People are collapsing from exhaustion and being left where they fall. There've been countless accidents, and there might even have been actual mutinies in places.'

'But?'

'But not enough to stop the incursion,' Hynard confirmed.

They were at the Council Hall. Several of the Company Leaders with whom he had been talking through most of the night had remained there, snatching such sleep as they could, sprawled across benches and tables. They converged on Marris as soon as he entered, but he allowed no debate, simply announcing his decision.

'The Greskilva Valley is well to the east of us. Making a stand there will start to pull the army away from where they are now, which is far too close. It's also very narrow and steep-sided and can be defended by a small group who'll be able to escape along it during the dark, when need arises.'

No one could argue with Marris's brief tactical summary, but the order to evacuate the village provoked more contention. He dealt with it as if he were explaining nothing more serious than the sowing of the year's crops.

'All the naturally defensible valleys like the Greskilva are, by virtue of that fact, uninhabitable. And all the habitable valleys, like this, can't be made impregnable. This you know. We've always relied predominantly on secrecy for our safety. If that army finds out where we are – and they may well – we're utterly lost. We can't hope to stand against such numbers, however disorganized they are. They'll wear us down by attrition if nothing else.' He looked round at his listeners: men and women he had known and trusted for many years, and several of whom he had turned from being ordinary, quiet citizens, into skilled fighters. Now the value of his training, and Ibryen's leadership would be tested to the full. 'You all know this too. Time we spend debating it will be wasted.'

Again his reasoning could not be faulted and, reluctantly, the discussion turned to the practicalities of the task. 'Anything that's not essential will have to be left and everyone will have to carry something,' Marris declared. 'Most of our supplies are already well hidden. With a little good luck they'll be too busy destroying our buildings and might not find them.' He could not forbear frowning at the thought but he did not pursue it.

'It's not going to be easy. With scouting patrols all over the ridges, we'll almost certainly be seen,' someone said.

Marris shook his head and frowned determinedly. 'No. This is to be an orderly withdrawal. Normal movement discipline will apply more than ever. And if attention's being drawn to Greskilva, there's no reason why we shouldn't move out unnoticed.' He answered the next question before it was asked. 'And even if we are seen, we still have the advantage. We'll be a comparatively small group, well-fed, well-equipped, disciplined, and bound by a common cause. We can move far faster than they can.'

'We won't know where we're going.'

'Nor will they,' Marris said forcefully. 'But *we've* enough portable supplies to sustain us for quite a long time, and we'll be heading towards Ibryen, while they'll be moving even further from their precious leaders and stretching their supply lines and communications to the limit within two or three days.'

Despite himself, his bewilderment at the Gevethen's actions found voice. 'If they *have* any supply lines,' he burst out, 'which I'm beginning to doubt. From a military point of view, what they're doing is insane.' He waved his hand apologetically to dismiss the topic. The last thing he needed now was to unleash general speculation about why

527

this attack was being made. 'We retreat as far as we have to until the first rush of their attack is spent. They can't sustain what they're doing for long, and when they withdraw we'll re-establish ourselves.' He sought to deal with another unasked question. 'We've done it before and we can do it again, this time using all the experience we've gained over the years.'

He was only partially successful. He and Ibryen had trained their people to think for themselves too well.

'We'll *never* defeat them from further in the mountains.'

The statement was unequivocal, although Marris noted with some relief that it was free from bitterness. He found it heartening too, that the speaker was still thinking in terms of defeating the Gevethen despite what was happening. He acknowledged her.

'Nor they us,' he replied, his face resolute and menacing. The power of his intent shook through the very depths of his long anger against the Gevethen. 'And consequences that we can't begin to foresee will follow from what the Gevethen are doing. A largely conscripted army, returning exhausted and demoralized, and *unsuccessful*! Returning to towns, cities, borders that have all been left unguarded. Dust blowing in the wind. Consequences.' He nodded to himself, then, clearing his throat brusquely, he allocated duties and sent the Company Leaders on their way.

A feint in the Greskilva Valley was a sound strategy, he thought, as he watched them leave; Ibryen would have approved of it. With a little good fortune they could emerge from this not only unscathed, but with the Gevethen perhaps fatally undermined.

In a strange reflection of the actions of the Gevethen themselves, Marris and the others began mobilizing their entire community. It was a dismal task and though there was little questioning of his decision, Marris was acutely aware of the gazes that followed him wherever he went: frightened, wide-eyed children, anxious mothers and mothers-to-be; fretful boys and girls, too young to fight, too old to be easily reassured; old people made angry by their failing faculties. Yet perhaps worst of all were some of the everyday sights he glimpsed in passing: a cottage door being gently locked, a child stooping to pick up a dropped toy then nursing it. The very ordinariness of such events carried them past the armour of activity he was sheltering behind and bit deep into him.

Once or twice the cry arose, 'We can't defeat the entire army! We should surrender, ask for mercy!'

Marris was strongly inclined to crush such appeals cruelly, but instead he yielded to them. 'The Gevethen drive others before them, Count Ibryen leads those who wish to follow. Anyone who wants to go down to the army is free to do so. All I ask is that you wait until the rest of us are gone.' The call did not take root.

Satisfied that preparations were well under way, Marris strode up the short grassy slope to join Hynard. 'Are you all ready?' he asked, indicating the men waiting nearby.

'As ready as we'll ever be,' Hynard replied.

Marris nodded. The task of the men mounting the diversion in the Greskilva Valley was going to be difficult. Combat in the mountains normally consisted of swift and terrifying attacks followed by equally swift withdrawals, bow and sword being the principal weapons. Now however, once the enemy had been engaged, Hynard's fighters would have to hold their ground for several hours in the narrow valley as though making a final, desperate stand. Unusually therefore, they were carrying large shields and long, makeshift pikes in addition to their other weapons.

There had been no shortage of volunteers for this expedition, but the men Hynard had chosen had all served in the army or the Citadel Guards under Ibryen. Nevertheless, 'You don't need me to tell you that this isn't going to be easy,' Marris said to them. 'We're all lucky enough never to have fought in a major battle so the only experience of this kind of fighting any of us have had has been on the training field.' He pointed in the direction of the Greskilva Valley. 'However, *they* don't even have that. You're going to have to get there at the double so you'll be tired when you arrive, but they'll be tired, frightened, driven, and facing a well-defended position. Keep your shield and pike wall tight and high. Protect your heads. Archers, wound as many as you can, and anything they throw at you, throw back harder. Engage the enemy as soon as you arrive. We'll go as far up the slopes as we can as soon as we're ready, but I don't want to start moving along the ridges until it's dark. You hold as long as you can, but take no unnecessary risks. We should be able—'

Suddenly, Hynard seized his arm and pointed. Someone was running towards them at great speed. Though he could not make out who it was, Marris could feel the runner's desperate urgency. His stomach turned.

When the runner arrived he was gasping for breath and could scarcely speak, but his fearful eyes and pointing hand were eloquent enough to confirm Marris's worst fears. Supporting the exhausted man, he glanced towards the village and the people gathering there in the bright spring sunlight. At another time they might have been waiting for the start of a festival.

'Very slowly,' he said to the runner, with a gentleness so controlled that it almost frightened him. 'Very slowly. Give me your message.'

530

The runner gulped violently and spoke between explosions of breath. 'They found the bodies. They're coming up from the lower valley. All of them.'

Marris closed his eyes and bowed his head. When he opened them, it was to see Hynard's face, pale and full of the agony of self-reproach. He knew that his own was the same.

'They'd have come looking for them anyway,' he said weakly, knowing that the statement was as unhelpful as it was accurate.

Hynard's men had gathered around them. Marris straightened up. 'Change of plan, gentlemen,' he said quietly. 'It seems the enemy are on their way. If they reach the Valley proper we'll never stop them. Same plan. Do what you can. I'll send reinforcements after you immediately and start moving out those who can't fight.'

Helsarn's horse stumbled again, almost unseating him. He swore and swung down from the animal. It would carry him no further up the slope to the Valley where the bodies had been found. He looked back. His men were a considerable way behind. Vintre also dismounted, and joined him. It was Helsarn who had sent Vintre out with a patrol to find the four missing men. Not from any great concern but because they were under his direct command and he feared they might have deserted, a matter which would have reflected on him personally. When Vintre returned with the news that they had been killed, Helsarn displayed the grim resolve for vengeance that was expected of him but inwardly he was elated – this was the first clear sign of the enemy's presence.

Unable to contact any of the other Commanders because of the general confusion, he had taken the risk of asking the Gevethen themselves for permission to send

531

a company to reconnoitre the valley. His request had been received with a cold silence, the Gevethen and their many images moving their heads from side to side as if scenting the air for Ibryen's presence. Then, colder than ever:

'Do as you must, Commander. Find Ibryen at all costs . . .'

'. . . at all costs.'

The mirror-bearers had folded about them and Helsarn suddenly found himself faced with a row of travel-stained Commanders. The memory of the gloomy tent, so like the Watching Chamber, lingered with him even in the sunlight as he clambered over the rocks.

'Do you think this is wise?' Vintre broke into his thoughts. He was glancing around nervously.

'Ibryen's many things, but stupid isn't one,' Helsarn replied. 'He's not going to ambush a force this size.'

'He might ambush *us*.'

Helsarn paused and wiped his hand across his brow. He shook his head. 'Ibryen's people never leave bodies where they've been killed. They panicked. And our men must have stumbled on to something important to get themselves killed so close to the main force.' He secured his horse to a spur of rock and started off again. 'There'll be no one here now – they'll have run like rabbits. And they'll have left tracks. There had to be at least eight of them to kill those four like that.'

Vintre gave a grudging grunt but loosened his sword in its sheath. In common with almost everyone else there, he did not like the mountains, such was the reputation of Ibryen's followers, but Helsarn's judgement was usually sound and there was no denying that if this trail took them to Ibryen's camp then the rewards would be considerable. They were certainly worth taking risks for. Also, this sortie was taking them away from the chaos of the main force and keeping most of their own men about them, which was no bad thing. The mood of the army was wildly uncertain. Old scores were already being settled in the confusion and once Ibryen was located and engaged, the opportunities would increase manyfold. At least Helsarn had always ensured that his companies were securely bound by ties of self-interest.

They moved on in silence until they came to the top of the slope and the valley began to open in front of them. They soon moved out of sight of their men as the slope levelled out.

'Where did you find the bodies?' Helsarn asked. Vintre pointed. Then the two of them swore simultaneously. Still some distance away but moving towards them, and moving quickly, was a large body of armed men.

First success in the battle fell to Hynard, his men reaching the top of the slope before Helsarn's. He did not have enough men to form a shield wall as solid as that intended for the Greskilva Valley, but it was adequate and it gave them a command of the high ground.

Helsarn had descended to his men with commendable restraint, knowing that, loyal or not, the sight of Vintre and himself charging over the skyline could well send his men tumbling back to camp in panic. As it was, they formed up in as good an order as the rocky terrain would allow, and moved up the slope cautiously to establish a line opposite Hynard's. Messengers were sent back to the base camp with express orders to take the news only to the Gevethen in person, while Vintre was sent to commandeer whichever unit was nearest for the purposes of making an initial attack. Helsarn had no intention of risking his own forces unless it proved absolutely necessary.

Hynard was glad of the delay. It enabled his men to recover from the pounding run they had made from the village. He watched Helsarn's Guards forming their line almost with amusement. The need for hunting in the mountains had, over the years, given Ibryen's forces more powerful bows than those carried by the army and the Guards, and Helsarn's line was well within arrow-shot. Hynard refrained from demonstrating the point however. It would be more effective if the Gevethen's men learned about it the hard way.

But despite his initial advantage, Hynard was far from complacent. He had a limited number of arrows and his men would be able to fight only so long before fatigue took its toll. And the same would apply to whatever reinforcements Marris sent. Worse, he knew that it would take only a moderate military thinker to realize that they could be out-flanked, even encircled, by a movement from neighbouring valleys.

He could certainly last this day out and, quite possibly, tomorrow. But after that, or if an attack was sustained through the night . . .?

From Helsarn's point of view, Vintre was most fortunate in the first army unit he came to and the two men exchanged knowing glances as he gave the order to open the line and allow the soldiers through. Their blustering captain, who was 'Going to show these Guards how these things are done,' was struck down by a heavy-bladed pike that suddenly appeared between two shields as he charged the defenders' wall. Several of his men went the same way, while others, breathless from the uphill dash, fell to swords and axes before the rest retreated. Hynard's line was undisturbed. In the lull that followed he sent out some of his men to retrieve the dead men's weapons.

The next dash fared little better and, in the end, the soldiers retreated, leaderless and sullen, behind Helsarn's line.

Gradually the slope up from the lower valley began to fill with a mixture of Guards and soldiers drawn there from the main force by a bizarre combination of confusion and curiosity. Helsarn searched for some time to see if there was any semblance of order in what was happening before he finally took command himself.

'Ibryen is to be found at all costs,' the Gevethen had said and he would get precious little thanks if he just waited aimlessly for a more senior Commander to arrive.

Thus, in the fading light, Hynard found his line increasingly pressed as Helsarn sent wave after wave of men against it. Screams and shouts and the clash of arms echoed down the rocky slope, and bodies began to pile up in front of the shield wall. It did not concern Helsarn that the attackers were little more than disordered mobs and that casualties were appalling, it mattered only that he was in command and that the defence was slowly weakening.

'For the Gevethen! For the Gevethen!' he shouted as he urged men forward up the slope. 'Bring the traitor Ibryen to justice!'

Hynard soon began to understand Helsarn's tactics. Reinforcements had arrived as Marris had promised, but even with them he knew that his men could not stand long against such reckless assaults. And once the wall was breached, all would be lost.

Then it was dark.

Hynard had little doubt that the attacks would continue through the night and he knew for certain that even if his force managed to survive that long, they would be destroyed the following day. They had no choice but to

535

withdraw if they were to be able to act as a rearguard to the fleeing villagers. Hynard stared down the slope, alive with torches and lanterns. Above the general clamour of the people gathered there, he could hear Helsarn's voice shouting orders. Another attack would be coming soon. He reached a decision.

Helsarn learned of it shortly afterwards when a wind-rushing sound presaged a hail of arrows. One snagged in his cloak and, in terror, he dropped the lantern he was carrying. It shattered and burst into flames. It was not the only one and, for a moment, by countless dancing lights, he seemed to see the whole slope alive with bright arrows, falling like streaking snow; with screaming men; with wild eyes and terrified faces; with flailing arms and manic shadows; as all around him the flight down the treacherous slope began. He heard himself cursing and swearing at the fleeing men then something struck him and sent him sprawling. As he struggled to his feet, another sound reached him out of the darkness ahead.

'For Ibryen! Death to the Gevethen! CHARGE!'

A clamorous din filled with roaring and angry cries rolled after it. And above it all came the sound of yet more arrows! As he turned to flee after his routed command, Helsarn lost his footing and tumbled into the darkness.

Hynard's men stopped shouting and beating their shields. They had not moved from their original line. Hynard stood for a moment, listening to the sounds of flight and self-destruction rising up the slope, then he whispered a command. His men turned and moved silently off into the night.

Helsarn had no measure of the time he lay on the ground,

but his mind was working before his body despite the distress it was in. There was noise about him but he could not identify it nor, from where he was lying, see what was causing it. Had Ibryen's people been more numerous than he had thought? Had they actually charged down the slope, sweeping the Guards and soldiers back down on to the main force? Fearful questions.

Yet there was no indication that he was in the midst of a triumphant army.

As quietly as he could, he moved his arms and legs, testing them for injury. His head was aching, but after a little while he decided that he was whole except for some bruising. When he cautiously pushed himself into a sitting position to look around, the discomfort in his ribs told him that he had only been winded when he fell. It could have been worse, he supposed. His relief was short-lived, for as his vision began to clear, the vague shifting shapes about him became bodies: the bodies of the men he had commanded, strewn over the rocky slope in postures of death and awful injury. The flickering lights of dropped torches and spilled lanterns gave an awful, twitching vitality even to those who were motionless. And the sounds he had been hearing became the groans and cries of injured men.

From deep within, a primitive fear rose up to fill him. Had he been slain in that panic-filled gorge and sent to some ominous netherworld for Judgement? He started trembling uncontrollably. With an effort he levered himself into a kneeling position. In the distance he could make out a pool of garish light. It seemed to be pulsating, resonating to his pounding heart. He shook his head to clear his vision completely.

As his eyes came properly into focus, his trembling began to ease. The light was the main army far below. For a moment he was tempted to run towards it and safety, but even as the impulse came to him, other considerations made themselves felt. He picked up a still-burning torch and looked around. Not only was there no sign of any triumphant army about him, such bodies as he could see were all either soldiers or Guards. He felt suddenly cold. Ibryen's men had never charged! They had unleashed their arrow storm, thrown up a great shout and ... Helsarn's grip tightened about the torch in rage ... fled into the darkness. Most of the damage he was standing in had been self-inflicted.

Almost immediately, a newer fear rose to displace the fading remains of the superstitious one that had just possessed him. It was no less awful. Whatever had happened here, it was a direct consequence of the disordered way the whole expedition had been mounted, but *he* would be blamed for it unless he could find a demonstrably plausible explanation.

A movement nearby startled him. Drawing his sword, he spun around. Holding both sword and torch in front of him he saw one of his Guards, arm raised to shade his eyes against the light. He was bloodstained and barely able to stand. The idea of deserting to avoid retribution had been forming in Helsarn's mind, but the sight of the Guard brought another one.

'Where's your sword?' he demanded.

The Guard looked at him vacantly.

'Where's your sword, man?' Helsarn shouted.

'I ... I think I dropped it,' the man stammered.

Helsarn sheathed his own and, taking the man's arm, shook him powerfully. 'Find another, quickly. Get a torch and get everyone on their feet who can stand. Do you understand? We must re-form the line and get to the top of the slope.'

Then, in an act of genuine leadership, Helsarn was moving through the carnage, dragging to their feet all who were capable of standing, and filling the shocked and wounded with his determination. Vintre, also only bruised and winded, was retrieved from under the body of a large soldier behind whom he had sheltered when he heard the second arrow storm being released.

'We withstood the enemy's charge, counter-attacked and beat them back,' Helsarn told him urgently. 'We stopped at the top to regroup and to prevent the advancing army from being ambushed.' The message was passed rapidly to the others – few were naive enough to question it. Most understood the Gevethen well enough to know that the choice facing them was that of being wounded heroes or executed cowards. The knowledge proved a better goad by far than any cursing, and Helsarn and Vintre soon found themselves herding their rump command up the slope like willing sheep.

On the way, Helsarn paused by a body to smear his sword and face with blood. As he did so he looked back down at the lights of the main army. Something was moving there but, not being able to make it out clearly, he turned and pressed on upwards.

The top was deserted as he had surmised. He had his 'gallant survivors' spread out a picket of torches then withdrew some way behind it. There could still be solitary archers out in the darkness and there was no point in taking unnecessary risks.

'Swords drawn, eyes front,' he ordered.

He and Vintre exchanged glances. The line of exhausted and wounded men looked good. That, and their story, might do much more than save their necks.

Helsarn looked back but the lights of the army were no longer visible due to the curve of the slope. He wondered how far the panic had spread, and what appalling damage had been done by the mass flight down the rocks. What a mess. What had possessed the Gevethen to mount this insane expedition?

He glanced back again.

The primitive fear that had seized him when he first recovered, returned in full terrifying force. Shapeless, shifting, and blacker than the night itself, a huge shadow was moving towards him.

Chapter 34

Helsarn's shaking grip tightened about his sword as the
apparition drew nearer, but his knees served him better
– they began to buckle. Thus when the Gevethen and their
myriad images appeared at the heart of the approaching
shadow, he was already almost kneeling. He was also
almost pathetically relieved to find himself facing a known
fear rather than an unknown one. Even so, the sight before
him was profoundly disorienting and it took him some
time to realize what he was looking at. What he had
perceived as a shadow was a huge canopy supported on
long, black poles. These were being carried by servants
who moved with the same silent and blank-eyed purpose
as the mirror-bearers, though it was hard to distinguish
them in the darkness. Other servants carried the edge of
the canopy, like a grotesque bridal gown, where it drooped
to the ground. In its shade within shade were the
Gevethen and the mirror-bearers and yet more servants,
these latter carrying lanterns, albeit they seemed to
deepen the darkness rather than throw light. Also there
was Jeyan, her face unreadable and her uniform mud- and
blood-spattered from the journey. Helsarn had a fleeting
vision of countless bodies covering the lower part of the
slope. The Gevethen and their entourage must have
simply walked over them.

The canopy passed over Helsarn and Vintre like an ominous cloud and the atmosphere about them became like that of the Watching Chamber. Helsarn quickly gathered his wits.

'Excellencies,' he said urgently. 'I must ask you to take care. There may well be archers nearby.'

'We are protected,' came the reply, voices colder than ever. 'None may approach.' A long line of Gevethen tapered into the distance, then became a circling crowd.

Helsarn prepared to account for what had happened, but the question that came was not what he had been expecting. 'Is the traitor Ibryen found yet?'

'No, Excellencies,' Helsarn stammered. Then, such dependence had he placed in the tale he was to tell that part of it blurted out anyway. 'His men fled when we held their charge and counter-attacked, and we were too depleted to follow them.'

'Advance!'

Helsarn and Vintre had almost to leap out of the way as the Gevethen suddenly moved forward. Helsarn had just enough time to shout a command to his makeshift line to open before the Gevethen walked over them also.

In the absence of any orders he took up a position at the front of the canopy and to one side. As he did so, he saw for the first time the long ragged crowd of Guards and soldiers struggling up the slope.

Hynard paused and, screwing up his eyes, peered into the distance. It took him some time to make sense of what he was looking at, and when he did, he could scarcely believe it. He could not see the Gevethen themselves, shaded as they were by their dark canopy, but the torches of the following army were spreading out across the valley floor like a glowing river.

It was a severe shock. After the panic-stricken rout he had witnessed, he had not expected any pursuit for several hours, and then perhaps only by a small force.

What he was watching did not seem possible.

For a moment, he considered leaving a few men to mount a harassing action, but he knew it would be a pointless gesture against such a force. However this recovery had come about, all he could do was make the most of such time as he and his men had gained, and follow after Marris and the others. It wasn't possible that this vast army could move across the ridges with such speed.

He was thus still quite optimistic as he pressed on back to the village.

The first blow to this optimism came with an unexpected challenge at the outer perimeter. 'What are you doing here?' he demanded of the woman occupying the post.

'*Everyone's* still here,' she replied. 'They didn't think you'd be able to stop the army. And with Ibryen gone they decided to stay and fight to the end rather than scatter into the mountains with all of you dead.'

Hynard felt the cold mountain air filling him to choking point and, for a moment, he could not speak.

'Did Marris have nothing to say about this?' he asked through clenched teeth when he had recovered.

'He was quite angry,' came the reply.

Hynard took another deep breath and out of the desperate confusion suddenly thundering through his head, snatched one simple, dangerous order. 'Strike your lanterns, but keep them low, and double as fast as you can.'

As he ran through the night, Hynard's mind sped over countless alternatives, chief amongst which was the hope that by the time they reached the village, Marris would have managed to talk some sense into the others and get them under way.

It was not so. They were greeted by a Marris who was verging on the distraught. Like most practical men, he did not bear helplessness well. 'I could do nothing,' he said, at once furious and almost tearful. 'I don't know what's wrong with them. They just set their minds to staying. Perhaps too much has happened too quickly.' Even as he was talking though, he was shaking off the mood, and Hynard was given no opportunity either to reproach or to console.

'Still, we can go now,' Marris announced.

It was too late however. The time that Hynard had won was lost as the villagers began the slow trek towards the ridges and their vanguard was barely up the lower slopes when the army swept into the valley, the Gevethen's black canopy billowing ahead of them like a great bat.

As the army circled about them, all those villagers who were armed formed an inner circle around the old and the young. Arrows nocked, swords, axes, pikes ready, they waited. As did the army.

'Why aren't they attacking?' Hynard hissed to Marris.

An opening appeared in the ranks of the army and the Gevethen's eerie chamber floated into it. As the Gevethen themselves came into view, several of the villagers raised their bows.

The soldiers facing them did the same.

'No!' Marris shouted to the villagers.

'Where is the traitor Ibryen?' Colder and more inhuman than even he remembered them, the Gevethen's voices made Marris's flesh crawl. No preamble, no bargaining, he noted. Everything now would be balanced on the finest of edges. And all he had was the truth.

'He's not here,' he replied. 'He's been gone for several days. He—'

There was a sharp command, then the sound of a single

arrow. An agonized cry followed by others, full of pain and rage, came from the crowd of villagers. Marris's voice tragically over-topped them all as again he restrained his archers.

Jeyan, standing by the Gevethen, flinched despite her control. It seemed that the Gevethen were becoming increasingly unstable as they neared their goal. The journey up from the base camp had been a nightmare: trampling over dead and dying bodies, the mirror-bearers still somehow performing their bizarre duties surefootedly over both flesh and rocks, and the black canopy flapping like a funeral flag. Now this. She pressed her hand against the knife secreted under her tunic, but still she could feel the unseen force that restrained her when she came too near the Gevethen.

The question came again. 'Where is the traitor Ibryen?'

Marris made no effort to keep the desperation from his voice.

'I tell you, he's not here. He'd be standing where I am if he were. You know that.'

There was another sharp command, then:

'HOLD!'

Ibryen's voice rolled like a thunderclap out of the darkness.

High on the ridge, Ibryen, pale and shaking, stood overlooking the lake of lights surrounding his followers. By him stood the Traveller, Rachyl and Isgyrn. Talking, laughing, arguing in the spring sunshine, they had been pursuing a leisurely pace back to the village, when Marris's runner had reached them. The remainder of the journey had been through the darkness. First the darkness that the news had spread over them, then the darkness of the night.

In the far distance, the sky was now beginning to grey.

'Carry my voice to them again,' Ibryen said to the Traveller.

The Traveller nodded, though he seemed weary.

'Release my people and let them go on their way, and I shall come to you.'

The Gevethen's heads moved from side to side as they peered into the darkness.

'You hear us, Ibryen?' they asked.

'I hear you.'

'Come to us now or we shall kill your people one at a time.'

'You can't go,' Rachyl said, seizing Ibryen's arm. 'They'll kill you and everyone else.'

A faint cry floated up from the Valley. The Traveller clamped his hands to his ears. 'They've shot someone else,' he said, his voice full of horror and rage. Ibryen felt him tensing.

'Do nothing,' he said sternly. 'Carry my voice down again.'

'But . . .'

'Do it!'

Once again, his voice echoed across the valley. 'Hurt no one else, I am coming. Be patient, it will take me some time.'

'I'm coming with you.' All three of his companions spoke at once. He turned to them. 'Rachyl, I'd rather you didn't, there's a fine life for you somewhere else in this world, but I know you'll follow me regardless. Just take care, Cousin. Sooner or later we'll come within arm's reach of our enemy.' Then, to the others, almost formally: 'Traveller, Dryenwr, it's my wish that you bear witness to what happens here and that you go your own ways, taking the tale with you so that others can be forewarned.'

'I can't abandon you,' Isgyrn said fiercely.

'Isgyrn, don't burden me further, this is no willing choice. You swore fealty to me, and this is my order: *Bear witness, and carry the news.* I thank you for your company and for the knowledge you've given me and I hope that my call to the Culmaren will bring your land to you one day.' He laid a hand on the Traveller's shoulder. 'Traveller, my thanks to you also, for more than I can find words to express. Read your Great Gate carefully when you come to it. Add our tale to it if you can.' Then he embraced them both. 'Look to one another. Live well and light be with you.'

He turned to Rachyl. She flicked her head to one side. 'After you.'

Ibryen turned up the lantern he was carrying and held it high. As he moved off down the steep slope, Rachyl took Isgyrn's hand in both hers and shook it. Then she bent down and embraced the Traveller. Isgyrn looked away. By the light of Ibryen's retreating lantern he could see tears in both their eyes. As she moved off, Rachyl let her arm swing behind her, holding the Traveller's hand until the last. Neither the Traveller nor Isgyrn spoke for some time, keeping their eyes on the slowly moving lantern.

'This is beyond tolerating, to stand idly by,' Isgyrn said eventually. 'What would I not give for a cohort of my Soarers.'

'What would I not give for the skill of a true Sound Carver,' the Traveller replied.

Rachyl and Ibryen too, spoke little. 'Remember, compliance with everything until we come within arm's reach,' Ibryen said. Rachyl nodded. It cut through all their many and complex concerns – focused the warrior in them on the only course that circumstances had left them. Perhaps

547

this, after all, Ibryen thought, was the way that the Gevethen could not have imagined. Simple and direct. A knife through the heart. Yet something was disturbing him. He reached out and sensed the Ways to the other worlds that were about him. The disturbance was there but it eluded him. Something was closing them to him. Something awful. He forced his attention back to the dark hillside and Rachyl.

It took the two of them a long time to descend from the ridge and make their way to the surrounded villagers. Helsarn and Vintre intercepted them. Ibryen recognized them. He looked at their soiled uniforms. 'Commander and Captain under your new masters, I see,' he said. 'It seems I was right to be rid of you from my service.'

'You only demoted me, if you remember, Count,' Helsarn said with a sneer. 'But their Excellencies know my true worth. Give me your sword.'

'We are protected. Bring him here!' The frantic impatience in the Gevethen's voices made Helsarn start, and taking Ibryen's arm he dragged him forward.

'You can keep your sword too, for all the good it'll do you, woman,' Vintre said to Rachyl. 'Just wait over there, you'll probably be needed afterwards.' He leered at her. 'When the sport starts. I'll look after you personally.'

Rachyl's face was impassive.

As Ibryen approached the Gevethen, the mirror-bearers began to weave about him but he ignored the bewildering images that they made. Instead, he stared at the two large mirrors which were being brought together. As they drew closer, so the disturbance he had felt on the way down returned to him, but worse by far. It was as if the fabric of the worlds about him were being torn apart.

And these were the cause!

There were many things he had intended to say should

548

he ever confront the Gevethen, but all he could do now was cry out as the mirrors finally came together.

'Abomination! What foulness conceived of this . . . device?'

The mirror-bearers fluttered to and fro and the Gevethen became an angry, gesticulating crowd. 'Take care, Ibryen, for you are going to open the Ways for us. His Ways. You are going to carry us to Him who made this miracle. You will not want such blasphemies on your lips when you look upon Him . . .'

'. . . look upon Him.'

'I will do nothing for you.'

There was almost humour in the reply. Now that Ibryen was here and trapped, the impatience had become mere excitement. 'You will, as you know, for we will kill your people, this raggle-taggle crowd that has so sorely taxed us these past five years. As you seem to value them, we will kill them – one at a time – quickly or slowly. You do not doubt us, do you?'

Ibryen moved towards them, but the force that held Jeyan away, held him also. He stiffened. 'No,' he said flatly, turning away from the Gevethen, not wishing them to see the pain in his face. 'I don't doubt you.'

He found himself looking at Jeyan. Her face slowly brought back her name to him.

'Jeyan?' he said softly, leaning towards her. 'Jeyan Dyalith? What are you doing here? I heard about your parents. I . . . I thought you'd been killed with them. I . . .' He hesitated. 'What are you doing in that uniform?'

The sight of the Count carried Jeyan back to years wilfully forgotten. To stand so close to the creators of all the horror that had swept those years aside and be unable to act was almost unbearable, but still she was a hunter, still, like Assh and Frey, she could wait. The moment must

549

surely come. In the meantime she must continue her part.

'I fled to the Ennerhald, then I killed the Lord Counsellor Hagen. Now I act in his place. I impose the will of their Excellencies upon the people.'

Ibryen stared at her, aghast, but the disturbance caused by the mirrors intruded on him again and he turned back to the Gevethen, his head inclined and his eyes narrowing as if he were facing an icy wind.

'Andreyak, Miklan. As you served my father, and he honoured you, turn away from this. Forces are moving against you, of which you know nothing.' He pointed to the mirrors. 'And this thing is an obscenity. Warping and twisting that which should be untouched. It should not be.'

At the sounding of their names, the Gevethen had frozen, watery eyes suddenly alive with horror. Then one of them stepped forward – an individual movement, unreflected by his brother. The mirror-bearers faltered and became still, and briefly there were but the two men facing Ibryen. 'Enough!' screamed the solitary figure. His brother stepped beside him and the mirror-bearers began to move again.

'Enough! You have the gift. This we know. You will open the Ways for us. You will carry us back to Him. You will take us now!'

Ibryen snatched at the discussions he had had over the past days. 'He is dead. Dead some fifteen years or more. As are His lieutenants. Turn away from this while you can.'

The Traveller covered his ears at the shriek of denial that followed Ibryen's outburst. He had been carrying Ibryen's and the Gevethen's word to Isgyrn, but that was beyond him.

'I heard that without your aid,' the Dryenwr said, his face pained.

He looked up into the slowly brightening eastern sky as if for relief from the darkness below and the horror he was hearing. Suddenly he gasped. The Traveller looked at him sharply, then followed his gaze. Glowing golden in the unseen sun, was a solitary cloud.

'No,' Isgyrn whispered to himself, his voice agonized.

'What's the matter?' the Traveller demanded urgently.

Isgyrn pointed to the cloud. The Traveller looked again. Then, as the cloud moved, he saw towers and spires glinting as they caught the sunlight. He let out a long, awe-stricken breath and closed his eyes. 'I hear it,' he said. 'It's one of the Culmadryen. Such sounds I'd never thought to hear again.' Abruptly, he was excited and his eyes were wide. 'Your Soarers, Isgyrn, your Soarers. They're here. They can rout this rabble of an army. Save the Count, and Rachyl and—' He stopped. The Dryenwr's face was awful. He was shaking his head.

'Many hours,' he said, scarcely able to speak. 'Even defying the will of Svara as they are, it will be many hours before they are here. It will be too late. My land will come too late. At best we will have only vengeance.'

He held up both clenched fists and let out a great cry of anguish. 'This cannot be. I am to be returned to all that I love when the man who made it possible is to fall to that carrion. I cannot allow it.' He stepped forward to the edge and swung the Culmaren about his shoulders like a cloak. The sun topped the farthest peaks and the Culmaren shone white and brilliant at its touch. 'Carry my words to them as you carried Ibryen's,' he ordered.

The Traveller closed his eyes, as though in pain, then nodded slowly.

'Know, Gevethen, that I am Arnar Isgyrn, Dryenwr, leader of the Soarers Tahren of Endra Hornath. Know too that my land approaches. Ibryen, Count of Nesdiryn is under my protection. Release him and his people or the consequences will be terrible beyond your imagining.'

The waiting army began to shift uncomfortably as Isgyrn's angry voice filled the Valley. The Gevethen inclined their heads, as if to listen but did not look to see from where the voice came. 'It seems you have more skills than we know of, Ibryen, but they will avail you nothing.'

Helsarn was less phlegmatic. First Ibryen's voice booming across the Valley, now this. And the army was beginning to look very uneasy. They had been pushed far too hard. He scanned the far side of the Valley.

'There is someone on the western ridge, Excellencies,' he said. 'Dressed in white.'

'A mountebank accomplice of the Count's come to play tricks on us. Nothing shall distract us now. Deal with him when we return.' They moved towards Ibryen. He made to draw his sword, but something restrained his hand. Then they were either side of him and leading him towards the two mirrors which had now become one. The mirror-bearers began to move about frantically.

Ibryen watched as his own image and that of the Gevethen moved towards him. The mirrors were more and more like a terrible rent in the reality about him. A hideous maw. They filled his entire being with emotions he had no words for. He struggled desperately but to no effect.

'Do not resist, Ibryen. Your destiny is with us, else why should He have brought us to *your* land? Why else would He have brought us together in the Ways? When you come to Him, bend your knee, prostrate yourself, show

552

humility. He is most generous to those who serve Him well.'

Ibryen wrenched his head away as, slowly, he and the Gevethen began to merge into their own reflections.

Eyes shielded, Isgyrn peered down into the Valley. The darkness there was deeper than ever now that the sun had risen. Far in the distance, the Culmadryen seemed to be no nearer.

Then, in a fury, Isgyrn drew his sword. It glinted bright in the sun.

The Traveller, slumped wearily at his feet, looked up at him. 'You can't do anything,' he said weakly. 'You mustn't go down there. We must do what Ibryen asked of us, however hard.'

'Carry my voice to them again,' Isgyrn said.

'My skill isn't sufficient, Dryenwr. I'm spent. Within the hour, perhaps, but . . .'

Isgyrn glanced down at him. The Traveller looked suddenly very old. Isgyrn reached down and squeezed his shoulder. 'Forgive me,' he said. 'You've done all you can, I see that. But I'll not have such a man walk alone into the darkness. I will send him what small aid I can.'

He held out his sword at arm's length, the hilt in one hand, the point in the other.

Helsarn, intent on the distant newcomer, put up his hand to protect his eyes from the sudden brilliant flash. As he turned away from it a movement caught his attention. It was one of the mirror-bearers. He was staggering as though he had been struck. Then he saw that the light from Isgyrn's sword was reflecting from mirror to mirror and flickering all about the inside of the gloomy canopy like captive lightning. The mirror-bearers seemed at once

553

terrified by it and unable to prevent its jagged progress. They became increasingly agitated.

Then the light struck the large mirror, just as Ibryen and the Gevethen disappeared into it. A terrible scream went up and one of the six bearers supporting the large mirrors tumbled backwards on to the ground. He twitched briefly then lay still. The two halves began to swing together like a great book. It was as though they had a life of their own, like a monstrous eye come suddenly into the daylight after aeons in the darkness. They were being held open only by the desperate efforts of their bearers. The light struck the mirror again and a second bearer fell.

Helsarn watched, helpless as the four remaining bearers fought to keep the mirrors apart. He did not know what was happening, nor what to do. One of the lesser mirror-bearers crashed into him, sending him sprawling. The light from Isgyrn's sword shone still. Scrambling to his feet, Helsarn drew his own sword and, pointing to the distant figure, screamed, 'Get up there! Stop him, now! Stop him!'

Citadel Guards, always wary of the moods of their officers, obeyed the order immediately and started running across the Valley in the direction of Isgyrn, despite the distance and the climb that would be involved in reaching him. A few soldiers started to move after them, then an increasing number. The restlessness in the watching army grew.

Jeyan too, was watching the scene in confusion, though for her it was dominated by the fading images of Ibryen and the Gevethen in the tottering mirror. Suddenly she realized that she was free. She snatched the knife from her belt and, weaving between the now frenzied mirror-bearers, she stabbed one of the four still supporting the closing mirrors. She was stabbing him again when Helsarn's cry stopped her.

'What are you doing?' he roared, running towards her.

With Ennherhald-bred fleetness she moved around him, and without hesitation, plunged into the mirrors. Helsarn dashed after her, but stopped fearfully in front of the mirror she had entered. He saw nothing but his reflection, eyes terrified and arms extended in futility. Tentatively he touched the mirror. It was cold and hard. Then, like something in a nightmare, Jeyan's hand emerged from the mirror and her knife slashed at his throat. Only reflexes he was unaware of saved him.

The knife was gone as suddenly as it appeared, but Helsarn, white-faced, backed away, sword extended.

Every fibre of Ibryen's being rebelled against the place he was in. It was beyond him that anything so appalling could have been constructed – for that is what it was – a construct – a mechanism – a device – something that tore out what should be gently yielded, forced a way where none should be. Yet, even worse, he realized, it was alive! What souls were being tormented to sustain this thing? The thought did not bear thinking. Desperately he pushed it away. He must concern himself only with the destruction of the Gevethen, no matter what the cost. Their creation, if theirs it was, was failing. Battering impacts shook it, lightning flashes filled it. He must destroy it utterly, as he might destroy an injured animal. Yet, despite this resolve, a part of him reached out in an attempt to quieten the tumult, to ease the pain about him.

'He is with us, brother,' he heard one of the Gevethen saying. 'Have faith. Soon we will be at His feet, our testing over.'

Then another sound came through the uproar. Dogs howling?

555

He felt the Gevethen hesitate and their hold on him lessen.

'Assh, Frey, to me!'

The piercing voice was right behind him. And amid the searing lights, there was another: a blade, slashing and stabbing. He had a fleeting impression of fluttering hands and snarling moon faces and skeins of blood, then the Gevethen's hold on him was gone and a powerful hand seized him and dragged him violently backwards.

And then he was rolling on the mountain turf, a different uproar all about him. In a glance he took in the mirror-bearers, frantic and screaming, as they tried in vain to escape from the light that Isgyrn's flashing sword had brought to them. And too, there was tumult from beyond the canopy as the din within it spread out to feed the growing unrest in the army, now in increasing disarray.

'Close the mirrors, Count! Close the mirrors! Seal them in the endless reflections.'

He looked up. Faint, behind the mirrors, he saw Jeyan's desperate face.

'Close the mirrors!' she cried again, her voice distant and fearful. 'Do it! Do it now! I can't hold them longer.'

Ibryen hurled himself at the remaining bearer supporting one of the large mirrors. Whatever power was invested in these strange individuals, it was considerable, for Ibryen found himself tossed aside as if he had been no more than a child's toy. He drew his sword, then hesitated. He could not cut down this wretched, unarmed creature, bound to its grotesque life by who could say what treachery.

Then he saw the image of one of the Gevethen forming in the tottering mirror. Their eyes met and Ibryen suddenly felt the power that had bound him before, returning. He swung round and with a single stroke cut off the head of the struggling bearer.

The two mirrors swung to. Ibryen fell to his knees as he felt the Gevethen's construction collapsing. It was as if he too were being crushed and ground into nothingness by the convergence of the countless worlds that it had held apart.

But even as it faded, something remained. A screeching, clinging, refusal to die.

As he looked up, he saw a solitary hand protruding from between the mirrors. And still he could feel the Gevethen's malevolent power reaching out to him.

He cut off the hand.

Still clawing, it moved almost two paces towards him before it stopped.

There was a fearful, echoing scream, then the mirrors closed and, with a sound like a long sigh, they bent and twisted and folded, and were gone.

Faintly, Ibryen heard dogs barking and a woman's triumphant laughter. Part of him reached briefly into the world where they were and touched them. It was like a blessing. Then they too were gone.

As was the darkness as the black fabric of the canopy floated to the ground. Ibryen needed to examine no bodies to know that the mirror-bearers and the Gevethen's other servants had died with their masters. The morning light washed over their enslaved bodies, now finally free.

As Ibryen came fully to himself he braced himself for combat. The Gevethen might be gone, but danger was still around him. The collapse of the canopy and the disappearance of the Gevethen however, merely completed the disintegration of the army and few even noticed him as he walked towards his followers. None raised a hand against him.

None save Vintre.

557

Ibryen saw him approaching and knew that he was virtually defenceless. Even had he not been drained from his ordeal, he was no match for Vintre, a skilled and vicious fighter. He levelled his sword at him. 'Put down your sword and surrender,' he shouted. 'You know you'll get a fair trial from me.'

'I'll forego the pleasure of that, *Count*.' Vintre spat the word. 'There are always people who value the kind of skills I have. I just want the satisfaction of killing you then I'll fade into the crowd here.'

'No!'

Vintre looked casually over his shoulder. Rachyl, sword drawn, was walking down a slope towards him. 'You said I might be needed later,' she said.

Vintre waved a dismissive arm and, with a sneer, turned back to Ibryen.

'Don't turn away from *me*, you rat's vomit,' Rachyl blasted. 'Or are you too afraid to face me?'

Vintre's eyes narrowed and he turned again. 'You first, then, girl. I'd rather have had some fun with you before I finished you off, but this'll be as good.' He took his sword in both hands and waited with scornful patience. Suddenly, with an incongruous little cry, Rachyl tripped. Arms flailing wildly, she took two ungainly strides but failed to catch her balance. The third stride sent her head-long down the slope. Vintre's lips curled in derision and he raised his sword to strike her when she had stopped. Rachyl's fall however, proved to be a wilful dive and before Vintre could react, she had rolled up on to her feet and run her sword clean through him in a single move.

Gripping his sword hilt, for fear of any dying stroke, Rachyl looked at his face, riven with both shock and rage. He was trying to say something.

' "Bitch" is the word you're looking for, *Captain*,' she said. Then she yanked her sword free and dropped him. It was the last killing that day.

Chapter 35

In the days immediately following the destruction of the Gevethen, there was much disorder as the largely conscripted army disintegrated together with much of what passed for Nesdiryn's civil administration. Many old scores were brutally settled. It was thus more than fortunate that Isgyrn's Culmadryen arrived and came to rest over the mountains. Visible even from parts of the city, its glittering tower and spires slowly changed and shifted at the touch of the sun and the wind, while beneath it, like the white haze of a distant snowstorm, the Culmaren reached down to touch the highest peaks, drawing such that it needed from them, yet leaving them apparently unchanged. It was a sight to instil awe and silence in the most garrulous, though talk of it was to last for generations. Its massive and mysterious presence seemed to spread a strange balm over the Dirynvolk as they looked up in their pain to find themselves free again, and when eventually it was gone, the horror of the memory of the Gevethen's rule was less.

Ibryen's return to Dirynhald was deliberately unspectacular. He knew that after the years of the Gevethen's domination it would be a long time before his country bore any resemblance to the one he had been ousted from, and that progress towards it would be best achieved slowly and quietly.

His first concern was that justice should forestall retribution and, to that end, only the more conspicuous of the Gevethen's followers were immediately arrested. As is the way with such people however, several were not to be found, not least amongst them being Helsarn. Reading matters more shrewdly than his erstwhile ally, Vintre, and also being sorely shaken by what had happened to him in front of the Gevethen's mirror, the Commander had shed his uniform and quietly slipped away with the rapidly dispersing army.

Those, such as Iscar who had worked to aid Ibryen from within, were duly honoured. Iscar not least for his assault on the virtually abandoned Citadel with a group of his followers even before news of the destruction of the Gevethen reached them. They tore down the shutters and sealed curtains and uncovered many of the mirrorways to flush the darkness from the place, it being their desperate intention to hold the place no matter what transpired in the mountains. It is said that it was the light that Iscar introduced into the Watching Chamber as much as the sunlight from Isgyrn's sword that destroyed the Gevethen's device, for all the mirrors there shattered on the instant.

Harik continued as the Citadel Physician and continued to affect an indifference to the changed regime, though his manner became noticeably easier.

Jeyan's name too was honoured, and the memory of her dogs, though none knew their names.

Floating high above his village, Ibryen gazed down at it yet again. 'Well hidden,' he said. 'It served its purpose well. We mustn't forget it.' To the north he could clearly see Dirynhald with the Citadel at its heart while to the south there hung the Culmadryen. He shook his head as he looked at it.

'There *are* words for it, Ibryen,' the Traveller said. 'But silence is the best in your language.'

'I'm sorry that you could not come to my land,' Isgyrn said. 'But it is too high. The lack of air would distress you. Perhaps when Svara's will has carried us here again our Seekers will have found a way for you to come there.' He leaned forward confidentially and patted his chest. 'They're doing a deal of thinking about me, I can tell you.'

Ibryen looked round at the cloud-island he was standing on. It was a bewildering place, with its strange terrain and unexpectedly angular buildings which constantly moved so that within the space of a few hours, one that had been at the top of a small hill, would be at the bottom of it. He could not make out how they had been built, but they were beautiful, shining silver and gold and white. Yet, for all their brightness, it was no strain to look at them, for there was an iridescence about the whiteness, and many subtle shadows about the whole that protected the eye. Amongst many other strange skills that they possessed, the Dryen-volk seemed to have a rare way with light, Ibryen mused.

He and his friends had been brought there by Isgyrn's Soarers, hanging from their brilliantly coloured Culmaren wings, for all the world like great gliding birds, yet as agile in the air as ravens. The journey had been a nerve-wracking prospect, and all freely admitted to taking at least the first part of it with both eyes tightly closed, despite being securely held. Subsequent to that however, it had been difficult for Isgyrn to persuade them to call an end to their swooping flights about the peaks and the valleys and to join the celebration that had been prepared on the island. Their hard-learned discipline of silence vanished that day and their excitement was a source of great amusement to the Soarers.

Now the celebration and the talking was over. It had

been a joyous interlude, not least for Isgyrn, finding his land unscathed and free from the darkness it had been threatened by when he was torn from it. And finding too, his family and kin.

Ibryen, to his considerable embarrassment had been treated with an almost overpowering deference though at the same time he was aware that he had been extensively interrogated about his disturbing gift.

'We are doubly in your debt,' he was told finally by the elder Seeker who had been discreetly leading the questioning. 'You have enriched us with your knowledge and with the return of our brave brother, long-mourned.' There was a hint of sadness in his voice though, and drawing Ibryen to one side, he spoke softly to him, away from the others. 'Few have been so blessed as you in your gift, Ibryen. But you must – you *must* – study it, learn everything that is to be learned. It was given to you for a purpose beyond what it has achieved so far, I'm sure. It must not be allowed to lie fallow because the immediate needs of healing your land are clamouring so.' He coughed awkwardly. 'You must forgive me speaking to you thus, elder to younger as it were,' he said. 'I don't normally regale guests with such lectures – Seeker's habit, I'm afraid – but had to speak how the mood took me. Please accept it in good part.'

Ibryen smiled and bowed. 'Your advice matches my intention,' he said. 'I regret that you can't remain longer to help me.'

But the time for parting had come. 'Svara's will can be defied only so far,' Isgyrn told his friends. 'The land must move on.' He embraced each in turn. 'It has been a time of great learning. It seems that the Great Corrupter may indeed have been destroyed – at least in this world.' He lowered his voice as though loath to darken the moment. 'But His touch lingers on and my land has been travelling in high and strange Ways since that time. We must concern ourselves more now with the middle depths. Learn what has happened to Him, for until He is destroyed utterly He will surely return. We will come here again.'

Then the Soarers carried them back to the sunlit ridge where Ibryen had first met the Traveller.

The little group watched in silence as the island began to drift back towards the Culmadryen. Like the mountains themselves, the scale of the great cloud-land deceived, and the island was scarcely visible long before it reached it. As it shrank into the distance, becoming the merest wisp of cloud, a single brilliant light flashed from it as once more Isgyrn's sword sent the sun to Ibryen. Then, slowly, the Culmadryen began to move away from them.

They stood for a long time, staring after it.

'I'll be off then.' The Traveller broke the silence.

'What?'

He flinched away from the combined exclamation. 'I'll be off,' he repeated weakly. 'I have to go.'

'Why?' Ibryen protested. '*Your* land's not blowing away on the breeze.'

The Traveller smiled. 'Neither is yours, Ibryen, but you've much to do. All of you. And so have I.'

Rachyl sat down beside him and put her arm around his shoulders. 'You can't leave us now,' she said.

The Traveller gently unwound the arm, but held her hand. 'It's been a noisy few days,' he said. 'Days such as I've never known before and may well not know again.' He looked at Rachyl. 'They've given me back many things I'd long forgotten about – renewed me. I must pay more heed to people in future. But I need to think. I need the sounds of the mountains.' Ibryen made to speak, but the Traveller continued. 'And my kin are returned,' he said, his eyes distant but excited. 'Isgyrn spoke of it when he first woke but we'd more pressing concerns then. Now the Seekers have confirmed it for me. The Ways of the Sound Carvers are being opened, the Great Song is being heard again.' The excitement reached his voice. 'And the Great Gate is *open*. I must find it, I have so many questions now.' He looked intently at Ibryen. 'And I must find those who can help you understand your gift and bring them to you, as well as spreading the news of what's happened here.' Then he cleared his throat and made a shooing motion with his hands. 'Go on now,' he said briskly. 'I'm not keen on goodbyes.'

There was nothing more to be said.

He took the hands of each as they left, but Rachyl remained sitting by him. He looked at her, eyes bright and full of life. 'You too,' he said.

'I know,' she replied.

He ran a finger down her cheek. 'Thank you,' he said softly.

'Thank *you*,' she said, taking his hand and squeezing it.

Then he stood up, hitched his pack on to his back and strode off.

He moved very quickly.

Rachyl stood watching him, one hand on her sword hilt, the other in her belt, patting her stomach thoughtfully.

'You *will* come again?' she asked, knowing that he would hear her.

'Oh yes,' came the reply. 'I'll be back.'

'When?'

'Ah . . .'

'I'll listen for you.'

'Yes.' His voice was growing fainter. 'Listen for me always.'

Then there was silence.
Rachyl leaned forward intently.
But there was only the sound of the wind.

A HEROINE
OF THE WORLD

*What chance did she have to attain
her heart's desire?*

TANITH LEE

'This card be called the Heroine, or the World's Girl.
Though it is also one of the cards of the She, the goddess
Vulmardra.'

The fortune teller spoke the words – showed Ara the cards
that predicted how she would become the focal point of
great events . . . But now, a defenceless captive of enemy
invaders, Ara could only wait and hope to discover her
true destiny.

Yet, in a world ruled by war, what chance did she have to
attain her heart's desire? Far from home, and alone among
strangers, only the will of the goddess Vulmardra could
protect and guide her.

But the path the Lady had started her on would lead Ara
into the very heart of conflict. And though she might gain
or lose great wealth, become pawn or key player in the
power games of princes, there was only one for whom she
would risk everything . . .

He was a soldier that some named traitor and others
liberator – and for him she would strive to become a
Heroine of the World.

FICTION / FANTASY 0 7472 4748 X

More Compelling Fiction from Headline Feature

DEAN KOONTZ

WINTER MOON

Eduardo, a retiree whose wife and son have died, lives on
his isolated Montana ranch. His life is peaceful – if
lonely – until he is awakened one night by a fearful
throbbing sound and eerie lights in the lower woods.
During the next several months, one mysterious and
disturbing event follows another. Increasingly, he fears
for his sanity and his life, until the terrible night when
someone – or something – knocks on his back door . . .

Jack McGarvey, a Los Angeles cop, is hammered by
submachine-gun fire when a madman goes berserk one
lovely spring morning. He barely survives. His partner is
not so lucky. Months later, still on disability, with no
idea of when he might work again, with Los Angeles
growing more violent by the day, he longs to move his
family to a more peaceful place. Though he would do
anything to protect his wife Heather and son Toby, Jack
seems powerless and without prospects.

Then, in their hour of desperation, the McGarveys find
salvation when they receive an unexpected inheritance. It
includes a sprawling ranch in one of the most beautiful,
peaceful places in the country. Montana. Excited by their
good fortune, the McGarveys set out from Los Angeles
to begin their new life – unaware that the terror-riddled
and unstable city will eventually seem like a safe haven
compared to what lies ahead.

FICTION / GENERAL 0 7472 4289 5

A selection of bestsellers from Headline